For my girls Claire, Erin & Emme, though only
one of you is old enough to read this book.

The Second Life of Nathan Jones

DAVID ATKINSON

OneMoreChapter

A division of HarperCollins*Publishers*
www.harpercollins.co.uk

One More Chapter an imprint of
HarperCollins*Publishers*
The News Building
1 London Bridge Street
London SE1 9GF

www.harpercollins.co.uk

This paperback edition 2019

First published in Great Britain in ebook format by Harper-
Collins*Publishers* 2019

A catalogue record for this book
is available from the British Library

ISBN: 9780008327880

Typeset in Birka by Palimpsest Book Production Ltd,
Falkirk, Stirlingshire

Printed and bound in Great Britain by
CPI Group (UK) Ltd, Croydon CR0 4YY

Chapter 1

Getting killed hadn't been part of Nathan Jones's plans for Saturday afternoon. Instead, he'd mapped out a nice relaxing time for himself on the sofa catching up on *The Walking Dead* boxset he'd got for his birthday.

His wife Laura and their three children were in the kingdom of Fife, visiting her mother, and weren't due back until the evening. He pottered from room to room, still in his pyjamas, revelling in the hush that had descended upon his normally noisy life.

Nathan polished off one of his favourite toasted cinnamon bagels, smothered with some of Tesco's finest jam, whilst flicking from channel to channel making the most of having sole custody of the remote control. Had he known what was in store for him when he left his flat, he would have remained safely seated on the couch and phoned for a takeaway dinner.

Instead, he got dressed, zipped up his coat and headed out into the windy November afternoon munching a bag of pickled-onion-flavoured Monster Munch crisps.

His planned destination had been the local Tesco but as he crossed the busy road adjacent to his flat he had an unfortunate run-in with a bus that subsequently changed everything.

When he pieced together the incident later, it appeared he had stepped off the pavement right into the path of the twelve-tonne vehicle. This was obviously a very silly thing to do and so unlike his normally cautious approach to life. He couldn't remember the number of times he'd drummed into his children's heads 'STOP, LOOK AND LISTEN'.

The ambulance arrived in record time, but a paramedic pronounced him dead at the scene and an A & E doctor confirmed the decision a short time later at the local hospital.

He remembered very little about dying. If pushed, he would classify it as a complete non-event. Nothing flashed before his eyes and no dead relatives stood beckoning him into the light. Even if they had, his relationship with his family had been such that the likely outcome would have been him running in the opposite direction.

If Karen Gillan had been tasked with bringing him into the fold he might have considered it, but she hadn't, probably because

1. She happened to be still very much alive and
2. He didn't merit a heavenly Hollywood A-list reception committee.

His first impression of death? A vastly overrated experience and he had no idea why everyone made such a fuss over it.

He'd felt that way about several things in recent years: the various royal weddings and births, the Brexit fiasco and the launch of the latest incarnation of the iPhone.

His poor impression of death might be down to the fact that, like many things in life, Nathan didn't do it very well. He was rubbish at lots of things. He couldn't ski, skate or work out quadratic equations and had issues with authority figures. He could now add dying to the list.

Thinking back to his childhood, Nathan recalled that his mum's main concern about death had been underwear.

'Nathan, you must make sure that every day you leave the house in clean underpants, just in case you're involved in any kind of accident. I don't want you showing me up in hospital.'

For that reason, whenever she left the house her underwear would be clean and as new as possible. Even as a relatively young kid, Nathan realised that if she ever got injured so badly in an accident that she needed hospital admission her underwear would more than likely be soiled to the point that it would have to be binned.

He never mentioned this to her, however, and had she still been alive, she would not have been happy that on the day her son's life ended, he'd been wearing very old and very threadbare boxer shorts.

Nathan first realised everything wasn't quite right with the whole 'after-death experience' when he became aware of a bone-numbing cold and that his arms had been strapped down. His face had also annoyingly been covered with cloth. Overall it felt as if he'd been swaddled in a similar way to that which his wife used with the kids when they were babies.

Initially he thought it might be a straitjacket hugging him tightly. Perhaps the increasingly fractious relationship with his wife had finally reached a stage where his sanity had cracked, leading to an extreme psychosis demanding he be sectioned and confined in a small space?

He could still breathe easily enough, though he learned his breath smelt none too pleasant as he received instant feedback from the fabric pressed against his face. He tried to move his left arm, but this resulted in such searing pain that it made him gasp and brought tears to his eyes. He tentatively moved his right arm. He felt some gentle tingling but no pain. He pulled it free of whatever restricted it, reached up and removed the fabric membrane from his face.

Free of the first prison, he then faced a second containment. He'd been enclosed in something dark, hard and metallic. As far as he knew, even the most dangerous mental patients were not placed in metal boxes. At least, he didn't think so, though he acknowledged he had limited knowledge of current UK mental health treatments.

Unfortunately, at this point some feeling started to return to the rest of his body and he ached. Not the kind of soul-ache that you got from being desperately in love with someone, which he could still recall (just), but the kind of all-over body ache that occasionally accompanied a bad bout of the flu when it felt as though a little man was running around your body stabbing your extremities with a hot needle. In fact, it felt very much as if he had been hit by a bus. Then he remembered with a start of realisation that that was exactly what had happened.

He started to shout. However, his croaky, weak voice only produced a pathetic whimper. He tried to bang the sides of the metal container with his good arm, but this only made the smallest of sounds given the lack of space at his disposal.

Nathan then discovered that if he banged his bare heels off the bottom of the metal prison it made much more noise. He did this for a few seconds then gave up, exhausted.

Then he suddenly felt himself moving forwards. It felt like the start of a roller-coaster ride but without any of the delicious anticipation, and suddenly he slid out of the darkness into a harsh white light.

As he squinted into the brightness a face emerged and peered curiously at him. An angel perhaps? If so, she was nothing like those depicted in Hollywood movies. Her hair was black, her eyes were black, her clothes were black, her earrings were black, her piercings were black, even her lips were black – although her teeth were pearly white. She smiled at him and said, 'Hello there.'

Chapter 2

My full name is Klaudette Ainsworth-Thomas (yeah, I know). I woke up on my tenth birthday, decided enough was enough and made a monumental decision. The first person I had to tell? My mother.

'Mum?'

Janice, my mum, could usually be found behind an ironing board. She ironed every day. Ironing was one of her many obsessions. If it got to 6 p.m. and there were no clothes left in the ironing basket she got all anxious and cranky and started to press things that had already been done, like my dad's shirts or something random like the bedroom curtains. She had even been known to remove the cushion covers from the couch and press them on a low heat.

'Mum?'

'Yes, Klaudie?' Now, there was another thing that annoyed me; even though my thoughtless parents had lumbered me with the triple-barrelled name from hell, they couldn't even be bothered to use it properly and invariably shortened it to Scotland's prevailing type of weather.

'I've made a decision.'

'That's nice, dear.'

'Mum, I'm serious.'

My mum put the iron down and stared at me. 'Klaudie, you're always serious, that's your problem, you—'

'No, Mum, that's not my problem, that's your problem. I am the way I am. I've decided that I'm sick of being called Klaudette, Klaudie and Klaudia, and I'm sick of Ainsworth-Thomas as well. From now on I'm only going to answer to the name Kat, K-A-T.'

'K-A-T?'

'Yep, Kat is much cooler and most of my friends call me that anyway.'

Mum returned to ironing her slippers. 'That's nice, dear.'

Despite my mum's apathy I stuck to my guns and from that day on I only answered to the name Kat. Eventually everyone, including my parents and most of the teachers, adopted my new alias, the only exception being the assistant head at my crumbling Glasgow high school, Mrs Brock, who insisted on calling me Klaudette. As a result, I ignored everything she said for the next five years.

The only issue with this impasse happened to be that Mrs Brock also taught me history for two of those five years. History, therefore, didn't turn out to be one of my strong points, not helped by the number of Harolds/Haralds mooching about in 1066.

The fault all lay with my mum. She'd met and married a John Thomas (yes, really) and they decided to join forces and hyphenate their names after they got married. I'd always thought someone who had grown up being called John Thomas would have had more awareness and sympathy about kids' names instead of lumbering his only daughter with such a mouthful. He'd even managed to become a professor of social anthropology to avoid using his first name. Even his bank cards only had 'Professor J Thomas' printed on them.

As a youngster, before I had the presence of mind to change my name, I had a plump, lumpy body, a squished face and little self-confidence. I used to come home from school, go into my bedroom and slip into a Cinderella or Snow-White costume from my dressing-up box and prance up and down in front of the mirror pretending I lived a different life, using clothes as an emotional crutch, an image to hide behind. I still did.

I've always felt that there was a certain cruelty involved, growing up as an only child, especially with parents like mine, who were too wrapped up in their own obsessions to notice my issues. All parents should be obliged to have two or more children or none. In my opinion, having only one kid could lead to them growing up lonely – well, kids like me who had real problems making friends would, anyway. If I'd had a sibling, they would have played with me and banished some of my loneliness.

Yeah, but knowing you they would have hated you so that would've made things worse.

'Things couldn't have been much worse.'

Wanna bet?

When I get stressed I often argue with my inner self, usually out loud, which can bring me some weird glances from strangers. Well, weirder than normal. Reminiscing about my childhood usually raises my stress levels so I try not to.

Despite the problems in high school I left with some decent grades, much to the surprise of many of my teachers, especially Mrs Brock, and won a place at Napier University in Edinburgh to study nursing.

I couldn't stand the thought of working in an office. I was a practical sort of person and initially believed that nursing would be a good option. I anticipated that it would provide a stimulating and fast-changing environment that would stop me getting bored. It didn't.

My first placement in an adult surgical ward saw me dealing with patients who were either waiting for or recovering from an operation. The ward was chronically under-resourced (like so many others), which meant I felt used and abused by everyone, staff and patients alike. On my first eight-hour shift my mentor said, 'Kat, the patient in room three needs some toast and tea. Can you get that for them?'

I rushed back to the nurses' station after I'd finished. My mentor said, 'Quick work, that. Can you change the two beds in room eleven, they're covered in blood and vomit, and after that could you be a dear and nip down to the shops for some sandwiches for me and Elaine, the staff nurse, as we both forgot to bring anything in for lunch?'

By the end of the day I felt more like a waitress and a chambermaid than a nurse. I also wondered why patients were called 'patients' as they were anything but, constantly pressing buzzers and shouting for anything and everything.

I could have probably put up with all that and carried on but for me the final straw came on the last week of my first placement. Whilst I was escorting an elderly male patient to the toilet, he suddenly turned and grabbed both my breasts in his bony (but surprisingly strong) little hands, thrust his head into my cleavage, sighed and expired on the floor.

Enough was enough, so I dropped out and began a medical internship at the local mortuary. Dead patients didn't grope me, or demand things, or speak to me, or stare at me, or assault me. In fact, they rarely did anything at all – except lie still. They occasionally stink a little, but you soon get used to that.

I applied myself and with the help of day release and evening courses I qualified as an anatomical pathologist practitioner, better known as a mortuary technician. I suppose given my view of the world and my relatively serious and introverted nature, the work suited me. I'd been working in Edinburgh's Royal Infirmary for nearly six years now and there wasn't much I hadn't seen, or, more pertinently perhaps, smelled.

Initially, my mum reacted in horror at my relatively unusual career choice and couldn't understand my motivation. Over time, however, she came to recognise that I enjoyed my job – as weird as that sounds – and never complained about it, the way many people did.

Monday, 23 November started out like most other early shifts. My alarm woke me at 5.45 a.m., I showered, ate cornflakes whilst drying my hair and staring at *BBC News* with the subtitles on, so I could understand what the presenters were jabbering about over the noise of the hairdryer. My thick hair always takes ages to dry.

After that I applied my Manic Panic foundation. If I was honest I liked the name more than anything as pretty much any pale slap worked for me. However, for the last ten years I'd only ever worn three shades of Rimmel lipstick: black, purple and, for special occasions, RockChick Scarlet but today being a work day meant boring Black Diva.

I then applied my black liner and smudged some light pink blusher on to contour my cheeks and make me look slightly less like one of my charges. In truth, as I'd got older I'd toned down the Goth persona. I supposed I'd got nobody and nothing to rebel against these days, but still liked the fact it made people wary of me.

I then pulled on my clothes, left my tiny rented flat in the Duddingston area of Edinburgh and drove to work. My workload scheduled for that morning should have been light as we had no post-mortems booked until the afternoon, so my plan had been to sort out a load of paperwork I hadn't bothered finishing on Friday. Another plus would be that I'd be working with Sid.

Sid's actual title was Dr David Ingles but his idol growing up had been Sid Vicious, so he'd taken the nickname. My only issue with this was that, in my opinion, Taylor Swift bore more resemblance to Sid Vicious than David did with his soft round face, big lips and gentle grey eyes. There was also the slight problem that as David, being only thirty-six, wouldn't have been born when the Sex Pistols were at their zenith but then who am I to criticise? Sid was my favourite forensic pathologist, which was a bit like saying he was my favourite teddy bear, given his nature. He started at Edinburgh's Royal Infirmary around the same time as me and although much more senior he didn't have the 'lording over' attitude some of the other doctors have and we got on brilliantly.

He was on my wavelength with so many things, and as we had absolutely no interest in each other physically it was easy to talk to him. I suspect he might be gay – in fact I'd stake money on it – but whenever I broached the subject (usually on a night out after a few drinks) he changed the subject of conversation immediately. He was firmly in the closet as far as I was concerned, so far in that he'd locked the damn thing and thrown away the key.

On this Monday, I managed to arrive before anyone else and opened the door to the large basement room where all the recently deceased were stored. Then, something made me stop in my tracks. I'd heard something. I didn't move for a moment, hardly breathing, then decided I must have been mistaken. I'd been alone down here hundreds of times before, both during the day and at night, and it didn't bother me any more. It had been a little creepy at first, but I'd soon come to realise that the dead couldn't hurt me (barring any kind of zombie uprising, of course), and life had taught me well that it was the living I needed to be wary of.

I quickly scanned the log, noting only one new entry, and as I turned to go and get changed I heard something coming from one of the drawers. How strange.

I cautiously approached the section where the banging emanated from and thought for a second that one of the medical staff might be playing a trick, but that sort of stuff was usually only reserved for 'newbies'. I slowly pulled out the offending drawer and peered down at the pale and bruised but incredibly cute face staring up at me. It blinked its bright blue eyes and I was immediately smitten. It had finally happened – I'd fallen for a corpse.

Chapter 3

Once I'd made sure my rather attractive 'corpse' was alive and not a figment of my too often fertile imagination, I called upstairs and got them to send down some of the intensive care staff. My 'patient' (I thought that sounded better than 'corpse' on the phone) hadn't been dead for long, if indeed he'd been dead at all. The doctors were understandably confused and fired loads of questions at me, most of which I couldn't answer.

Fifteen minutes after I'd discovered the patient – Mr Jones, according to his label – had been moved to an intensive care bed, wired up to the moon and subjected to all manner of poking and prodding. After they finished their tests, they loaded him up with painkillers and left him to sleep. The IT consultant told me that, 'Nathan Jones is a medical curiosity, a walking miracle – well, he will be. Currently, he's a lying-down moaning miracle.'

At the end of my shift I pottered upstairs to see how my first 'living corpse' had fared. He intrigued me but, more than that, he'd unsettled me. I'd never developed feelings instantly for anyone before, alive or dead or maybe somewhere in between, as Mr Jones appeared to be.

I knew I'd stepped onto dodgy ground but couldn't help the way I felt.

I stopped by the nurses' station on the way and got an update from Jan, the staff nurse on duty. We'd known each other for years. She'd 'taken me under her wing' (her description not mine) when I'd first started in the hospital, and even confessed to me one night when we were both a bit drunk that she suspected she had bisexual tendencies but didn't want her husband or teenage son to find out. Given that new information, I hadn't been sure at the time whether her 'taking me under her wing' might be a sign that she liked me or a sign that she *liked* me, but – to my relief – nothing more than her drunken confession had happened.

She filled me in on what she knew and that he remained asleep. I slipped into his room and sat staring at him for a while, wondering how on earth he'd managed to get pronounced dead and yet still be alive.

I'd just decided to get up and head for home when his eyes flickered open. 'Hello there,' I said brightly.

'Can you say anything else?' he mumbled with an English accent, running his tongue around dry lips. I poured him some water and handed it to him. His left arm had been encased in plaster but his right one seemed fine and he took the beaker from me.

'Are you right-handed? That's lucky.'

He nodded. 'Yeah, I don't feel that lucky just now. I think I need to thank you ... you know, for finding me.'

'You were being very noisy. The morgue is usually quiet, like, well ... a morgue, I suppose.'

'Not too noisy, I hope – not enough to wake the dead.'

'I didn't check but I think you were the only live one there.'

'Has that ever happened to you before?'

I shook my head. 'Nope, you're my first zombie. You were definitely dead when they shut you in the drawer again yesterday.'

'Again?'

'Yeah, I wasn't in over the weekend, but it seems after your wife identified you on Saturday night, they moved you around a fair bit because they were servicing the fridge mechanisms, so you haven't been in the drawers much. Thing is, you'd think all that moving about would have woken you up.'

'I don't understand.'

'Neither do I, nor the doctors. You've got a lot of people confused and all worked up. They don't know why you're alive and that bothers them.'

'They'd rather I'd stayed dead?'

'Probably; and if you'd stayed in there much longer you'd likely have frozen to death anyway. They're saying you've been subject to the Lazarus Syndrome.'

'What's that?'

'Well, it's also known as autoresuscitation after failed

cardiopulmonary resuscitation, which is the spontaneous
return of circulation after failed attempts at revival.'

'What does that mean?'

'You're very lucky.'

'You said that already. What's your name?'

'Kat.'

'What, as in pussy? Sorry, that sounds rude.'

'It's fine. No, K-A-T.'

'Oh, okay. As in short for Katie or something.'

'Yeah, something like that. Look, I really came to see if
there's anything you need?'

'A new body, maybe.'

I laughed. 'I can't help you there. I think your wife
stopped by earlier.'

'Did you speak to her?'

'No, I was downstairs at that point helping saw the top
off someone's skull.'

'I probably didn't need to know that.'

'Sorry, the staff nurse said she couldn't hang around
because of your kids but they've called to let her know that
you're awake. She said she'll come tomorrow.' I scratched
my nose where a black piercing emerged from my left
nostril. I noticed Nathan watching me intently. I must admit
being overcome with a feeling of disappointment when I'd
discovered he had a wife. My taste in men wasn't getting any
better the older I got. 'It must have been a shock for her.'

'What? That I'd died?'

'Well, yes, that you'd died. And then that you were

suddenly alive again.' I noticed his face darken and a frown appeared, making him look older. 'What's wrong?'

'Apart from being broken?'

I smiled. 'Yeah, you look upset about something.'

'No, just in a bit of pain, I think.'

I didn't believe him but whatever was bothering him wasn't really any of my business.

'Well, as your wife isn't able to come and see you, who else can I call?'

'Ghostbusters,' he said, smiling.

'Seriously – there's no one? Your mother?'

'She's been dead for seventeen years.'

'Father?'

'Dead for twenty.'

'Brothers, sisters?'

'I'm an only child.'

'Lonely child, more like. What about friends?'

Nathan sighed. 'You could have called my mate Graham, I suppose, but he's on holiday in Thailand.'

'Have you told your work you're likely to be off for a while?'

'I mainly work for myself, freelance, so no need.'

'Freelance what?'

'Just freelance. You're very nosy.'

'Are you lonely?'

'With a wife and three kids? You must be joking.'

'Outside your family circle there doesn't seem to be very much for you though.'

'I'm a very busy person.'

'That's what lonely people say.'

'Is it?'

'Yes.'

We were both silent for a moment and I noticed his eyes closing.

'I should go. You're obviously very tired and you need to sleep.'

He nodded. 'You've got to get back to work, I expect?'

I shook my head. 'No, I've just finished my shift so I'm heading home now.'

'Is your boyfriend waiting?'

I wondered why he'd asked that and it slightly annoyed me. Maybe he'd been a serial cheater, and, if so, no wonder his wife hadn't rushed back to the hospital.

I said rather sharply, 'I don't have a boyfriend. Do you think I'd be sitting here if I had anywhere better to be?' I could tell my question and tone of voice had taken him aback.

'Probably not,' he said, chastened.

Perhaps that had been a bit harsh. 'Sorry, that didn't come out as I meant it to.'

'No, it's fine, I appreciate it. I wouldn't have had any visitors at all today if you weren't here.'

'I probably won't come to see you again. I really only popped by to see if you needed to contact anyone else – now that you've told me you don't ... well, that's fine.'

'Thank you for bringing me back to life.'

I smiled and shook my head. 'I don't think I did but it's a nice idea. Goodbye, Mr Jones.'

'Nathan.'

'Goodbye, Nathan.'

*

The next morning Nathan awoke early. Mainly due to the clatter and clashing that went on in hospital wards at that time of day. He'd had a troubled sleep and his dreams had been haunted by the mortuary girl, and then pain when his medication had worn off. A nurse had stopped by to take his blood pressure at some ungodly hour, though, and thankfully administered more pain relief.

During the morning his wife appeared with their youngest daughter, four-year-old Daisy. Daisy jumped onto the bed and gave him a hug, which felt lovely. They also had Millie, ten going on thirty-five and Chloe, six.

'Where's the other two?'

Laura smiled. 'At school, of course – it's Tuesday.'

'They could have missed a morning to come and see their dad.'

'They're confused enough. I spent the last two days trying to stop them crying about you being dead. Now they think I've been lying to them about it and Millie especially is hardly speaking to me.'

'Sorry for upsetting your life.'

Laura's phoney smile vanished. 'Don't start, Nathan. I've

had a traumatic few days. You've no idea how hard it's been coping with everything. We all thought you were dead.'

He nodded. 'I'm not going to apologise for still being alive, Laura. It was the Lazarus Syndrome.'

'What's that?'

'Something to do with pulman circumnavigation or ... anyway, I didn't do it on purpose to complicate things.'

Laura blinked and looked away. 'Yeah, I know. Sorry. How are you feeling?'

He sighed. 'Sore. I've got a lot of broken things.'

'Yes, I know, they told me.'

'You could have come yesterday.'

'I did but the girls were playing up and I ... might have been in shock. When they told us we had to go it seemed easier to just agree.'

'Shock?'

'That you were still alive; as I said I'd spent two days ...'

'Yeah, telling the girls I'd died, you just said.'

The next few minutes passed in silence until Daisy announced, 'I need pee pees.'

Laura went with her to the toilet on the other side of the room and Nathan took a moment to try and see things from his wife's point of view. He accepted that she'd been shocked by his death, and their three daughters could be a handful, but if the situation were reversed would he have waited patiently to see his wife? No, he would have demanded the hospital staff let them in rather than giving up, for the girls' sake if nothing else.

21

He sighed and tried to remember the love he'd once felt for Laura but found it difficult; they hadn't been close for so long. Occasionally they had a good day or more likely a good night when she was horny, and their love-making brought them together physically and mentally, but those episodes had become less frequent.

Laura came back and sat with Daisy on her knee. His wife had jet-black hair, her natural colour. In all the years he'd known her she'd never changed it. Even now with many grey hairs appearing she still resisted colouring it. Her small nose sat like a cute little button on her pale and lovely face. Dark emerald eyes that once captivated him and gazed upon him with love and devotion nowadays more often expressed impatience and scorn.

'Well, I suppose I'd better get home. Daisy needs her lunch and I've got to pick the girls up from school at three.'

Nathan didn't argue; the silence wasn't comfortable, and he needed to sleep. The painkillers made him drowsy and irritable. Minutes after she left he slipped into a fitful slumber. His dreams were rarely pleasant any more.

Chapter 4

Laura brought the girls to see him every evening whilst he remained in hospital and although seeing his daughters acted like a tonic, staring at his wife's stressed and unhappy face had the opposite effect. He was glad when, after four days, they let him go home.

The consultant appeared on the Friday afternoon with a clipboard and a printed list of things he wasn't allowed to do once they handed over the strong painkillers and released him from their care.

Motocross
Hang gliding
Parachuting
Rally driving
Water-skiing
Boxing
Bull riding

Nathan had never attempted any of those things and it left him wondering if he'd been missing out on life somehow. He signed the bottom of the form, promising not

23

to do anything dangerous, though he had to remember he'd ended up in the morgue by simply trying to cross the road.

The young-looking consultant – too young to be a senior doctor in Nathan's mind – took the signed disclaimer from him and ticked another box on her clipboard and said without looking up, 'Now, you shouldn't drive or operate machinery whilst taking these pills either.'

He waited for her to look up and wafted his sling and plastered arm at her.

'Oh, yeah, sorry, I'm on automatic, but you'd be surprised at what some people try and do.'

'Like bull riding.'

'Sorry?'

'It's on your list of prohibited activities.'

'Is it?'

'Yeah, right at the bottom.'

She peered at the form then looked up and smiled. 'Yeah maybe give that a miss for a few weeks at least.'

'I'll try, but there are so many opportunities to bull ride in Edinburgh that it might be unavoidable,' Nathan informed her.

She ignored his sarcasm and left his discharge forms on the bottom of the bed.

Apart from the obvious sling and a few cuts on his forehead, Nathan looked none the worse for his experience. Underneath his shirt, his broken ribs were bound tightly, and his damaged skull bore no marks, but he'd been told to be careful because, although the linear fractures required no treatment as such, he had to return immediately if he experienced any unexpected or severe headaches. Heading home to a grumpy wife and three young kids meant the chances of developing a severe headache were somewhere near one hundred per cent.

Despite this, mentally, he felt elated. It might be down to some sort of post-death high, but he reckoned that, as there wouldn't be many discussion groups available who'd shared his experience, he'd probably never know.

Laura arrived to take him home in an unusually animated and chatty mood and did most of the talking. As his head hurt and he felt drowsy this suited him fine. He spent most of the weekend watching TV and falling asleep unexpectedly. One minute he would be watching a re-run of an episode of the *Antiques Roadshow*, the next he'd be snoring, although he suspected this might be more to do with the programme than the pills. Chloe woke him up. 'Dad, how can you sleep when you're snoring so loudly?'

'I don't know, Chloe.' He yawned, and Laura came over and made a fuss of him, which he really enjoyed.

Then Daisy jumped onto the couch and gave him a huge cuddle. Dying had certainly made his two youngest daughters very appreciative of him. It probably wouldn't last so he needed to make the most of it – once they sensed he'd recovered fully they'd be back to normal. Daisy jumped down and tripped over his foot.

'Shit.'

'Daisy, don't say that; it's not a nice word,' scolded Laura.

'Daddy said it.'

'He shouldn't have. Nathan, don't say shit.'

'I didn't.'

'Shit,' squealed Daisy with delight.

'Daisy, stop it.'

'You said shit again, Laura, that's why she's doing it.'

'Shit!' yelled Daisy again, gleefully.

'I didn't, did I? Shit, I didn't mean to.'

'Shit,' said Daisy, bouncing up and down on the rug.

Laura put her head in her hands. 'We need to stop saying shit. I hardly ever say it – it's you she's learned it from.'

'Why's everything my fault?'

'Because it usually is.'

'Shit,' cried Daisy as she walked over and picked up her doll. She took the doll into her bedroom whispering, 'Shit,' into its ear.

On Monday, Laura dropped Daisy at her day nursery and went to work, leaving him alone at home for the first time since he'd come back from hospital. His wife had been making an effort to be civil to him and he felt guilty about the recent disingenuous thoughts and feelings he'd had when she'd so easily given up on coming to see him in hospital that first day. He hoped it might be a sign that they could begin to patch things up.

Their marriage had started off amazingly well considering the circumstances under which they'd got together. After Millie had been born they'd remained close; people even referred to them as 'devoted' when they saw them together.

26

He couldn't put his finger on when exactly things had begun to turn sour. He supposed it had been a gradual process. Somewhere between falling pregnant with Chloe and the birth of Daisy everything had changed. They'd not had a lot of time together as a couple before Laura fell pregnant with Millie. Perhaps if they'd been given that time socialising, holidaying and doing the normal stuff that young couples did then the relationship might have run its course and ended. Kids complicated everything. They naturally became a priority and somewhere in the mix Nathan and Laura had got lost. Money had only started to become an issue after Chloe came along. At that point Nathan's work had dried up – companies took more decisions and jobs in-house meaning contractors were used less. The practice had begun to reverse in recent times, but good contracts remained elusive.

Going back further, Nathan suspected that part of Laura's initial attraction to him could be put down to the fact she'd thought him posh. True, he'd gone to boarding school, but his private education had come about more from the fact he'd been an inconvenience to his parents rather than any aspirational hopes they'd had for their son. He'd interfered with their lifestyle, so he'd spent most of his pre-school years in assorted day nurseries and most weekends with babysitters or childminders. (He still didn't understand the distinction between the two.)

Shortly after Nathan's birth, an elderly aunt had died, leaving her entire and considerable estate to his mother.

He learned later that she had been waiting years for this happy event, and his parents had spent many hours planning exactly what they were going to do with the money – which included a lot of travel, some nice cars and a holiday home in France. The inconvenience of having a brat would be something they'd deal with as long as it didn't cramp their style.

'Mum, why did you have me?' he'd asked her once.

'I don't know, Nathan.'

'What do you mean you don't know?'

'Well, you weren't exactly planned, let me put it like that.'

'So, I'm an accident?'

'Kind of. Once I found out, though, I decided to keep you. Auntie Caroline had hung on longer than anyone expected so I thought you might be a welcome diversion, something to help pass the time.'

The only family trips they ever made were to the house in France. Even then, he only got to go during the summer holidays, which he suspected had more to do with the fact it was cheaper to hire a childminder in Brittany, where they had their cottage, than to pay for one in London. His babysitters in France were more colourful than the middle-class young girls they employed in London.

One evening, just after his ninth birthday, his parents engaged Monsieur Masson to look after him while they went to a party. As soon as they were gone Monsieur Masson's mistress arrived and they left Nathan to his own devices while they made full use of his parents' huge four-poster.

By the time his parents returned home Nathan had managed to shave his eyebrows off, using his dad's razor and shaving foam. During the process, he'd nicked the skin above his eyes in numerous places, leaving his face a mask of blood. It made him resemble some demonic child from a cheap horror flick. He then attempted to make a meal by smashing eggs into a large stainless-steel bowl, adding a liberal portion of tomato sauce and grated cheese before putting the whole lot uncovered into the microwave. The resulting multicoloured explosion took weeks to scrub clean. Monsieur Masson didn't get asked back.

A few days after his fifteenth birthday his father, aged only fifty-six, died of a heart attack. Perhaps the hedonistic lifestyle he and his mother had undertaken could be blamed, or perhaps it could be put down to faulty genes. In any event, the loss of his father curtailed his mother's excesses for a while and Nathan started attending the local comprehensive in south London as there was no sense in needlessly wasting money on private education any longer than necessary, according to his mother.

Despite the disruption he found that he enjoyed the local school much more and, although his mum could never be described as 'doting', at least she took an interest in him for a while.

Laura's upbringing was in stark contrast to his. She came from a poor background in Fife, growing up in a cramped flat. The glamour of being associated with someone from his background, despite it being completely dysfunctional, might have been intoxicating for her. Nathan admitted it was possible he played the 'posh' card a little too much with Laura in the beginning, but as she had been so exceptionally gorgeous he'd felt he needed every advantage he could get.

His wife now worked for a venture capital firm. She'd started as an administrative assistant but, after taking dozens of exams to 'better herself and her chances' (her description), she'd progressed to operations manager – a remarkable achievement given she'd had three children along the way. She still wasn't satisfied with that, though, and continually moaned about how much more she could earn if she moved back to London. Nathan had grown up in the capital and had no wish to return, yet another thorn in their relationship.

The postman noisily shoving something through the letterbox pulled him from his thoughts, and he padded down the hall to retrieve the mail.

There were four items; the first two were a bank statement, which wouldn't make good reading – he left that to one side – and a small catalogue for children's books, which had Laura's name on it. He placed that on top of the bank statement. The last two envelopes intrigued him. They were of the white windowed variety and, although both were addressed to Laura, he could see underneath the window on one of them and noticed his name and a policy number. On the back, the name and address of the sender: The Corporate Mutual Insurance Company.

Nathan opened it and read the script:

Dear Mrs Jones

<u>*Mr Nathan Jones – Policy Number CM2345GY98*</u>

We were sorry to hear about the recent death of your husband. As discussed with you in our telephone conversation on 23 November please find enclosed the requested information. We apologise for the delay in forwarding this to you but due to an issue with our systems we had not realised this request had not yet been actioned. We apologise for any distress or inconvenience this may have caused you.

Enclosed is the relevant claim form for completion to enable us to consider the claim under this policy.

Please note, in order to be able to pay the proceeds, under policy number CM2345GY98 we will need sight of the original death certificate and for this reason we recommend you return the completed form together with the death certificate by recorded delivery to ensure no delay is caused by lost documentation.

Our thoughts are with you at this difficult time, and if you need to speak to us directly, please call our confidential customer helpline on 0804 345 6788. The phone line is staffed between the hours of 8.30 a.m. until 5.30 p.m., Monday to Friday.

We trust that you will find this to be in order.

Yours sincerely

Mr K Stanton
Senior Claims Executive
Encs.

Relevant Claim Form

Nathan sat down on the couch, stunned. The morning he had been found alive by the mortuary girl his wife had been on the phone to the insurance company chasing money. No wonder she'd been so 'shocked' to find him still living. He knew his wife could occasionally be, well, if he was honest always, 'money orientated', but his body had hardly been cold and the first thing she'd decided to do was cash in on his death. Nathan had two life insurance policies, the one referred to in the letter and another joint one with Laura that covered the mortgage. He'd no doubt that she'd been on the phone chasing that one as well. What a cold-hearted bitch.

He decided to open the other envelope, fully expecting it to be from the other insurance company, but this one turned out to be even more bizarre as it contained his death certificate. As he sat staring at it he suddenly shuddered, as if someone had just walked across his grave. He then comforted himself with the thought that not many people got to read their own death certificate.

*

He decided to wait until all the girls were asleep that evening before confronting his wife. She'd poured herself a large glass of Shiraz and slumped down onto the couch to watch TV. Nathan sat opposite in an armchair and watched her, wondering if she really could be as hard-hearted as her actions appeared to suggest.

It was clear Laura could feel his eyes on her. 'What is it, Nathan? Why are you staring at me?'

'I opened some letters today.'

Laura sipped her wine and smiled. 'That's nice; highlight of your day, was it?'

He nodded. 'In a way, yeah. The first letter came from The Corporate Mutual Insurance Company.'

He watched the colour drain from her face. 'Nathan, I can explain.'

'Go on, then.'

'Err, well, I had concerns that they'd cancel the policies before I could register a claim – you know what these insurance companies are like, they'll try and weasel out of paying any way they can.' Laura smiled, obviously happy with her quick thinking.

'Why would they cancel the policies, Laura? They were up to date and as far as they were concerned I'd been killed legitimately, so why would there be any issues?'

'Well ...' Laura paused and chewed on her bottom lip. 'Yeah, but the premiums came out of your bank account and with you dead all your accounts would have been frozen. The bank wouldn't have paid so I wanted to make sure I got the claim in before they could cancel due to non-payment of premiums.'

'Is that why you were so fast to get my death certificate as well?'

Laura nodded. 'Yeah, they said they needed that to process the claim.'

Nathan thought that over for a moment. He really wanted to believe her, but the problem was, he knew his wife inside out. 'Doesn't exactly tally up with your earlier claim to be really upset and grieving, though, does it?'

Laura sighed and put her glass down on the floor. 'I don't know what you want me to say, Nathan.'

Neither did he. Did he want his wife to beg for forgiveness, admit she was cold and unfeeling towards him and tell him that everything would change? If she did he wouldn't believe her anyway; they were too far gone for that and he knew it. 'We could go to counselling.'

Laura stared at him for a moment, blinked several times and dismissed the suggestion. 'I don't believe in that sort of thing.'

'What do you mean, you don't believe in it? You can

maybe get away with not believing in fairies, UFOs and leprechauns, but marriage counselling is real, proven and helps loads of couples.'

'I think our marriage is beyond fixing, Nathan, and has been for a long time.'

'What you mean is, you don't want to fix it.'

Laura picked up her glass, took a gulp of wine and shook her head. 'I can't be bothered, Nathan, and I think that's worse. It just seems like too much effort. I wasn't glad when you died but, I should tell you, I was relieved. I know that sounds cold-hearted and unfeeling but it's the truth. It meant I wouldn't have to deal with this, deal with you, deal with us. I wanted to wait a little longer until you were completely healed but ... well, there you are ... you forced it out of me.'

'It didn't take much.'

'No, it didn't and there's the problem, isn't it? I need to leave and move on. I need more from my life than you.'

'What about the girls?'

'It'll be hard at first, but they'll adapt. In the long run it'll be better for them not to have to live with our arguing and ... what would I call it ... apathy?'

'Indifference.'

'Yeah, see, you get it, don't you? Deep down you know I'm right. It'll let you move on too, maybe find someone new.'

'I don't want anyone new. I want the Laura I married.'

Laura smiled sadly at her husband. 'That Laura died a

long time ago. You killed her slowly over time, strangled the life out of her.'

'That's horrible.'

Laura shrugged. 'It's the truth.'

'It's *your* truth.'

*

Laura looked at her husband for a moment, trying to remember what it had been like to love him. She'd changed over the years while he'd remained pretty much the same, stuck in a rut. Maybe it had been unfair of her to expect more given his family and background, the very family background that had made him so attractive in the first place. Laura knew she had an ambitious social-climbing streak in her at a time when it had become increasingly unfashionable to admit to such a thing. In her mind, quality mattered and whatever else she thought about her husband he had quality – if such a thing existed. It helped he was good-looking, but he never seemed to realise that, which over the years had been at times a comfort and at others a curse. He attracted people to him with his easy manner and chilled-out personality. That personality trait annoyed her the most, though – he didn't worry about things. Appointments to Nathan were vague arrangements, deadlines something to work towards, the future ... what future?

She could have had anyone; at the time she probably

hadn't realised that, but it had been true. She'd been intelligent, beautiful and outgoing. Nathan was so loyal, so devoted like a little puppy, and almost as cute.

Over time, though, loyalty and devotion became wearing and irritating. With Nathan dead her plan had been to sell up and relocate to London. The life insurance money would have come in handy, especially given the costs of living down there, but, in any event, she'd get by.

She sighed. 'It doesn't matter whose truth it is, Nathan. I'm going to make it easier on everybody and move out. I've applied for a transfer to London and as soon as that's approved I'll leave. You can live here with the girls and that way they don't miss out on their schooling and stuff. I'll see them at weekends and holidays.'

*

Nathan sat in shock; he hadn't known how the conversation would end. He hadn't anticipated a happy ending but Laura's returning to London hadn't even been on his radar. 'If you want out, London's a bit drastic; couldn't you just stay with your mum and dad for a bit and see how it goes?'

'I know you can't, but, if you could, would you go back and live with *your* parents?'

Nathan shook his head. 'I barely lived with them the first time around, so no. But why London? You were the one desperate to get away from there years ago.'

Laura nodded and bit her lip. 'Yeah, that was then, this

is now. The world's changed, I've changed. This way life will be much more pleasant for everyone.'

'Much more pleasant for you, you mean, living it up in London.'

Laura shook her head. 'I won't be doing any of that, Nathan. I'll be working hard to try and build a better future for myself and the girls. And you know what? For the first time since I was nineteen I'll be doing it on my own.'

She waited for a reply and when none came announced, 'I'll be out of here in early January. What we need to do over the next few weeks is pretend that everything is normal for the girls' sake over Christmas. That shouldn't be too difficult for us really – it's what we've been doing for years.' She tossed back her hair and the rest of her wine and stomped out of the room.

Nathan switched off the TV and sat back in his chair, thinking. He couldn't contemplate life without Laura, despite their problems. He'd somehow always believed that things would get better, fix themselves in one way or another. Her cold determination left him reeling.

After a while he went to bed and slipped in beside his sleeping wife – well, he assumed she'd gone to sleep as she made no movement when he snuggled up beside her. He'd been sleeping like this for over a decade now, he couldn't imagine doing anything else, but some time soon his bed would be cold and empty. Would he be able to cope?

Chapter 5

Christmas and New Year passed with a black cloud hanging over the flat. No matter how he tried Nathan couldn't shake off the gloom. Even the usual manic Christmas morning present fest had a hollow feel about it. The girls returned to school and nursery and the time Nathan had been dreading was nearly upon him.

This would be his last weekend at home with his wife. He'd been trying to come up with a plan to make her stay but, so far, he'd drawn a blank. He'd pleaded with her a few times over the last few weeks, but she wasn't interested. He'd considered trying to emotionally blackmail her with the girls but didn't want to use his children so blatantly. Besides, he'd decided, if her daughters had meant that much to her she wouldn't be leaving anyway.

The whole thing had come about due to that stupid afternoon when he'd stepped in front of the bus. Laura had said it had only hurried up the inevitable, but Nathan wasn't so sure. Laura had glimpsed the potential of a life without him when that had happened, and it had been the catalyst for everything else that had followed. It wasn't as if he thought their married life had been perfect, far from it, but, in his head, they had stayed together for the good of their family. In his maybe old-fashioned view of the world this appeared to be perfectly acceptable if it meant they remained together. Miserable, but together.

He smiled at his own analysis. He didn't want a miserable marriage any more than his wife did. He wanted their old relationship back, the one they'd had when they were first together, the first few months of wide-eyed wonder they'd shared after Millie's birth when everything had seemed filled with promise and novelty.

Millie and Chloe would be home from school soon. After that he planned to cook up some steaks for Laura and himself. Millie would have a little bit and he'd do some pasta for the younger girls, who wouldn't touch steak. He'd already bought a nice bottle of expensive Shiraz; well, a tenner seemed expensive for him. He'd sauté some potatoes and serve them and the steak with green beans, pepper sauce and onion rings, the height of sophistication for Nathan. It also felt a little like the last meal for a condemned prisoner or, perhaps more fittingly, the last meal for a condemned marriage.

He'd been so busy in the kitchen that he almost forgot to get Daisy from nursery and had to zoom up the road in his car. He made it just as the last of the parents were leaving the building. When he bustled into the classroom he found Daisy sitting on Mrs Ridgwell's knee, crying.

Mrs Ridgwell, a severe woman in early menopause, always appeared to be mad at everything and everyone.

'Daisy's been upset all day, Mr Jones. She says her mummy's leaving – is that true?'

Nathan frowned. They'd deliberately agreed to limit what they said to Daisy, deciding she would be too young to grasp the reality of their situation. Of course, her older sisters had been subject to no such censor and he suspected they'd been telling Daisy more than she needed to know.

'She's going to be working down south a few days each week, that's all.' He wasn't willing to share more than that with strangers.

Mrs Ridgwell looked over the top of her glasses at Nathan and pouted. 'Daisy is very upset about it. I think your wife should reconsider going if this is the effect it's going to have on her children.'

Nathan initially reacted with anger at her poking her nose in where it had no right to be, but then he realised she echoed his own sentiments exactly. So he relaxed and said, 'I'll mention it to her, Mrs Ridgwell.' He prised his daughter free from the clutches of the scowling teacher and guided her to his car.

Daisy's demeanour brightened considerably when she arrived home and into the loving circle of her sisters, a relationship so complex, enveloping and at times contradictory that Nathan, as a man and a father, would never completely understand it. However, as he stood and watched Chloe and Millie making a fuss of their youngest sibling he decided, whatever happened between him and Laura, he'd always put his girls first.

His wife arrived home from work tired and stressed as usual. She said a quick hello to everyone, accepted a glass of wine from Nathan and disappeared to soak in the bath.

*

Later, after dinner, Laura and Nathan sat in silence at the dinner table. The plates had been cleared and stacked in the sink and Laura pulled out a notepad from her handbag. She poured the remainder of the wine into their glasses and said, 'Right, Nathan, you're going to have your hands full on Monday, so you need to make a list of what needs done and when.'

'Do I?'

'If you want to have any kind of life you do, yeah.'

'I like my life just as it is.'

Laura sighed. 'Well, it doesn't really matter what you like, does it, Nathan? It's going to change and you either accept it now, or in a week, or in a month's time. It'd be easier for the girls if you could at least pretend to be an adult and listen to me.'

Nathan bristled but checked his anger. He didn't want the rest of the weekend to be a battleground. 'I'm listening,' he said tersely.

Laura ripped a few pages out of the pad and passed

them over; digging into her bag, she produced a pen and handed that over too.

Nathan picked the pen up and waited. 'So, I'm your secretary now, am I?'

Laura smiled. 'Just for a little while. Now, I know you spend a lot of time with the girls doing the fun stuff. What you also need to do now, is the mundane stuff, like ironing and prepping.'

'I do prepping.'

'You occasionally iron a skirt or fill a water bottle. Right, we'll start with school stuff. Millie and Chloe need their uniforms washed and ironed at the weekend. I'll make sure there's a week's worth ready but next weekend you'll need to be prepared. You'll need five white blouses each, five skirts, and either tights or socks depending on the weather. Probably tights will be the order of the day most of the time.' Laura paused and nodded as Nathan took notes. 'Daisy just needs normal clothes for nursery but, if it looks like it's going to be wet, try and pick older outfits as she'll end up covered in mud. Before the girls go to school you need to do their hair. Millie likes a little side-pleat and you need to use tiny little hairbands for that—'

'I don't know how to do pleats.'

'Millie will show you; it's not difficult. You need to make sure Millie and Chloe have a snack for the morning and a bottle of water each. Yes, before you speak I know you do them, but with all the other stuff going on you might forget so write it down. They both eat school lunches, so you don't need to worry about that, but Daisy needs a packed lunch every day. She likes ham or cheese in her sandwiches but not both together, despite what she says. She also needs at least three bits of fruit, though she only ever eats two.'

'So why not just put two in, then?'

Laura glanced up. 'Because if you put in two pieces, she'll only eat one.'

'What happens if you put four pieces in?'

'She still only eats two. Now, you also need to make sure you've got the list of stuff they do after school and nursery. You already do most of this, but let's run through it anyway. Monday at 5 p.m. Millie goes to dancing and Chloe to football.'

'Daisy stays with me.'

'She does. Tuesday and Wednesday are free nights. Thursday Chloe has swimming lessons at 4.30 and Daisy goes to Gym Tots; they're both in the same place so that's easy but remember Millie's iPad. Saturday morning Millie and Chloe go to drama but I'm not sure Chloe's that keen, so you might have to let her drop out.'

'I thought she loved it.'

'She did, but now I'm not so sure. Sunday is free as you know, but instead of watching the football you'll need to catch up on your ironing and cleaning. Most evenings try and get Millie and Chloe to do their reading and homework before you put the TV on for them because, as you know, otherwise it's a nightmare trying to get them away from it.'

'It all sounds like a riot.'

'You'll cope, but I'll put everything on a list, so you don't forget. You need to hoover every day, the kitchen floor needs cleaning with the steam mop every night after the carnage that is dinner time is over, but you usually do that anyway, and the fridge needs cleaning at least once a month and sometimes more. There's loads more, but that'll do for now. I'll write everything down on a master list for you, so you have it all handy. I'll also email it all over to you because, knowing you, you'll lose the list in a day or two.'

'I won't.'

'You will. This way you'll always have a copy.'

'A reminder of how much my wife loves me.'

Laura sighed. 'A reminder that, regardless of what you think, Nathan, we need to put the girls before everything.'

'Running away from them isn't exactly a good example of that, is it?'

'I'm not having this conversation with you, Nathan. It's pointless, we've been there already. I'm doing this for everyone's benefit. Now, tomorrow I'm taking the girls into town as I need to get some new clothes for work and there's a sale on at Clarks, so I'll try and get Chloe some new school shoes because she's nearly grown out of her last ones. Sunday we'll try and do something as a family, but we need to try and be civil to each other so that it's not a total disaster, okay?'

Nathan nodded. 'Maybe the zoo if the weather looks nice?'

'Yeah, good idea, that'll keep everyone busy and we can visit your relatives.'

'My relatives?'

'Yeah, the chimps.'

He managed to laugh.

Chapter 6

I'd just finished working with Sid on what we called a 'stinker'. Not a nice description but an accurate one. This poor old soul had died about a month ago in her council flat in Leith and had lain undiscovered throughout Christmas and New Year, until a neighbour had phoned environmental health about the 'smelly drains'.

We didn't know much about her, as was often the case with 'stinkers'. Although the weather had been very cold she'd had the heating set at maximum when she'd died so the decomposition had advanced considerably and bits of her had started to fall apart like an over-cooked Christmas turkey – except there would be no gravy, pleasant aroma or feel-good factor associated with this one.

The cause of death couldn't be established from our post-mortem and Sid hoped the lab reports would give some clue to any grieving relative that came out of the woodwork.

I felt a little sad even though I'd worked on dozens of these over the years. It always surprised me that so many people in our digital and fast-moving world died seemingly friendless and unnoticed. Maybe one day we'd all have little devices built into our bodies that sent out a signal when we were about to die. At least then she could have updated her status on Facebook with a message saying: 'sorry I can't watch the video of your daughter singing an out of tune song because I've just died'. Then she might not have lain undiscovered for weeks.

We cleaned ourselves up, changed into new scrubs and went for a bite of lunch. When I first started in the mortuary the thought of even looking at food after such a stomach-churning morning would have made me ill but it's amazing how time and exposure dull your senses. My tummy rumbled at the promise of some watery National Health canteen soup.

Sid said he'd started a diet, though I wasn't sure why as he had virtually no body fat at all. I'd asked him about it and he'd replied, 'I have cellulite everywhere' – words I'm pretty sure a straight bloke would never utter – and then he ordered a baked potato with no filling. Personally, I'd rather eat cardboard.

'So, Kat, how's your love life?' Most of our conversations started this way. He had an unhealthy interest in my love life, which tended to be a short conversation. Occasionally he'd announce, 'I'm going to a punk reunion gig this weekend.' I had real problems picturing him among some of the throng of gobbing pseudo-violent psychopaths that must attend those things. Sid always reminded me of

Marcus from Nick Hornby's novel *About a Boy*, a real fish out of water at the best of times.

'My love life is still going through a dry period Sid. No, that's wrong; suspended animation would be a better description.'

'You need to get out more, Kat. You have to be seen to be dated. I mean, nobody's going to turn up at your door, are they?'

'I had two Jehovah's Witnesses around last night.'

'Were either of them cute?'

'They were both cute, smartly dressed and glowing like someone had just buffed them up with a leather chamois and a bucket of car wax.'

'Maybe you should try the internet.'

'Online dating? My friend Hayley did that. It wasn't good for her.'

'She's the hot one?'

'Yeah, so hot she's on fire.'

'But it might be different for you, Kat; you're not so ...'

I pointed my spoon, dripping with lethal minestrone, at him. 'Watch what you say here, Sid.' I laughed as he struggled to find words.

'Obvious, you're not as obvious as her, so you would probably attract less weirdos.'

'I'm Goth, Sid, I'm a weirdo magnet.'

'You're being too hard on yourself. I think you're very pretty. There's absolutely nobody on the horizon?'

The desperately cute image of a sleeping Nathan Jones

flashed into my mind and for the thousandth time since I'd met him, I wondered how he'd fared since going home, but as usual I dismissed it. He had a wife and three kids to boot. 'No, Sid, nobody at all.'

'Maybe drop the Goth thing, then?'

'I don't think I can. I've never felt comfortable in my own skin. Even as a kid when my mum used to cart me off to birthday parties dressed in sequinned silver party dresses, I felt like I stood out like a sore thumb and that everyone would be staring and judging how ridiculous I looked, like a gorilla in hot pants.'

'I bet you didn't.'

'No, I know that now, but back then, well, that's how I felt.'

A few minutes of pleasant silence passed between us as we finished eating before I brought up the subject of family. 'How's your folks?'

'Mm,' Sid mumbled while swallowing a fork-full of potato. 'They've started on a new project. Recreating the Settle to Carlisle line, in 1:64 scale.'

'Sid, that made about as much sense to me as the number eleven.'

'Eleven?'

'Yeah, I've always thought it should be onety-one. I assume the thing your mum and dad are doing is something to do with trains?' Sid's parents were model railway enthusiasts and they'd met at a fair, or whatever they called places where train weirdos got together. He'd regaled me with stories of his childhood, he and his brother foraging in the fridge for food at mealtimes, sitting alone with his teacher on parents' evening because his mum and dad had become so engrossed in their latest project they'd forgotten all about everything else.

I noted the bewildered look on Sid's face as he tried to work out the 'onety-one' thing, then he shook his head and said, 'Yeah, the Settle to Carlisle line is the highest railway line in England and—'

'Yeah, thanks, Sid. I could probably have lived out the rest of my life quite happily without knowing that, thank you very much.'

'Me too, but you did ask.'

'I did.'

'What about you – have you been home to see your mum and dad recently?'

I finished chewing on a rubbery piece of bread crust. 'Not for a few weeks. I'll need to make the trip next weekend, I suppose, seeing as I'm not working.'

'"Make the trip"? You make it sound like it's hundreds of miles; it's only Glasgow.'

I laughed. 'Yeah, but a trip home always makes me feel like I've entered *The Twilight Zone*.'

Sid smiled at me. 'What's your dad got in his sheds these days?'

'I dread to think. It's an ever-changing smorgasbord.'

'Does your mum still have her ironing fixation?'

'Ironing, hoovering, washing her hands, cleaning the light bulbs ...'

'Cleaning the light bulbs?'

'Yeah, that's one of her new ones. A few months ago, the light in the hall needed a new bulb and when she went to change it she felt disgusted, that was her word, "disgusted", to see how dusty and dirty it had become, so she's now taken to cleaning all the light bulbs in the house ... and other people's houses.'

Sid put his cup down. 'Other people's houses? I can't really imagine she goes and knocks on their door and says, "Can I come in and inspect your light bulbs, please?"'

I laughed. 'I wouldn't put it past her, but no, my dad had to take her home from their friends' house last week because she started doing it there. My dad has his foibles too, but I think my mum is getting worse; we used to think the menopause might be partly responsible but she's past that now, so we don't have that excuse. Her latest, apart from the light bulb cleaning, is that she's got a thing going with the fridge.'

'A thing going?'

'Well, yeah, it's one of those big American models and she stood for half an hour opening and closing the door.'

'Why?'

'She wanted to make sure the light went out when she closed the door.'

'But you—'

'I know.'

'That's—'

'I know.'

'What did your dad say?'

'He took the bulb out.'

'That'll work.'

'Smart man, my dad, but it doesn't work in other people's houses.'

'No, it wouldn't.'

'They don't visit much just now.'

'No, I don't suppose they do.'

'That's why my dad spends much more time in his sheds, looking at sheds online or even better if he can sit in a shed talking online to other people about their sheds. He's going to enter "Shed of the Year" this year. Actually, that's not true. He's entering two of his sheds for the "Shed of the Year".'

Sid shook his head and gave me the same look he always did when we talked about my parents, the one that said, 'How the hell did you make it out of childhood with only a Goth persona and confidence issues?'

The worry is that one day I'll end up like my mum. True, I don't have to go back home three times every day to make sure I've switched off the cooker and unplugged the kettle or check seven times that I've locked the door before getting in my car and I don't always need to count to twenty-five when ordering a coffee from Costa or to eighty-one in Starbucks. I know that sounds kind of random, but my mum needs to multiply the number of letters in the coffee shop's name by itself (Costa – five letters times five letters equals twenty-five). If she ever visits a café in that weird Welsh village with the ridiculous name, I might never see her again.

Although I've not reached that level I have enough issues to know I might get worse and become un-dateable – perhaps I already have.

Chapter 7

The plane sat at the top of the runway awaiting clearance from air traffic control. Permission granted, it thundered down the runway and into the air. After watching Edinburgh shrink to 'Toytown' proportions then disappear into the distance from her window seat, Laura sat back and felt guilty. She knew she'd be back in a week or two but the pain she suddenly felt at leaving her daughters behind hit her like an unexpected punch in the gut. She stifled a sob, glad she had a row of seats to herself. A few minutes later Lilly, one of two BA cabin crew on the one-hour-thirty-minute flight to Heathrow, poured her a large glass of white wine, which helped numb the pain somewhat.

Her guilt extended to Nathan as well. Deep down she knew he'd be fine. He had the girls to keep him busy and eventually he'd come to realise it would be the best solution for everyone. He'd pleaded with her not to leave with tears in his eyes and she'd almost caved, before remembering that in the whole of her adult life she'd never had the chance to be by herself.

Getting pregnant at nineteen had robbed her of the years her friends had enjoyed partying, experimenting, travelling and learning who they were. She'd never figured out how to be comfortable in her own skin or to set her own life expectations. Nathan had denied her all of this and she'd always be bitter and resentful about that, even though deep down she knew she'd been partly responsible. She felt justified in shifting most of the blame onto him as he'd been the older out of the two of them when they'd met and should have known better, even though over the years she'd come to realise that Nathan had never really grown up – perhaps men in general never did, never had to.

She sipped her drink and tried to put the negative thoughts to the back of her mind. She settled back into her seat, loosened the seat belt and tried to relax, telling herself that for the first time in years she'd broken free from the shackles of motherhood, free from Nathan and free from the fractious nature of their relationship. The problem seemed to be, though, as soon as she reminded herself about her husband it inevitably brought the girls back into focus and she ended up trying to analyse it again. Yes, she'd loved Nathan once – back in the days when he'd had fire in his belly and ambition in his heart.

When the girls had been born, though, it felt as if each one of them had robbed him of a little bit of that fire. After Daisy had appeared it had all gone – no ambition and no get up and go. It appeared as if his mission in life had been fulfilled with the birth of his daughters and now he channelled all his efforts into them. Helping Millie with her school project work, dancing competitions and drama, spending countless hours with Chloe to make sure her reading and writing were perfect and even devoting time to Daisy's scribbled drawings and silly songs.

In Laura's mind it wasn't normal for a father to do all that. Maybe she had old-fashioned views, but she expected her husband to be a provider, a hunter who went out into the world and made a niche for himself that allowed him to bring home money, so she could kick back and take it a little easier, possibly do some of the things that Nathan took it upon himself to do. To be the care-giver, the mother, the educator, even though she much preferred being at work verbally jousting with adults across a boardroom table to arguing over who had the pink pram first and whose turn it was to choose which DVD to watch.

Now that she'd broken free, at least for a week or two, she could make some decisions. Belatedly decide where she wanted her life to lead, where she would live and maybe one day who she would live it with. Turning her musings to her new life cheered her up. It would be exciting and scary. She'd rented a small flat in Putney, south of the river and only a short journey from her new office in Fulham. Even though it had only one bedroom the rent came to nearly £1200 a month. The flat would be cramped whenever the girls came to stay but they'd manage. It would be like camping, at least that's how she'd try and sell it to them. She'd arranged everything online and hadn't yet, set foot in the apartment. That afternoon she'd pick up the keys at the letting agency and sign the last of the paperwork.

The expectations of her bosses would be higher too, now that she'd relocated to the head office, but she looked forward to having that pressure. It would mean long hours and hard work but all of it had to be easier than being a mum.

The plane bumped down onto the tarmac at Heathrow and she noticed with dismay the rain lashing against the windows and the strong wind making the water ripple across the ground. *Great*, she thought.

She spent an hour and a half travelling across London, dragging two suitcases and a laptop bag. Thankfully the evening rush hour hadn't started yet, which made the Underground bearable. She emerged from Putney Bridge Tube station and discovered the rain still hammering down with very little shelter nearby. Even though the letting agent's office could only be a five-minute walk, she hailed a taxi. She had too much baggage, both physically and metaphorically at that point, to travel any distance on foot in this weather. Even the short time it took to clamber into a taxi left her soaked. As the water dripped down her face it hid the tears that she tried to stop spilling from her eyes as they made their way along Fulham High Street onto Fulham Palace Road, where the taxi sloshed to a stop outside the pokey letting agent's office.

She pulled herself together, paid the driver and entered the agency. Inside an older man with Greek or Turkish heritage greeted her. He reeked of stale cigarettes and stared at her cleavage the whole uncomfortable ten minutes it took to complete the last of the paperwork.

'Will you be living alone, Mrs Jones?' he asked creepily in a heavily accented voice.

'No, my husband will be here later. He had some business to attend to in the City.' She lied, allowing a small smile to creep across her face at the thought of Nathan having anything to do in the City apart from maybe drink coffee.

Laura detected an expression of disappointment flick across the man's face as he handed her two sets of keys. She almost fled from his presence and then hailed another taxi. Ten minutes later it deposited her outside a large brown sandstone building. She stood on the pavement staring at her new home. Guarding the main entrance were two wilting New Zealand palms that looked as miserable as she felt.

She entered the communal hallway, which smelled old and mildewed, and trudged up the four flights of stairs (no lift) to the fourth floor where her new home awaited.

Four numbered doors, 11–14, confronted her on the landing. Her flat, number 14, had a grey door and as she inserted the key and pushed the door open it bounced back, locking itself again. She opened it more carefully this time and discovered a badly built inner wall that stopped the door from opening fully.

She struggled inside with her cases and eventually managed to squeeze the front door shut. She left her bags where they lay on the floor and toured her new home for the first time. It didn't take long. A small living room and kitchen, an even smaller bedroom with a double bed and a tiny built-in wardrobe. The mattress on the bed displayed some suspicious-looking stains and she decided she wouldn't be sleeping on that for long.

The bathroom, just off the bedroom, only had a shower cubicle so no soaks in the tub after a long day for her. She sighed and sat on the edge of the stained bed. The whole place smelt stale and unloved, which pretty much described how she felt as well. This time she let the tears come and they flowed down her face as her body shuddered with huge sobs. She'd never felt so lonely and so alone.

Chapter 8

Nathan should have been ready for the tears and the bad behaviour from his girls on the day their mother left but how did you prepare for something like that? He didn't know. His own emotions were raw, which made dealing with his daughters' feelings even harder.

Millie withdrew to her room and cut all the hair off two of her Bratz dolls. Chloe demanded to watch a documentary about elephants. Nathan searched all the channels and the various on-demand options, finding programmes about lions, rhinos and even hippos but nothing on elephants. Chloe cried and flung herself to the ground like a two-year-old. Daisy sat and played with her Sylvanian Families, occasionally coming into the kitchen to check that her daddy hadn't left and to bash him on the head with a large plastic hammer that she'd recently taken a shine to. Then she promptly peed her pants for the first time in nearly a year.

Thankfully the first day represented the peak of their discontentment; next morning everyone had to attend school or nursery and were too busy to worry about much. Finally, left alone, Nathan sulked for a while, partly about Laura leaving and partly about the ridiculous amount of work he had to do in getting everyone ready and out of the door in time for everything.

Laura had been right about that – he really hadn't known what it involved. By the end of the week he'd managed to get into a sort of routine, only interrupted by the evening call that Laura made to speak to the girls. This went reasonably smoothly for the first few weeks, then one Friday Laura announced to Nathan, 'Next weekend I want to bring the girls down here for a few days.'

'That's a hassle, Laura. They'll hardly get there, and they'll have to turn around and come back.'

'Not really; it's only an hour on the plane and they've got an in-service day at the school on the Monday, so they don't need to be back until Monday night so that gives me an extra day with them.'

'How—?'

Laura interrupted him. 'My mum's going to bring them down; all you need to do is drop them all at the airport for 3 p.m.'

'You've worked it all out, huh?'

'I'm organised, Nathan.'

'You said your flat's tiny.'

'It is, but we'll manage as it's only for three nights.'

Nathan had detected a hint of regret in Laura's voice on the phone each evening. Perhaps having the girls over a weekend would be a good thing and she might realise how much she missed both them and him. Well, them, at any rate.

Nathan hadn't imagined Laura would completely abandon her kids, but he'd expected her to fly up and down at the weekends, not drag them all down there. So far, she'd only made it home once since leaving, but she said this had been down to having to work extra hard, including weekends, to 'make her mark' in the office.

On the following Friday he dutifully drove everyone, including his mother-in-law, to the airport and waited until the flight took off before heading home to an empty house. He hadn't made any plans to do anything so when his friend Graham phoned and suggested a beer he readily agreed.

Nathan arrived at the pub first, but, it only being five minutes from his house, this wasn't a surprise. He ordered two pints and went to sit at a table near the back where he could see the TV. Some lower-league football match played out for single lonely males who had nothing better to do on a Friday night. Nathan's local wouldn't be described as lively; it lacked the thumping dance music and flashing lights of uptown bars. The muted dark atmosphere attracted a certain clientele, older with less testosterone. During the week some of the patrons were local MSPs from the parliament building nearby.

As it was a Friday most of the MSPs had returned to their constituencies, but Nathan recognised Steven Cowley, a large sweaty man sitting alone at the bar nursing a glass. He'd been all over the news in recent weeks, having been caught having an affair with a young intern. His wife had taken their children and left.

The affair had been revealed on the Channel 5 breakfast show hosted by ex-celebrity chef Lance Donaldson. The show tended to focus on the more salacious news items and frequently wheeled in those in the public eye who'd become embroiled in some scandal or other, though Lance's team wasn't averse to using ordinary members of the public if celebrity scandals were thin on the ground.

Nathan didn't usually take much notice of such things, but this stuck in his mind because the intern had been exceptionally pretty, and he couldn't understand what a young girl saw in such a fat oaf as Cowley. Power must be a powerful aphrodisiac to attract someone like that to him. Well, he'd paid a high price, as the intern had dumped him in the end, unable to cope with the publicity.

He got pulled from his thoughts by the arrival of Graham, who waved across the bar and made a drinking motion with his hand. Nathan shook his head and pointed at the two drinks already on the table. Graham sat down opposite him.

'How's things?'

'Oh, fair to crap, I suppose.'

'Laura's taken them all weekend?'

'Yeah, the flat's so quiet.'

'I wish Alison would take our two and disappear for the odd weekend.'

Graham had two children, Jack and Emma, with his partner Alison. They weren't married, which didn't appear to be an issue for either of them.

'Yeah, but it'd be different if Alison had left you. You wouldn't be so keen then.'

'Does that mean you're going to sit and mope about for three days?'

'I like moping about.'

'It's not good for you.'

'How would you know? Have you been studying up on the dangers of moping?'

'It's not healthy; you need to get out and about, do something new.'

'Like what?'

'I don't know – maybe you should try and find a girl-friend.'

'What?'

'A girlfriend. Laura's not coming back, you know.'

'How do you know that? You know nothing about it.'

Graham smiled. 'I know enough about you two to know you've been unhappy for years. One of you had to make a move and now that she's done it, she's not going to come back.'

'She might realise how much she misses our life and—'

'You make each other miserable.'

'We don't.'

'You do. I've listened to you for years go on and on about it; so has Alison.'

Nathan sank the rest of his beer in silence, knowing his friend was right but not wanting to admit it in public. Graham went to the bar and came back with more drinks and changed the subject. 'I've got some work coming in over the next few weeks that I can send your way if you're up for it?'

'Yeah, of course, I've not got a lot on the go right now, so that would be really useful.'

'Okay, the first one is from one of our farming clients. It's not a huge account but they need a campaign put together to sell their range of nettle drinks.'

'Nettle drinks – what, like stinging nettles!'

'Yeah, they had fields full of nettles, so they decided to harvest them and make them into a range of drinks. Nettles are good for you.'

'Is that the slogan you want me to use?'

'Mm, maybe something a bit more imaginative will be needed; the public perception of nettles isn't great.'

'What kind of drinks do they make from nettles?'

'Well, they make nettle-ade, which is I suppose is like lemonade with nettles instead of lemons, and they have nettle iced tea, which is like—'

'Yeah, okay, I get the picture.'

'I'll send you some of it over on Monday, so you can try it.'

'Have you had some?'

'Yeah.'

'Well?'

'I suppose you'd say it's an acquired taste.'

'You mean it's disgusting.'

'Yeah, pretty much.'

'Thanks, mate.'

'You're welcome. The other thing I'd like you to look at is in the pet-care line, but I'll send it over rather than try and describe it.'

'Pet-care?'

'Yeah, I'll talk to you once you've seen it.' Graham smiled. 'We're definitely not out on the pull tonight, then?'

Nathan looked around the bar. Besides Steven Cowley still drowning his sorrows there were three blokes in overalls, an old chap with stained brown trousers and a large backpack-wearing tourist worrying the barman with a map and exaggerated gesticulations. 'Nah, I'm not in the mood. Besides neither of us have pulled anything for more than a decade. I wouldn't know what to say any more.'

'Nobody would be interested in you anyway in your current state. You'd scare any woman away with chat about your wife.'

Nathan supposed he might be right, but the image of Kat flashed into his head. Her dark eyes, pretty face and white teeth occasionally appeared in his dreams, but she didn't deserve to be burdened with his troubles. She probably had enough of her own to be going on with. He downed his drink and headed for the bar.

*

The next morning, he awoke with a mouth that felt, and probably tasted, like the bottom of a budgie's cage and a head that thumped incessantly. It even hurt to move his eyes. He hadn't been drunk for a long time and could only vaguely remember getting home. He still had his clothes on from the night before so obviously he'd just fallen into bed.

He very slowly made his way to the kitchen and swallowed two paracetamol and a bottle of water before returning to bed to wait for the painkillers to kick in, thankful for the first, and only, time that weekend that his girls weren't there.

Later in the afternoon he went for a walk in Holyrood Park to clear his head and ordered Chinese for dinner. He needed some stodge to make him feel better.

After his Friday night excesses, he spent the remainder of the weekend in the flat tidying and getting the girls' stuff ready for the next week at school. On the Monday, Graham couriered over some of the nettle drinks, which were even more disgusting than he'd imagined. Selling them would be a challenge. The pet-care thing he'd deal with tomorrow.

Later, with the girls back from their first long weekend with their mother, his world descended once more into comfortable chaos. Laura had brought them back late in the evening, tired and irritable, partly due to the lateness of the hour and partly due to the fact they hadn't slept well over the weekend, crammed into her tiny flat.

Nathan felt annoyed at Laura for bringing them back

so late, especially with Millie and Chloe having school the next day. Despite this he bit down his irritation and they worked in partnership once more as they'd done for years. Within an hour all three of their drowsy daughters were tucked up and asleep.

It almost felt like old times as they both collapsed onto the couch and sipped red wine whilst watching the ten o'clock news.

'I don't think I'll do that again in a hurry; my flat's too small. I'll try and get a bigger place soon.'

Nathan didn't reply as all he'd have said was, 'There's a big flat here you could stay in,' and the argument would have started up all over again. Apart from that, it felt reasonably normal – that was if he ignored the fact that, although Laura would be sleeping beside him in their bed, they'd be miles apart mentally, then tomorrow after she'd helped get the girls ready she'd be out of the door, leaving for London on a lunchtime flight. Then none of them would see her for weeks. It was an arrangement that suited only her.

*

Nathan awoke to an empty bed, which he'd grown used to by now. He could hear the shower in the en suite bathroom and glanced at the clock beside the bed: 6.12 a.m., an early start even by her standards. He rolled over, clutched her pillow and breathed in the familiar scent. He sighed and closed his eyes. A few minutes later his wife appeared wrapped in a big fluffy bath towel. She even managed a smile as she caught him staring at her legs. She walked over to their wardrobe, which still contained many of her clothes due to the lack of space in her London pad. She dropped the towel and quickly pulled on a pink G-string and matching bra. Nathan watched in rapt appreciation; he could feel himself becoming aroused simply by the sight of his wife putting on her clothes. He knew he could do nothing about it and it was a relief for both of them when he pulled a towel from the ottoman at the foot of the bed and went for a shower, possibly a cold one.

After a mad breakfast and the usual morning chaos only Nathan, Laura and Daisy remained in the flat.

'I'll drop Daisy off on my way to the airport if you want?' offered Laura. 'Spares you going out and means you can get some work done, and it would be nice to spend a little bit of extra time with her before I go.'

Nathan thought but didn't say, *You could spend as much time with her as you want if you only decided to live with her.* Instead he said, 'Yeah, okay. Thanks,' and wandered into his study and shut the door. Having her home, even for an evening, had been hard on him. He knew that she'd left him but somehow this coming and going made life difficult; it meant he couldn't ever get any perspective on his feelings. He imagined it might be like that for lots of couples with kids who split up.

An hour later she came into his study and sat on the

only other chair in the room beside his desk. Nathan noticed she'd dressed impeccably in a new Paul Smith black V-necked dress with black Kurt Geiger Chelsea boots that she'd proudly shown him the previous evening. He'd commented that she worked in Fulham so she'd better be careful wearing Chelsea boots. It had made her laugh and his heart had ached when she'd smiled at him.

He noticed her make-up had been perfectly applied and her hair, which had been straightened and tumbled down over her shoulders, no longer had any traces of grey in it. Even that pained him as she'd not bothered to do that when she'd been living with him. It felt as if every action she took had been carefully designed to hurt him. She'd also changed her perfume to a subtler product that reminded him of apple blossom.

*

Laura noted his pained expression; she'd expected it. She knew her coming back to the flat to stay would be hard on him. It felt uncomfortable for her too. She found it difficult to stay angry when she didn't see him every day. Maybe the old saying about familiarity breeding contempt had more than a ring of truth to it. She missed her daughters much more than she'd expected, but she'd come to realise that she could never come home. Nathan would drive her bonkers, especially now when she had other distractions in her life. She forced a smile. 'Right, then, that's me off.

I'll drop Daisy at nursery; don't forget to get her at three o'clock.'

'I haven't forgotten any day when you've not been here so I'm not going to start now.'

'Yeah, sorry.'

He sighed. 'Laura, can we not try again? All this coming and going is silly. We could sell up, buy a new bigger place and start afresh.'

'We've been over this – all we would do is take our problems with us. It's not like we can pack them in a box and leave them in a cupboard somewhere. Anyway, we couldn't afford to move; you hardly make enough to cover the mortgage as it is with your fannying about on the internet.'

'I don't fanny about. I run a top-end advertising consultancy.'

'Any time I've ever come in here, you're on some football website.'

'I only do that whilst waiting for inspiration and sometimes it's just research.'

'You must do an awful lot of waiting for inspiration, then. Also, how many football accounts are you working on?' she asked with a laugh.

*

Nathan sighed. He found it hard to be mad at Laura when she knew him so well. He wondered if he would ever have that again with someone, that intimate 'knowing' that took so long to establish.

'What are you working on just now?'

He opened a drawer in his desk and pulled out a small plastic photo frame and handed it to Laura. On the bottom of the frame a tiny fan whirled around.

'Is it a photo frame that keeps you cool?'

'That would probably be easier to sell.'

'What is it, then?'

'It's a fish comforter.'

'A what?'

'Yeah, that's what I said when they sent it to me. Basically, there's a small battery inside that powers the fan, which is actually a propeller.'

'I'm still none the wiser.'

'The idea is that people who own pet fish, aquariums and the like, stick a photo of themselves in the frame, then drop it in the water and it kind of buzzes around the tank reminding the fish of what their owner looks like when they're not there; thus, comforting the fish that they've not been forgotten about.'

Laura cocked her head to one side and gave her husband a strange look. 'I don't know much about fish, but I don't think they're that bright. In fact, I would think that being chased around a fish tank by the disembodied head of an absentee owner is likely to add more to their stress levels than anything else. Who's going to be stupid enough to buy something like this?'

'Good question. One in ten UK households now have pet fish, probably because they're relatively easy to look after and make no mess.'

'And they all worry about their pets suffering separation anxiety when they're out?'

'Not yet, they don't.'

'Oh.'

'The idea is to create anxiety and then sell this to them to satisfy that anxiety.'

'Don't you ever feel, Nathan, that what you do is completely pointless?'

Nathan laughed. 'Most of the time.'

Laura stood up and kissed him on the cheek. 'Right, I'm off. I'll phone later to speak to everyone. Look after my girls.'

Nathan longed to grab her, pull her onto his knee and lock his mouth onto hers as they'd done years ago, but instead, with a whoosh of black hair and Paul Smith, she vanished, leaving behind a faint delicate scent of apple blossom, which would haunt his office for the rest of the day.

*

Later that evening, whilst Daisy and Chloe were playing in the living room, Nathan glanced up from washing the last of the dinner plates and noticed Millie fiddling with her empty plastic glass.

'Do you want some more orange juice, sweetie?'

'No.'

'Have you had enough to eat?'

'Yes.'

It felt as if his eldest daughter was growing up fast, and although he considered her to be wise beyond her years, which he deduced happened to older siblings, she hadn't yet become a teenager. Her monosyllabic answers were out of character, signifying something was worrying her.

Given their current disastrous domestic arrangements, this didn't come as a huge surprise. When Chloe and Daisy were upset they manifested this in displays of bad behaviour and petulance and had been testing his patience a lot lately. However, Millie had grown beyond that stage and now had fewer options left open to express any distress. Nathan wiped his hands, closed the kitchen door and sat down opposite her at the table.

'What's wrong, Millie?'

'Nothing.'

Nathan started with the easy option. 'Is school all right?'

'Fine.'

'Something's bothering you.'

'I'm fine.'

'You're not fine. I know all this with Mum being away is hard, but I can't change it, not just now anyway; it's complicated.'

'You and Mum haven't been getting on for ages, Dad, I get that.'

He frowned. 'What is it, then?'

'I don't want to move to London.'

He sat back, startled by her answer. 'Who said you're moving to London? The reason we are living in this mess is because ...'

Now he had a problem. They'd agreed that, despite what either of them might think or feel, they were to present a united front to the kids. No laying guilt trips on them, no using them as tools to hurt the other. They were to pretend that their current arrangements were perfectly normal, but Millie knew that it had been her mother's decision to move away. 'I just need some space,' Laura had said countless times in those last few weeks.

Nathan took a deep breath. 'Millie, the reason Mummy is working in London is because she can make so much more money there. One day she'll come back home and in the meantime we all stay in Edinburgh and carry on like before.'

Millie bit her lip and tears formed in the corners of her eyes. 'I know, but what if Mummy doesn't want to ever come back here? Then she'll take us all to London and leave you here all alone.'

That puzzled him. What had Laura been saying. 'Why do you think that?'

The tears started to pour down Millie's face and he shuffled his chair around beside her and held her. Between snuffles and snorts she said, 'Mummy's got a boyfriend.'

That rendered him speechless.

It took a few minutes to calm his daughter down and gather his own thoughts. He got Millie some water and sat beside her. 'So how do you know Mummy's got a boyfriend?' he asked sceptically. Laura had only been in London for two months and he found it hard to believe she'd been able to break their wedding vows, for what they were worth, so quickly or indiscreetly – and, more to the point, to reduce their eldest daughter to such a state.

Millie smiled weakly at her dad. 'There were two pairs of men's boxer shorts in the washing basket in her flat.'

He tried to think of an innocent explanation for that, and, although he couldn't immediately come up with one, he decided to give Laura the benefit of the doubt. 'That doesn't mean anything, Millie. She might just have bought them for me as a present and decided to wash them before giving them to me.'

Millie stared at him, bestowing a look of pity upon her father for being so stupid. 'Dad, I checked her phone as well one morning and she had loads of dirty texts from a guy called Simon Kedward – some were way beyond stuff you see online, and others were all lovey-dovey yucky stuff. There were some pictures of them together as well. They'd all been taken in London last week. He's got blond hair and in one of the pictures he's got his hands over Mum's boobs. So, I know he's not just a "friend" like she said.'

Nathan reeled from her confession and the shock that she'd confronted her mum. 'What did Mummy say when she knew you'd been looking at her phone?'

Millie narrowed her eyes and wrinkled up her nose and stared at him as if he'd gone way beyond stupid this time. 'I didn't tell her I'd looked at her phone.'

Maybe Nathan *was* stupid. 'So how ... why did she say he's just a friend if ... I don't understand, Millie.'

Millie smiled and shook her head at his bafflement. 'Because he came and gave us all a lift to the airport in his car.'

Laura hadn't mentioned anything about a Simon or the fact that she'd technically been unfaithful.

'What does this Simon guy do for a living?'

'I don't know but he makes "oodles of cash".'

'How do you know?'

'He said so.'

'He's got a bit of money, then.'

Millie smiled and wiped her eyes. 'Yeah, oodles of it.'

'Mm, this Oodles guy – that's what I'm going to call him – do you think that's why Mum likes him?'

'Dad, you're asking me about grown-up relationships – not exactly my specialist subject.'

'What is your specialist subject?'

Millie bit her lip, thinking. 'Mm, probably Little Mix or *The Voice*.'

He hugged Millie and she squirmed uncomfortably. 'Don't mention any of this to your mum until I can speak to her, okay? As for you moving to London, I think the fact she's got a boyfriend probably makes it less likely as having you lot around doesn't exactly give her a lot of freedom.'

'His last text to Mum said: *I can't wait to meet your girls, perhaps one day we could all be a family, wouldn't that be something?* So, I wouldn't be so sure about that, Dad.'

Millie picked up her iPad and left the room. Nathan frowned. She seemed to have left in a lighter mood. He couldn't be sure if she'd been genuinely reassured by his words or by the fact that she'd unburdened her secret. Maybe a combination of both.

He got a large glass from the cupboard and poured himself some wine. He needed to think. He had about half an hour before everyone needed to be in their pyjamas and ready for bed. He'd been genuinely shocked by Millie's revelation, but it at least explained the newly dyed hair, clothes and perfume, plus Laura had changed in another way that he couldn't initially put his finger on; she seemed to walk taller, with more of a spring in her step ... Then it dawned on him: *she was happy*.

That depressed him, but the fact some other man wanted to form a family with his wife and kids disturbed him the most. Millie might have picked it up wrong, of course – it seemed unlikely that another man would be so ready to take on another woman's children quite so quickly. He couldn't imagine doing that, but then he didn't know anything about what had gone on. Perhaps Laura had laid down an ultimatum: *love me, love my girls*. He wouldn't put it past her.

Nathan knew somewhere deep down that one day Laura would meet someone else. In fact he reckoned it had been part of her plan in moving to London. It was always easier to jump if someone was waiting to catch you. He just hadn't expected her to jump so soon.

Chapter 9

Going home always brought about mixed emotions. I loved my parents and I enjoyed spending time with them partly because they were more bonkers than me and, in a perverse way, that made me feel better. However, this was inevitably tempered with some apprehension of discovering what new shenanigans they might be involved in.

Arriving to see them on the Saturday morning, I parked outside the semi-detached stone villa that had been my home growing up and remained so in many ways. My room still contained my old bed and the wardrobe still held a selection of my clothes that I hadn't felt the need to take with me. The chest of drawers in the corner was full of old black scarves and jumpers. Officially the room had been designated as a 'guest' room but the last guest to sleep in it had been me, four months ago, on Christmas Day. My parents didn't do 'guests' well. The bedroom door still had my name on it, 'Kat' shaped from the silhouette of a bat with blood dripping from its wing tips. I still liked that and might take it with me one day.

I used my key to open the door and found my mum standing on a pair of steps just inside cleaning the coving with a bottle of Dettox and kitchen roll.

'Hi, Mum.'

'Oh, Kat, I didn't know you were coming over today. You usually phone.'

'Thought I'd surprise you.'

My mum didn't like surprises. I once booked a weekend away to London for her and my dad for their wedding anniversary with tickets to see *Cats*. With her control issues she'd spent most of the time in the capital on TripAdvisor, investigating what the highest-rated weekend wedding anniversary trips were. At that time, it had been a spa break in Bath. She phoned me and asked, 'Why didn't you do some research and book us on a spa weekend in Bath?'

'Err, because they don't have *Cats* playing in Bath at the moment.'

'Ahh, so it's a musical theatre break you've organised for us.' The fact I'd handed her the show tickets in an envelope along with the hotel booking should have given that away really. She'd hung up but then phoned me back fifteen minutes later whilst they were on their way to the theatre to see the show.

'Kat.'

'Mum.'

'If you'd done your research you'd have discovered that *The Lion King* is the most popular show on in London now, so next time—'

I hung up on her.

That happened to be the first and last surprise break I ever organised for them.

Back in the hall my mum got down from her steps and moved them along three feet to get at the next bit of offending ornate plasterwork. 'You'd better tell your dad you're here.'

'Where is he?'

'It's Saturday morning and it's sunny; where do you think he is?'

'In a shed?'

'Where else? Number two, I think.'

I plonked my jacket onto the back of a kitchen chair and went out of the French doors. Our back garden stretched back almost ninety feet with a load of trees and shrubs clustered at the far end. Grass and sheds took up most of the space, though using the word 'sheds' to describe my father's pride and joys did them a huge disservice.

Number one had a flat slated roof, large double-glazed windows and a seven-point locking door with toughened safety glass making it very difficult to break into or, as we discovered, out of. I suppose I'd describe it as a glam-shed. Inside, mounted on the wall was an HDTV, two comfy couches and, in the corner, a desk with a PC and internet connection. It also had independent LPG heating. Shed number one doubled as my dad's escape from reality. He'd sit in there for hours in the summer watching the test match or peering at the PC screen, researching stuff for his work or talking to fellow shed enthusiasts. Shed number one had also been the site of his run-in with authority when he'd locked the local MSP, Moira Cleethorpes, inside for not agreeing to challenge the local planning authority who'd refused him permission to build an extension onto the back of our house.

Moira had used her mobile to call the police, who had arrived and duly cautioned my father for false imprisonment despite his argument she'd had the third day of the England versus South Africa test match on HDTV to watch and a jug of homemade lemonade to keep her cool.

I approached shed number two from the 'blind side' (the side with no windows) and noticed a pile of fixtures and fittings on the grass. Shed number two had recently been decked out to resemble an artist's studio with two easels, selections of paint, acrylics, charcoal and canvases. The fact neither of my parents had any kind of artistic ability or interest whatsoever hadn't seemed to cross his mind when he'd been planning it. Now that idea had obviously been changed and a new project had started.

'Hi, Dad.'

'Kat.' My dad jumped, startled. 'I didn't know you were coming today. Does your mum know you're here?'

'Yeah, she's cleaning the cornicing.'

He nodded. 'Still? She started that yesterday. Keeps her busy, I suppose.'

'What are you doing here?'

'I'm cleaning out space for my new project.'

'Which is what exactly?'

'Llamas.'

'Llamas?'

'Llamas – they make excellent pets.'

'I'm not sure they do and why do you want a pet? No disrespect, Dad, but you and Mum have a hard enough time looking after yourselves.'

'They make very good guard animals, especially against small predators.'

'Dad, this is Glasgow; the only small predators around here usually hail from a sink estate, are malnourished, have substance-abuse issues, a bad attitude and a Stanley knife in their pocket, oh, and maybe a pit bull in tow.'

'Llamas don't like dogs.'

'What's that got to do with anything?'

'I don't like dogs either.'

'I'm not sure picking a pet based on a mutual dislike of something is necessarily the way to go about it but, for argument's sake, let's say it is – why not just opt for a cat?'

'I can't sell cat poo online.'

I stared at him for a moment. 'I'm sorry, Dad, I thought you said you "can't sell cat poo online".'

'I did.'

'I'm not following you.'

'Llama poo is called "beans" and is very prized by gardeners due to its very rich texture and high phosphate content. It retails for around £35 a kilo.'

'You're going to get a llama for its poo?'

'Two. I'm going to get two. They're sociable pack animals and like company, and two pooing llamas are better than one, and I might even breed them, so I'll get two females to start with.'

Although nothing my parents did really should surprise me any more I had to admit this had set me back a little – also if he planned to breed them he'd surely be better with a male and a female unless he'd decided to utilise some sort of artificial insemination technique. The picture dropped into my head of my dad approaching the rear end of a female llama with a large syringe filled with llama semen. I shook my head to get rid of the image and instead continued with my llama objections.

'Aren't they noisy?'

'No, they hum a little.'

'What, stink?'

'No, hum as in humming a tune.'

'They hum tunes?'

'Well, now, I don't know,' he said, scratching his head. 'I don't think so. They just make a delightful little humming noise. There's a website that shows some llamas humming. Do you want to see?'

'Not right now, thank you. Don't they spit at you?'

'No, that's a myth. They don't do that unless they're badly treated or stressed out.'

I reckoned anything, llama or otherwise, living with my mum and dad would be likely to get stressed out damn quickly but I didn't share my thoughts. 'You must need a licence or permission from the local authority, then?'

'No, nothing at all, they're an administrative joy. I might even invite our local MP over to view them.'

'She probably won't come. Is there enough space out here?'

'For Moira?'

'No, not Moira, the llamas?'

'Yeah, just about, if I provide some hay or fodder to supplement the grass, which, by the way, I'll never need to cut again.'

I'd run out of llama objections.

'Do you want some coffee?' My dad smiled, having outlasted me. 'I've just brewed some in the "church". Come on.'

I followed him around to shed number three, which had been designed and built as a small scaled-down version of the original church from Salem village, Massachusetts (as depicted in Arthur Miller's *The Crucible*) complete with a small, square bell tower, clock, and double oak-panelled doors. I wasn't sure what the Reverend Samuel Parris would have made of the irreligious interior though. As you stepped over the threshold the inside was reminiscent of an old country pub, complete with a shiny mahogany bar and wooden hand pumps connected to ale caskets underneath; a large TV sat on the wall and even a fully functioning fruit machine bleeped away in the corner.

Even though I'd been in here loads of times its authenticity always made me smile. When he shut the door, blocking out the views of the garden, you'd almost swear you were privy to some old-world pub lock-in event.

'Can I tempt you with a pint of Leg Spreader?'

'DAD!'

'That's what it's called. Look.'

He pointed to the picture on the hand pump, which depicted a smiling buxom girl in a short skirt sitting on the ground with her legs open. A strategically placed pint glass of frothy ale hid her embarrassment.

I had to smile. 'Yeah and I'm sure you just got it because it tastes nice.'

'It's a good pint actually. Bob likes it too.'

'I'm sure he does.' Bob is my dad's best, and sometimes I think only, friend. Bob lives a quarter of a mile away, and, as well as sharing my dad's love of wooden huts, is a web designer and fellow lecturer at my father's university. He's a lover of real ales, online gaming and collecting vintage comic books. Unsurprisingly, he's also single and stares at my boobs whenever he sees me, which thankfully isn't very often.

'I'm fine with coffee, Dad, and I'm driving.'

'You could always stay over; the house isn't the same since you left.'

'Dad, I've been gone for seven years now.'

'I know, and I've still not got used to it.'

'You should have had more than one kid, then.'

'We should have but that wasn't down to me; your

mother had been so traumatised by your birth we barely had sex for—'

'Ouch! Too much information, Dad.' At least I knew where I got that trait from.

'Oh, sorry, Kat, anyway, we're fine now. We just miss having you around.'

He handed me a steaming mug of coffee and I sat on a bar stool while he stood behind the bar, polishing some glasses like a caricature publican. 'Any change on the boyfriend front?'

Why did everyone need to know about my sex life, or, as it happened to be, my non-sex life? 'No, Dad, no chance of any grandchildren any time soon.'

'You're nearly thirty now, Kat. You need to get out more. You spend too much time mooching about at home and, let's face it, your job doesn't exactly offer up the opportunity to meet anyone, does it?'

'I had a cute corpse in recently. He sat up and said hello.'

He didn't believe me. 'Yeah, sure, Kat. You could tone down your make-up as well – you probably scare most men away.'

'Dad, I'm Goth. It's not a werewolf mask or anything. Underneath I'm a nice person. If I have to change who I am to try and attract someone, what does that say about me and what does it say about that person who'd only want to be with me if I pretended to be something I'm not?'

My dad blinked at me a few times, put down the

glass he'd been polishing and said, 'I've obviously hit a nerve again; maybe we should go back to talking about llamas?'

I laughed; my dad had always been great at dealing with my outbursts. 'I think we've exhausted the llama dilemma. What does Mum think about it?'

'She's not said much. I suspect she thinks I won't go through with it, but I will. I need a new hobby.'

I drained my mug and for the briefest of moments considered trying the Leg Spreader, but opted for another coffee instead. 'I did actually meet a cute corpse, Dad.'

My dad stared at me for a moment, then shook his head. 'Kat, that's not even funny. You spend too much time in the morgue; it can't be good for the mind, staring at corpses and doing whatever ghastly things it is that you do to them.'

'Ghastly?' I spluttered in disbelief, choking in laughter. 'Did you actually say *ghastly*? Have we gone back to 1952?'

'Ghastly is a perfectly respectable modern word, especially in relation to what you do to those poor dead people.'

'They're dead, Dad – well, usually – so they don't know anything that's happening to them. But it's true, I had a live one recently. You might have read about it in the papers; he got mentioned in a few. He'd been brought in on the Saturday and I found him still alive on the Monday.'

'I didn't read anything about it in *The Telegraph*.'

I smiled. 'No, you probably wouldn't have. Anyway, he's a cutie called Nathan Jones.'

'That's nice.'

'He is.'

'What's his family history?'

'I'm not really sure.'

I watched my dad as his brain whirred. 'Jones, that's a Patronymic name.'

'What does that mean?'

'It's a very old name meaning 'derived from the father'. Back in the day some poor people didn't have or know their surnames, so they only had a first name, usually John.'

'What, everyone was called John?'

'Not everyone, but lots of people, so they took the second name John as well.'

'What, John John?'

'Yeah.'

'That's silly. You can't go around being called John John.'

'Well, they did, becoming known as "two Johns", which eventually morphed into "Jones". That's how it came about. There are other examples like—'

I held my hand up. 'No, no, that's enough, I'm bored now, but I'll be sure and tell him that. I'm glad he's called Nathan and not John – he's cute.'

He wasn't listening. 'If we go into number one we could look it up on my database?'

'Maybe in a minute, but I'm not sure it's worth it.'

'I thought you said he was cute.' He had been listening.

'He is, but why do I need to know his ancestry at this point?'

'Might give you something to talk about on your next date.'

'What date?'

'Well, you said ... I just assumed ... Is he disabled after whatever happened to him?'

'No, he's married.'

'Oh, that's worse.'

'What, being married is worse than being disabled?'

My dad laughed. 'No ... well, it feels like it sometimes ... but no, I mean in terms of liking him, if he's married then it's a non starter.'

'His wife's left him or is about to or something like that anyway.'

'How do you know that? Has he told you?'

'Just my intuition.'

'Sounds a bit messy, Kat; do you really want to get involved? Can you not just try internet dating or something?'

'Hayley did that. She hated it.'

'Hayley's too fussy.'

'And you're saying I'm not?'

'I didn't mean you, I meant Hayley. You're fussy too but in a different way.'

'I didn't know there were different degrees of fussiness.'

'There must be. Dr Dave.'

'Don't mention Dr Dave.'

'I just did.'

'I wish I'd never brought him to meet you – biggest mistake of my life.'

'Bringing Dr Dave to meet us? He did come across as a queer fish.'

That shocked me. If my parents thought that about him, given their own eccentricities, he must have been a bloody borderline psychopath. Dr Dave Ross had worked with me some years before, and I'd unwisely become involved emotionally with him. Thankfully, he now lived and worked in London, far away from me. 'Yeah, I shouldn't have got involved with him in the first place. He wasn't good for me.'

My dad knew better than to poke around in that sore. 'What are you going to do about Mr Jones?'

'Find out about his ancestry; c'mon, let's fire up your search engine.'

'And while we're there I'll show you the humming llamas.'

'Great, I can't wait.'

Sarcasm always missed my dad. 'Right, we'll look at that first, then, shall we?'

Chapter 10

'I'm taking the girls to London for Easter, Nathan. The schools break up on the Thursday and we'll get the teatime flight down.'

Nathan hadn't expected that. 'You can't, Laura. It's Easter – I thought you'd be here, so we could at least pretend to be playing happy families. I won't get to see them or—'

'Look, I don't want to be here with you. I want to be in London with—'

'Simon.'

The name struck home; he could tell by the silence on the other end of the phone. Eventually she recovered her composure. 'Well, I suppose you had to find out some time, but I hadn't planned on mentioning him. I want to be in London with the girls; there's so much to do now the weather's getting better. It'll be a whole new experience for them and I want them to see it.'

'What about me?'

'You're not invited,' she said cruelly. 'Look, Nathan, I don't want to fight about it. I don't want to spend Easter with you, but I do want my girls with me. They should be with their mum during the holidays; I don't get to see them enough.'

'Yeah, well, whose fault is that?'

'I'm not going to fight with you, Nathan.'

'But it's not fair.'

'No, it's not, but I'll only keep them for a week and you can have the second week of the break. I've taken the two weeks off work so that'll still leave me with a bit of time to tidy up and sort stuff once they've gone.'

'And gives you some alone time with Simon?'

Laura paused. 'Maybe. I didn't want you to find out about him yet. I'm not sure how I feel; it's all very early. How did you find out anyway ... Millie?'

'Yeah, she'd got really upset about it.'

'How did she know? She only met him the once when he gave us a lift to the airport.'

Nathan didn't want to reveal his daughter's clandestine surveillance techniques, which also meant he couldn't mention the whole happy families bit either, at least not directly. 'I think she just put two and two together. She's very perceptive. She said he told her he makes oodles of cash.'

'Oodles?'

'That's what he told her.'

Laura considered that for a moment. 'Yeah, that's the sort of thing he would say. Not one of his best features, I have to admit.'

'How did you meet?'

'He works in the office down here. He's an accountant in a different department.'

Nathan snorted. 'Love over the water cooler.'

'Jealousy doesn't sit well on you, Nathan. It never has.'

'You're my wife. You shouldn't be shagging someone else.'

'Nathan, our marriage is a sham. It has been for years. I'm surprised one of us hasn't done anything before now ...'

'You mean you're surprised you haven't?'

'If I'm honest, yes. I needed to get away for my own sanity. I didn't expect to meet anyone, nor did I go looking for it, if that's what you're thinking. I don't know what'll happen. It's early days.'

'Why would he want to get into a relationship with someone with three kids?'

'Simon loves children.'

'Does he have any of his own?'

'No.'

'Does that not strike you as a bit weird?'

'Not at all. If he wants to be with me then he knows I come with baggage.'

'Is that how you described your daughters?'

Laura snorted down the phone. 'Good try at winding me up, Nathan, but I'm above that sort of comment now. I just need someone to hold me and tell me everything is going to be okay.'

'I could do that, Laura. I used to do that.'

'I know you did, but I don't believe you any more;

nothing about us works. We're broken. Our marriage is broken and it's not fixable.'

'We could—'

She interrupted. 'No, Nathan, we couldn't, and I don't want to, that's the thing. If someone came along and said, "Here, take this pill and everything will be okay between you and Nathan," I wouldn't take it. It's over. You need to accept that, Nathan. We can't keep going over this old ground. It's not good for anyone.'

They were both silent for a few moments before Laura said, 'Anyway, that's why I'm not coming back for Easter. I did think about it, but I couldn't deal with the arguments and resentment, so I think it's best if I'm away. I'll bring them back on the Sunday and you can have them until they go back to school.'

Nathan hated the fact she'd started seeing someone else, but he couldn't do anything about it. He didn't want it to eat him up inside and destroy what little self-confidence he had left so he had to try and learn to live with it. His marriage *had* been a sham for a while, he knew that – although he'd tried to fool himself otherwise. He'd started to wonder if Laura had been unfaithful before, but he'd stopped himself. That train of thought would take him to another dark place he didn't want to visit.

*

He'd made it to Wednesday and the girls had been away for six days now. He missed them, but they were due back on Sunday, so he had a few more days to kill. Daisy and Chloe had been excited to be going on a long train journey, but Millie knew the reality of the situation and had been difficult and huffy. However, at the age of ten she still did what her mother told her, albeit reluctantly. Laura had moved to a larger flat a few weeks ago and had tried to placate her with a room of her own. It didn't work.

Thankfully Nathan had been busy working on another commission that his friend had pushed his way.

Graham had phoned and said, 'I need your help on a health campaign, Nathan.'

'Nothing to do with nettles?'

'No, though I wouldn't put it past them to come up with some health thing to do with them; no, this is for kids. Constipation is on the increase due to poor diets and increased obesity.'

'Is it?'

'Apparently.'

'So what is it?'

'A suppository for under sevens.'

'A what?'

'A suppository, you know, that you stick up—'

'Yeah, I know what you do with it. How are we supposed to sell that?'

'That's why I need your brains on this.'

Later, as he sat staring at a picture of the product

98

on-screen Nathan realised why it had been given to him. The infantile staff in Graham's office would have wasted hours joking and mucking about instead of expending any serious energy working out how to sell it.

Sending it to him made a perverse kind of sense – he had nobody to joke around with.

As he sat and thought about the products and their purpose he asked himself how the hell he could persuade anyone to buy them.

The target market was mothers – what made mothers buy things for their kids?

To make them happier, cleverer, healthier or safer. Nathan spent hours mulling over ideas and trying to work out an angle. Around lunchtime he took a break and remembered he had his last (hopefully) hospital appointment in the afternoon. He'd had the plaster cast from his arm removed by the GP weeks ago and today would be his last visit unless they found something else wrong with him. He welcomed the interruption from thinking about infant constipation and how he could persuade a mother to somehow think it would be a good idea to shove a hard white pellet up her kid's bum at bedtime.

The hospital had also scheduled a session with the psychiatrist that had visited him soon after his miraculous return from the dead but, given his current delicate mental state and his preoccupation with toddlers' suppositories, Nathan might give that a miss.

He drove to the general vicinity of the hospital and

parked on a quiet street rather than be forced to pay the exorbitant car-park fee. An icy wind cut across the road and open land around the hospital, making him pull up the collar of his coat. The warmth of spring had yet to reach this far north; London would feel positively balmy compared to Edinburgh. The sky had darkened considerably since he'd left his flat and rain looked imminent. He waited in the outpatient department half an hour past his allotted time before being ushered into a cramped and dimly lit consulting room. A middle-aged consultant, Dr Spencer, reviewed his case notes whilst periodically peering over the top of her glasses at him as if to convince herself that he really existed and wasn't the figment of someone's imagination.

She closed the file, sat back and gazed at him. 'Remarkable.'

Nathan nodded but remained silent, not knowing how to respond.

'What did you feel when it happened?'

'When what happened?'

'When you died?'

He sighed. 'Nothing, but then I wasn't really dead, was I?'

'Weren't you?'

'I don't know, you're the doctor.'

'You know it's called Lazarus Syndrome?'

'Somebody did mention that, yes.'

'Named after the man that Jesus brought back to life.'

'Okay.'

'There are well-documented cases around the world, and probably many others that don't get recorded, but, in your case, we think you had a cardiac arrest when the bus hit you, and at the scene the paramedics couldn't revive you. Then later, probably in the ambulance, your heart started spontaneously, but possibly with an extreme bradycardia arrhythmia which made it difficult to detect. Then your severe concussion kept you unconscious until you became normally responsive in the mortuary.'

'You've lost me.'

'It doesn't matter, you seem fine now, but I'm not sure why we didn't pick up any life signs when you arrived at the hospital. Perhaps the equipment was faulty or maybe the autoresuscitation didn't happen until later. We still have more questions than answers. Are you spiritual, Mr Jones?'

'I've never seen any ghosts.'

'That's not quite what I meant. Do you believe in God?'

Nathan had to think about that. 'I don't know. I don't think so, but I've never really given it much thought.'

'I take it you're not a regular churchgoer, then?'

He shook his head.

'Shame.'

Nathan wondered if she worked on the side as a lay preacher, trying to convert or recruit lost souls into religion.

She took off her glasses and pinched the bridge of her nose. 'I've never reviewed a case like yours before. I suppose now that you're physically healed – all except your skull, that might take a few more months to knit together fully – the only issue is your mental well-being. I see you've got a psychiatric evaluation scheduled after you're finished here?'

He nodded.

'Well, as I say, physically you're on the mend. I do think that you might need some spiritual counselling but, of course, that's up to you. However, for the next six months or so you need to take care not to damage your head. Do you play football?'

'Err, no.'

'That's good, as I wouldn't recommend you head any footballs. Do you take part in any other contact sports?'

'No.'

'Good. Do you regularly crawl into small spaces?'

Nathan stared at the doctor. 'I don't make a habit of it, no.'

'That's good – just in case you bang your head, you see. People who crawl into small spaces, especially when they're older, do suffer some serious head injuries. Do you jump up and down a lot?'

'Not usually no, and again it's not something I've got planned.'

'Good – it wouldn't be good either. I recommend you try and remain as sedentary as possible for a few months. What's your occupation?'

'I work in advertising.'

'Right, well, that should allow you to stay relatively calm, shouldn't it?'

'Physically yes, but it's mentally challenging at times. Is it okay if I think a lot?'

Dr Spencer completely missed his sarcasm. 'Yes, that should be fine. Everything in moderation though.'

He left the consultation room with an overwhelming sense that he'd wasted an hour of his life. He headed towards the main entrance, having no intention of meeting with a psychiatrist who would no doubt try and recruit him into the Masons or Rosicrucians. He remembered an old joke about psychiatrists. How many psychiatrists does it take to change a light bulb? Only one but the light bulb needs to want to change.

Chapter 11

I rushed into the waiting area beside the outpatient section and spotted him immediately, smiling as if he'd just come out of a brilliant comedy show. I think I startled him when I asked, 'Something funny?'

He stopped in his tracks and his smile vanished when he saw me. Not a good sign.

'Oh, hello, I didn't expect to see you today. Sorry, what did you say?'

'Doesn't matter. How are you?'

'Better than the first time you saw me anyway. Just here for my final evaluation.'

'I know, that's why I came up, just to say hi. I got delayed and thought I might miss you.'

'You nearly did. How did you know I'd be here anyway?'

'You were in the computer. I've only got about twenty minutes, busy day in the morgue, lots of doctors not doing their jobs properly.'

Nathan frowned at me, his sense of humour obviously

a million miles from mine. 'Just a joke,' I said. 'Would you like to grab a coffee, as long as you've got time?'

'Yeah, okay. I could use a drink.'

'Tough afternoon with the doctors?'

He smiled. 'Just one. She seemed more worried about my spiritual rather than my physical well-being.'

'Dr Spencer?'

'How'd you know?'

'She's well known as a God botherer, though I didn't know she did that with patients too. You must have come across as a lost soul.'

We were both silent for a moment before Nathan asked, probably quite reasonably, 'What's this about, Kat?'

'What's what about?'

'Well, maybe I'm missing something, but you came down to meet me like you had something to say?'

'I just wanted to say hello, like I explained.' *You're so cute – I could wrap you in cling film and keep you in my fridge.* Uh-oh, did I just say that out loud? I stared at him for a moment but, as he didn't flinch, I thankfully must have kept it inside.

'You mean you broke all sorts of data-protection protocols just to come and say hi?'

Yeah, he wasn't buying into the whole 'I just wanted to say hi' scenario. 'I didn't break anything. You're technically one of my patients.'

'I'm no longer dead.'

'True, but you were registered as deceased in my system.'

'That might make getting a mortgage a little tricky.'

'Do you need a mortgage?'

He shook his head. 'It's not important right now.'

'Is your wife divorcing you?' Oops, I think I sounded pleased.

'How'd you come to that conclusion?'

'Well, the mortgage thing, I suppose, and because she couldn't be arsed fighting to see you in the hospital.' Better – slightly more like an emotional detective and less like a stalker.

'I need to go, Kat. In case the psychiatrist I'm due to meet appears.'

I've offended him. No surprise there. 'You're avoiding him?'

'Yes, I'm not in the mood.'

'Sounds like you really *should* go, then.'

He smiled. 'Maybe, but my wife and kids are in London this week and I'm missing them.'

'Why didn't you go, then? A break would probably do you good.'

'It's complicated, Kat, and I don't really want to discuss it.'

'She's left you, hasn't she?' Oops, none of my business but I couldn't help myself.

He scowled at me. 'Kind of.'

I drained my mug, trying to think of a response. 'How can someone "kind of" leave you?'

'As I said, it's complicated.' He stood up and gave me a

strange look. If I didn't know better I'd think he might be appraising me; if so he'd probably conclude that I had a large pot at home to boil bunnies in. 'Thanks for the coffee, Kat. I've got to get back to work. I'm trying to figure out how to make inserting a hard white tablet into a child's bum a pleasant experience.'

I stared at him open-mouthed as he walked away. I'd no idea what that last sentence meant but strangely enough I found it quite comforting, as it meant he might be a bit bonkers. We'd get on famously.

The thought encouraged me and as he walked away I decided I needed a plan. Nathan had something about him that intrigued me – well, let's be honest, I had the hots for him; just the sight of him made my bits tingle and that hadn't happened for a long time, if ever. I hadn't expected the physical attraction to continue, I'd thought that my initial feelings for him were down to him being vulnerable and injured but, no, they went *way* beyond that. Shame he had a wife, kids and multiple complications. Still, nothing worthwhile ever came easy. I also recognised some of me in him; he seemed to have loads of insecurities and doubts and I knew all about that.

So how could I get closer to Nathan? And would he want me to? I had no idea, but I did know where to go for inspiration – my BFF Hayley.

Hayley Dunlop had been my best friend since high school and the best friend a girl could *ever* have.

I think it would be fair to say we were 'forced' together at first. Hayley had been an awkward overweight teenager with a speech impediment, and I'd been a similar outcast due to my dress and attitude, both of which had been more extreme back then. As a result, nobody wanted to sit beside either of us, so we sat together. I spent countless hours beside Hayley in History refusing to answer any questions.

'Klaudette, can you tell the class which king had to be forced to introduce Magna Carta?'

As usual whenever Mrs Brock spoke to me like that, using my 'official' first name, I ignored her. I kept my head down. I used to be able to recognise most of my classmates simply by their shoes, I spent so much time with my eyes down trying to avoid conversation. I stared at Mrs Brock's foot as it tapped impatiently. Whilst waiting for the moment to pass I noted the horrible wedges that complemented perfectly the hideous tweed skirt and faded grey cardigan. Mrs Brock, as well as being a cow, had a fashion sense akin to 1957.

As usual she moved on to torment Hayley. 'And how about you, Miss Chatty Pants? Can you tell the class which group of medieval noblemen forced King John to seal the document? In fact, Miss Dunlop, don't bother trying to answer, we've only got fifteen minutes of the period left and we don't want to spend it listening to you trying to string a sentence together.' The other kids in the class screamed with laughter and jeered like opposition MPs during Prime Minister's Question Time. Poor Hayley sank down as low in her seat as possible.

That day I readjusted my view of Mrs Brock. As well as being a cow she had a cruel, vindictive streak that should have barred her from ever being a teacher. Hayley suffered from a stammer at school and Mrs Brock knew it became worse whenever she got put on the spot and made to speak aloud. Most of the other teachers knew this and made allowances but not our bitch of a history teacher – she went out of her way to make Hayley as uncomfortable as possible.

Our misery wasn't restricted to history lessons and the taunts were usually accompanied by a barrage of paper pellets fired at us whenever a teacher turned their back.

Although we had to endure this in other classes it always felt worse with Mrs Brock, who condoned our treatment as outcasts by doing little to intervene in the torture. I knew I'd been ostracised by insisting on my self-imposed name estrangement and dress-noire. The misery didn't lessen though, just because it happened to be self-inflicted. I only ever wore black. Some of the kids even referred to me as Grim – as in the Grim Reaper – but I secretly quite liked that taunt and wrote it on the front of all my notepads.

Hayley, as well as her speech issues, pushed the scales around to a hefty twelve stone at age fifteen. She did her best to hide the excess flesh in dark baggy outfits dotted with small patterns accentuated with a light belt around her midriff to draw attention away from the obvious, but it only went so far.

Hayley's worst day at school (though there were so many to choose from) came about when the coolest guy in school, James Cochrane, turned his attention on her. He also happened to be totally gorgeous and for some reason walked like a panther, positively prowling the halls of our high school leaving teen girls breathless in his wake. Part of his appeal undoubtedly lay in the fact that he sang lead vocals in his own grunge-rock band, The Fluckers. In addition, he had considerable artistic ability and, unfortunately, he used this talent to draw a picture on the whiteboard in Mrs Brock's classroom. He did this just prior to a double period of torture using a permanent black marker. He drew the Michelin man of Michelin tyre fame with his new girlfriend, an even larger blown-up tyre girl with rolls of fat spilling down her body, called Dunlop Girl.

Mrs Brock made things worse by leaving it on display for weeks and referring to Hayley as Dunlop Girl for the rest of the year. Even when rubbed out, the permanent marker meant a faint image remained as a reminder of how shit her life had become. I'm not sure how long she could have taken this but something remarkable started to happen later that year as she approached sixteen. The latter stages of puberty subjected Hayley to an unexpected late growth spurt that also kicked her metabolism into overdrive. It had the effect of changing her body shape forever. Once the transformation started she augmented it by shunning the sweet drinks and fatty snacks all the rest of us guzzled with abandonment.

Her face began to reflect the changes and her visage went from pudgy puffy panda to sculpted smooth sophistication. High cheekbones emerged, so did a slim aquiline nose. She also began to experiment with make-up techniques that accentuated her new features and the transformation could only be described as breathtaking. Hayley's cornflower-blue eyes and natural blonde hair that had been lost in the lumpiness together with the other changes meant her teenage-boy rating shot up from 'untouchable' to 'totally shag-able'.

She blossomed academically too and after studying law at St Andrew's University she joined a Glasgow law practice and had recently been made up to partner. She lived in a small flat in Glasgow's trendy West End with a perpetually nervous cat called Whisky.

I buzzed the intercom at the outside door of Hayley's flat. A gust of icy wind blew some light rain into my face, making me shiver. Hayley's voice sounded tinny from the tiny speaker and I smiled as I bounded up the stairs, glad to be out of the rain that had started to get heavier. My friend waited for me at the top of the stairs with a hug and the warmest welcome I got anywhere. Hayley had changed physically and mentally over the years we'd known each other, but her affection for me remained as solid and loyal as it always had.

Hayley ushered me into the living room where the large

picture window had views of the river and busy expressway running alongside. I watched the headlights of the cars bouncing off the dark water.

'Did you drive?'

I shook my head. 'No, I took the train. Just as well as I think it's going to be a filthy wet night on the roads.'

'Yeah, good call – wine?'

'Chablis?'

'Of course.'

'Yes, please.'

Whilst Hayley fetched a drink I wondered how best to broach the subject that had brought me here. In the end Hayley made it easy.

'I haven't seen you for weeks, so what brings you up, babe? Don't tell me you've met a man at last?'

I giggled. 'Yeah, in a way. I've met a guy, or at least I think I have.'

Hayley shook her head and sipped her wine. 'Well, you either have or you haven't.'

'I don't know if he likes me. He probably doesn't.'

'Then you've not really met anyone, have you?'

'It's complicated.'

'It always is with you, Kat,' she said with kindness in her voice. 'What's his name?'

'Nathan, but he's married.'

'That's not good.'

'I think Nathan's a nice name.'

'Yeah, it's fine; it's the married bit that bothers me.'

'He's cute, especially when he's sleeping.'

'Yeah, you probably shouldn't tell him that, and how would you know that if you've not been ... with him?'

'That's complicated too, and why shouldn't I tell him that?'

'It's not the sort of thing I'd want to know.'

'You're not a guy.'

'No, but I'm a human and I wouldn't like it.'

I thought about that for a moment. 'Maybe I'll leave it for a while.'

'Has he got kids?'

I bit my lip and nodded slowly.

'That's even worse, Kat. Is he on Facebook? Can I get a look-see?'

'I don't know, he might be.'

'Let's see, shall we? Do you want more wine?'

'Yeah, might as well. I'm not driving.'

Hayley booted up her iPad and opened the Facebook app. 'What's his name?'

'Nathan Jones.'

'How did you meet?'

I hesitated. 'Err, I met him at work.'

'Oh, he's not a doctor, is he – not another Dr Dave?'

I laughed at the horrified expression on her face. Hayley hated Dr Dave. 'No, I met him in the morgue.'

'So, he does what you do?'

'No, he's a ... actually I'm not sure what he does; he's quite evasive about his occupation.'

I watched as she wrinkled up her nose in puzzlement. 'I don't understand, then. What's he doing in the morgue if he's not working? It's not the sort of place anyone has on their bucket list to visit before they have to.'

'He was dead.'

'Dead?'

'Yep, dead.'

'I don't understand – did you give him the kiss of life? Is he a zombie?'

'No, he woke up on his own. I heard a noise from one of the drawers. I opened it up and found him just lying there.'

'Gross. How did he end up in there?'

'He got hit by a bus.'

'Ouch. And you've fallen for him? I've always wondered about your taste in men, Kat, but going for a married dead guy, I don't know, that's stretching it, even for you. You're really living up to your high-school nickname.'

'He's cute.'

'Okay, let's see ... there's a Laura Jones married to a Nathan Jones.'

'That'll be his wife.'

'Wow, look, she's in a bikini on here; a dark Latin type. Hard to believe that body's squeezed a kid out.'

'Three kids.'

'You're joking? That's worse. So, your best-case scenario is that you'll end up a surrogate mother to three brats while the father pines after his beautiful ex-wife.'

'Well ...'

'You've not even thought that far ahead, have you? You're hopeless, Kat, hopeless.'

I pointed to Laura's Facebook page. 'There's a picture of Nathan there, down in the bottom corner.'

Hayley enlarged the image and examined it closely. 'Well, he doesn't look like a zombie, I must admit. Mm, he's cute, but you'd expect that, given the wife. I'll maybe give him ... eight out of ten. He might have squeezed a nine if he'd been single.'

'As I said, he looks even better when he's sleeping,' I said mischievously.

Hayley shook her head. 'You're weird, Kat. I think maybe working with all those dead bodies is getting to you. There must be a better way to meet a man than hanging around waiting for a stiff to wake up.'

'You're not doing any better.'

'This isn't about me. You hardly know the guy, by the sounds of it, and I just don't want you getting hurt and disappointed again. I know our thirtieth birthday alarms are going off ...'

'Even my dad mentioned that.'

'Yeah, well, my mum goes on about it as well. Look, Kat, I know you want the whole white wedding and the 2.3 kids thing, but—'

'Black wedding maybe.'

'Whatever, the point is you're not going to get either with him, are you? Well, you'll end up with the kids by default but there must be easier targets.'

'I'm not targeting anything.'

'Exactly, you don't have a man-plan.'

'A man-plan?'

'Yeah, you don't want to be on your own, but you don't do anything about it. I mean, you're a sexy lady, but you don't really push it out there, do you? Your clothes could be a bit ... I don't know, tighter?'

'Tighter?'

'Go to Topshop; everything they sell is tight, especially the tops.'

'That's down to your boobs, Hayley. Mine aren't as big as yours.'

'You've got great boobs, a tight tummy and lovely arse but nobody can see it.'

'Are you coming onto me?'

Hayley giggled. 'If I don't get a shag soon I might.'

'I never blossomed like you did.'

'You never needed to. You've always been pretty; you've just never made the most of it. You undervalue yourself even now, throwing time away on a married man. Kat, I just want you to be happy and find the right guy.'

'How do you know Nathan's not the right one?'

'Because he's someone else's right one already.'

'I don't think he'll be married much longer.'

'Like I've never heard that before. Remember Chris, the bloke I met on the beach in Crete, and how he told me he'd left his wife? As you know, it turned out the only time he ever left his wife was to come and shag me and the "getting over her" holiday in Crete turned out to be his brother's stag do. You can't believe a word a man says to you.'

'Hayley, that's just one example. You just need to get out more as well.'

'Yeah, maybe, but it's harder when you get older. My social circle has reduced so much. You remember my twenty-first birthday? I practically filled a nightclub. For my thirtieth, it'll probably be me, you, Liz from work and maybe my dad. How sad is that?'

'Aw, Hayley, that's not true; you've got lots of friends, but I suppose you could always try internet dating again.'

'I don't think I could. It just feels like an interview for a shag every time you meet someone, plus the last date I went on put me off forever. The guy looked great in his picture and even better in the flesh, and you know how often that happens, but, God, it was hard work. The problem is, any guys that are still single in their thirties or, God forbid, their forties are single for a reason.'

'Maybe you should join a divorced dating site.'

Hayley groaned. 'Then you've got to listen to them prattle on about their ex-wives and their kids and all the baggage that comes with that, like your bloke will do, and there's the small point that I'm not divorced.'

'You could lie – everybody lies online.'

'I could but I won't, not if I'm ever going to meet "the one". I've got to at least start out honestly.'

'You're such a romantic, Hayley. Your "one" has probably got side-tracked and married someone else by now.'

'That's a depressing thought but, yeah, you're probably right. I can live in hope, though.'

'Aww, sweetie, you could just go out and meet someone for meaningless sex, you know, in a nightclub or something.'

'Maybe five years ago I would have, but I can't be bothered, getting all dressed up and spend the night being chatted up by blokes to maybe find someone I like enough to drag home. It all feels kind of desperate.'

'You *are* desperate.'

'Not *that* desperate in fact it makes waiting around the morgue waiting for some dead guy to wake up seem pretty attractive. Does that happen often? Maybe I could come and hang out one day with you, see what pops up?'

That reduced me to a fit of giggles. 'It doesn't happen often. Nathan's my first but sometimes ... you get what we call "Angel Lust".' I giggled again.

'Right,' said Hayley in a commanding voice, 'no more wine for you. What is "Angel Lust" exactly?'

'Sometimes we wheel a corpse out and it's got a huge erection. It's a symptom of rigor mortis – even though it's pretty rare, I've still seen quite a few. So, if you fancy it, next time I get one I'll phone you and you can nip over and ... hop on.'

Hayley laughed. 'Well, at least I wouldn't have to make small talk afterwards.'

We were both silent for a moment, staring at the picture of Nathan Jones, before Hayley squealed.

I jumped out of my skin. 'What is it, Hayley?'

She bounced up and down in excitement. 'Guess who came into our office today? God, I can't believe I forgot. I meant to tell you as soon as you arrived.'

'Who?'

'Guess.'

'Err, Brad Pitt?'

'Don't be silly. Why would he come into our office?'

'Is he not in Glasgow filming again?'

'Is he?'

'I think so – I read it in the *Metro*.'

'Oh, it must be true, then. No, c'mon, Kat, *guess*.'

I tried to think of someone who would make Hayley so excited. 'Give me a clue.'

'Someone we hated at school.'

'Mm, that doesn't narrow it down all that much, to be honest ... Mrs Brock?'

Hayley shuddered. 'God, no; I would hope that evil old witch is dead by now. Honestly, Kat, if I saw her I'd probably run away and hide. I wouldn't have survived school without you with me in her classes.'

'Sharing the abuse.'

'Yeah, you scared her. She just hated me for some reason.'

I stared at her. 'Scared of me? I hardly think so.'

'Uh-huh, because you were happy being different. I couldn't help it.'

'I can tell you I was far from happy.'

Hayley squeezed my arm. 'I know, sweetie; that isn't

119

quite what I meant – you'd chosen to stand out from the crowd, express your individuality, and she didn't like that. She liked everyone to be quiet little sheep. Anyway, you've got me off subject. You've got one more guess.'

'I can't, Hayley – apart from you and Mr Dobbie, the PE teacher who always let me skip his class, I hated pretty much everyone at school.'

'I'll give you a clue: The Fluckers.'

I squealed. 'Not James Cochrane?'

'The very same.'

'My God, we haven't seen him since prom night.'

Chapter 12

The end of year prom became a watershed moment for Hayley. Like me, she usually endured such events by hiding in the toilets or hanging around outside. Our school had the unusual practice of having one combined prom for the 4th, 5th and 6th year kids. The idea belonged to the penny-pinching headmaster Bill White and probably had more to do with saving money than, his claim that it "brought the school together". This year the pupils of the senior years had predictably voted James Cochrane 'King of the Prom'. An archaic practice that only further raised the confidence and expectations of a kid who needed very little of an ego boost in the first place. Then on the night of the event the king had to choose his queen from the assembled gaggle of giggling sixteen, seventeen and the few eighteen-year-old girls – most of whom had been slugging cheap cider behind the gym block. It did nothing to further the ambitions and confidence of already angst-ridden teenage girls, but state education didn't really seem to take any account of that.

We were sitting in a corner watching the proceedings with a detached air, laughing at the three or four meringue-dress-wearing blondes, limbs lathered in St Tropez burnt orange and desperate to be picked so they could live off the experience of being selected Prom Queen for the next twenty years.

I'd managed to squeeze into a black frock I'd picked up in a charity shop on Byres Road. My mother bought me a pair of black kitten heels, even though I'd insisted I would be quite happy wearing my Dr. Martens with the dress. After staring at myself in the mirror for a few minutes I eventually decided that the Dr. Martens and strapless black dress didn't quite measure up, especially with the black tiara I'd spent so much time on. Black tiaras were hard to find, or at least they had been back then, so I'd painted a cheap silver one jet black with a tin of gloss gutter paint I'd found in the cupboard under the stairs. It had needed three coats and the smell of the paint remained quite over-powering. I spent more time than usual on my make-up and hair so that when I eventually appraised myself in the hall mirror I felt quite pleased. It must have been good because my mum shook her head and tutted the whole time. She wanted me in a meringue.

My efforts, however, paled into insignificance when I met up with Hayley. She'd gone for a figure-hugging blue pageant dress that pushed up her already generous boobs. The tight waist gradually tapered outwards once it passed her hips until it reached the floor. The sweetheart neckline showed off her shoulders and, with her blonde hair piled on top of her head in what Hayley had described as a 'messy updo' (which I think meant she'd done it herself), she looked stunning. An overused description, even back then, but in this case, given the transformation Hayley had undergone in the months leading up to this evening, it felt appropriate.

She'd finished off the look with a smear of Charlotte Tilbury Red Vixen across her lips and added Eye Candy 50's style lashes to her eyes. Although she'd gone to great lengths to get ready, she remained oblivious of the reaction she got from those around us. I'd noticed both sexes nudging each other and pointing as we walked past.

We found a quiet corner and tuned out of the long boring speech from the head teacher, who waxed lyrical about how this had been the best group of seniors he'd ever known – something he said every year. We only started listening when he introduced this year's King of Green Park's Prom, James Cochrane. James swaggered up and accepted the cheap plastic crown, shoved it onto his head, and, as instructed by a beaming Bill White, set off across the dance floor in search of his queen.

I laughed when he completely bypassed the expectant pouting face of Lyndsay Crowther, one of Green Park's premier bitches who had been one of my and Hayley's chief tormentors over the years. He then turned and headed towards our corner. I wasn't surprised as sitting two seats down from Hayley happened to be Carly Boyd, a beautiful redhead who James had been 'going out with', as the kids called it, for most of the summer term. She smiled as he approached, stood up and pushed some imaginary creases from the hem of her fabulous coral dress, touched the side of her hair to make sure the matching flower hairclip remained secure and stepped forward in anticipation. A wave of shocked mumbles passed through the hall when James brushed past Carly and instead knelt in front of Hayley.

'Hayley Dunlop,' he said into the microphone as he began to recite a speech he'd obviously been rehearsing all day, 'Tonight I have chosen the most beautiful girl in the whole of Green Park High School to be my queen. Will you join me on the dance floor?'

Hayley and I stared at the kneeling figure of James Cochrane with our mouths hanging open. In the tradition of the prom, James then placed the microphone into Hayley's hand. I wondered for a moment if this might be another cruel joke as handing a microphone to a stammerer like Hayley would be akin to dropping a tarantula into the lap of an arachnophobe. Initially my fears were justified as a shocked Hayley stared at her hand as if he'd just whipped out his willy and slapped it down onto her palm.

I became acutely aware of the open-mouthed staring from most of the school year but particularly the venomous glare from the red-haired and now very red-faced Carly Boyd.

The room hushed as everyone waited for Hayley to

speak. Normally the lucky girl just mumbled some inane nonsense and joined her king on the dance floor but tonight Hayley delayed speaking.

She stared down at the expectant gorgeous face of James Cochrane, his long, gelled hair styled perfectly by his hairdresser mother, his pressed suit immaculately tailored to his toned frame and she began to speak, not taking her eyes off him. It became the most wonderful and memorable moment of my young life.

I was pretty sure that necking at least three bottles of Bacardi Breezer before arriving helped get her going – that and the fact she'd endured six months of speech therapy. 'James Cochrane, I have to ... to ... say that this is a huge surprise.' *Oops, Hayley – you need to avoid the Ts if you can,* I thought.

James beamed and relaxed.

Hayley continued, warming to her task, spurred on by alcohol and four years of indignation. 'Who'd have guessed "Dunlop Girl", the Michelin Man's girlfriend, would ever be selected as Prom Queen?'

There were a few nervous laughs amongst the girls in the hall and I noticed the forced grin of Bill White begin to slip.

'Now, my experience of boys, as you will all know, has been ... well ... very limited, if I'm honest, for obvious reasons.' She paused, and a few laughs greeted her self-deprecation. 'However, I'm not completely naïve and I suspect that James choosing "Dunlop Girl" for his date has more to do with him hoping I'll be so shocked and grateful just to be picked th ... th ... that I'll do just about anything to reward him.'

James's face fell as his ulterior motive, which he'd thought so subtle nobody would ever guess, had suddenly been exposed to the whole of the senior school. Just to avoid any doubts whatsoever, Hayley raised her voice and said, 'I'm sure th ... th ... th ... the King would expect, at the very least, a post-party blow job behind the gym block.'

I squealed with laughter along with most of the hall. Bill White's grin vanished altogether at the mention of 'blow job'. When the noise had died down a little Hayley carried on; there would be no quieting her now, not after the confidence boost she'd got by managing to get 'post-party blow job' out without stammering.

Bill White started to move, but from the other end of the hall he had to squeeze past the hormone- and alcohol-infused bodies of nearly a hundred and fifty teenagers to get near us, which allowed Hayley to carry on.

'Life for people like you, James, is so easy and so ... so ... so pleasant. Nobody ever rattles your cage or ruffles your feathers. But for us lesser mortals life is never so sweet or so easy. You've no idea how hard it is to ... to muster up the energy every morning to drag yourself into school only to know you're going to be abused and made fun of all the time. Maybe to ... to ... tonight you and everyone else can understand, ju ... ju ... just for a moment what it's like to be me. To ... to ... to be an outcast, to be taunted, to be unloved.'

The laughter in the hall died down, and a strange silence descended upon the crowd as Hayley stood and stared around us. Her eyes filled with tears and she tossed the microphone to a shocked Bill White, who'd managed to squeeze through the teenage throng. She pushed past him, and the crowd of bodies parting like the Red Sea to let her out.

As she neared the exit some kids began to clap and soon the whole hall filled with spontaneous cheers and whoops. A watershed moment for Hayley and in a way for me too. I followed my friend outside, defiantly glaring at Lyndsay Crowther as I left.

Hayley had grown used to receiving stares and comments due to her weight so now she didn't even notice the stares and comments she received due to her beauty. She remained a little uncomfortable and self-conscious and I doubted that would ever leave her, which, in my opinion, could only be a good thing. The speech therapy eventually allowed her to conquer even the letter 'T'. She still had the occasional lapse, notably when she got very drunk, but nobody except me ever noticed.

My stock rose slightly on the coat-tails of my friend's metamorphosis and, although I became tolerated rather than embraced, it made my final year at school bearable. I wouldn't be rushing back to any school reunions any time soon, but then neither would Hayley.

'So, what was he doing in your office?' I asked, desperate to know the juicy details.

'He had a meeting with David Ross, our family law guy. He's getting divorced.'

'No way?'

'Yeah way, he caught his wife in bed with someone, a builder, I think.'

'Can you believe it? James Cochrane, Green Park High's epitome of cool, loses out to Bob the Builder. How'd you find out? Isn't it all supposed to be confidential when you come and see a lawyer? Attorney-client privilege?'

'Well, yes, but I can find stuff out, especially as I'm doing a bit of family law just now, so I have access and I couldn't *not* tell you.'

'But they don't know you know him?'

Hayley giggled and shook her head. 'No and I'll keep it that way and just make sure I'm out of sight if he ever comes in.'

I couldn't help but ask, 'What's he look like now?'

Hayley laughed. 'He's still gorgeous. He's put on a bit of weight but, given how skinny he used to be, that's no bad thing. He still walks like a panther, which is weird, and he works for the BBC now. I'm not sure what he does there – his file says "Technical Support" but that could mean anything. I'm not sure how much money he makes, but he didn't look flash or anything.'

'He made your life such a nightmare with that drawing.'

Hayley sipped some wine and nodded. 'Yeah, but my life had already hit rock bottom and, to be honest, in a weird way it helped. When I started to lose weight, I used the memory of that drawing to help me keep it off and it stopped me eating junk. It still does, actually. In fact, I wish I had a copy of it now. I could stick it on my fridge as a deterrent. Besides, I got a pretty good revenge on him.'

'He never came back to school after the summer break, did he?'

'No. I wondered about that – you know, if it had anything to do with me or if he'd planned to leave anyway?'

'We'll probably never know.'

Hayley tipped the remaining wine into our glasses. 'Anyway, enough of Mr Cochrane, and I know I shouldn't be encouraging you, but what are we going to do about your dead boyfriend?'

'He's not my boyfriend, and he's not dead – well, not now, he isn't.'

'Whatever, we need a plan.'

'A man-plan?'

'A dead-man-plan.'

Chapter 13

Hayley's suggestion that I drop in on Nathan when passing his house and say, 'I thought I'd stop by just to make sure you're okay,' probably wouldn't be believed any better than my hospital excuse of, 'I just thought I'd say hello.'

I couldn't be sure how Nathan would react to me turning up on his doorstep but once I decided to act on something I just kind of did it. The next evening, I decided to carry out my plan and had illogically become a little pissed off with him as I hadn't realised he lived in such a dodgy area, which I'd have had little excuse to be driving through otherwise. To top it off, the rain had been hammering down for most of the evening.

You're going to get soaked on this fool's errand, my inner self warned.

'Thanks for that, and what's a fool's errand when it's at home exactly?'

Something from Shakespeare probably, but you're going to get wet; you shouldn't have come.

'But Hayley said to "strike while the iron is hot".'

She's not out here risking rape and death in the rain, though, is she?

'Can you see a parking place anywhere?'

No, too many double yellows. Maybe you should just go home.

'Not now that I've come this far.'

It's only a few miles.

'Yeah, mentally, not the actual distance, you numpty.'

Don't call me a numpty. Look, there's someone leaving; quick, get the space.

'I see it.'

Hurry up, you silly cow; someone else will get it.

'Don't call me a cow.'

I won't call you a cow if you don't call me a numpty.

'Deal. You need to shut up now – I'm going in.'

Good luck.

'Thanks, I think.'

I got out of my black car (what other colour would I have?), grabbed my bags and coat and squinted at the intercom on the wall outside the door. It had grown very dark and water had started to drip down the back of my neck, making me shiver. I pressed the button beside his name and waited. No response. Maybe he'd gone out, which would be bloody typical after all the effort I'd gone to. I pressed again, keeping my finger on the buzzer. Eventually a voice said, 'Hello?'

About bloody time. 'Hi, Nathan, it's Kat, can I come up?'

Surprisingly he didn't say a word and pressed the buzzer

to open the door. I trudged up the stairs leaving wet foot-prints all the way. He opened the front door and I bustled in, not waiting for an invitation. I felt annoyed at being soaked so I shook some rain from my hair.

'Jeez, it's pissing down. I wouldn't have come if I'd known it was going to rain like that. Also, I didn't realise you lived in Dumbiedykes.' I dumped the three full Sainsbury's plastic carrier bags onto the floor as the plastic handles were digging into my skin.

'I didn't know you were coming, and actually I don't think I ever said where I lived. Finally, I don't live in Dumb-iedykes, I live in Holyrood.'

I shrugged off my black coat and looked for somewhere to hang it. There were no pegs or cupboards or anywhere obviously designated for coats, so I folded it over once and dropped it in a neat pile on the floor.

I noticed Nathan staring at it, probably wondering what it would do to the carpet, but that was what he got for not having any hooks.

'Holyrood? Nah, don't think so – if it quacks like a duck, walks like a duck and tastes great with plum sauce, it's a bloody duck.' I had to admit most of our conversations so far had been a little strange, but then much of my life felt like that.

'It's definitely not Dumbiedykes, Kat.'

'Yeah, well, we'll need to agree to differ on that. I didn't want to park my car outside in case it got stolen.'

'What did you do, then?'

'Well, in the end I *had* to bloody park it outside your block, didn't I? Besides, I couldn't lug these bags about. They're too heavy.'

I watched as he rubbed his hand across his face. He asked, quite reasonably, 'What are you doing here?'

I looked carefully at him. 'You're tired.'

'I just woke up.'

'If you've just woken up you shouldn't look tired. I think maybe you left hospital too soon. Also the issues with your wife and kids are probably taking their toll on you.'

'I didn't know you were a doctor and a psychiatrist. Anyway, I've been out of hospital for ages now.'

'I've had enough medical training to know you should have stayed recuperating for longer and any stress will make it worse, regardless of how long you've been home.'

'Do you need medical training to work with dead people?'

'You do actually, but I didn't start out in the morgue. I trained as a nurse.'

'What happened?'

I didn't want to have that conversation right now. I picked the bags up. 'I'll tell you later. Where's your kitchen?'

He pointed to a closed door opposite where we were standing. I staggered down the hall, noticing he didn't offer to help. I pushed the kitchen door open with my hip. Pleasantly surprised to find a large and modern kitchen, I tipped out the bags onto a worktop and opened the fridge. It was filthy.

'Your fridge needs cleaning. It's really dirty.'

'I'm only at number fourteen on my list. Cleaning the fridge is number twenty-four. I kind of hoped I'd get to it by next week.'

I didn't understand what he'd said so I popped my head around the kitchen door and noticed he hadn't moved from the front door. Would he just stand there all night? 'What did you say?'

'Nothing important, I just haven't had a chance to go to the supermarket and, to be honest, I've been a bit nervous about going to Tesco.'

'Why Tesco?'

'Well, I'd been going there when .... my accident happened.'

'Is it just Tesco supermarkets you've got a phobia about?' 'I don't know.'

'Well, if you're going to pick one I'd suggest Waitrose. It's expensive and full of posh folk. The one near me has even got a security guard on the fruit and veg.'

'Is the stuff that good?'

'Nah, it's just that across the road is a mental health day unit and some of the patients like to wander in and lick the tomatoes.'

'Why?'

'How would I know?'

'Anyway, I think it's just Tesco.'

'Good, as all the stuff I brought is from Sainsbury's. Go and sit down before you fall down, and I'll bring you a drink.' I knew he'd be wondering why I'd turned up and probably how I'd acquired his address. The former I couldn't be sure about myself, the latter I'd pulled from the computer. I tipped a large bag of crisps into a salad bowl and poured two glasses of wine and carried the whole lot into the living room. Nathan flipped off the TV just as I entered. I dumped the crisps onto a small side table.

'What were you watching?'

'Nothing, I just had it on for company.'

'That's sad.' I handed him a glass. 'Well, now you've got me for company, so we can talk.'

'We're not very good at that, or at least we weren't in the hospital.'

I took a huge gulp of wine and relaxed. I waited for him to do the same. 'That's better.' I put my glass down on the table. 'Now we can have a proper chat.'

'Okay, I'll start. Why are you here?'

'You need some company ...' I nodded at the now blank TV screen '... and my BFFF Hayley suggested I come and see you.'

'BFFF?'

'Best Female Friend Forever.'

'Oh, right, well, that's nice of her. I'd fallen asleep.'

'She said you'd be lonely.'

'Is your friend psychic?'

'I don't think so. She used to be very fat, now she's very beautiful. I always thought she was beautiful even when she was a size gazillion. She pretty much lives on wine and rice now.'

'That sounds like a fun diet.'

'I was exaggerating.'

'I did get that.'

'Oh ... okay. Anyway, she's right; you are lonely.'

'Am I?'

'Absolutely. Lonely people sleep a lot. So do teenagers and cats.'

'What about lonely cats?'

I ignored his comment. 'When's your wife due back?' I quickly scanned the flat in case she happened to be lurking in another room. I really should have checked before turning up unannounced.

'Not today anyway – Sunday maybe – why?'

Phew, thank God for that. 'Just wondering; I don't want her getting the wrong idea about us.'

'Us?'

'We're not a couple.'

'I never thought we were.'

'I'm not a lesbian either.'

'I never said you were.'

'Did you think it, when I talked about my friend being beautiful?'

'Err, no, I can honestly say your sexuality hadn't crossed my mind.'

'My sexual orientation, not my sexuality. Because I dress differently some people naturally assume I'm a lesbian.'

'I don't know much about lesbians.'

'Neither do I, so that's something we've got in common already. Another thing – you should have stayed longer at the hospital today, then I wouldn't have had to come out here in the rain, risk getting raped, and wouldn't have had to spend sixty quid in Sainsbury's.'

'I'll give you the money—'

'I didn't ask for any money.'

Nathan sighed. 'Okay, I won't give you any.'

I refilled my glass and munched some crisps. 'I feel a bit drunk now, but that's okay. I trust you not to take advantage of me now that you know I'm not a lesbian.'

'That's nice, I think.'

'Now, why don't you tell me why you're so lonely?'

'My wife and kids are in London.'

'That's not what I mean. Even if they were all here you'd still be lonely.'

'Would I? I'm usually quite happy with my own company.'

'That's what lonely people say.'

'Is it?'

'Yep, all the time. What happened with you and your wife?'

Nathan laughed; it lit up his face. 'Where do you want me to start?'

'How old are you?'

He frowned.

'Don't frown. It makes you look old.'

'I'm thirty-five.'

'Oh, you *are* old. What music do you have on your ... phone or ... maybe iPod?'

'I don't have an iPod, and my phone I only really use for calls.'

'Oh, dear, that's positively dinosauric. How do you listen to music, then?'

'Dinosauric?'

'Yeah, as in "being a dinosaur".'

'Oh, right, well I've got some CDs I play in the car and I've got some music files on my laptop.'

'What was the last CD or song you bought?'

'Err, I can't remember ... maybe something by One Direction.'

'Jesus. Are you a fifteen-year-old girl in disguise?'

'I don't think so. I guess that's not very cool, is it? What should I be listening to? What do you like?'

'I'm not really into all the dark music Goths normally like – it's too depressing. I recently downloaded some tropical house.'

'I'm sorry, I don't know what that is. It sounds like something you might find at the Botanic Gardens.'

'You're hopeless.'

'Obviously I'm too uncool for all that. How old are you, Kat?'

'You shouldn't ever ask a girl her age.'

'Why?'

'It's rude, but if you must know I'm twenty-nine, thirty

this year on the twelfth of November if you want to get me a birthday present.'

'What would you like?'

'You can surprise me.'

'This is another strange conversation.'

'That's because we don't know each other very well. Let's change that – tell me what happened with your wife.'

He frowned again, noticed me watching and put on a pretend smile instead. 'I don't really know.'

'People that say, "I don't really know" always know. So, come on, tell me; I'm a good listener.'

'We started out okay. We used to party a lot and—'

'Why did you ask her out?'

'Err, I fancied her, I think.'

'You think? Has your accident affected your memory?'

'Not that I know of.'

'How old were you?'

'Twenty-three, nearly twenty-four. Laura had just turned nineteen.'

'What did she see in you?'

'Sorry?'

'Yeah, I didn't phrase that well – I meant did she fancy you too?'

Nathan laughed, which made me smile. 'I think so, I assume so, we were all over each other all the time we—'

'Spare me the details – I get the picture. Where did you meet?'

'At a party in a friend's flat in London. This gorgeous

girl kept making eye contact with me and I couldn't believe she liked me. I suppose you'd describe it as a whirlwind romance. We started going out and saw each other every day – it was really intense. The first time I met her parents I had to tell them their darling daughter was three months pregnant and we were going to get married.'

'I bet that went down well.'

'Yeah, you can imagine. She had to drop out of university, the only reason she'd moved to London in the first place. Her parents had struggled to fund her education and their first reaction with me in the room was, "Laura, you have to have an abortion. You can't throw your life away on a loser like this."'

'You made a good impression, then?'

I watched him shake with laughter. 'Yeah, and it didn't improve much over the years. She didn't listen to them anyway and moved into my tiny flat.'

'What did you do for a living?'

'At the time I worked in an office.'

'Doing what?'

'Advertising executive – a rather grand title for what I did.'

'Sounds exciting.'

'Mm, it had its moments, I suppose. Most of the time I'd describe it as organised chaos. Imagine a room full of creative types ... no, don't. Imagine a home for emotionally immature adults who spend most of their days playing with computer games, making up friends on Facebook, taking turns to run to Starbucks or if the boss, Woody, happened to be off sick – which happened a lot – surfing porn.'

'Did you work in an office full of men?'

'Mainly but not exclusively.'

'With a boss called Woody?'

'Yeah, he resembled a woodpecker with a sharp beaky nose, protruding eyes, and he waddled rather than walked. He wasn't really the boss. "Vaguely in charge" would be the best description, I think. He'd been a senior partner who'd suffered burnout and so they gave him the task of overseeing the office. He spent most of his days, when he turned up at all, wandering about making unhelpful suggestions.'

'And you got paid for that?'

Nathan laughed. 'Yeah, crazy, but London is full of places like that – advertising agencies, PR firms, IT contractors – where people can get away with pissing about all day in the name of creativity.'

'What do you do now?'

'The same thing except now I'm freelance.'

'So, you work for yourself?'

'Kind of. I have a few firms that pass me some regular stuff. They get a contract and then hire out the work. It doesn't pay that well and Scotland has very few ad agencies. My mate Graham runs one of the London spin-offs based in Glasgow and he uses me whenever he can get away with it.'

'Have you done anything I'd have heard of?'

'I suppose Simpson's Sheets would be one of my most memorable. If you can remember the series of adverts a few years ago: "If crinkled beddin' does your head in – buy some Simpson's Sheets".'

'I do remember that. They did a whole series of TV ads with all sorts of people having problems with their lives that were miraculously solved when they bought new bedding and didn't have to straighten and iron their sheets.'

'Yeah, a bit over the top but it kept me busy for the best part of a year.'

'I bought some.'

'Did you? That shows you the power of advertising, then. I suppose the thing I like about working the way I do now is that I can do it from here most of the time. Sometimes I need to go and meet people and one or two days a week I might work from Graham's office in Glasgow if there's something I need to collaborate on. The rest of the time a few phone calls and emails are enough. I also don't have to deal with all the nonsense that comes from being part of a "team".'

'I'm bored with your job chat. Tell me about the pregnant teen.'

'Oh, right, well, the baby was due in November. We'd initially planned to get married first but getting ready for a baby turned out to be more expensive and stressful than we'd expected.'

'When did you get married?'

He smiled, happy memories obviously. 'Three years later,

when Laura fell pregnant with Chloe. We had a little more money, Millie got to be a flower girl, so cute and—'

'I take it Laura felt vulnerable being pregnant again?'

'Maybe, but we'd talked about it loads before then—'

'Insecurity is a terrible reason to get married.'

'We were in love.'

'Had her parents forgiven you?'

'Eventually ... well, her mum did, anyway.'

'What about her dad?'

'He died.'

'When?'

'The year before we got married.'

'Poor girl. Pregnant, grieving and planning a wedding that her dad would never see. I'm surprised she didn't crack up.'

'No, she decided to save that until later.'

Chapter 14

I gawked at him, open-mouthed. I closed it, then opened it again to ask, 'When?'

'I'm not sure. I suppose shortly after Daisy came along.'

'How old's Daisy?'

'Four.'

'She cracked up four years ago.'

'Not exactly; it was a gradual thing.'

'What did you do?'

He took a sip of wine. 'What do you mean, what did I do?'

'When she started to crack up, what did you do?'

'I didn't do anything.'

'Let me get this straight: your wife is looking after three kids, probably still grieving for her father, she starts to crack up and you do nothing?'

'What could I do?'

'Get her some help.'

Nathan sighed. 'I tried to get Laura to go and see

someone, a therapist, her GP, anyone, but she insisted that she didn't need any help.'

'In denial, probably. There's something you're not telling me, isn't there?'

'Is there?'

'You've not mentioned *your* parents once. You must have issues with them.'

'I don't have issues with my parents.'

'Everyone has issues with their parents.'

'Do they?'

'Absolutely.'

'Do you?'

'Of course, why do you think I'm a Goth?'

'I thought that maybe it had something to do with rebelling or belonging to some kind of tribe or ... excuse my ignorance, my Goth knowledge is ... well, pretty non-existent.'

'Yeah, obviously, but you are probably right about the rebelling thing. My parents are so ... well, you'll see if you ever get to meet them. I think this ...' I held out my palms and gazed down at my clothing '... is a way of keeping people away.'

'Not a big fan of crowds?'

'Not a big fan of people.'

'Is that why you ended up working as a mortuary girl?'

'That's not the technical description of my job. I'm an anatomical pathologist.'

'Is it okay if I just call you mortuary girl?'

'Yeah, but the story of why I am one probably dates back to my tenth birthday when I changed my name.'

'Are ten-year-olds allowed to do that?'

'This one did.'

'By deed poll?'

'No, by obstinacy.' I laughed; I still found that funny even though I must have said it a thousand times by now.

'What did your name used to be?'

'Klaudette Ainsworth-Thomas – Klaudette with a K, hence K-A-T. I hated it and from that day on I only answered to the name Kat. Eventually even my teachers got used to the idea, all except the assistant head at my high school, Mrs Brock. She insisted on referring to me as Klaudette so I ignored her for five years.'

'I know your name is maybe a little long, but it doesn't sound that bad.'

'We need to get back to your parental issues. I put your details into one of my dad's search engines—'

'Your dad's search engines?'

'Yeah, he's a social anthropologist, boring as rabbit shit.'

'So, you know all about my family?'

'Not really, the information's a bit sketchy – births, deaths and that your name came about from being poor and called John John.'

'John John?'

'John John.'

'I have to say you doing that is a bit creepy, Kat.'

'Is it?'

'Yeah, I think so. It feels like you're spying on me.'

'Sorry, I guess I never thought about it. That's what happens when you're brought up by someone like my dad. I haven't checked out your Instagram page, if that helps.'

'I don't have one.'

'Okay, and I didn't open up your wife's Facebook page either.' (This was true – Hayley did that.)

'Okay, I'll forgive you. My upbringing's not been straight-forward either. I didn't see much of my parents growing up as they packed me off to boarding-school, but I'm not sure I've got that many issues with them.'

'You're in denial again – in denial about your failing marriage, mentally unstable wife and your family. You're a serial denialist.'

'You just made that up.'

I shrugged. 'Did not, it's true. What happened to your father? He died quite young, didn't he?'

'You've done your research. My parents inherited a load of dosh just after I was born and set off on a series of adventures and spending sprees. I got in the way so that's why I ended up in all-day nurseries and boarding school. I think the hedonistic lifestyle ended up killing my dad.'

I thought about that for a moment. 'That's very sad.'

'I'm over it now.'

'I don't think you are – you never will be. But you've learned to live with it. What did your wife think about it all?'

'She liked it, or more the idea that somehow I came from

this posh privileged background. Whereas for me private education represented a punishment for being born – a reminder that I simply got in my parents' way of having a good time.' Nathan smiled. 'Maybe I do have some issues with them. After my dad died I got to know my mum a little better. She brought me home to London, for company probably, and I went to the local school instead. After about a year she got itchy feet again and started going on cruises and long-haul holidays on her own or in groups for single or widowed women. At which point I'd got to the age where I could fend for myself.'

'What happened to your mum?'

'She went overboard.'

'Oh, that can happen when someone loses a partner – they can't cope and start doing all sorts of strange out-of-character things and—'

'No, no, she literally went overboard – she fell off a ship.'

'Eh?'

'Yeah, somewhere near the Greek island of Kos – I don't know for sure as they never found her body.'

'Oh, my God, that's awful. Wouldn't I remember it from the news or something?'

'It happened a long time ago and it's quite common.'

'What is? Falling off ships?'

'Yeah and nobody noticing – anything between twenty and thirty people do it every year. It's not that surprising if you think about it – pissed pensioners and boats, not a good mix.'

'I don't know what to say.'

'Nobody does – as I said, it happened a long time ago. She didn't turn up for breakfast so the folk she'd been hanging out with raised the alarm, but nobody could find her. She'd pretty much run through all the money by then so maybe she jumped. Who knows? I'm over it.'

'So is that how you ended up in a maisonette flat in Dumbiedykes?'

'Yeah, well, as I said, the money had gone. It's a duplex and it's in Holyrood.'

I smiled, took a slurp of wine and said, 'You're in denial about everything, aren't you?'

He laughed again, lightening the mood.

'When will the divorce be finalised?'

Nathan spluttered, and wine dripped down his chin.

'Attractive,' I said, laughing.

'Divorce? What divorce?'

'Well, that's what happens, isn't it?'

'What?'

'I've not had that many relationships and I've never been married, but when your wife moves out and gets as far away from you as possible, surely the next thing is divorce. Your marriage is now a Humpty Dumpty.'

'Humpty Dumpty?'

'Yeah, all the king's horses and all the king's men couldn't put it together again.'

Nathan shook his head. 'We've not talked about it.'

'Given your communication issues that doesn't surprise me. But it'll happen, you need to realise that.'

'I do?'

'You do.'

I passed over a tissue. 'You've got wine coming out of your nose.'

'Sorry.'

'It's okay; I've seen worse things.'

'I'm sure you have.'

'You know what you need?'

'A psychiatric evaluation?'

'Maybe. It wouldn't do any harm, but that wasn't my first thought.'

'Right, so what else do I need, then?'

'Food.'

'I am a little hungry.'

'There's nothing in your fridge. What have you been living off?'

'Baked beans and bagels.'

'I'll make something. Not involving beans and bagels.'

'That'd be nice.'

'You're a mess, Nathan; you need to sort yourself out.'

'I had a shower and shaved this morning ...'

'That's not what I mean. You're a mental mess. Anyway, I'm off to the kitchen.'

I left him sitting and pottered into the kitchen. I felt very comfortable in his flat for some reason. I pulled some stuff out of the bags and found the pots and pans in a cupboard under the sink. They were filthy too, so I started washing them. The running water must have piqued his interest as he poked his head around the door.

'What are you doing, Kat?'

'I'm washing the pans, they're filthy. Do you have a dishwasher?'

'Yeah, it's over there next to the washing machine.'

'Why don't you use it, then?'

'It's broken.'

'How long has it been broken?'

Nathan shrugged. 'A few weeks, I think.'

'You need to sort yourself out and get on top of things.'

'Kat, I know, but you nagging me isn't going to help.'

'I'm not nagging.'

'You are so. I don't need you to do that; I've got a wife for that, thank you very much.'

'No, you don't.'

'Okay, I *had* a wife for that, then, and I don't need a stand-in.'

I felt annoyed again but wasn't sure if it was down to his manner or my mood. 'I don't think I like you, Nathan.' I wiped my hands on a large piece of kitchen roll.

'That's good, Kat, because I don't think I like you either.'

'Why?'

'Why what?'

'Why don't you like me?'

'I hardly know you and yet you keep poking your nose into my life and I don't need that right now.'

'You don't know what you need, Nathan; that's your problem.'

'Look, you turn up here uninvited and start analysing me. I'm a grown man with three kids. I don't need this shit.'

I'd gone from irritated to angry now (so it probably *was* him) and I dropped the pan I had in my hand onto the counter, where it clanged and bounced onto the floor. 'I'm doing a nice thing here, trying to help you out.'

'I don't want your charity.'

'Is that what you think this is?'

'I don't know, you tell me.'

'I came over because I know you're in pain, you've had a really traumatic time and I thought, "Here's your chance, Kat, to do something for someone else for a change," you know, stop being so self-absorbed and narcissistic—'

'I don't know what that means.'

'Narcissistic?'

He nodded.

'It means being overly concerned with my appearance.'

'Oh. So, is this all about me or is it about you? I—'

I didn't let him finish his sentence and instead popped a huge chunk of cooked ham into his mouth. I needed a few moments to think about what I'd just said. I'd engaged my mouth before my brain again and needed to check if I'd said anything I shouldn't have. Thankfully I hadn't mentioned anything about liking him but the whole narcissistic thing had just emerged from my gob fully formed with no input from my frontal lobe whatsoever. I shuddered and tried to cover my discomfort by focusing on him. 'You need to eat, Nathan. Your brain needs sugar.'

I broke off a lump of crusty bread, smothered it in butter and pushed it towards his mouth. He swallowed the ham and bit into the crust. 'Mm.'

What fun. I hadn't fed anyone other than myself since Lesley Ashcroft, a nurse I knew, brought her three-month-old baby into work one day and let me feed him. I didn't think Nathan had become such a basket case that he needed to suck a bottle, but you never knew. I popped the remainder of the bread into my own mouth.

What next? I had butter all over my fingers. Might be time to try the bottle test. I slowly licked the butter from two of my fingers, not breaking eye contact. My little finger remained coated in slightly salted butter and instead of licking it off myself I slowly offered it up to him. His tongue darted out, but I pulled my finger away before he could touch it.

Interesting.

I dipped my fingers into my wine glass and sucked the wine from them, then repeated the action, except this time I locked eyes with Nathan again and held them out to him. He approached cautiously this time, not wanting to be duped for a second time, but I had no intention of pulling them away. I wanted him to suck them. I wanted my fingers inside his mouth. I desperately wanted him to run his tongue between my fingers; I wanted to feel the warm wetness of his mouth. I'd become completely absorbed in the moment.

Slowly, he leaned forward and wrapped his hand around my wrist. He pulled my fingers into his mouth, sucking the wine from them. It felt incredibly intimate and erotic and I didn't even think the black nail varnish bothered him; in fact I didn't think he noticed. My stomach flipped over, and I could feel every inch of me becoming charged with electricity and lust. I hadn't planned or wanted this but found myself staring into his pale blue eyes, searching for something – what I couldn't be sure – but his face had glazed over with need. Just as we leaned closer to each other the house phone on the kitchen wall trilled gratingly, destroying the moment.

The lustful expression left his face as he answered the call.

'Hello?'

His face darkened, and he hung up almost immediately. Uh-oh, I thought. 'Was that your wife?'

'No, someone wanting to know if I need a new kitchen.'

I laughed with relief and couldn't believe the comic timing of it all. My body had drained of most of its horni-ness – probably a good thing as I'd had no intention of complicating Nathan or my life more than necessary, not yet anyway, but I liked the fact he found me attractive.

'You probably *do* need a new kitchen.'

'It just needs cleaned.'

'Especially the fridge.'

'You told me that earlier.'

We sat down opposite each other at the table like normal people instead of horny rabbits.

I'd completely lost my appetite but assumed that, as he'd been living off tins of beans, his need for food would be greater. I pushed things towards him: smoked ham, crusty bread, strawberries, grapes and a triangular slab of Brie. 'Eat,' I commanded and poured myself some more wine while I watched.

He spread some Brie on the bread and shoved a big chunk into his mouth. Some of the cheese got stuck to his cheek and breadcrumbs rained down onto the table.

'This is like watching a pig eat.'

'Thanks.'

'You're welcome.'

'Do you know what else you need?'

'A bib?' he mumbled.

I laughed. 'Probably, but you also need a friend, maybe a girlfriend.'

'I do? Why?'

'You've been through a traumatic experience. Not many people get to die and come back.'

'Vampires do.'

'Does that mean you're going to bite my neck?'

'Do you want me to?'

'I'll think about it. I can't be your girlfriend just now, though.'

'You can't?'

'No, not while you're married.'

'Right, okay, I forgot about that.'

'Yeah, that tends to happen when the little head takes charge of the big head.'

'Thanks for pointing that out and reminding me of my domestic strife.'

He appeared to be a little sad, which lifted my spirits and made me decide to ignore Hayley's advice.

'You're beautiful when you sleep.'

His brows knitted together. 'I don't think I am, and how would you know anyway?'

'When you were all drugged up I watched you sleep for a while.'

'That's weird, Kat, and a little creepy.'

I nodded. 'My friend Hayley did say I shouldn't tell you that.'

'She sounds like a wise woman. You should listen to her more.'

'She doesn't know you.'

'You don't really know me either.'

'I knew I liked you as soon as I saw you.'

'I'd been dead when you first saw me.'

'Fair point, but the moment I pulled you out of that drawer I just knew – as long as you survived, of course. I'm not into necrophilia.'

'Just as well, given your occupation. It's possible that you might need professional help too. I've got some good mental health people recommendations recently – maybe I could arrange for you to see one of them.'

I laughed. 'I'm one hundred per cent sane. I just know what I want. I go out of my way to avoid people, but when I like someone, which doesn't happen often, I tell them straight off.'

'I've noticed.'

'You fancy me.'

'I do?'

'Of course, you do, your eyes don't lie.'

'My eyes?'

'Your pupils dilate every time you look at me. You want into my knickers.'

'I do?'

'You do. But you're not getting into them, not yet anyway.'

'Why?'

'We've already had that conversation.'

'Have we?'

'Yeah.'

'I must have forgotten.'

'Oh, dear, amnesia too. You should go and see Dr Spencer again.'

'She wants to introduce me to Jesus.'

'I've heard he's a nice guy.'

'We won't have anything in common.'

'Oh, I don't know – he came back from the dead as well.'

'I forgot about that.'

'See? Amnesia.' I stared at him for a moment, wondering what fascinated me. Yeah, he looked good, but there must be something else, possibly that mysterious stuff called chemistry. He wouldn't have been my first choice as he was confused, had three kids in tow and was heading for a messy divorce. Hayley was right – I must be a sucker for lost causes.

I smiled at my thoughts and said, 'I'm going to tidy up in here, then get a taxi home. I can't drive because you've made me drink too much. If my car gets broken into or stolen overnight, I'll send you the bill.'

'Fair enough.'

'Keep an eye on it – it's a black Fiesta – and text me if anything happens.'

'It'll be fine.'

'I hope so.' I gave him my number anyway.

He texted me later to make sure I'd got home okay, which was nice of him. He then texted me to say, *I hope you get a good night's sleep.*

Thank you.

Thanks for dinner.

You're welcome.

Are you tired?

A little bit.

OK goodnight.

Goodnight Nathan.

In the morning I woke to a plethora of messages:

2.11 a.m. Sorry I can't sleep, you are haunting my dreams.

I wasn't sure how I could be doing that if he wasn't asleep.

2.16 a.m. What are you doing for breakfast? Do you want to meet up?

Needy or what?

2.19 a.m. Sorry, that sounds like I'm really needy.

Glad he agreed.

2.31 a.m. I know you are worried about me being married and having kids and still hankering after my wife and all that stuff and I suppose you're right to be worried (I'd be worried) but having a friend at this time would be nice. Will you be my friend?

He sounded like a child.

2.35 a.m. I shouldn't have sent that one, it makes me sound pathetic, lonely and about five years old. Sorry.

At least he could be quite self-aware.

2.43 a.m. I'm going to sleep so I'll stop texting you now, but let me know if you'd like breakfast, or lunch or brunch (depending on when you collect your car). I'm sorry about the texts I'm not used to texting pretty girls. PS your car is fine.

I lay in bed, thinking and working on a mental checklist. On the plus side he was cute, vulnerable, funny, didn't take himself too seriously and had a bonkers streak running through him that had probably been shaped by a weird childhood. (The last item might have been a red marker for most folk, but a green one for me.) He also liked me and fancied me and said I was pretty.

On the negative side, he was married, had kids, hadn't got over his wife yet. (Would he ever? Did married people ever get over splitting up?) His life was in turmoil and he lived in Dumbiedykes, despite his denials.

It was too late for breakfast anyway, so I texted back:
Let's have brunch but not in Dumbiedykes.
   Holyrood.
   Yep, in denial.
   See you soon, Nathan x.
   Our first kiss!

Chapter 15

When I got off the bus I noticed him standing beside my car. I hoped he'd not been guarding it all night.

'Hi, Nathan.'

'Hi, Kat.'

We stood staring at each other awkwardly before I said, 'I'm hungry.'

'So am I.'

'Where will we go, this is your end of town?'

'There's a nice place not too far from here, I sometimes take the girls there for lunch.'

'OK, your car or mine?'

We took mine. We ended up in the Elephant House Café and squeezed into a tight corner table near the toilets. The waitress took our orders and a few moments later delivered us coffee.

'Why are all these people taking selfies?' I asked Nathan as he read the menu.

'This is the place where J. K. Rowling wrote the Harry Potter books – well, the first one or two at any rate.'

'Oh.' I watched lots of foreign tourists come in the door, pose for a selfie and disappear without buying anything.

'I'm sorry for texting last night. I'm not used to texting girls, except Millie.'

'Who's Millie?'

'My eldest daughter.'

'Oh, okay.'

'I hope I didn't disturb your sleep.'

'Nah, once I'm out I sleep like the dead.'

'That's a gruesome description, Kat.'

'Thanks.'

'I'm not sure I meant it as a compliment.'

'You should have.'

'Well, all right. That might take some getting used to. Last night, well ... I think I was trying to sort out my feelings.'

'That'll take more than a few texts to a sleeping girl.'

'You're probably right.'

'I am right. Now, if you want to talk about your feelings, that's fine, but as you know I like you, and you like me. That's the easy bit. The more complicated issue is that you've got loads of baggage to sort out and I'm YFS.'

'YFS?'

'Young, free and single. Well, quite young; younger than you at any rate.'

'With no baggage, so why would you want to get involved with me?'

'Oh, I've got baggage, but you're right – you've got three

162

children and they might not like me. I'm nothing like their mother.'

'That's a big plus for me.'

'That remains to be seen. Let's talk about your wife. What's she up to?'

'She's working, in London.'

'Yeah, you told me that, but what else? Has she got a boyfriend?'

'Oodles.'

I stared at him for a moment. 'What, loads of boyfriends?'

'No, just one called Oodles.'

'That's a strange name and, believe me, if I think that, it's true.'

'He's called Simon. He's got oodles of money – that's why we call him Oodles.'

'Who's we?'

'Me and Millie.'

'Ah, your daughter knows.'

'She told me about him.'

'Oh.' I tried to process that. 'So, your wife's quite open about it, then?'

Nathan nodded and took a bite from his bagel.

'If your wife has introduced your kids to her new boyfriend, then your marriage really is a Humpty Dumpty. I was right.' He nodded again. 'So you need to move on.'

'I know.'

'I assume that's why she moved to London?'

He frowned. 'Why?'

'To be with Oodles.'

'Laura said she's just met him.'

'And you believed her?'

He nodded again. Aw, bless, what a trusting soul. 'The first thing we should do, if you want to see how things might pan out, is introduce me to your daughters. It will be awkward but necessary if you want to move on.'

'I want to move on, I think.'

I laughed. 'That's an honest answer, at least. I don't want you to do this for the wrong reason. I don't want to be used as a pawn or a lure to tempt Laura back.'

'I don't think I understand. How would I do that?'

I studied him for a minute to see if he was being obtuse, but he genuinely seemed puzzled, so I let it go. 'There will be plenty of bumps in the road so be prepared.'

'Okay.'

I wasn't completely convinced, but I fancied him, and he needed me. I liked that. I didn't often feel needed; in fact, I couldn't remember the last time anyone needed me, apart from Sid to help open up a cadaver or to compare notes on our dysfunctional families.

'What shall we do, then?' I asked, sipping my now lukewarm coffee.

'I had planned on taking them to the safari park on Monday. It's a school holiday. You could come with us? It'll be on neutral ground and with other things to occupy their minds. I'll just say you're a friend. Oh, but won't you be working?'

'One of the good things about shift work, perhaps the only good thing about shift work is that my work-patterns are quite varied. I'm off Monday. As for being a friend, I suppose, for the time being, that's all I am. It might be fun. I've not been there for years and we can visit your relatives.'

'My relatives?'

'The chimps.'

'Are you sure you've not been speaking to my wife?'

'Why?'

'That's what she said when we went to the zoo.'

'Must be true, then.'

Chapter 16

That evening I caught up with Hayley.

I'd bagged a quiet table in The Fall Guy, an old bistro pub in the Grassmarket area. I'd already finished a glass of red wine while watching the door for her arrival.

The waitress had been over twice to see if I'd decided what I wanted before Hayley showed up. Her timekeeping had always been terrible.

'Sorry,' she said quietly, chewing her bottom lip. She looked uncharacteristically flustered.

'Busy day?'

'Every day's a busy day now. I even have to go in tomorrow just to catch up, but I don't want to bore you with my work stuff.' She smiled at me and waved the waitress over. I ordered penne-pasta with meatballs, considered another glass of wine but opted for caffeine free diet coke instead.. Hayley went for a lean chicken salad and sparkling water. 'Do you know what's in that stuff?' she asked, pointing at my drink.

'It's diet, caffeine-free Coke, so practically nothing, it's just dirty fizzy water. It must be okay though, as they tested it on kangaroos in the Australian outback.'

'How do you know?'

'I read it in the *Metro*.'

'Oh, well, must be true, then, but it's got that sweetener stuff in it that your body changes into formaldehyde.'

'We use that in the morgue.'

'There you go, then, it can't be good for you – and on the subject of the dead, how are things with your dead boyfriend?'

'Well, he's still not dead, or not any more – you need to stop calling him that – and he's not my boyfriend.'

'I know you gave me the basics over the phone, but what's your plan?'

'I'm going out with him and his kids on Monday.'

'That's a big step. What if he gets back with his wife? What if he decides it's too early to date someone new? What if he just wants a shag?'

'He's not like that. His brain doesn't work that way, at least I don't think it does, plus, his wife has introduced his daughters to her new boyfriend.'

'That was quick.'

'I think she's been seeing him for a while.'

'Oh, did Nathan tell you that?'

'No, common sense.'

'You might end up as a surrogate mother that he can dump the kids on and bugger off to the pub.'

I laughed. 'He wouldn't do that – leaving *me* in charge of children, can you imagine?'

Hayley put her finger to her lips, pouted and raised her eyebrows, pretending to be thinking deeply about my child-caring abilities. It just made her look dipsy. 'Stop it. I'm not that bad.'

'Yeah, okay, but have you thought this through? You hardly know this guy and yet are thinking of taking on his kids.'

'I'm not taking on anything. It's a day out and nothing more.'

'Whatever. I reckon he still might just want a shag and I think you're wasting your time with him.'

'He needs me.'

'The wife won't like it.'

'She's done it to him.'

'Is this his idea of payback?'

'It was my idea.'

Hayley laughed. 'For some reason that doesn't surprise me. Still, it can't be worse than Dr Dave.'

'Don't swear.'

'Listen, I've got some news.' I watched Hayley chew her lip again and twirl some of her hair in her fingers, avoiding looking me in the eye.

'What's happened?'

'Um, I'm not sure how to tell you this but ... well, I've met someone.'

'You have?' I squealed, a little too loudly, as everyone in the pub turned and stared at our table.

'Shhh, Kat, too noisy.'

'Sorry,' I said, bouncing up and down on my seat. 'How, where and when?'

'I kind of met him at work, I suppose.'

'What? Another lawyer? I thought you hated—'

'He's not a lawyer.'

'Right, so ...' I tried to think what other males worked in Hayley's office. 'Is it that cute paralegal guy that you wanted to snog last Christmas?'

'Alex? No, he's moved on anyway.'

'So, who is it? Come on, Hayley, don't keep me in suspense here. You never mentioned anything the other night; how did this happen so quickly?'

'You're not going to like it, Kat.'

'Why won't I like it? Who could ...?' Suddenly the penny dropped. 'No-o-o-o-o.' I gasped. 'You can't. You haven't. It's not right, it's not decent, it's like ...'

Hayley smiled guiltily. 'I couldn't help it. He came in yesterday morning when I'd been sitting in the open office and I didn't have time to hide and, well, we just got to talking and—'

'Hayley, what are you thinking? He made your life hell.'

'Yeah, but it was a long time ago and, in a way, also helped save me. That drawing he did was the final push I needed to stop eating crap and start losing weight.'

'Your weight loss was hormonal, wasn't it? That's what you've always claimed.'

'Initially, yeah', she confirmed. 'But, later, I had to work at it.'

'It still doesn't make it right, Hayley.'

'How can I *not* go out with someone that walks like a panther? Besides, well, the way I see it is what better way to lay a ghost than to lay the ghost?'

I couldn't help laughing despite my shock. 'You've slept with him already?'

She nodded.

'You tart. You slept with him on your first date, that's not like you?'

'I know, crazy and it wasn't really a date. He came back at the end of the afternoon, we went for a few drinks and it kind of progressed from there. Anyway, it was you who told me to join a divorced dating site.'

'Yeah, so you could meet some random divorcee, not grab one that's not even divorced yet. What if he gets back with his wife? What if he decides it's too early to date someone new? What if he just wants a sh—?'

'Does any of this sound familiar to you, Kat?'

I stopped and thought about what I'd said and watched the deadly serious face of my friend. Slowly I noticed a small twitch appear on the left side of her mouth, then it spread to the other side, then seconds later we were both screeching with laughter. I said eventually, between breaths, wiping tears of laughter from my eyes, 'What are we like?'

Chapter 17

Monday arrived sunny and warm and I donned a pair of black leggings, matching tunic top and my black military minx jacket. Given I felt like I might be heading off on some kind of military campaign, the choice was apt. I also went for my black Berghaus boots with the ermine faux fur around the tops as they were comfy. I toned down my make-up a little, but then had to rewash my hair after I dripped jam from my toast onto my GHD straighteners without noticing and then applied the sticky mess to my lovely dry locks.

For some reason I felt more nervous about meeting his kids than I had been on the evening I'd turned up at his flat unannounced.

'What if they hate me?'

They probably will, my inner self answered.

'Thanks for that.'

My pleasure. Think about it; their mother has pissed off down south, then you waltz into their dad's life. Hardly a recipe for a magic meeting.

'That's what I love about you – your optimism.'

Just pointing out what might happen.

'I need to think positive.'

No point in talking to me, then.

'Okay.'

I knew very little about children, except that little girls were complex things – I used to be one once and I was very complex.

I arrived outside Nathan's flat and switched off the engine. The area looked a little better in daylight, but I had to remind myself that everywhere looked nicer when the sun shone. I got out, locked the car and pressed the buzzer. Nathan's tinny voice said, 'Just stay there, we'll be right down.'

A few minutes later he appeared dressed in black Superdry cargo trousers and a white polo shirt. He had a canvas jacket in his hand and dark desert boots on his feet. He looked as if he'd just stepped out of a catalogue with his casual look and roughly gelled hair. Behind him were his three beautiful daughters, all with jet-black hair and dark emerald eyes. I felt outnumbered and outclassed.

Nathan smiled and said, 'This is Millie, Chloe and Daisy, in order of age and size.'

I smiled and said, 'I'm pleased to meet you all.'

For a fraction of a second, I didn't know what to say next. My first thought had been to compliment the way they looked, but I remembered when I was a little girl that was all anybody ever said to me, even though I knew I had a fat body and squished face. In fact, I reckoned that was where some of my neuroses began – not the fact that I had a fat body and squished face, but that people ignored my obvious shortcomings and said, 'Aw, she's lovely.'

Instead I knelt in front of Chloe. I instinctively knew she'd be the key to our introduction. Daisy didn't really understand the ins and outs of the situation due to her age, Millie knew fine well, which left Chloe as the perfect in-betweener. 'How are you feeling, sweetie?'

'I want to see the lions and I miss my mummy.'

Wow, all her emotions in one short sentence. 'That's fine. I want to see the lions too and, you know what, even though I'm a grown-up I sometimes miss my mummy too.'

Her eyes were wide with surprise. 'You miss your mummy? Is she dead?'

I laughed. 'No, she's not dead, she lives in Glasgow and I don't see her as much as I should.'

'You should visit more, then.'

'You're right, Chloe, I should.' I noticed Nathan watching me and said, 'I miss my daddy too.'

'Is he dead?' Chloe asked with a serious face. Her obsession with death intrigued me. I remembered having a similar fixation at the same age – who was I kidding? I still had it – even their dad had been dead when I'd met him.

I smiled. 'No, sweetie, my dad is very much alive. He likes sheds.'

An adult would be taken aback by such a statement, but Chloe took it in her stride. 'Urgh, sheds are full of spiders.'

'My dad's sheds are spotless, Chloe; no spider would dare set up home in one of his sheds.'

'Why not?'

'What's your favourite thing in the whole wide world?'

'Hannah.'

I raised my eyebrows to Nathan, who said, 'Hannah's her "real life" baby doll.'

'Real life doll? That makes about as much sense as bumblebees.'

'Bumblebees?'

'Yeah, bumblebees make no sense at all.

'Don't they?' asked Nathan.

'No.'

'Okay.'

I turned my attention back to Chloe. 'So, listen, honey, would you let Hannah get all dirty and covered in spiders?'

She squished up her features, almost reminding me of myself at that age, and said, 'Urggh, no way.'

'Well, that's how my dad feels about his sheds.'

Nathan knelt beside me. 'Sheds, as in plural?'

'Yeah, he's got three sheds.'

'What does he do with three sheds?'

'He keeps stuff in them.'

'What stuff?'

'Just stuff. He locked the local MP inside one for three hours once but that didn't end well.'

I stood up and stretched my back. Millie, I knew, had not

taken her eyes off me since I'd arrived. She stepped forward and asked, 'Why do bumblebees not make any sense?'

I smiled. 'Because they are big and bumble about all over the place and probably shouldn't be able to fly but they can.'

I could see Millie taking in what I had just said. 'Oh. But they give us honey.'

I hesitated. 'They don't really, we get honey from honey bees, not bumblebees, but they do pollinate flowers, which is very useful. Now, what are you looking forward to today?'

Millie smiled. 'Lions, tigers and bears ... oh my.'

I burst out laughing and noticed that only Millie and I understood the joke. Nathan just looked at us with a strange look on his face and Chloe and Daisy were oblivious. I grabbed Millie's arm and we skipped to Nathan's car saying, 'Lions, tigers and bears, oh my!' I'd made connections with Chloe and Millie and I was sure I'd get Daisy onside by the time we got to the safari park.

Nathan's car, a large Ford Mondeo estate, meant lots of room for everyone and the large picnic cool box he'd shoved in the boot before leaving.

On the way I picked up the leaflet he had on the safari park and noted that it charged quite a lot of money to get in. I had an idea that might give everyone a good laugh and save us a few quid into the bargain. I checked his satnav, which said we had about eight miles left to go or twelve minutes. I swivelled my head around and said to the girls, 'Right, who's up for hiding in the boot?'

The three girls squealed and all three thrust their hands in the air. Nathan said, 'What are you talking about?'

'We're all going to hide in the boot until we're safely inside the safari park.'

'Why?'

'Firstly, it's fun and, secondly, it'll save us some money.'

'But it's not safe.'

'Oh, don't be such a killjoy. Stop a mile or two before the entrance and we'll all sneak into the back.' I could tell Nathan wasn't happy but today was about the girls and not him, so a few minutes later we all crawled into the back and Nathan reluctantly drove on.

A few miles down the road we stopped at the tollbooth at the entrance to the park and I could hear the muffled voice of the girl talking to Nathan. I tried to stifle a giggle but couldn't, which set the girls off and all four of us started giggling. Thankfully Nathan drove off just as the giggles turned into full-scale laughter. Once we got out of the car I took one look at Nathan's grumpy face and started laughing again.

'What's wrong, Nathan? We just saved a fortune.'

'What if we'd got caught?'

'But we didn't. You can't spend time worrying about things that didn't happen – that won't lead you anywhere good.'

I could see him trying to process my last statement in his overly cautious brain. I supposed his reticence had something to do with having kids and needing to think differently from me, but eventually he worked it out and smiled. 'Yeah, okay.'

The sun had his hat on and the temperature hovered in the mid-sixties in old money and that, for Scotland in April, was about as good as it got. We sat at an outside table under a shady parasol and ate the lunch Nathan had packed, supplemented by coffee and ice cream from the nearby café.

Nathan, I'm sure, would have been happy to sit there all day and watch the girls playing on the huge play frame in the shape of a boat situated a few metres away, but I'd come to see the animals so I rounded everyone up, which took some time.

We first headed off to see Nathan's relatives on Chimp Island. This involved standing in a queue for twenty minutes before being herded onto a boat, which circled the island and then headed back to shore. I spotted one chimp, which appeared to be busy smacking another one on the head with a coconut.

'What's the monkey doing with that coconut?' asked Chloe.

Nathan scratched his chin and said, 'I don't know.'

I jumped in. 'I think he's trying to crack it open.'

'Wouldn't it be better smacking it off a rock?'

'Probably, but monkeys aren't that bright.'

'They share a lot of the same DNA with us,' argued Nathan.

'Exactly,' I said, smiling.

After the boat ride we stood and watched two rhinos trying to shag each other for a few minutes; they were soon joined in the same enclosure by some amorous zebras. Maybe it had something to do with the sunshine or maybe we'd come on 'animal porn day'.

Thankfully the remainder of the afternoon passed without any further sex scenes and Nathan relaxed as the day wore on. By the time we saw the birds of prey at 3.30 p.m. he'd started smiling. I realised that he'd been really stressed, like a tightly coiled spring. I didn't know if this had anything to do with me meeting his daughters or if it represented his default setting since his wife had buggered off. In any event he needed a chill pill.

On the way out, we eventually visited the lion enclosure and watched the most boring bunch of lions I'd ever seen. They sat under an old tree sleeping and didn't move a muscle despite the hordes of cars driving past. They were the lion equivalents of lazy scroungers. I suppose being kept in a safari park meant they didn't need to hunt for anything and park employees chucked them a dead cow every other day to chew on.

The girls were very quiet on the way home. I put it down to tiredness, but I suppose the fact they were missing their mother might have had something to do with it.

I had planned on heading off home as soon as we got back but Nathan insisted I stay for dinner. His plan to order Chinese takeout went down well.

In the flat I initially sat on the couch in the living room

while the girls went to their rooms. Nathan had disappeared into the kitchen – probably to polish the fridge in
case I did an impromptu inspection. After a few minutes
of sitting on my own I wandered down the hall, knocked
on Millie's door (I perceptively spotted the name 'Millie'
stuck on it) and went in. What struck me most? The sheer
tidiness of the place. Not a thing lay on the floor, there
were no clothes on the bed and not a speck of dust could
be detected. I imagined it to be like an army billet – I'd
never been near an army base so I was guessing here, but
it felt as if everything had been made ready for the sergeant
major's inspection.

Millie wasn't there. I heard voices in the next room and
found her in there with her sisters. Chloe and Daisy shared
this bedroom and again, not a thing seemed to be out of
place. Little girls shouldn't be this tidy. It didn't feel right.

'When did you last make a mess?'

Three pairs of dark green eyes focused on me, as if I'd
just suggested we should gut a kitten.

'When did you last come home all muddy and wet?'

Same reaction, three girls staring at me like the kids from
Village of the Damned except they were all dark, not blonde.

'When did you last make a den?'

Millie blinked, then said, 'A what?'

'A den.'

'What's a den?'

I couldn't believe she didn't know. 'A den, a secret place
away from adults.'

Chloe piped up, 'Mummy doesn't like secrets.'

That explained a lot, and the identity of the sergeant major. 'Right, this way, we're going to build a den.' I marched into the living room with them trailing behind me like an impish sprite about to lead them into mischief.

'Right, Chloe, you take all the cushions off the couch.'

'Why?'

'You'll see.'

'Where do I put them?'

'On the floor for now.'

I watched while she followed my instruction.

I then moved the couch around, so it sat across a corner leaving a gap. I then picked up the cushions and laid them on the back, so they formed a roof over the dark corner making a 'secret space'. Well, okay, not that secret but I had to start somewhere.

Six eyes continued to watch me.

'There you go. It's not great but it's a start.'

'What do we do with it?' asked Millie, assuming the role of chief spokesperson to the lunatic.

'You crawl into the space and sit there.'

'Why?'

'It's fun; it's called playing – you've got a space away from all the adults.'

'There's only you and Dad here.'

'True, but it gets you away from us.'

'Do you want rid of us, so you can be alone? We can play in our rooms.'

What was wrong with these kids? 'No, I don't want rid of you. It's the other way around – you need space away from adults to play and, well ... to do naughty things.'

'Mummy says it's not good to be naughty.'

I felt so sorry for them I wanted to cry. They'd end up more screwed up than me at this rate and that would be saying something.

I crawled into the den and reluctantly they followed me in. We all sat there in the shady corner.

'Now what?' asked Millie.

'Now you use your imagination. Have you not got any secret things that you'd like to bring into the den?'

Eventually Daisy said, 'Mr Mistyfluffs.'

I smiled at her. 'Who is Mr Mistyfluffs?'

'He's a cat I got from the bear factory.'

'Wouldn't you get him from the cat factory?'

Daisy crinkled up her nose. 'Where's that?'

Millie piped up. 'There isn't a cat factory, Daisy; only a bear factory, where they also sell cats, dogs, goats, monkeys and Minions.'

'What's a Minion?' I asked, intrigued.

Millie darted a glance at me. 'You're joking, right?'

I shook my head.

'They're blue and yellow.'

I nodded, none the wiser. 'Why don't you go and get Mr Mistyfluffs, Daisy, and maybe get a Minion too so I can see what it is?'

Away she went.

'Chloe?'

'I could bring my jewellery box in.'

'Good girl, go get it, then.'

'Millie, what about you?'

'I've got my princess diary with the padlock on it.'

'Excellent – now we're getting somewhere.'

A few minutes later they were well into the swing of it and the den had filled up with a selection of toys and possessions, including an annoying square Minion figure that had Tourette's tendencies and kept saying, 'Wayhay,' for absolutely no reason at all.

Daisy had started pretending to be a cat called Bella. Her sisters were petting her, and she purred.

Nathan then appeared and nearly spoiled it all. 'What's going on in here? Who's making a mess?'

I popped my head up out of the top of the den and said, 'Me.'

Daisy popped up and said, 'Meow.'

The Minion said, 'Wayhay.'

'What are you doing, Kat, messing up the room?'

'Wayhay.'

'Who keeps saying that?'

I didn't answer him. I crawled out of the small space and escorted him by the arm out of the room into the kitchen. 'The girls are playing.'

'They're making a mess.'

'Yes, they are and it's healthy.'

'It's a mess.'

I sighed. 'Nathan, you and Laura have these girls living like little mice, too scared to even squeak.'

'What are you on about now?'

'When did the girls last come home dirty?'

'We don't really go anywhere dirty.'

'Why not?'

Nathan paused while he thought of an answer. 'I don't know. Because Laura likes everything neat and tidy.'

'When were you last at the beach?'

'I don't think we've ever been to the beach.'

'What?' I almost shouted this at him, which made him take a step back. 'You live, what, within a couple of miles of Portobello and you've never been to the beach?'

'We've been to Portobello loads; the girls cycle up and down the promenade.'

'When it's nice and sunny and dry.'

'Yeah, mostly.'

'But not on the sand, no paddling and getting all muddy, sand in their hair, seaweed on their legs, wet knickers and leggings from falling over.'

He shook his head.

'Oh, Nathan, what a shame.' I genuinely felt sorry for all of them, bless.

The girls coming into the kitchen saved him further pity. They'd attached a small belt to the lapel of Daisy's top and she crawled along on all fours, meowing. Chloe had the Minion under her arm slightly muffling the 'Wayhay'.

'Bella's thirsty,' announced Chloe.

I laughed. 'And what would Bella like to drink? Some milk for the pussycat?'

Daisy/Bella shook her head. 'Apple juice,' she mewed.

I got a plastic cup from the cupboard, but Chloe said, 'Cats don't drink from cups. They drink from a saucer.'

I poured some apple juice on a saucer and put it on the floor. Chloe said, 'C'mon, pussy, come and drink your pussy juice.'

At that point I exploded with laughter, as did Nathan, and even Millie laughed though I don't think she should have. The Minion said, 'Wayhay.'

I left his flat just as the girls were getting tired and irritable. I didn't want to complicate their bedtime and didn't fancy at that stage getting involved in reading bedtime stories or whatever people did with their kids these days at night. Nathan escorted me to my car, very chivalrous of him. I still glanced around in case any would-be car thieves were lurking nearby. He awkwardly bent to kiss me as I opened the driver's door. I started to kiss him back, happened to look up and noticed three heads peering down from his living-room window. 'You've got an audience.' I laughed as he followed my gaze. I jumped in, started the engine and drove away smiling.

That went well.

'It's not like you to be positive.'

I know, I must be coming down with something.

'Well, keep it to yourself, please.'

My shift pattern meant I'd be working nights most of

the rest of the week and it'd be the next weekend before we could meet up again. As much as I'd enjoyed my day with the girls, now I really wanted some alone time with Nathan.

*

After Kat had left, Nathan got his brood ready for bed, Millie being last as usual. As he got her settled she said, 'Mummy want's us down in London again this weekend.'

'I know.'

'Gran's going to take us.'

'I know.'

'Can't I stay with you?'

'I think mummy wants you all together.'

'It's not fair.'

'I know.'

Millie was silent for a moment then asked, 'Are you going to marry Kat?'

'Where did that idea come from?'

'Inside my head.'

'Yeah, but apart from that, I'm still married to Mummy.'

'Not for much longer, though.'

'How did you work that out?'

She shrugged and yawned. 'Well, she's with Oodles now and you're kissing Kat. These things happen.'

'You're too grown up.'

'Someone has to be around here.'

Nathan laughed. 'I've just met Kat.'

'But you like her.'

'I do.'

'We like her too. She's funny and naughty.'

'She is, but it's complicated, Millie, and there's a lot going on just now.'

'I know.' She was quiet for a moment then asked, 'You still really like cinnamon and raisin bagels, don't you?'

'I do.'

'If you only had one left, would you give it to Kat if she wanted it?'

'Yeah.'

'You've got it bad.'

Nathan laughed, ruffled his daughter's hair, kissed her goodnight and said, 'You're too smart for your own good at times.'

Chapter 18

Early, the following Saturday morning, Nathan's phone buzzed and the words 'Laura's home phone' flashed up in green. He answered quickly.

'Hi, Nathan.'

'Laura, what's happening? Is everyone all right?'

'Everything's fine. I just phoned to let you know that we're having a really nice time.'

Nathan's antenna was twitching. She wouldn't phone just to tell him that, but he played along to see what happened next. 'Listen, Nathan, the girls won't be home tomorrow.'

Here we go, he thought. 'Why not?'

'There's much more room for them here, now that I'm in a bigger flat.'

'Yeah, Laura, whatever, that's nice for you, but what about the girls? They've got school on Monday.'

'They're not coming back, Nathan.'

'What do you mean they're not coming back?'

'I thought I'd made myself very clear. They're going to stay down here with me and go to school locally. I've

187

managed to get them into a fabulous little primary school just down the road from my new flat in Brixton. I've agreed with the head teacher that we can start them in two weeks.'

'Brixton used to be a war zone.'

'It's changed and gone upmarket now, the flat's got a lovely little garden and—'

'Laura, I don't give a shit about your flat. You can't just decide to keep the girls in London. It's—'

'If you're going to become abusive, Nathan, I'll hang up.'

'How do you expect me to react? This is the first I've heard of your hare-brained scheme. What do the girls think about it?'

'I've been talking to them on and off about it and they can see the benefits of going to school here.'

'You mean you've poisoned their minds or bribed them or—'

'I'm their mum, Nathan. That's the thing you've got to think about.'

'You buggered off and left them.'

'You're swearing again.'

'What the fu ... hell do you expect me to do?'

'Talk like an adult, calm and measured.'

Nathan gathered his thoughts and wondered whether Laura could do this legally. He needed to be sure before he went down that road. 'Why the change of mind, Laura? You left us behind so fast there were practically scorch marks on the carpet.'

'That's a bit of an exaggeration, Nathan, but I never

really wanted to get away from the kids, just from you. Now I want my girls with me here, simple as that. They can have a much better life with me.'

'You said you wanted them to stay here because they'd have a more settled life in Edinburgh.'

'I've changed my mind.'

'You can't do that.'

'Of course, I can, I just did.'

'I won't see them, Laura; this isn't fair.'

'Of course, you'll see them; you can see them whenever you want. You just have to let me know in advance when you're coming.'

'Laura, that's ridiculous; you want me to book an appointment to see my girls?'

'It's hardly like that, Nathan, just a little notice would be required, that's all.'

'I can't go flying up and down to London; it's too expensive.'

'I did it.'

'You chose to do it, for Christ's sake. That's hardly the same thing.'

'You're being abusive again, Nathan. I think I might need to start recording our telephone conversations.'

Nathan took a deep breath and tried to calm his temper. 'Laura, you know this isn't fair; especially not the way you've told me. You should have let me know ages ago.'

'I only decided in the last few days, Nathan. Look, I know this is difficult for you, but try and put your

David Atkinson

personal feelings to one side and you'll realise this is the best thing for the girls. A girl needs her mother more than her father.'

'That's not true, Laura, and well you know it. I've always been there for the girls.'

'Well, it's my turn now, then. Also, look at how many single mothers are bringing up children; it's almost the social norm now so that proves my point. Besides, I'll have Simon as support. We've talked about getting a place together.'

'That was quick and he's an arse – what good's he going to be? They're not his daughters. He doesn't have their best interests at heart. He only wants into your knickers.'

'He'll be there for moral support. He gets on great with the girls, which helps as I'm sure it can be tough being a single parent. As for my knickers, well, if you must know, when I'm with Simon I don't wear any.'

Nathan knew the last comment had been designed to get his blood boiling but despite this he could still feel his face getting red. He decided to play the 'legal card' anyway. 'I'm not happy about this, Laura, I don't think what you're doing is legal.'

Laura sniggered. 'Of course, it's legal; I'm the girls' mother.'

'I'm their father; don't I have rights too?'

'I'm going to go now. I'll phone you in a few days, once you've had time to think about things a bit more and cool down. Please don't contact us meantime; the girls need a few weeks or months to get used to the idea. I'm working long hours for the rest of this week, so I can take next week off and show them how great living in London will be.'

'Who's looking after them during the day, and what do you mean by months?'

'They're booked into a wonderful activity centre this week near Fulham Football Club. It's really geared up for younger kids during term time, but they've agreed to take them for a few days. It'll help burn up all their excess energy.'

'And allows you to have a nice quiet evening to yourself.'

'Well, after working hard all day I deserve it, don't you think?'

'No, I don't "think", and Millie hates sport.'

'Millie's just spoiled.'

'She's not spoiled, she's just old enough to know what's going on.'

'She has been a little difficult.'

'I'm not surprised. It's a huge disruption and all her friends are here. You never answered my question – what do you mean "months"?'

'I said weeks *or* months, depending how long it takes them to settle, especially Millie. She needs to get used to the idea. They all will.'

'You're a complete cow, Laura.'

'Thanks, Nathan. That makes me feel better. Bye.'

Laura hung up and Nathan's spirit sagged, as if a heavy weight had suddenly been placed onto his back. He found it difficult to move and breathe. Laura had obviously been

David Atkinson

planning this for some time; she'd ambushed him, but he probably should have seen it coming.

The girls had only been away for a day and he missed them already. He'd planned on spending the morning preparing their clothes and uniforms ready for school and now ... well, now he wouldn't have to. He'd never do it again; months, she'd said months. He felt sick and didn't know where to turn, then suddenly he did.

Chapter 19

Nathan didn't say much on the phone, but I could tell something had happened, as asking me to come over seemed out of character. He'd texted me only an hour ago and he'd been lovely, we'd planned a nice evening in town with a meal and drinks and ... well, I hadn't thought too much beyond that.

Yes, you have, you liar.

'Don't you start.'

You had this whole fantasy in your head, back to his flat with the whole bodice-ripping thing going on.

'I don't own a bodice.'

You know what I mean. You were wearing one in your fantasy.

'You shouldn't be watching my fantasy.'

I don't have much choice, do I?

'You could close your eyes.'

My eyes were closed.

'Well, you could have looked the other way.'

What and miss that? No chance.

'I need to go.'

Don't forget your bodice.

'Shut up.'

I didn't know what to expect when I cautiously parked outside his home, once again looking out for car thieves and dodgy characters, but every person wandering around at that time in the early afternoon in Dumbiedykes looked shifty to me.

I hurriedly buzzed his flat and quickly closed the door once he'd let me inside the vestibule. When I reached the top of the stairs he opened his door and stood waiting for me; his red eyes and dark expression made me think the worst. 'What's wrong? Has someone died?'

'No, of course not.'

'Right, sorry, whenever I, we …' I didn't want to explain my and Sid's default situation on crisis management. 'Never mind, what's happened, then?'

'Laura's keeping the girls in London.'

'For how long?'

'Forever.'

We went into his uncannily tidy living room and I sat down on the couch opposite Nathan, who slumped down into a chair. I hadn't expected that answer. 'Can she do that?'

'Yeah, it seems that she can.'

'Can you not see them at all?'

Nathan snapped, 'I don't know, eventually, she said months.'

'Don't shout at me. I'm not the one taking your kids away.

I'm on your side. I'm just trying to find out what's going on. I know diddly squit about child access custody shit.'

Nathan tried to smile. 'Sorry, Kat. It's diddly *squat*, not diddly squit.'

'You choose now to correct my grammar?'

'I could do with a hug.'

'You're not very huggable right now and I'm not in the best of hugging moods but I'll try, okay?'

I sidled over and squeezed into the armchair and pulled him into my arms. He snorted. I grimaced, but my bits still twitched even though I had in my arms a snivelling, miserable ex-corpse. I was either smitten or a raving loony. 'Nice. It must be true love for me to be sitting here doing this. You're a mess, Nathan.'

'You keep saying that to me. you'll give me a complex.'

'I think you're about as complex as it's possible to get. Hayley's right, I shouldn't have got involved with you.'

'I wouldn't blame you for walking out of here and never coming back; my life is a mess.'

'I'm a sucker for lost causes.'

'Am I a lost cause, then?'

'You're the king of lost causes.'

'At least I'm good at something.'

We were quiet for a minute or two before I thought the time had come for him to stop feeling sorry for himself. 'So, what are you going to do?'

'What do you mean?'

'About your girls.'

'I don't know. I've only just found out. I haven't really thought about it.'

'Right, well, first let's get out of here. You need some air to clear your head. It's a lovely afternoon – let's take a walk up the high street.'

'I don't feel like moving.'

'That's exactly why you should – c'mon, let's go. I'll phone Hayley on the way; some legal advice might be useful.'

Half an hour later I'd managed to relocate his gloom from his flat to a comfy leather chair in Starbucks. It felt as if he had one of those little cartoon rain clouds following him about. To make matters worse, it'd started to rub off on me and my spirits were falling. We were sitting at a window table watching groups of happy tourists walking by, waiting for Hayley to phone back. Nathan's latte had grown cold and had a skin on the surface so that when he took a sip some of it was stuck to his lip, giving him a caramel moustache. I watched him lick it quickly, as he rightly assumed it wasn't a good look.

My phone rang. Hayley; good timing. The place was quiet, so I put her on loudspeaker. 'Okay, Kat, I'm assuming there's no formal agreement in place yet around custody?'

I looked over at Nathan, who shook his head.

'There's not,' I said.

'Well, then, currently, both parents have equal custody rights.'

'What does that mean?' Nathan asked.

'Well, as there's no legally certified agreement yet, there's no restrictions on you seeing your children. The downside of that is that there's no agreement as to when you *have* to see them either. So, if you like, possession is nine tenths of the law. She's got your children and until something is agreed in writing she can manoeuvre things so that you are kept away from them, indefinitely. How was it left between you both?'

'Not good,' Nathan said gloomily.

'What does "not good" mean?' Hayley asked.

'She said months.'

'Months?'

'Months.'

'That's quite a long time,' Hayley said, her tinny voice resonating on the table. 'A divorce where children and property are involved can take up to a year to resolve.'

'A year?' asked Nathan, his voice pitching towards hysteria.

'Thanks, Hayley,' I said, deciding that Nathan had heard enough.

'Kat, call me later?'

'Will do, bye.'

After we'd hung up I stared at Nathan, who sat with slumped shoulders in his chair. 'What can I do?'

I felt very sorry for him. I couldn't really empathise as I wasn't a parent but there must be hundreds if not thousands of men across the UK (and some women) in the same or similar positions. 'Nathan, you need to realise that she holds all the aces here. She has them in her care in her flat in London, some four hundred miles away.'

'I know, and her boyfriend, Oodles, seems very happy with the arrangement. I'm not sure why, but he is.'

'Okay, you could move to London, but that doesn't guarantee you'd see them any more often than if you stay here, but at least you'd be in the same city.'

'I don't really want to move back to London. No matter what I do, she's not going to let me see them, is she?'

'I don't know.'

'She just expects me to accept it and get on with things.'

'Probably – what else can you do?'

'I don't know.'

I wished I could think of something to lift our moods, when suddenly I had a brainwave, one of those ideas that only lived once and streaked across the mind like a fizzing, fading shooting star, the kind of idea that you needed to act on immediately or it vanished forever. I turned to Nathan, all excited, and said, 'Nathan, I've got it.'

'Got what?'

'A camper van.'

'A camper van? I thought you had a Fiesta?'

'I do. But we could *hire* a camper van. I've always wanted to drive about in one ever since I was a kid. My dad's friend used to park his old Volkswagen caravanette outside our house when he visited. It was diarrhoea brown, covered in rust, and had a huge hole in the floor that meant you could watch the road whizzing past when you travelled along.'

'You're not selling this to me very well, Kat.'

'Yeah, that's because you've got no imagination.'

He gave me that kind of hang-dog look associated with someone about to be patronising. 'Kat, I know you're only trying to cheer me up by suggesting this holiday idea and, believe me, in different circumstances the thought of heading off with you to a beach somewhere in a camper van is lovely but ...'

'You don't understand. I'm not suggesting you and I go off alone, though now you've mentioned it that does sound quite tempting, but no, I thought we could hire one, shoot down to London, snaffle the kids and then, whoosh, we're gone. It'd make us really hard to track down.'

Nathan sat bolt upright. 'Whoosh?'

'Whoosh.'

'That's a great idea. It's probably kidnapping but I like it.'

'I'm not sure how it can be kidnapping when they're your children and you're allowed to see them as much as you want. How is it more like kidnapping than what she's doing? Possession is nine tenths of the law, remember?'

'True.'

'Also, after we've got them, you can call your wife and explain that you'll bring them back but not until there's an official agreement in place. That way she can't keep them away from you for months – tables turned.'

'We'd need a bigger camper van than your dad's old friend used to own, hopefully with less rust.'

'You can get them in all shapes and sizes now but best not to go too big otherwise it's

hard to drive. Plus, you want one that doesn't stand out.'

'Why?'

'If the police start looking for you, we aren't so easy to find.'

'The police? I thought it wouldn't be kidnapping?'

I thought for a moment. 'Well, I don't know that, do I? There might be a restraining order or something on you.'

'Wouldn't I know about it?'

'I don't know. Probably.'

'We're not very good at this, are we?'

I laughed. 'No, but we'll be expert kidnappers soon, just you wait and see. Now, we need a plan.'

Nathan paused and frowned at me.

'What?'

'I don't understand why you really want to get involved with me and all my ... baggage.'

I had wondered that myself; in fact, I hadn't come up with a plausible answer to satisfy myself, let alone him, especially as ten minutes ago he'd started to drag me down. I fancied him, I liked being with him even when everything seemed to be a constant crisis, and he made my bits twitch. Nobody had ever done that before, at least not fully clothed. Maybe I was a complete weirdo but perhaps that wouldn't be the best kind of reply, so I dredged up something I'd seen on an old episode of *Kung Fu* I'd watched on an obscure cable channel a few weeks ago. 'There's an old Chinese proverb that says, "Whenever someone saves another's soul they need to stay until they're whole, or something like that.'

'What hole, like a hole in the road?'

'Eh?'

'What? Never mind, and, technically, did you save my life?'

'I don't know. I think I might have – if you'd been left in the drawer much longer you would have died of hypothermia.'

'Thank you again.'

'You're welcome, but I have to admit that ever since I set eyes on you lying dead – or rather *un*dead – in your shroud I've been unable to get you out of my head.'

'Sounds like you've got issues.'

'Yeah, I think I have, but you've become my latest in a long line of lost causes and, whether you like it or not, I'm sticking around.'

'I like it.'

'Good.'

Nathan moved over and sat close to me on the couch. Then he leaned over and kissed me gently on the lips. 'Thanks for helping me.'

Uh-oh. My body betrayed me; everything inside had gone liquid. What a shame we were sitting in a busy Starbucks. I wanted him to tear my clothes off and drag me onto the floor, and wondered about that. I obviously had some clothes-shredding fantasy thing going on, which, unless I happened to be wearing something old and threadbare from a charity shop,, would only result in some stretched necklines, chafed skin and the odd popped button.

Don't forget the bodice.

'Shut up about the bodice.'

'What was that, Kat?'

Oops.

'Nothing, just thinking aloud.'

'About bodices?'

'Erm, yeah, I need to get a new one.'

'I'd like to see you in that.'

I bet he would.

'Shhh.'

'Okay, sorry.'

'No, I wasn't talking to ... never mind.'

I'd also determined that when we eventually 'did the deed' the time and place had to be just right. I didn't know when or where, but it had to be my decision, and it didn't look as if it would be any time soon now this latest crisis had hit.

Jesus, I hadn't realised what a control freak I'd become or why I'd got myself worked up about it, given the variety of places I'd had sex in my life; a muddy tent, a smelly toilet and a grubby Ford Transit came to mind, but I tried to rationalise this by thinking this man was still married and worried about his children. Surely, I must be just an added complication right now, despite the fact my body was screaming at me to grab him and hold on. Of course, it might just be that it'd been so long since I'd had a shag my body was desperate for anything. I laughed into his mouth at the thought.

'What?' he asked, pulling back.

'I'll tell you later. Let's go and plan our road trip.'

Chapter 20

B ack in his flat, the gloom had lifted now that we had a plan of action. We sat staring at Nathan's laptop while we surfed Scottish websites showing camper vans for hire. Most of the prices were extortionate, asking nearly £1200 a week. I tutted. 'That's stupid money; you'd be better off buying one.'

'Really? How much are they new?'

'Well, this one here is about fifty grand.' I pointed at the screen.

'Okay, so maybe *not* better off buying, then.'

Suddenly I had another brainwave. I was on fire today. 'These are Scottish sites, that's the problem.'

'Is it? Why?'

'Because there's so much less choice up here. Let's look at places inside the M25 corridor – makes it easier to get there too. If we hire a van locally we'll have to drive it all the way down and that'll take ages.'

I scrolled through various screens and came across a site. 'Look, the very same van at ...' I squinted at the screen '... somewhere near Oxford. It's called Motorhome World and the price is only £500 for a week – that's like less than half price.'

'Weird.'

'More choice. More competition. Right. Now give me your credit card. I'll book this before it goes.'

While the information uploaded Nathan asked, 'Where will we go once we've got the girls?'

'How about the Highlands? I've never been there.'

'Me neither, but you're Scottish and lived here all your life. I'd have thought you'd have gone with your parents.'

'You don't know my parents. Tramping around the Highlands wouldn't be their thing. I think the furthest north I've been is Aberdeen. I had a weekend training course there a few years ago entitled "Advanced Decomposition of the Exposed Corpse".'

'Sounds like a blast.'

'The pubs were good.'

The website pinged, confirming our reservation. 'That's it done. We pick it up Monday morning.'

'That's quick work. So we need to get to Oxford tomorrow or Monday?'

'Monday – I need to pack a bag and tidy up my flat.'

'Tidy up your flat?'

'Of course. I can't go away and leave a messy flat.'

'Why not?'

'Just because. You book the trains and I'll see you at the station Monday morning.'

I got the feeling that Nathan hoped I'd hang around for a bit longer but then I might just end up going all liquid again and losing my resolve and probably a few items of clothing as well.

'It'll be fine, Nathan. We'll get your girls and have a ball. Tomorrow you need to pack some stuff for your girls, and yourself. Travel light if you can.' I gave him a quick peck on the lips, wishing just for a second that I could stay, and left.

*

After she'd gone, Nathan fetched a beer from the fridge, popped it open and stared out the window across to Arthur's Seat in the distance.

He hadn't initially been that keen on the camper-van idea, but the more he thought about it, the more he believed it was the only way to make Laura see sense. He could, of course, try and reason with her, but he'd be wasting his breath. Sharing a life with her for over a decade had taught him that much.

His flat felt empty and quiet now Kat had left. He suddenly realised he missed Kat when she wasn't there as much as he missed his daughters. Now that was a real revelation to him.

Chapter 21

Hayley phoned me on the way home from Nathan's and I put her on hands free as I drove.

'Sorry, Kat, I can't talk long. I'm at work catching up.'

'It's Saturday, Hayley.'

'I know, but I had to go into the office for a few hours to prepare for my Monday meetings, then I'm going to the gym. What's happening with Nathan and his kids? Have you made any plans?'

'Yeah, we're going to snatch them back.'

'Sorry, say that again. I thought you said you were going to snatch them back.'

'I did.'

'Uh-oh, that's not a good idea. Maybe you should just step away now and not get involved in any sort of hare-brained scheme.'

'It's *my* hare-brained scheme.'

'Strangely enough, that doesn't surprise me as much as it should.'

'He looked so sad. I don't like him sad.'

'Still, it's a bit extreme, don't you think?'

'His wife's a cow.'

'Playing devil's advocate, you don't know her – she might be lovely, and he's just driven her potty.'

'I don't think so. How many women do you know would move away and leave her kids behind?'

'Not many; but she's not leaving them, is she? She's now taking them back. It seems like this might have been her strategy all along.'

I hadn't thought of that until today. Hayley was a much smarter cookie than me. 'Well, that's even worse, she's a devious cow.'

'My advice is don't get involved.'

'It's too late for that, Hayley, but I need you to do me a favour.'

'What?'

'I need to know if Nathan snatching his children is illegal, like kidnapping or a felony.'

'It's not a felony.'

'It's not?'

'No, because we don't live in America.'

'Oh, okay. What about UK laws? Is it illegal?'

'Well, as I said earlier, possession is nine tenths of the law, so I don't think so, as long as they're not being endangered or missing school or stuff like that.'

'We're only taking them for a week maybe, just so his wife knows Nathan isn't going to sit about for months until she decides he can see them.'

'He could just ask her.'

'He says that won't work.'

'There must be easier ways of settling things.'

'You're right, there probably is. I'll talk to him again later. We'll be away for a week, then we'll come back to Edinburgh.'

'What happens after that?'

'I don't know; we haven't thought that far ahead.'

'That doesn't surprise me either. I say again, you shouldn't get involved, Kat.'

I knew she was probably right, but I didn't want her to put a downer on things, not now that we were about to set off on an adventure. I had this nagging doubt that perhaps I had some selfish reasons for the escapade, to inject some excitement into my mundane life, but I felt something special whenever I spent time with Nathan. Most of my life I'd felt inferior, uncomfortable, maybe even unequal, in my relationships with men. I always seemed to be the one compromising and making allowances. I could never just be myself around them. With Nathan things were different. It could be something to do with the way we met. Perhaps everything would change once he'd sorted his life out but for now he needed me, and I liked that.

*

At 7 a.m. Monday I spotted him standing outside WHSmith in Waverley station – our agreed meeting point – with a small rucksack on his back and a small silver case by his feet. I dragged my very heavy and very large suitcase behind me, the small castor wheels on it beginning to buckle. I'd probably packed too much. I always did.

'Kat, you said travel light.'

'This is me travelling light. You have no idea how hard it was to leave stuff behind.'

'It looks like your whole wardrobe.'

'This isn't all my wardrobe, not even close. This is only the basics.'

'Well, I suppose if we can't get a camper van we can use your suitcase to hide the girls in.'

At least he'd remained cheerful. 'What platform do we need?'

'Six.'

'Okay, let's go.'

Five hours and two train changes later we left Oxford mainline station and hailed a taxi. Nathan helped me lug my suitcase in and gave the driver the address and postcode and we were on the final leg of our journey.

The taxi eventually weaved into a run-down industrial estate and deposited us outside some large grey metal gates, strewn with razor wire and secured by a large chain and padlock. Attached to the left gate a large sign warned 'Beware of the Attack Dogs'. Not the most welcoming of places, I had to say.

An intercom had been screwed onto the fence. Nathan pressed the buzzer and waited. Eventually a male voice asked gruffly, 'Yes, what is it?'

'Err, we're here to pick up a camper van?'

'Have you made an appointment?'

'Well, no ... but we booked online and paid a deposit with a credit card.'

'You're supposed to make an appointment.'

'Well, we didn't know that, and we've come all the way from Edinburgh.'

'You should have made an appointment. What would have happened if I'd been out?'

Nathan looked to me and shrugged. 'Err, I don't know.'

'Exactly,' said the voice triumphantly. 'That's why the website asks you to make an appointment.'

'Sorry, we didn't read that bit. We've got a very big suitcase with us.'

I heard a dramatic sigh through the hiss of intercom static. 'That's what everyone says. As for your suitcase, we at Motorhome World don't like large suitcases. They scratch the paintwork.'

That made me wonder how clear the appointment malarkey could be if everyone said the same thing. I peered through the fence at the scrubby patch of land that encompassed Motorhome World. I couldn't see any motorhomes at all, which struck me as strange. I would have thought that somewhere called Motorhome World would be packed full of the things. After a minute of silence Nathan pressed the intercom again.

'Yes?'

'We're still here.'

'I know, I'm just putting my shoes on. I'll be with you in a minute.'

'He's just putting his shoes on,' Nathan repeated.

'I heard.'

'I wonder why he's got his shoes off?'

'Maybe he's got sore feet.'

A few minutes later a large man with a sweaty complexion and greasy black hair ambled into view. Mr Sweaty, as I immediately named him, approached the gates and stopped a few feet short of the fence. He nodded as if coming to some monumental decision and leaned forward, opened the padlock, removed the chain and swung one of the gates open. We stepped inside, and he hurriedly closed the gate and padlocked it again. I shivered despite the warm afternoon sunshine and hoped Mr Sweaty wasn't familiar with John Kramer of the *Saw* movie franchise. I could imagine him trapping us here and subjecting us to various lab-rat-type tests before systematically chopping off bits of our limbs. A strange scent drifted to my nose from the man, a mixture of sweat, cigarettes and aftershave or deodorant used liberally to try and mask the other two smells.

He turned and walked away without speaking. We assumed that we were to follow him, the alternative being to stand and stare at the gate waiting for the attack dogs to show up.

We trailed warily a few yards behind, mainly because my suitcase didn't trundle very well on the rough tarmac. Eventually, he paused at the door of a run-down Portakabin with dirty windows. I still hadn't spotted a single camper van. He smiled creepily and beckoned us inside. I had become more and more convinced that we would walk inside to find an accomplice ready and waiting in a hockey mask ready to fire up a chainsaw.

Instead we found a paper-strewn desk with several stained coffee mugs perched precariously on the edge. Mr Sweaty sat down behind the chaos and indicated we were to sit in the chairs opposite.

He punched some keys on an ancient computer keyboard. 'Name?'

'Nathan Jones.'

Punch, punch. 'Yeah, I've got you here. Now, you've booked one of our newest models, a Swift Exit 39.'

I thought I'd like to make a swift exit right now, especially as the confined space only served to enhance his strange body odour.

'Do you know much about motorhomes?' He didn't let us answer. 'I assume not, as you referred to it as a "camper van". Let me make it very clear: we do not stock, nor have we ever stocked, nor will we ever stock camper vans. In fact, in my opinion the camper van ceased to exist in 1967 when Volkswagen ended the manufacture of the split-screen version.' I had no idea what he was on about but sensed, somehow, we'd made a mobile home faux pas.

Mr Sweaty smiled (I wished he hadn't) and said, 'Motorhomes are the most luxurious and comfortable fun you can have outside your bedroom.'

He directed his smile towards me at that point and I felt my sex organs shrivel in response. I'd seen more attractive decomposed corpses, but I nodded in the hope that by humouring him we'd get out of there faster. 'I've got it – motorhome, not camper van.'

Mr Sweaty scowled and wiped his face with the grimy sleeve of his black pullover. 'Fine. Now, before I complete the paperwork and get copies of your ID and driving licences I need to ask a few questions. Firstly, are you going to take this to some weird music festival and get it all muddy? We don't like our deluxe models all muddy.'

As his questions seemed to be directed at me for some reason, I answered, 'No, we definitely won't be going to any music festivals.'

Sweaty nodded and ticked a box on his form. 'Who will be travelling? Is it just the two of you?'

'Well, no, we will have some children with us.'

Mr Sweaty didn't appear to like this answer. 'We, at Motorhome World, don't like children – they tend to have sticky, dirty fingers and be prone to bouts of vomiting. Bouts of vomiting and motorhomes don't go well together. Are your children subject to frequent bouts of vomiting?'

Nathan answered quickly, 'No, they're good travellers.'

Sweaty didn't look convinced. 'Well, if on returning the vehicle there is any evidence of vomit we will withhold your deposit pending a full valet.'

Obviously unhappy at renting a motorhome to someone so vulgar as to want to transport children in it, Mr Sweaty completed the formalities with little further conversation, apart from relieving Nathan of an extra £150 for insurance. He then took us around the back of the Portakabin onto a tarmacked area where, lo and behold, sat a single solitary motorhome.

Despite a reluctance to engage in any kind of chit-chat with Sweaty, I had to ask, 'Why is this called Motorhome World if you've only got one?'

Sweaty peered at me and a bead of perspiration dripped down his forehead. I watched it until it reached the end of his nose and dripped to the ground.

'We have lots of motorhomes for hire, but we don't keep them here.'

'Where do you keep them?'

'In Cumbria.'

'Cumbria?'

'Yes, it's a large English county in the north near—'

'I know where Cumbria is,' I said. 'So, when we're finished with it we could drop it off in Cumbria rather than drive back here?'

Sweaty considered the question for a moment then nodded. 'Yeah, probably.'

He handed me a set of keys and used another set to open the door of the white and blue vehicle. There was then a brief explanation of both the mechanical and practical aspects of a Swift Exit 39. I wasn't sure what the 39 referred to and I immediately called it the SE39, much less of a mouthful. Then Sweaty said we were allowed twenty minutes to familiarise ourselves with it before we had to leave. He'd be at the gate in exactly that time to let us out.

Nathan said he'd driven a few Transit vans before when moving stuff from flats, but this represented a much bigger proposition. It had an automatic gearbox, which helped, and after a few minutes fiddling about he seemed reasonably happy with the controls. I hadn't planned on doing any driving unless I absolutely had to, so I didn't want a turn. We decided to use some of the quieter roads around the industrial estate to practise before venturing onto any busy A roads and motorways.

We made it to the gate in time to be let out and drove the large vehicle around the wide but quiet roads of the industrial estate. Once I'd grown confident in Nathan's ability to manoeuvre the thing, I said we should head off or it'd be too late to get the girls before Laura took them home. We eventually found our way onto the A40 and headed south towards London.

I sat beside him and watched the built-in satnav as it mapped out our progress.

Nathan sighed. I put my hand on his arm. 'What?'

'I wish we didn't have to do this. It all seems a little extreme. We used to be so happy.'

'When? I thought your marriage had been buggered for years.'

Nathan laughed. 'Well, yeah, it was, but once upon a time we were happy.'

'Cheryl and Ashley Cole were probably happy for a

while too, and Cheryl Fernandez-Versini and Mr Fernandez-Versini and Cheryl Tweedy and Liam Payne but look what happened there.'

'They're all one person, aren't they?'

'Yeah.'

'Well, that's not very representative, is it? She's maybe just been unlucky.'

'Probably, but sometimes it works out, a lot of the time it doesn't. I think expectations are too high. Also, most people are too busy to notice whether they are happy or not. Personally I think people like being busy as it stops them from having to think about the big questions in life. Maybe that's why the world is so manic now, too many people in denial, putting off making the big decisions until it's too late to make them. Life moves fast. "If you don't stop and look around once in a while, you could miss it."'

'Is that another of your Chinese sayings?'

'No, Ferris Bueller. Wise man.'

I could feel Nathan's eyes on me for a moment, but I didn't meet his gaze. Eventually he said, 'So tell me again about what your friend said about what we're about to do.'

'Okay, Hayley has confirmed what you're doing is definitely *not* kidnapping. They are your children and as such they only need one responsible parent to be with them at any one time. As long as they are not being subjected to any physical or moral danger—'

'What's moral danger?'

'I don't really know; letting them watch porn, maybe.'

217

'Have we got any porn with us?'

'I don't think so.'

'Is there none in your suitcase? It's certainly big enough to have just about everything in it.'

'I've definitely not brought any porn.'

'Is there anything else in it that could subject them to moral danger?'

'I don't think so.'

'That's a shame.'

*

As we edged closer to London we came across a problem we should have foreseen. Driving a seven-foot-wide and twenty-one-foot-long vehicle in London streets turned out to be nigh on impossible and after about fifteen minutes we pulled into a Tesco car park near Wembley and reconsidered our approach. In my head I had a vision of us screeching up in a camper van, bundling the girls inside and screeching off again. In reality, we'd have to slowly edge along the road, letting every car and van past before trying to find a gap in the traffic to make our escape, and the only screeching would probably have come from Nathan's wife, who would easily have been able to follow us on foot and retrieve her children.

We noted that we could park up to two hours for free and set off for the nearest Tube station.

'Where's this place Laura sends them during the day?'

'It's near Fulham football ground.'

'That's a bit vague.'

'How many places full of kids can there be?'

'Well, given its term time there's those pesky things called schools to consider.'

'Oh, yeah.'

We got off at Putney Bridge Tube station and walked for about fifteen minutes before arriving outside Fulham Football Club. 'Hugh Grant used to work here,' I said, gazing up at the hulking structure.

'I didn't know he played football.'

'I don't think he did.'

'What did he do, then?'

'I don't know, swept up or something after matches. I just read it in a magazine. Right, well, now what? I don't see or hear any kids.'

'I don't know; maybe ask someone.'

'What's the name of the place?'

'I don't know.'

'So you want to ask someone if there's somewhere near here that we can go and watch young children playing?'

'Well, yeah, when you put it like that we might get a better outcome if *you* ask.'

'Nathan, the only outcome we'll get if either of us ask is a night in the local nick. Wait until I check my phone.'

'Are you going to call Hayley?'

I glared at him for a moment before saying sharply, 'Hayley? Why would I call Hayley?'

'You always seem to call Hayley when you need help with anything.'

I thought about that for a minute. He was probably right, but not on this occasion. 'I don't think Hayley will know where your kids are being looked after, Nathan, but Mr Google might.' I tapped in 'children's activity centres near Fulham Football Club' and got loads of suggestions but only one fitted the bill. I opened the map helpfully listed on the website of Grange Children's Activity Centre and started walking. Being a paedophile must be a doddle these days.

A few minutes later we stopped at a large concrete structure surrounded by green fences with razor wire along the top. I had to say it looked more like a concentration camp than a place of fun and relaxation.

The sign on the gate said 'Grange CAC for all ages'. One day I may have children, and if I do, I'm not sure that I'd want them going to a place that was quite happy to include CAC in its title, but perhaps I'm just being a little picky. It also listed some of the activities: football, cricket, tennis, hockey, climbing wall, archery and javelin. Again, I might be off the mark, but I'm not sure that allowing kids access to pointy, spiky things like arrows and javelins would necessarily be a good thing but I assumed it would be strictly controlled. We now needed to extract the girls from this Gulag without bringing the authorities down upon our heads.

Nathan walked a little further down the fence line and

spotted a small number of younger kids having lunch outside on picnic tables.

He stuck his head against the mesh and beckoned me over. Sitting together at an old picnic table away from the other children were the girls. They appeared to be picking at some dry-looking food.

There didn't seem to be any adults supervising the kids but, given the nature of the security, they'd be there somewhere, probably wearing dark uniforms with fascist insignia on the lapels.

'Pssst,' said Nathan ineffectively.

'Millie,' I hollered. She looked up at the mention of her name and came running over, closely followed by her sisters.

'Dad, Kat,' she yelped. 'What are you doing here?'

'We're here to get you out,' Nathan explained, grinning.

She smiled then the smile faded. 'Mum says we're staying in London forever.'

'Well, maybe not forever, but she did say she wants you to go to school here for a while. Anyway, we can talk about that later. Now, how do we get you out of here?'

Millie peered back over her shoulder. 'Security is pretty tight inside the building. There's no way to pass the lady on the door without signing in or out. The back is well guarded too, the main gates in and out are electric and covered by CCTV. There's a side door down by the kitchen but that's always kept locked. There's CCTV everywhere but only one camera out here and that faces the eating

221

area.' She pointed to a large wooden pole with a camera mounted on top.

'The staff do regular patrols out here, every five minutes or so. They've just been so

we've got maybe four minutes tops before they do the next pass.' I wasn't surprised that Millie had already considered escape routes.

I walked up to the fence and pulled the wire. 'It's pretty thick but not reinforced. Wait a minute.' I fished about in my handbag and pulled out a small pair of pliers. The bottom of the plier head had two pincer blades that should be more than enough to cut the wire. I handed them to Nathan, who gawked at me.

'What?'

'Why have you got pliers in your handbag?'

'I've always got pliers in my handbag, also an emergency loo roll, a set of mini screwdrivers, a spare tampon, a clean pair of knickers, nail scissors and a scalpel, just in case.'

'Just in case of what?'

'Just in case. Anyway, are you going to cut the wire before we get caught or question me about my handbag all day?'

He blinked a few times, smiled in admiration (I hope) and started snipping the wire at the bottom of the fence. It took a few minutes and I anxiously kept watch in case any of the staff appeared. A few of the kids looked over but as they couldn't see exactly what we were up to they didn't seem to be too bothered, though I'm pretty sure they'd raise the alarm as soon as we pulled the girls out of the wire and legged it.

Twenty minutes later we were on a Tube train heading north. We had to change at Edgware Road and again at Baker Street but eventually we made it out into daylight at Wembley Park and headed for the motorhome.

The girls hadn't said much during the journey except when we'd explained we'd be going on a trip in a motorhome, which had brought squeals of excitement. Millie, ever the practical one, had said, 'Dad, but we've not got any clothes.'

'It's okay, I've brought a suitcase full. It's in the van.'

'What about Laura?' I asked as we walked towards the Tesco car park.

'What about her?'

'Well, I'm sure by now she's called the police, or the centre staff have. Shouldn't you tell her that the girls are with you?'

'Maybe I should let her suffer for a while.'

'Maybe not, as it means the police are looking for us. Once they know they're with their dad they maybe won't bother.'

'I'm not phoning her, though. I'll send her a text then switch my phone off as I don't want to listen to her going berserk..'

I watched as he quickly sent her a text and turned his phone off.

'How will she react, do you think?' I asked, already knowing the answer.

Nathan stopped and smiled into my eyes. 'This family is now at war. First blood to us.'

Chapter 22

We headed north then west to pick up the M6 and stopped at a service station near Birmingham for some food.

As we were coming out a police car screeched to a halt near the entrance and two officers rushed into the building.

I jumped, then remembered that technically, taking your own children wasn't wrong, even though it felt wrong. I glanced over to Nathan, whose expression told me he shared my feelings.

'They're not looking for us,' I said.

'No, I know,' Nathan replied.

Chloe smiled at us before asking brightly, 'Are we all going to prison?'

'No, we haven't done anything wrong.'

'Mummy won't be happy,' stated Millie.

I agreed. 'No, she won't, but hopefully she can't do anything except kick up a fuss.'

'Mummy's good at that,' said Millie.

'I'm sure she is,' I replied as we opened the motorhome.

Nathan got the girls in their seats while I sat in the passenger seat and buckled up. As we drove off I had the curious feeling that my idea to rent the motorhome had perhaps not been one of my best. For the money we'd forked out we could have driven in Nathan's car to a Euro-camp in the South of France or somewhere equally warm and further away from Laura Jones.

That evening we parked up at the back of a lorry park in a service station in Westmorland. We used the showers in the services and ate a surprisingly tasty meal from the restaurant.

The motorhome felt a little cramped despite the fact it had been advertised as a six berth. I slept in the little raised platform on my own. I really wanted to snuggle in with Nathan in the double bed at the back, but Daisy had wangled her way in there, having got upset and angry just before bedtime. I'd bide my time; trying to have a shag with Nathan whilst his daughters were next door, separated by a paper-thin wall, probably wouldn't be a licence for a night of unbridled passion anyway.

You haven't got your bodice either.

'How do you know?'

I know everything you know, and quite a lot that you don't.

'That's scary.'

I know.

As I drifted off to sleep I wondered if Nathan's wife would give up. Somehow, I doubted it.

*

The next morning, we ate breakfast in the motorhome watching some kids' cartoons on the TV that neatly folded into the wooden unit in the lounge/kitchen area. My phone vibrated on the table, signifying a text. It was from Hayley and simply said, 'Channel 5 NOW!!!'

I picked up the remote and flipped over to Channel 5 despite protests from the girls. As I took in the picture on the screen the remote fell from my hand and Nathan dropped his spoon. There, sitting on the couch in a plush TV studio, was Lance (silver spoon) Donaldson appeared to be a little flustered this morning as he couldn't get Nathan's wife to say anything; she just sat and sobbed into the camera.

I gazed around at Nathan and the girls; they were all watching the screen intently. I could see Chloe's eyes filling up at the sight of her mother crying. Even Nathan looked close to tears and I must admit she'd affected me too. Thankfully the camera moved away from her and focused on Lance, who spoke intently and seriously into the camera. 'Well, unfortunately Mrs Jones is too upset to answer any further questions at this point. We might return to her later, but, just to recap, she has appealed to the better side of her husband's nature and asked him to bring her children home safe and sound. As we now know, yesterday he took them without telling anyone from the Grange Activity Centre in south-west London, severely damaging the perimeter fencing and endangering the safety of other children in the process.'

'What a load of crap,' Nathan said. 'We cut a little hole in the fence and—'

'Shhh.' We all shushed him, wanting to hear the rest of what Lance had to say.

'Mrs Jones claims that her husband has been influenced by a punk girl he began an affair with when she started commuting to work in London.'

'I'm Goth, not punk.' This time I got shushed.

'Mrs Jones says she'd been shocked and hurt to learn about her husband's infidelity and feels betrayed that he'd do something like that while she'd been simply trying to earn extra money to provide a better future for her family.'

'What a pack of lies,' Millie said quietly. Nobody shushed her.

Lance summed up. 'So, although Laura Jones is at this time too upset to say anything further, I'm appealing on her behalf to Nathan, her husband. For the sake of your children and your beautiful wife, please come home.'

I flipped the TV off.

Nobody spoke for a few minutes, then I said, 'Well, I think that's round two to Mummy.' It broke the tension and everybody, even Daisy, smiled.

*

Given the publicity Laura had generated, we were looking forward to arriving in the sparsely populated Scottish Highlands. We set off soon after breakfast and, apart from stocking up in a local supermarket just north of Glasgow, we drove non-stop. As the scenery became more and more beautiful and towns and traffic less and less, I started to relax. We were now in the middle of nowhere and it felt wonderful.

I alternated between sitting with Nathan and playing games with the girls. They were all strapped in seats facing the TV but after the third Disney DVD and fourth bag of Maltesers they were beginning to grow restless and hyper. Daisy announced, 'I need a pee poo.'

'Nathan, you need to slow down or stop, even. Daisy needs to go to the toilet.'

He shouted back to me, 'I can see a wide bit coming up; I'll pull over.' The motorhome slowed as he steered it onto the grass verge. I squinted out of the windscreen and noticed what Nathan hadn't. The verge wasn't just a widening of the road but a junction, although that might be too grand a description. The road that led from the main A86 could be described as a dirt track in comparison. I got up to unstrap Daisy, then fell over onto my bum as the vehicle went into reverse and then lurched forward.

'Nathan!' I yelled.

'Sorry, I'm still getting used to the controls. I thought I'd look up here to see what's what.'

I got up rubbing my coccyx (the bit where my tail used to be when I was a monkey – if you're an evolutionist) and walked towards the front again. We were bumping along a rutted tree-lined road and tree branches bounced off the side of the vehicle as we edged along. 'Where are we going, Nathan?'

'I don't know.'

'That's comforting. Why are we off-road? This isn't exactly a Range Rover.'

'I just saw this little track, and something told me to check it out.'

'Uh-huh, so we're running on intuition?'

'If you like.'

'I don't "like", actually, I—' My breath caught in my throat as the road ended and widened out to reveal a small secluded glade just wide enough to allow Nathan to turn the van completely around should he wish. We were enclosed on three sides by small hills dressed in purple heather and yellow gorse. At the end of the space a tiny stream dropped down a few metres in a gentle waterfall. Nathan brought the vehicle to a halt and switched off the engine. I stepped out into the most peaceful and beautiful space I'd ever seen. I looked back to the way we'd come in and I could hardly see the old dirt road hidden by trees and bushes – our very own Brigadoon.

Beside the stream about ten feet from the waterfall I noticed the remains of a ruined cottage. Only the gable ends and a section of the back wall remained. The rest had either fallen or been removed. The three girls emerged behind Nathan and stood transfixed by the beauty of the spot.

'Wow! Someone used to live here, Nathan,' I observed. 'Imagine, someone used to own this little piece of heaven.'

'In the height of summer maybe, but I can't imagine the winters were much fun.'

'Oh, I don't know, a roaring fire, some blankets, red wine and I'm sure we'd be fine

while it snowed and snowed and snowed. Can we stay here tonight?'

Nathan appraised the glade. 'Don't see why not. We've got plenty of food, it's nice and quiet and we need a rest.'

'I still need a pee pee,' Daisy piped up just as my phone started ringing.

Nathan grinned. 'And what do you know? We've got network coverage. I'm definitely not switching my phone on.'

I wandered over towards the old cottage, pressing the phone to my ear while Nathan took Daisy to the toilet.

'Hi, Kat, it's Hayley.'

'Hi, sweetie, I'm pretty busy right now. What is it?'

'Just calling to say I love you.'

'You've got a man now, Hayley, so you don't need me.'

'Whatever happened to girl power and we'll be friends forever? Do you want me to send you one of those little "Friends Forever" teddies to prove it?'

'Nah, you're all right, I believe you.'

'You're famous.'

'Infamous more like – as the bitch from hell.'

'You did see it, then? I think Mrs Jones has the whole nation on her side.'

'Well, the bit of the nation that watches early morning

Channel 5 chat shows. Besides, that's not what's happening, Hayley. *She's* the one that stopped Nathan seeing his daughters.'

'I know that, but the world at large just sees a poor heartbroken mother who's had her children stolen and her husband's run off with a punk.'

'Don't you start.'

'Sorry.'

'She's a first-class cow.'

'That's not how it's coming across. You need some help to get your point of view over and aren't you lucky? Because that's exactly why I'm phoning you.'

'You've lost me. Help me do what?'

'I'm going to help you with the media.'

'Hayley, I love you and you're a great lawyer ... I think ... but dealing with—'

'James is here.'

'That's nice. Is he surgically attached to you now?'

Hayley giggled. 'Not exactly, though it does feel like it sometimes. He wants a word.'

'I don't really have time to speak to him, Hayley. We've just stopped in the most beautiful little glade and then—'

'You *need* to hear what he's got to say. Hold on.'

I listened to some muffled voices in the background followed by my friend saying, 'I'm going to hand my phone over to him, okay?'

'Kat?' The male voice on the line instantly transported me back to my high-school days. Not the best of memories.

'James, it's been a long time. I hope you're treating my friend better than you did all those years ago.'

'Thanks for reminding me. If you remember, though, your friend's revenge meant I had to leave school before I wanted to. I couldn't come back and face everyone after that.'

'Welcome to our world. You had one night of it, we had a lifetime's worth.'

James sighed. 'I've already had all this from Hayley. I should have got you both together and you could have both unloaded both barrels at me. I've apologised to Hayley, and now I'm doing the same to you, and if you can put your anger to one side I think I can help you.'

'Help me?'

'Well, you and your boyfriend.'

'How could you possibly do that?' I asked sceptically.

'I work for the BBC news team.'

Now, I'd been vaguely aware from Hayley's numerous ramblings that he worked for them, but I hadn't known it had anything to do with the news. 'I've never seen you on the TV.'

'Not everyone can be in front of the camera. There's a whole bunch of us beavering away behind the scenes, editing, choosing the items to run, scheduling and various other things that are too dull to talk about. Anyway, the point is I've been following the very one-sided coverage of this situation and, as Hayley's explained, legally there's nothing Laura can do about Nathan taking the kids, at least until they start missing school. So, what she's doing now is playing the "helpless mother" card and painting you as the dark bitch from hell – a real-life Cruella De Vil – and punk temptress who's also lured away her husband.'

'Goth, not punk.'

'Yeah, whatever, but punk plays better with the media as they associate them with deviant and violent behaviour. She's doing a great job of playing up to prejudice and scare-mongering. What I'd like to do is give the other side of the picture, show what it's like for a father to be denied access to his children and how they're totally powerless when this happens so that you are forced into taking drastic action. The issue I've got is that your angle is very weak now.'

'Angle?'

'Yeah, sorry, news-speak – what I mean is there's very little going in your favour. All the world can see is this road movie going on, which appears to be a dark version of *Thelma and Louise* where the baddies have kidnapped some children and the distraught mother is pictured in interview after interview crying and pleading for you to bring them home.'

'Thelma and Louise? Didn't they die in the end?'

'Yeah, they drove off the edge of the Grand Canyon.'

'I don't fancy that much.'

'Well, there are alternatives. I think the biggest reason this has captured so much attention, apart from it's been a slow news week, is that the girls are all angelic little things and their mother, well, she's an absolute knockout.

Flowing dark hair, green soulful eyes, I mean, shit, I bet half the country has fallen in love with her by now. She's the ultimate Yummy Mummy—'

James's voice got cut off as Hayley punched him somewhere painful. He returned somewhat chastened. 'Yeah, okay, maybe a bit over the top; sorry, but you did see her this morning? I mean, anyone devious enough to get old "silver spoon" Donaldson flustered must be doing something right. I don't think I've ever seen anyone sit and cry on prime-time TV for five minutes. They couldn't get a word out of her, very effective. You see what you're up against? To burst her bubble, you need something really strong.'

'I could get Nathan to cry on camera ... I think.'

'Nice idea, but the world would just view him as a wuss, where nothing pulls on the heartstrings like a beautiful woman crying. I do have an idea or two, and I've got a certain amount of expertise I could bring. Also, I've been in touch with an organisation called "Dads for Daughters", which is a group, as the name suggests, that fights fathers' causes where and whenever it can. They think they might be able to help you present your side of this so far very one-sided story.'

'James, neither of us know anything about Dads for Daughters or dealing with the media.'

'Exactly, that's why you need some help.'

'Why do you want to get involved in this, James? It can't be in your best interests.'

He paused before saying, 'Well, Hayley asked me to, and

maybe I could use it as some sort of atonement for being such a complete twat to the both of you at school? Also, if I'm being totally honest, as I do try to be with Hayley nowadays, it might benefit me in the long run. I've been working as a content assistant in the BBC Scotland news and current affairs team for three years now and I really want to move on, get myself noticed, and because I kind of know you guys this gives me an edge I might be able to use.'

'Not a completely selfless act after all.'

'No, but if you think about it that can only be a good thing. If it's a win-win situation then there's a real incentive in it for everyone.'

'Why don't I trust you, I wonder?'

'Nothing is ever black and white, Kat, but what is being portrayed by Laura now is a very one-sided view of the world, which is very black for you. From what I can gather from what Hayley's told me, there's been no mention of the truth in her statements so far and no mention of her rich boyfriend, which is something Donaldson will love. I've spoken to the producers of his show and they're up for us doing a bit to show the other side, as long as you're in the footage.'

'Why me?'

'You're the evil bitch that's lured her husband away.'

'Thanks.'

'Yeah, well, as I said, that's where we are with it right now.'

'What do we do?'

'We'll need to get some film of you guys and before that we need to do some coaching so that Nathan looks and reacts well on camera.'

'But we're hiding in the Highlands.'

'We could come up to you. Where's the nearest airport?'

'Err, no idea. The nearest train station I think is Tulloch; we drove past it a few hours ago.'

'I've no idea where that is.'

'That makes two of us. We've stopped in this idyllic secluded little spot.' I gazed around me. 'It would look incredible on film.'

'Okay, leave it with me. Don't move on anywhere else until I can work out how to get there.'

'Okay, James, I don't think we are in any hurry to move; it's lovely in the Highlands apart from the midges.'

'Ouch.'

'Yeah, well, they don't bother me much, but although we've only been here a few minutes I can see a cloud of them around Nathan.'

'Maybe your perfume's keeping them away.'

'James, you are really cruising for a bruising.'

'No, I didn't mean that. Last year when my wife and I were in Spain the mozzies didn't bother her and we discovered they didn't like her perfume.'

'What kind of perfume? I might get some.'

'I don't know.'

'That's helpful.'

'Leave it with me, I'll organise everything.'

'The perfume?'

'No, not the perfume, forget about the perfume.'

'You mentioned it, not me.'

'Yeah and I regret it already. I need to know where you are.'

'The Highlands.'

'That doesn't narrow it down much.'

'The West Highlands.'

'Again, not a huge help.'

'I'll get the coordinates or whatever is in the satnav and text Hayley.'

'Okay, thanks.'

'Don't forget the perfume.'

He hung up.

We spent the next half an hour working out how to unfurl the awning attached to the motorhome, then another twenty minutes trying to get the sides to zip up and the front pinned back. Eventually Millie stepped in and pointed out the hidden clasps that pulled the plastic front up out of the way.

For dinner we had a barbecue with sausages, burgers and thin steaks all bought from the supermarket where we'd stocked up. We'd also invested in some beer, red wine, crisps, bread rolls, along with milk and cereal for breakfast. Nathan sipped a beer watching me and the girls munching burnt meat squeezed into crispy rolls with too much tomato sauce. I smiled at him as grease dribbled down my chin. It somehow felt normal, even though I'd never seen myself in any kind of maternal light, least of all with kids that weren't even mine.

I suppose everything had a kind of unreal quality about it as we were so far from the hustle and bustle of everyday life – and Laura. I watched Nathan visibly relax for the first time since we'd been to the safari park. His recent stress levels must have been off the scale.

I decided to enjoy tonight and worry about tomorrow ... well, tomorrow. It might be fun being coached for the camera. We hadn't mentioned it to the girls yet; the next morning would be soon enough.

I finished shoving all the debris from the barbecue into a black bin bag and lay back onto the rug we'd spread onto the grass and squinted up at the sky. I hadn't done this for years and I watched all the little white clouds float by. There were some darker ones gathering in the west but for now I enjoyed the warmth of the evening sunshine.

I hadn't expected the heat. I'd thought the Highlands would be cold and wet, especially in May, but we'd had the air con on in the van since leaving Glasgow. The heat seemed to have subdued the midges for the time being, or perhaps the smoke from the barbecue had kept them at bay. Suddenly a stream of ice-cold water splashed across my face followed by Millie yelling, 'C'mon, lazy bones, Dad's got your water pistol. It's kids versus grown-ups.'

I jumped up and went to join the fun. The girls had started to learn to play properly and I didn't want to discourage them.

Chapter 23

That evening after we'd got the exhausted trio to bed, Nathan and I sat outside under the extendable awning on folding chairs. The air had turned oppressively muggy, and the rug we'd draped over our knees to ward off any chill as darkness fell had been dumped on the grass. We were working our way nicely through a bottle of Merlot and our third family-size bag of crisps.

I'd become more than a little tipsy. 'So, tell me about all your old girlfriends.'

'Where did that come from?'

'I'm curious, and slightly drunk, *again*. You're a bad influence on me.'

'I'm sure it's got nothing to do with me. I didn't force it down your throat.'

I smiled and kept my eyes straight ahead; the wine made me daring. 'Are we still talking about wine here, Nathan?'

'You've got a very dirty mind.'

'True, but you've not answered my question.'

'What question? I've forgotten.'

'No, you haven't, you're being evasive – old girlfriends.'

'Well, this'll be a short conversation. I've been with Laura for over a decade and before her I'd never had a proper girlfriend.'

'You were a virgin when you met her?'

'I didn't say that.'

'Okay, then, so who was your first?'

A wind sprang up, a warm breeze like my GHD hairdryer on its lowest setting. With it came a few spatters of rain that fell on the awning and drummed on the motorhome roof. Nathan glanced back inside anxiously to see if the rain would disturb the girls.

'Don't worry about them, Nathan; they're exhausted. It'll take more than a few drops of rain to wake them. It's been quite a day. Who was she?'

'Why do you want to know this?'

I giggled. 'As you once said to me before, I'm a nosy cow.'

'I don't think I called you a cow.'

I shrugged. 'Bet you thought it, though – I would've – so, come on, answer my question.'

'My first was a girl I knew from my biology class in school. I bumped into her at a party about a year after we'd finished our A levels. It was weird because at school she'd been pretty but didn't really get my attention, then, when I saw her, I hardly recognised her. In fact, I didn't recognise her when she came up and started talking to me. She'd kind of filled out in all the right places ... I'm not sure how to describe it, really, she'd just changed.'

240

'It's called growing up, Nathan.'

He chuckled. 'Yeah, maybe, she'd also dyed her hair blonde and, on the night, had squeezed herself into a really tight black dress. She looked amazing.'

'Eyes on stalks.'

'Eh?'

'I bet your eyes were out on stalks like a cartoon character.'

He nodded thoughtfully and smiled. 'Yeah, good description. Anyway, that evening we just talked, but agreed to meet up a few days later. Her parents were divorced so we went back to her mum's flat. She was at work, which meant we had the place to ourselves. When we were finished, and all snuggled up with her head on my shoulder, she told me that she was heading off to New York with her twin brother for a joint gap year. I didn't know she had a brother; I hardly knew anything about her at all. I really liked her, but I never saw her again.'

'Were you her first?'

'I never asked but I don't think so.'

'Is that it?'

'No, after her I met a girl called Angela. She worked in my office. She came from Northern Ireland and I used to tease her all the time about her accent; then one Friday night after work we went for a few drinks in a pub and I asked her out. We kept it secret because working together and being involved was quite difficult. Then I met Laura.'

'This all happened when you lived in London?'

'Yeah, we didn't leave London until after Millie was born.'

'How did Angela react when she found out about Laura?'

'I didn't tell her. I just said I didn't want to see her any more. We'd only been together a few months so—'

'How did she take it?'

'Very well. We weren't in love or anything. I got the impression she was quite relieved. I just remember it being easier than I expected.'

'Then Laura came along. Why did you leave London?'

'Because she wanted to be closer to her mother in Fife.'

'Laura's Scottish?'

He nodded.

'And you've never been unfaithful to her?'

Nathan shook his head. 'No, never.'

I had to think about that. He'd been very loyal despite the problems they'd had. I wondered if Laura had been equally loyal. From what I knew about Oodles, probably not.

'What about you?'

'What about me?'

'Who was *your* first?'

'I need more wine. Let me get some more from the fridge.' I stood and leaned into the door of the motorhome, opened the fridge and pulled out another bottle, Shiraz this time. 'I like that – from fridge to glass in two steps.'

'I've never had chilled red wine before.'

'I'm a philistine but if I'm drinking something it has to be cold unless it's tea or coffee.'

I poured us both a plastic mug full and sat back in my seat, took a swig and smacked my lips.

'My turn. Not much to tell, I'm afraid. My first two came along almost together like buses. Eleven years ago, shortly after my eighteenth birthday, I met Ross, a grungy drummer from a local rock band. I must have been about the last in my year to lose my virginity, no surprise really given how uncool I was. He was bonkers in a bad way, which, ultimately, wasn't a good thing. My mum hated him, which unfortunately made him even more attractive to me at the time. We had six months of lust- and alcohol-fuelled sex before I pulled the plug on it, otherwise I might have become addicted in more ways than one. He was a bad boy and I knew he'd been cheating on me pretty much from the minute we got together but I put up with it for the sex and the fact I had someone to talk to who didn't mind me being forthright and honest.'

I sipped from my cup and continued not looking Nathan in the eye. 'A few weeks later I met Noah. He was much older than me, around twenty-seven. He'd been divorced twice from the same woman and was just looking for somewhere to park his penis for a few months.'

'Nice description.'

'Thanks. Accurate, though. I knew he'd go back to his double-ex-wife eventually. I can laugh about it now and, to be honest, I liked the fact that I had no expectations. I had fun, so did he and it didn't last long. Eventually he moved back in with his wife and soon afterwards they upped sticks and moved away.'

'She probably made him leave to get away from you.'

'Yeah, more than likely.'

'What did your mum make of him?'

'You're joking. I never told my mum. She still doesn't know, doesn't need to.'

'There's a bit of a theme here – both boyfriends so far have been bonkers.'

I giggled and nodded. 'Well, the theme continues, I'm afraid. After Noah I endured a couple of years of celibacy until I met Dr Dave.'

'Dr Dave?'

'Yep, Dr Dave. He made me call him that all the time as well.'

'Was he a real doctor?'

'Oh, yeah, a consultant pathologist, not much to look at, to be honest, but initially great fun and we got on for some reason.'

'Bonkers?'

'Definitely. He used to come over to my flat and say, "Okay, Miss Kat—"'

'He called you Miss Kat?'

'He did. All the time. "Okay, Miss Kat, Dr Dave needs to do an examination – legs up, panties down, please."'

'Too much information.'

'Yeah, sorry, anyway, after a few months when he still

244

wanted to do that it got a bit odd and when he carried on after that it felt weird, then downright creepy, and I broke it off.'

'His cock?' Nathan asked, smiling.

'No, I should have, though. I reckon that's why he became a pathologist; his bedside

manner would have got him disbarred in a heartbeat.' I laughed out loud, then remembered the sleeping girls and bit my lip and giggled instead.

'How long ago was that?'

'Must have been about seven years.'

'You've not been with anyone since?'

'Nobody serious. I had a fumble in a tent with a bloke at a music festival and spent

a passionate few days with Alex, an Irish bloke I met in Dublin on a hen weekend. I really liked him.'

'What happened?'

'He had terrible problems with his memory.'

'What?'

'He forgot to tell me he was married.'

'Oh.'

'Yeah, well, all that makes me sound pretty trashy, I know, but I'm not at all. I've not

actually been with anyone at all for about three years – it might even have healed up by now.'

'Kat, too much information again.'

I giggled at my confessions. Without the wine I wouldn't have told him half of what I had, nor mentioned my unwanted celibacy. I could probably live without the sex, but I missed the intimacy of being close to someone and sharing things. Yeah, I knew my appearance sometimes caused an issue, but usually my attitude was what caused problems with men, and some women if I was being honest.

In my more introspective moments I knew my discomfort with everyday idle chit-chat and pleasantries, which most of the rest of the world seemed to love, caused me problems. Whenever someone said casually, 'How are you?' it took me years to realise the question was largely rhetorical and that people didn't want to know that I'd hurt my knee on the coffee table that morning or that I was suffering abdominal cramps or had a cold.

In the end I decided I really couldn't be bothered with such stuff, and if my appearance and, more likely, my attitude stopped that happening, well, I could live with the downside it created. It didn't mean I shunned human company – I craved it like any other warm-blooded woman – but it had to be on my terms. Saying all that, I was fine at work with my colleagues and on nights out with other staff, maybe because they expected anyone who worked in the morgue to be a bit quirky. To be fair, most of us were.

Sid had got his whole 'gay denial' and ex-punk singer thing going on, Gina, who did the same job I did, was living with a boyfriend she no longer loved but was too comfortable to break up. 'I can't leave Gary, Kat; that'd mean moving into a crappy flat and no more Caribbean holidays, Christmas trips to New York or Michelin-star restaurants.'

There was also Paula, who'd just started as a pathologist, replacing Ken Gordon, who retired. We hadn't worked Paula out yet, but she owned six cats, which probably wasn't a good sign.

Only Sid knew that I'd started seeing Nathan, or 'the zombie' as he'd named him (I probably wouldn't tell Nathan that bit). I wasn't sure what the reaction at work would be now that they'd have seen the whole sorry saga on TV. Personally, I didn't see anything wrong with it ethically, but I supposed it might be viewed as a little weird. The thing was, speaking to Nathan was easy and I felt relaxed in his company, which was rare for me. Maybe he was bonkers – too, which would fit in with the pattern of my love life perfectly. I fixed him with a stare and said, 'Yeah, sorry, I kind of speak first and think later.'

'I've noticed.'

'Is it a problem?'

'Not for me. Laura's always been a bit like that too, so I've got used to it.'

'What do you want to do now?'

'Sit here and chat some more?'

'We could, I suppose, but I think it's time we had sex.'

I laughed as he choked on his wine. When he recovered from his coughing fit he said, 'Do you?'

'I do. We've been circling around this for a while now and I think it's time, plus I'm

very horny.'

'It's the wine.'

'No, it's hormones; my nipples are hard and—'

'Err, too much information ... again.'

'Yeah, sorry. Go and get the double quilt off the bed, then we can stay out

here without disturbing the girls.'

Nathan needed no further encouragement. In fact, it was the fastest I'd seen him move.

While he was away I quickly zipped up the insect netting, effectively sealing us into a canvas cocoon. I then stepped out of my jeans and pulled my top over my head and wished I'd taken the time to wax my bikini line in my flat before we'd left. I'd borrow his razor in the morning. I hoped he had some spare blades as my legs were going to need doing again too. I had anticipated this evening and, after getting soaked earlier in the water-fight, I'd changed into my red Huit underwear.

I felt Nathan's eyes on my back.

'What is it, Nathan? I know you're standing staring.'

'Your underwear's red.'

'It is.'

'I'd expected it to be black.'

'Sometimes I like a change.'

'Your body's in great shape.'

I smiled but didn't turn around. 'Well, as you know I don't have ... didn't have a boyfriend and not much of a social life, so what else do you think I do with my time?'

'Makes sense. It's just in your normal clothes you can't see very much.'

248

'And that's a bad thing? Do you want other men lusting after me?'

'I don't know.'

'You'd rather I wore tight clingy clothes that made other men stare at me whilst having carnal thoughts?'

'Maybe.'

'You mean you'd like other men ogling your girlfriend?'

'I don't know – are you now officially my girlfriend?'

'You don't know much.'

'I know lots, just not much about women, I suppose.'

'You and the rest of the male species and, yes, I'm now your girlfriend. The media have me down as your girlfriend, so it must be true.'

'I don't believe everything I read.'

I spun quickly around, pleased to see his eyes meet mine and not drop to my boobs. 'So, you want other men lusting after me?'

'I think men like to think that their girlfriend is attractive to other men.'

'It's like a validation thing, then?'

He shrugged. 'Probably.'

'Men are weird.'

'We are. Shall I get my coat?'

'Oh, no, I don't think so – putting clothes back *on* is not what I've got in mind right now, my nipp—'

'Yeah, yeah, you've said all that.'

I smiled and stepped into Nathan's space and gazed into his eyes. I leaned into him and when our lips met my body suddenly felt it was in the presence of superior genetics and in a rush of adrenaline it liquefied.

My breath caught in his mouth and I felt him stiffen against me in more ways than one. He slipped his hands down my back and pulled me in close. One of his hands slipped instinctively lower, touching the elastic of my knickers, and as he slipped his thumb just under the fabric I was sure he could feel the sweat that had accumulated on my lower back just above my buttocks. It felt incredibly intimate, him touching my perspiring skin.

An I felt his hand sink lower I allowed myself to relax into him. The moment I'd been denying myself for so long had arrived and I wanted to enjoy every second of it.

I pulled his tee shirt over his head while he fumbled with his belt and jeans. Now we were both standing in our underwear staring into each other's eyes and gasping. A fleeting thought about suggesting we both shower first flashed across my bizarre brain as neither of us had bathed in the last twenty-four hours (excepting the water fight, but that hardly counted). The scent coming from him, all male and musky, made me forget all about the shower; I didn't want to wash any of that away. Before I could think about anything more Nathan pulled me onto the duvet.

Nathan hadn't been with anyone but Laura for a decade.

I hadn't been with anyone for ages.

I worried that I'd be inadequate in some way, unable to match up to Yummy Mummy Laura. My self-doubts and fear that our first encounter would be crap had played a role in delaying us getting together. What I hadn't bargained for was it being amazing.

Nathan rolled on top of me, pinning me under his body, and the storm that had been building broke in more ways than one as the first fork of lightning sparked across the sky. Hormone-soaked lust took over and everything felt natural and easy, as if we'd known each other forever. I only wished I could have shared the mind-blowing feeling I could feel building and expanding outwards. As I rushed towards climax the lightning flashed, momentarily freeze-framing Nathan's face distorted in ecstasy as he too neared his zenith. The sight pushed me over the edge and I couldn't help crying out as the thunder rumbled dramatically over-head and rain began to hammer on the canvas above us.

When I came to my senses I lay clutching Nathan's body, slick in sweat and arousal, and could detect above the intoxicating scent of our own bodies the subtle but unmistakeable metallic sparky smell of ozone. I didn't normally notice smells and scents much, probably because I'd desensitised myself from years of working in the morgue, but for some reason tonight my sense of smell had height-ened. I panted like a thirsty collie and wondered how incredible the world must be for dogs with a sense of smell forty times more sensitive than ours.

'Nathan?'

'Mm,' he mumbled.

Still coming down from my orgasmic high, I giggled. 'It must be amazing to be a dog.'

'Eh?'

'It must be amazing being a dog.'

'We can do doggy in a while if you want. I need a few minutes.'

I slapped his sweaty but cool bum. 'No, I didn't mean that. Dogs have such sensitive noses they can smell everything, loads more than we can.'

'Not sure that's very romantic, Kat.'

'Can you smell heather?'

'Who's she?'

'Not who – what. The heather, it's kind of like herbs.'

'I don't think heather is a herb. It might be though – I didn't do botany at school.'

'What can you smell?'

'I can smell you. You're delicious.'

'Thank you. Anything else?'

Nathan moved off and lay beside me and pulled my head around and kissed me deeply. 'I can't really concentrate now. You're so beautiful I can't take my eyes off you.'

I laughed nervously. I wasn't good at afterglow chat, nor could I accept compliments gracefully, so I kept quiet, kissed him back and asked, 'What are you thinking about?'

Nathan sighed. 'Why do women always want to know what you're thinking? Laura used to ask me that when we first got together. I wasn't thinking anything.'

'You were thinking about nothing?'

'No, I wasn't thinking anything. Thinking about nothing

implies I was thinking about nothing and my brain had been engaged in thinking, but it wasn't.'

'You can't not be thinking about something.'

'That's a double negative and I don't deal well with that sort of question, but why not?'

'Because it's not possible – everybody needs to be thinking about something. You can't walk about with an empty head.'

'But I can. Most blokes I know are quite capable of sitting about not thinking about anything at all. When I worked in the London ad agency some of the blokes managed it spectacularly well with an accompanying vacant expression. Some managed to do it pretty much all day, judging by their work output. We men don't have this conveyor belt of stuff trundling past us 24/7 like women seem to have. It's not that we never think or worry about things, as my current situation shows, but generally if I'm not thinking about mundane stuff or nothing at all then I'm thinking about work problems or sex or occasionally football, or if there's an England test match on then I might be wondering—'

'Okay, stop, please, stop ...' I laughed. 'I'm sorry I asked now. I won't—'

Nathan grabbed my shoulders and stopped my reply by engulfing my mouth with his. The wind suddenly picked up as the thunder and lightning drifted away. I shivered deliciously and snuggled into Nathan. He pulled the duvet around us and this time we made love slowly, listening to the sound of our breathing and raindrops falling all around us. Afterwards, he lay with his head resting on my tummy, which felt incredibly intimate for some reason. 'Are you comfortable down there?'

'Yes, thanks.'

I giggled, which made his head jiggle up and down.

'What is it?'

'I just had a thought – I've got a head for bodies and a body for heads.'

'Very good, Kat; don't give up the day job.'

'I work nights too.'

'Don't give up the night job, then.'

I punched him gently on the back. 'That's us now, mated.'

'You make us sound like swans.'

'Nice analogy; swans mate for life.'

'I didn't know that.'

'You do now.'

We must have drifted off to sleep because the next time I opened my eyes dawn light had started to bathe the grass and heather-clad hills in crimson light. I sat up and then gazed back down at my still-sleeping boyfriend. He'd moved up beside me at some point during the night. He really was beautiful when he slept, lips slightly parted revealing perfect white teeth. He had to be the most gorgeous man I'd ever slept with, ever kissed in fact, punching well above my weight. One thing I knew – I was done for, totally smitten. I'd been waiting my whole life to feel what I was feeling now and although there were huge obstacles in front of me I didn't care. I didn't know how he felt about me and, until I did, I didn't want to blurt out my thoughts as that would just put undue pressure on him, especially as the split from his wife was so recent and so raw.

That made me a little worried; he must have compared me to his wife. A woman like Laura – in a similar way to Hayley – must be aware of how her looks made people react. Men would listen to her, open doors for her, stare after her when she passed them and even women would view her differently. Some would envy her, some would admire her. The one thing nobody would do was ignore her.

He must have compared you to his wife when you were shagging, my inner voice whispered.

'I know, she's very beautiful, but she's a bitch,' I whispered back.

A beautiful bitch.

'He wouldn't be with me if he didn't like me.'

He likes you, but does he love you? Could he love you?

'I don't know.'

You forgot the bodice.

'So, I did, damn.'

I watched as Nathan's eyes opened, at the look of surprise on his face to see me gazing down at him. 'Hi,' he said sleepily.

I put my insecurities to one side and tried to live in the moment. I leaned down to kiss him.

Nathan reached up and pulled me down on top of him. I laughed just as we heard Daisy's voice: 'DADDY, DADDY! Where are you?'

Nathan groaned, and I laughed. 'You'd better go, Daddy.'
Nathan reluctantly pulled away from me. 'Later?'
I nodded. 'Definitely.'
Nathan stood up and started to walk towards the open door of the camper when I noticed something he hadn't. 'Nathan?'
'Yeah?'
'Clothes.'
He looked down and, realising that he was still naked, he quickly pulled on his boxers and jeans, both of which appeared to be damp from lying on the grass all night.
'DADDY!'
Nathan sighed. 'Coming, Daisy, I'm coming.'

*

As he went inside to tend to his daughters, Nathan felt as if he were walking on air. He hadn't experienced emotions like these in years. All his pain and anguish had vanished; he had made a connection with another human being both physically and mentally that felt incredible and he wanted it to last forever.

Somewhere deep down, he suspected that there would be a price to pay for all of this joy, but, for now, he tried to ignore it and let the feelings of new love (and lust, if he was being honest) wash all over him.

Delirium, that would be the best description he could think of. He remembered reading somewhere that love was a kind of madness that didn't last, but that didn't mean you couldn't enjoy it. If it evolved into something deeper, more satisfying, you were lucky. He hoped he'd be lucky.

Chapter 24

The Second Life of Nathan Jones.

I opened the netting and looked around for my underwear that I'd hastily discarded the previous evening. I found my bra but the bottom half of my twin-set had vanished. I wondered for a moment if Nathan had an underwear fetish and had secreted them away, but he'd not even had his own boxers in hand when he'd got up.

I gave up searching and avoided the girls by slipping into the shower cubicle. I stood under the warm water for longer than I should have, given that we only had a finite amount available. I came out to find Nathan waiting for his turn. He kissed me quickly and said, 'You're amazing, oh, and Millie's got some questions for you.'

'What questions?'

'You'll see,' he said cryptically as he slipped past me.

I put on some clean underwear, a black Melrose lace top and a pair of slashed leggings – black, of course. I reapplied my dark eye make-up, discarded any thought of wearing my kitten heels (no idea why I'd packed them or why I'd thought I'd ever get to wear them on a trip like this). Instead I laced up the black trainers I'd been wearing since we left Edinburgh. I brewed myself a mug of coffee and made ready for Millie's interrogation.

'Kat?'

'Millie.'

'Do you like my dad?'

'Yes, Millie, why do you think I'm here?'

'Can I ask the questions just now, please?'

I laughed at her serious face, and decided she'd make a great police detective. 'Okay, sweetie.'

'I'm also speaking for Daisy and Chloe this morning. We've already got a mum, you know. I'm also old enough to know that my parents haven't been getting on for a long time, but if you and my dad get together what kind of role will you have in our lives?'

'That's a very grown-up question, Millie, and I'm not sure your dad and I are really at a stage to answer it yet.'

Millie nodded. 'Okay, but, if we assume that things progress and you "stick around", what will you be?'

'The evil stepmother?'

'You're not taking this very seriously, are you?'

I laughed again and shook my head at the serious face staring back at me. 'Millie, you're so ...' what was the best description? '... grown up. Why is that?'

Millie rolled her eyes, 'Somebody needs to be on the ball around here.'

'Your dad and I are on the ball, Millie. We—'

'I heard you last night.'

'Oh.' I didn't know what to say to that. 'One day you'll ... I'm sure ...' I was useless at patronising and decided being honest was what I was best at. 'I love your dad, Millie. I'm not sure he knows it yet, but I do. Last night was just an expression of that love.'

Millie smiled, enjoying my discomfort. 'It was a very loud expression.'

I laughed and blushed.

'Anyway,' Millie carried on, 'I'm glad for him. He and Mum, well ... they didn't, don't make each other happy, I think they only stayed together for as long as they did for us.' Millie paused and squinted at me through her fringe. 'When he got killed Mum seemed happy and that can't be a good thing, can it?'

I slowly shook my head. 'No, I don't think it is.'

'If everyone gets to be happier, then I think that's a good thing even though it'll be confusing for us.'

'How did you feel about changing schools and staying in London?'

'Not happy. All my friends are in Edinburgh and I wouldn't get to see Dad much. Daisy and Chloe aren't old enough yet to understand and just kind of do what they're told, but I said to my mum I didn't want to stay in London.'

'What did she say?'

'"You'll get used to it."'

'That wasn't very nice.'

'No, it wasn't.'

The mention of her mother seemed to knock Millie off her stride and she said, 'Okay, that's all my questions for now.'

'Did I pass?'

Millie smiled and flicked her hair back. 'I'll let you know later.' She wandered outside, and I got the feeling I'd been let off lightly.

*

Nathan and I sat close at breakfast. I wanted to be near him and the feeling was obviously mutual. He kept touching me, my hand, his knee pressed against my thigh, stealing kisses when the girls weren't watching.

After we'd tidied away the plates, I got a text from Hayley saying James would be arriving in about half an hour. We got the girls dressed and ready the best we could. Millie was still playing with my GHD straighteners (switched off, of course) when I heard a car engine pull up and stop outside.

I stepped out of the door and Hayley emerged from the car. I ran over and we hugged. It felt great to see her and, on the verge of tears, we both did that strange dance that women did when they were trying not to cry, bouncing and fanning our eyes with our hands.

I pulled Hayley over to meet Nathan. 'Nathan, this is Hayley.'

'I'd gathered that,' he said, staring open-mouthed.

'Eyes on stalks, Nathan,' I warned.

'Sorry.'

'She is gorgeous, though, isn't she?'

I watched and could see him wondering if agreeing with me would land him in trouble, but if he'd learned anything about me at all he'd know I expected everyone to be honest even if that expectation was rarely satisfied. He smiled and said, 'Stunning, definitely eyes on stalks.'

'What is this "eyes on stalks" business?' asked Hayley.

'You know, babes,' I answered. 'Like those cartoon characters when they see something amazing – their eyes pop out on stalks.'

'Oh, okay.'

I glanced over her shoulder. 'I didn't know you were coming. I just expected James and the Dads for Daughters bloke.'

'I couldn't resist tagging along. Besides, I don't think James wanted to come on his own in case you beat him up.'

'I've never beaten anyone up in my life. I'm a pussy Kat.' I giggled at my own joke.

'Yeah, well, it's probably because I've given him such a hard time that he wanted some reinforcements. Here he comes now.' Hayley stepped back to let James into our little circle.

'Kat, it's good to see you again.'

'James,' I said coolly. 'It's not really, is it? Under different circumstances maybe. This is Nathan.'

Nathan shook hands very formerly with James, just as a large dark-bearded man pushed into the group. James introduced him. 'This is George from Dads for Daughters, also known as the bearded wonder.'

'Especially by my wife,' he added.

'Too much information, I think,' I said, wondering why someone would say something like that in front of strangers. Maybe he suffered from the same foot-in-mouth syndrome that I did.

'What a drive,' James said, changing the subject. 'It took us four hours from Glasgow. It doesn't look that far on the map and we must have driven past the opening to your little hidey-hole about five times.'

James gazed out across the little glade and said, 'What a beautiful place.'

I beamed. 'It's amazing, isn't it?'

James then spotted Millie, Chloe and Daisy standing nervously a few feet away. 'Wow, your girls are gorgeous, and, if you don't mind me saying so, little dark-haired carbon copies of their mother. In fact, you know what they remind me of? Little Russian dolls, each one a smaller version of the previous one.'

Nathan smiled. 'Someone said that once before when we were in Turkey on holiday. Kat says you know each other from school?'

James nodded. 'Yeah, and that's how I know Hayley too.'

'What, like childhood sweethearts? Kat never told me that.'

I watched as James shuffled uncomfortably as Hayley answered, 'Well, that's not *exactly* how it happened, to be honest. We hadn't seen each other in years, then one day he turns up at my work.'

'Looking for a job?'

'Looking for a divorce.'

'So, you asked out the lawyer handling your divorce?' Nathan asked James in a surprised tone. 'Isn't that a conflict of interest or at least unethical?'

I watched my friend squirm uncomfortably. 'Well, technically I'm not his lawyer, and we'll keep it secret, obviously, until James's divorce is finalised.'

Nathan nodded, and noticed me shaking my head. He took the hint and changed the subject. 'Okay, James, so what do you want me to do?'

'We'll spend the remainder of the morning coaching, how to look at the camera, how to hold yourself—'

'Hold myself?' Nathen interrupted, puzzled.

'Posture and eye contact mostly, then we need to pick up any tics that you might have.'

I said, 'There's lots of midges but I've not seen any ticks. Don't you get them from sheep? I haven't seen any sheep.'

'Not that sort of tick, nervous tics, like mannerisms and habits. We want to make sure that when we're talking the focus is on what Nathan is saying, not on what he's doing.'

'I didn't know it'd be so complicated.'

'You wouldn't believe how complicated it gets, but all I'm after is some good interview footage with everyone. George here will be sympathetic and provide some advice and hopefully a few shots of you all playing with the girls.'

I didn't understand. 'Why do you want me involved? I'm the wicked witch, remember?'

James scratched his head. 'Yeah, exactly, we need to dispel that myth as well. In many ways this is as much about you as it is Nathan. At the beginning of the Donaldson interview they made out that you've led Nathan astray. They even suggested that you might have been the cause of all the Joneses' problems.'

I couldn't believe that. 'What a crock of shit – is that what she's saying? We must have missed that bit.'

Chloe appeared behind me and tugged on my top. 'Wait a minute, Chloe, I'm talking to James,' I said kindly.

Nathan came over and put his hand on my arm. 'Don't get annoyed. You'll get the girls upset if you start slagging off their mother. We both know it's a pack of lies but we just must try and deal with it and fight back – that's what James and George are here to do. The thing is, I'm not one hundred per cent sure why we're even bothering.'

Chloe said, 'Kat, Kat ...'

'Wait a minute, Chloe.' I still hadn't looked at her.

James stepped in. 'Good point. When you get back to civilisation Laura will be waiting for you. She wants the girls to live with her and you want them with you. She'll have everyone on her side now, so you need some ammunition to fight with. Currently you have nothing.

'In this wonderful setting they can't fail to look happy and content and that is probably the most important and powerful thing we can do – show your girls happy and playing with you both. That one shot will probably do more good than all the other footage we put together, but it's all about building a picture completely contrary to that being painted by your wife.'

'You make it sound like a war,' Nathan said.

'In a way it is, I'm afraid, whether you like it or not.'

Nathan sighed and said, 'Okay, what would you like me to do?'

'Kat!' Chloe said very loudly.

I turned around. 'What is it, Chloe?'

'Are these yours?' Gripped between her forefinger and thumb, very gingerly she held up my missing knickers for everyone to see.

'Oh,' I said, turning beetroot.

'I found them over there near the bushes. Did you lose them doing a pee pee?'

Everybody roared with laughter as I grabbed them, tucked them into my pocket and said, 'Yeah, something like that.'

James came to my rescue by saying, 'The weather's not looking too promising so let's get a move on.' He noticed Daisy scooping mud from a puddle. 'Can we keep them clean, do you think?'

Everybody followed his gaze and started laughing again. 'She wouldn't have dared do that a month ago,' Nathan observed.

'Why not?' asked Hayley.

Nathan nodded towards me. 'Because someone's taught

them how to be naughty and they've become proper little tomboys.'

I punched him playfully on the arm, glad the attention had been taken off my underwear. 'I taught them how to have some fun. They were timid little mice before I appeared on the scene.'

James switched his gaze between me and the girls. 'So, it's your fault they're playing in a muddy puddle, then?'

I shrugged. 'And *Peppa Pig*'s. They were watching that this morning.'

Hayley noticed the darkening sky and said with her practical head on, 'It also means that we might need somewhere to stay overnight,' as she walked over to the motorhome. 'Ooh, what a lovely camper van.'

'Motorhome,' I corrected.

'Is it?'

'Yeah. The camper van ceased to exist in 1967, apparently.'

Hayley stared at me for a moment, shook her head and asked, 'Can we sleep in here tonight?'

'You and James?'

'Yeah.'

'No, there's not enough room, and, anyway, I don't want to listen to you two shagging all night.'

'We won't.'

'You will too. Besides, he farts a lot.'

'I do not,' protested James.

'You do so. Hayley told me.'

James frowned at Hayley. 'Do you tell her everything?'

Hayley nodded. 'Pretty much.'

I giggled. 'What about me?' asked George.

'Do you fart a lot?'

'Not unless I've had lentil soup.'

'Have you had any?'

'No.'

'Well, you can't stay anyway. There's not enough room.'

*

We managed to finish filming the boring 'talking head' bits with the bearded wonder in under an hour, then they filmed me playing 'piggy in the middle' with the girls, which got a bit out of hand when Daisy started crying because she couldn't catch the ball. I ended up hugging her.

James smiled. 'That'll look great on playback; you came over as caring and fair.'

He wandered off and I watched the love-sick puppy look of longing that Hayley sent after him.

'Hayley, you've really got it bad, haven't you?'

She blushed. 'Yeah, well, it's like he's come alive since we started planning this. He's full of passion about making films and documentaries. That's what he did at college and what he wants to do. That passion spilled over into last night. I don't think we slept much, to be honest. We're running on oxytocin today. Thank God George did most of the driving.'

'Oxytocin?'

'The sex hormone.'

'Oh, I should probably know that with my background.'

'Not much call for oxytocin amongst the dead.'

'No, I suppose not.'

James interrupted us. 'Well, that's about it. I need to get all this home tonight, a quick final edit and—'

'We don't get another night in a cosy Highland hotel?' Hayley asked, disappointment dripping from her voice.

'I'm afraid not, babes. I need to get this over to the Channel 5 team tonight before the story goes cold or something else happens.'

'Like what?' I asked.

James shrugged. 'Anything. Some MP caught with his or her trousers down, a celebrity *ménage à trois*, anything like that. The only reason this story has had any air time at all is because there's not much happening at the minute and some researcher, or maybe Lance himself, fancies Nathan's missus.'

'Isn't he engaged to that actress that used to be in *Holly-oaks*?'

James shook his head. 'Nope, that ended last month, so he's single and on the prowl again.'

'That's crazy. Why would he want to get involved with Laura and her whole domestic mess? I mean, what sort of person would do that ...?'

I stopped speaking as both Hayley and James locked eyes onto me and raised their eyebrows at the same time.

David Atkinson

I'm not sure what surprised me most: the realisation that I'd just described my own situation perfectly or the fact that they'd only been together a short time but, already, had managed to synchronise their eyebrow raising.

Chapter 25

James, Hayley and the bearded wonder packed up their equipment, stowed it into the boot of their car and headed off. I'd hugged Hayley before she'd left and we'd agreed to meet up in Edinburgh in a few days to compare notes. In the meantime, Hayley would let me know if James managed to get our footage on the air.

Nathan and I had planned to head across country to a huge campsite just north of Pitlochry, where the girls could join up with other kids and enjoy the entertainment programme and swimming pools.

Personally, I could cope with being the other woman if it meant we could stay in our little holiday bubble a little longer, and Nathan seemed keen for the girls to have some fun.

I'd hoped for another night under the stars with Nathan, but the rain really started lashing down just as twilight closed in and we were destined to spend the night cramped inside.

With three kids in there with us there would be no

chance of Nathan and I snuggling up. 'Kids are great contraceptives, aren't they?' I asked, smiling.

'Yep, best there is.'

'Makes you wonder how anyone ever has more than one kid.'

'Nature always finds a way.'

'My dad said that he and my mum didn't have sex for ages after I came along.'

'Your dad told you that? I didn't know parents talked to their children about such things.'

'Yeah, well mine do, unfortunately. The last time I went home he offered me a pint of Leg Spreader.'

Nathan blinked a few times, opened his mouth to speak, then closed it again. He'd likely be wondering how my family managed to escape the attention of social services. I probably shouldn't have mentioned that; it was up there with the 'you're beautiful when you're sleeping' line and would have been better remaining firmly in my head. Still, he recovered well and suggested, 'Maybe we could sneak outside when the rain stops?'

Unfortunately, by the time we got the girls to sleep the rain had begun to rattle off the roof so hard we could barely hear ourselves whisper so we had a steamy snog and retired to our respective ends of the van. I lay in my little bunk frustrated and horny, but consoled myself with the thought that we had all the time in the world in front of us.

*

After a late breakfast we packed up all our stuff and headed out. We planned to arrive early to mid-afternoon to make the time worthwhile. I made sure everyone had strapped themselves in and that the *Trolls* DVD had started. Daisy sat holding her Minion character, which continued annoying everyone periodically with its cry of 'Wayhay'. I hadn't managed to work out how to switch it off or even how to remove the battery, as there didn't appear to be any kind of access to the damn thing's insides.

Millie watched me try to find an off switch or battery lid. She smiled smugly and said, 'All the Minions come from a special factory where each figure has embedded within it a magical sprite that speaks the word of the Minions everywhere, "Wayhay". So, you won't find a battery because the spirit within doesn't need any power.'

I must confess for a moment she spooked me but then I decided that Millie watched too much adult TV. 'So how do I get it to shut up, then, smarty pants?' I asked her.

'You don't,' she replied smugly. 'You have to sit and listen to it all day.'

'I don't. I could throw it out the window.'

Millie nodded, the smile leaving her face. 'You could, but Daisy might not like it.'

The way Daisy *now* held her Minion, rather warily by its leg, made me believe she probably wouldn't be too bothered, but I left my options open and buckled myself in the seat beside Nathan.

The sunny morning that had greeted us at breakfast

David Atkinson

had clouded over and the sky had darkened considerably since then; no doubt more rain would follow. My initial assessment about the spring Scottish weather being warm and sunny in the Highlands had to be reassessed, given the amount of rain we'd endured since then.

About an hour into our journey the heavens opened, almost like a cloudburst, and the narrow road became slick with water. Nathan slowed down and started to look for somewhere to pull in and wait for it to pass. Suddenly a deer sprang out of the undergrowth and ran straight into our path. Nathan slammed on the brakes and wrenched the wheel to the right. The tyres squealed, and the motorhome lurched onto the verge of the road and, almost in slow motion, began to tip over. I screamed, and Nathan twisted his head towards me and I saw the look of terror on his face as we plunged down the grass verge into the trees.

The first thing I noticed when we eventually stopped was the silence and the disorientating sensation of looking at the world upside down. A fine layer of dust covered me, and an acrid smell permeated my nostrils. I glanced over at Nathan. His eyes were closed, and he had a large red circular bruise on his face, but I couldn't see anything that could have caused it. Then I wondered in horror if he might be dead again. Thankfully, he quickly dispelled that thought by groaning and opening his eyes. Then he started awake, shouting, 'The girls!'

I suddenly came to my senses and carefully unbuckled my seat belt and dropped to the roof, a strange and disconcerting thing to do. I then helped Nathan out of his seat.

My shoulder ached, and I could feel a bruise beginning to form on my bum, but nothing seemed too serious. I didn't bother to ask Nathan how he was feeling as he'd already clambered into the back of the van. I crawled back with him, hoping against hope that the kids were okay.

Daisy had a huge smile on her face and still clutched her Minion, which predictably uttered, 'Wayhay'. Daisy giggled and asked enthusiastically, 'Can we do that again?'

I laughed; it was impossible not to, especially as I noticed that Millie and Chloe were fine too. Upside down, still harnessed into their seats, but fine. Millie said in a grumpy voice, 'I suppose this means we're not going to Pitlochry now?'

We got everyone out of the SE39 and seated under a large umbrella on an overturned log far enough away in case the motorhome blew up (though I suspected this only really happened in movies). We remained close enough for the emergency services to find us when they eventually arrived. Nathan had been surprisingly reluctant to phone the police and suggested maybe the RAC would be able to get the van back on the road. I'd shown him the crumpled rear-corner section of the thing and he'd come to his senses and immediately dialled for help. We'd given them the grid reference from the satnav, then I'd gone back and retrieved my handbag from the footwell, which now formed the top of the van.

The police and ambulance arrived together. They didn't have any flashing lights or sirens as I'd told the dispatch person that we were all fine and, although nobody had any life-threatening injuries, we did have young children with us and would like them to get checked out as soon as possible. There were two police officers – an older male with greying hair and a young woman with red hair tucked under her police cap.

The paramedic called Julie examined the children first, making sure nobody had any broken bones. Satisfied that they were fine, she said, 'Right, girls, I'll just make sure your mum and dad are okay.'

'She's not our mum,' said Chloe.

'Our real mum's in London,' clarified Millie. 'That's Kat.'

Julie paused for a moment, then smiled with recognition. 'I saw you on the TV this morning. They played a clip of you being interviewed and playing with the children.'

I wondered why James or Hayley at least hadn't told us it had gone out. I pulled my phone out of my bag; it had no power. I'd forgotten to charge it up. I didn't know how long it would be before I could do that again, given our current predicament. I could get by without clean clothes or even a shower for a day or two if necessary, but not having a working phone would be really irritating.

'How did it come across?'

'Well, I'm ... I hadn't seen yesterday's programme so I'm not that up on your, err ... situation?'

'Situation is as good a word as any.'

'Yeah, well, as I say, I didn't see the other point of view, but I suppose my overall impression is that you all looked happy.'

'We were having a great time ... well, until now.'

Julie nodded. 'Well, yeah, I don't suppose this will help your case much.'

My brain hadn't caught up with events yet, but now I understood Nathan's initial reaction and his reluctance to call for help. In the end, though, we'd had no choice and we were just glad everyone got out uninjured. Nathan's only visible injury was the nasty bruise on his face. Julie had prodded it and announced, 'That'll be the result of the airbag going off. Most people in accidents don't even notice the airbags deploying because there's too much else going on.'

That explained the acrid smell I'd noticed just after we rolled to a stop. I had a strained muscle in my shoulder and a bruise on my bum, which Julie reckoned came from bashing it on the door handles.

The police stayed in the background, occasionally answering their radios or phones or whatever it was they used now. When the paramedic eventually gave us all a clean bill of health the female officer came over and spoke to Nathan. 'The nearest hospital is Fort William, but it seems that you've been really lucky and none of you need any urgent attention, so we can arrange for a recovery service to come and retrieve the motorhome from the ditch. We can't give you all a lift in the police car as there's too many of you, so what I've done is to arrange for the local taxi firm to take you to the nearest railway station where you can catch a train back to Glasgow. Unfortunately, there isn't a train until noon, so you'll have to wait around for a while.'

'I need to get our clothes out of the motorhome,' I said, panicking at the thought of being separated from my clothes.

'I'm not sure the vehicle is safe enough for you to do that—' The male officer started to explain but I'd already gone; I wasn't going anywhere without my stuff.

Twenty minutes later I'd managed to drag my suitcase and most of Nathan's and the girls' items from the van. Nathan lent a hand when he spotted me struggling up the slope with my huge case.

'You didn't need to bring it all up with you. You could just have got the essentials.'

I glared at him. 'These are my essentials.' I lugged the shiny silver case up onto the tarmac and sat on it.

*

Later, as we sat on the train home, Nathan said, 'I don't suppose the man at Motorhome World will be too happy with us.'

'No, I guess not, but that's what you paid the insurance for. Looking on the bright side, at least neither of us need to drive it to Cumbria now.'

Nathan's phone started whistling. He answered it and then passed it to me. 'It's your friend,' he said.

'Hayley, you got my message, then?'

'Yes, oh, my God, are you all right?'

'Yeah, amazingly, we're all fine. We're still a bit shaken up but thankfully we weren't travelling all that fast at the time. That's why nobody got hurt.'

'How are the kids?'

'They're annoyed that we've had to cut short our holiday but, apart from that, fine. We're on a train home so if we get cut off you know why.'

'Okay, listen quickly – did you see the Lance Donaldson show this morning?'

'No, we missed it, I—'

'But I texted you.'

'My phone had died by that point.'

'Oh, right, well, I think you came over really well, and they couldn't get Nathan's wife to come back on and face up to some of the lies she'd told, so in the end it makes you guys look a lot better. The bonus, I suppose, is that James says it's becoming a non-story and likely nobody will be that interested in you two now – that and the fact a Premiership football manager just got caught in bed with Samantha Wentworth.'

'The prime-time newsreader? When did that happen?'

'The story broke this morning and has kind of swept everything else off the news agenda.'

I poked Nathan. 'Some football manager got caught in bed with Samantha Wentworth.'

Nathan squinted at me and said, 'Who?'

'Samantha Wentworth, she reads the news.'

'Does she?'

'Oh, you're hopeless.' I returned to the phone. 'I've got no internet access here; I feel like I'm cut off from the world.'

'When will you be home?'

'We're due into Glasgow about half two, then we'll need to get another train to Edinburgh. We'll be home for teatime, I think.'

'You could come and stay at mine if you like *if you're* you going to Edinburgh. We can have wine and a catch-up.'

I knew she wanted to rave about James and, as pleased as I was for my friend, I couldn't face an evening of her rambling on about the man who made my school life hell. I couldn't quite forgive him for that, well, not yet, anyway.

'I think I need to be with Nathan, babes; we've had a pretty traumatic day so far.'

Hayley remained silent for a moment before saying, 'Well, maybe tomorrow. You're not working this week, are you?'

'No, I'm off until next Monday.'

'Okay, I'll text you later. Bye.'

Hayley's clipped sentences worried me; she obviously had something to tell me and it wasn't just to rave about her boyfriend. It would have to wait. I handed Nathan his phone just as it started to ring again. He frowned at the screen and declined the call. 'Laura,' he said by way of explanation. He sent a brief text and then switched it off. 'I just told her we'll be back in Edinburgh tonight. That should shut her up for a bit.'

The rest of the journey seemed to take forever as the girls were getting bored and restless. We grabbed some sandwiches and crisps in Glasgow before boarding the train to Edinburgh. An hour later we arrived at Waverley and fed the starving girls at the nearby Burger King. Then we piled into a taxi and soon arrived outside Nathan's flat; he paid the driver and we wearily trudged up the stairs and inside. I parked my humongous case in his hallway.

I helped him get everyone settled then decided to go home. I felt weary and my bum hurt. I did think about staying over and satisfying the sexual itch that I could feel just below the surface, and the look on Nathan's face when I announced my departure told me we would've had a nice time scratching it.

I promised to phone him in the morning and suggested we could maybe do something with the girls to make up for some of the disappointment of not making it to the holiday park in the Highlands.

I took what I needed from my case and stuffed it into a smaller bag. I couldn't face dragging the case another step. I also knew that if I took my case home tonight I'd want to wash everything and wouldn't be able to stop myself.

I left the flat and remembered I had no car. I stood outside his apartment and wondered which direction the rapists and muggers would come sprinting from first. I walked quickly to a nearby bus stop and jumped on the first bus that came. It dropped me near Easter Road and I walked home from there. I tried to make sense of the last few days, the description 'emotional roller coaster' not really coming close. I'd fallen in love, had mind-blowing sex during an electric storm, appeared on TV (yes, it had only been a cameo appearance but an appearance nevertheless), suffered an interrogation about my sex life from a ten year-old girl, been bashed and bruised in an incident and met up with James Cochrane again after all these years. I'd also managed to spend a few days cooped up in close quarters with other human beings without making a complete arse of myself and for that reason alone I thought I deserved a hot bubble bath and some wine.

Any hopes I had of having a quiet evening alone were dashed when I arrived home, as parked outside my flat in her BMW convertible was Hayley Dunlop. I briefly wondered why she hadn't just phoned or texted, then remembered my phone still wasn't charged.

Hayley literally jumped out of her car when she spotted me. 'Where have you been?'

'Well, I started the day in this beautiful Highland glen, then my boyfriend managed to total a seventy-grand vehicle, then—'

'Yeah, very funny. I meant in the last hour or so.'

'We had something to eat in town before heading back. Apart from that, sitting on trains.'

'I thought you'd be back sooner. I need to talk to you.'

'Okay, I'm listening.'

'Not out here, inside.'

'It's a bit messy.'

'No, it's not; you always say that, and it never is.'

'That's because my idea of messy and your idea of messy are miles apart, Miss Dunlop.'

'Yeah, whatever, just get in, oh, wait a sec ...' Hayley went back to her car and brought out a bag. 'Nearly forgot.'

'Nearly forgot what?'

'Wine. C'mon, let's get in out of the cold.'

I didn't think it felt cold, but then I'd been exposed to public transport and the elements on my walk whilst she'd been cosseted in her heated cream leather seats.

I dropped my bag inside the door, turned up the thermostat for Hayley's benefit and sat on my couch.

'Right, we need some glasses,' Hayley announced as she came in and sat beside me. 'Oh, and before I forget I'm so glad you're all right.'

'I've got a sore bum.'

Hayley's nose twitched like a rabbit. 'How did that happen?' she asked suspiciously.

'The accident.'

'Oh, right, of course. I thought for a moment that Natha ... No, never mind. Right, glasses.' She bounced up and into my tiny galley kitchen and returned with some glasses.

'What's going on, Hayley?'

She poured us two large glasses of Chablis and sighed. 'Best friends forever.'

We clinked glasses and I took a drink. She then bit her

lip and as I watched tears started to form in the corners of her eyes and then she fell on me bawling her eyes out. I spilled some of my wine onto her hair, but I didn't think she noticed.

Between sobs she said, 'I'll have to wash my hair now.' She'd noticed.

'Hayley, what's going on? You turn up out of the blue with wine and now you're upset; what's going on?'

'It's James's wife.'

'What about her?'

'She came into the office today and registered an official complaint against me.'

'Why?'

'Why do you think?'

'But you said you'd kept it all secret.'

'She found out.'

'How?'

'James told her.'

'But, I mean, well … I'm not sure I really understand.'

Hayley sat up, put her wine down and blew her nose into a tissue. 'The Law Society of Scotland are going to carry out an investigation into my conduct, on the grounds of unprofessional and unethical behaviour.'

'She's a bitch. She's the one that cheated in the first place.'

'True, but there are rules and regulations and I might have breached some.'

'Might have?'

'That's what they said.'

'Sounds pretty vague?'

'It's to do with law, of course it's vague.'

'What happens now?'

'I don't know. I'm suspended.'

'Aw, sweetie.'

We sat for a moment, the only noise breaking the silence being the odd sniff from Hayley.

'What did James say?'

'Oh, he's really upset. It seems she wound him up and he just blurted it out and I don't think he realised she'd take it that far, nor the consequences for me.'

'What happens next?' I asked, holding Hayley's hand.

'We finish the wine and I spend the night on your couch.'

That set us both laughing, lightening the mood a little.

'I meant with work?'

'Who knows? I'm not allowed back until the investigation's finished, which could take weeks. If they find against me I might be disbarred – that's unlikely, but possible. One thing's for sure, I'm glad I made partner before this happened. They wouldn't have offered it to me now.'

'I suppose it gives you some extra time to see James.'

'Yeah, I suppose.'

She didn't sound very enthusiastic, but I kept my opinion to myself.

Chapter 26

I had to wait until the next morning for my bubble bath. I don't think I'd ever had one while nursing a hangover before. After the Chablis we'd managed to polish off a bottle of Pinot Grigio and three cans of cider that Hayley had discovered lurking at the back of my fridge.

My friend had already showered and left earlier, wisely deciding to take the train back to Glasgow. She'd arranged to meet with an employment lawyer to discuss her case. I would have thought she'd be able to work all that out for herself, but she insisted that another lawyer would give her an objective view.

I'd agreed to drive her car back to her flat later and share a takeaway tonight. Sober this time – well, *soberish*.

As I lay soaking in my bubbly bliss I heard my now fully charged phone ringing. I ignored it; nothing would entice me out of the water for at least another half-hour. It rang twice more but I decided whoever and whatever could wait.

Eventually I had to move and, after towel-drying my hair

and wrapping myself in my black fluffy bathrobe, I picked up my phone. All the missed calls were from Nathan and he'd also sent a text saying, '*Kat phone me ASAP!*'

How on earth had that man ever managed to get by without me? I phoned him to see what new crisis had befallen him. 'Nathan, what's up?'

'Can you meet me at the civil court in Chambers Street in an hour?'

'Court? Why, what's happened?'

'I'm not sure.'

'What do you mean? Is everyone all right?'

'I think so.'

'What's happened, then?'

'Laura came by this morning.'

'Did she?'

'Yes, and she had company.'

'Her boyfriend?'

'No, that would have been easier. She had social workers.'

'Social workers, plural?'

'Yeah, and they took the girls away.'

'Away where?'

'I don't know. All I do know is that I have to be at the court for eleven.'

'That doesn't sound good.'

'No, it doesn't. I don't suppose your friend Hayley's around, is she?'

'She went home to Glasgow this morning.'

'Can she come back?'

'I doubt it. Anyway, she's got her own problems to deal with.' I briefly outlined what had happened. 'I doubt she'd be able to help.'

'She knows her way around a courtroom.'

'She probably knows where the café is to get coffee; anything else I'm not sure about but I'll get there as soon as I can.'

*

I texted Nathan as I arrived, and he met me at the front door of the imposing building. He looked shell-shocked.

'Laura's taken out a non-molestation order against me.'

'Have you been molesting her?'

'Not for a long time but that's not what it means. She's done it to stop me seeing the girls.'

'Can she do that?'

'She's done it.'

'What does it all mean, Nathan? I don't really understand.'

'She's in there now; sitting before some lawyer-type person telling them a pack of lies.'

'What's she saying?'

'Well, I don't know exactly, do I? I'm not allowed in and I'm out here speaking to you, but she'll be laying it on thick that I'm a danger to the girls and reckless because I crashed the motorhome.'

'How did she find out?'

'Millie told her on the phone yesterday.'

'Well, I suppose you did crash it, though, didn't you? So not much you can do about that.'

'Whose side are you on? It was an accident. I didn't want to hit Bambi.'

'Bambi's mother, more like.' I noticed how red his face had become and I wondered if his blood pressure had risen to dangerous levels.

He might be about to have a stroke.

'Don't be silly.'

'What do you mean don't be silly? I'd have killed it.'

'Killed what?'

'The deer.'

'Oh, yeah, so what happens now?'

'After I got off the phone to you I did phone a legal firm, one that specialises in family law, but they told me at this stage I'd be wasting my time and money as the court would almost certainly grant her the order and it's only after it's in force that I can challenge the terms of it.'

'That doesn't sound right to me, but then what do I know?' I tried to think it over. 'Don't you think it'd be much harder to stop an enforcement order being enforced after it's in force?'

Nathan blinked at me. 'I didn't understand that sentence.'

Before I could elaborate the door opened and Laura appeared. I'd seen her on TV, but she'd been crying her eyes out and I had to say, grudgingly of course, she radiated beauty even with an angry frown. She had behind her what I can only describe as an entourage. She led a group of grim-faced, blue-suited men, with a well-preserved skinny blonde lady bringing up the rear holding a pile of papers. Laura halted when she noticed Nathan and let the blonde push her way to the front. She pulled the topmost of the papers out of her bundle and spoke without making eye contact with anyone. 'The judge has granted Ms Laura Connor a non-molestation order against Mr Nathan Jones effective immediately.'

I leaned over and said into his ear, 'Laura Connor?'

'That's her maiden name.'

'Are you divorced now?'

'If we are nobody's told *me*. Maybe she's got a very efficient legal team on her side.'

Skinny blonde lady pulled out another piece of paper and handed it over to Nathan. 'This is a copy for your records pursuant upon and from said previously alluded to order being granted, implemented and enforced by the Edinburgh & Lothian Civil Court in line with the terms set out under and crystallised in the Children (Scotland Act).

'You should seek and retain individual and independent legal counsel in connection with this enforcement and in any event ensure you adequately familiarise yourself with the pertinent and relevant restrictions and clauses set out in said document to ensure you do not involuntarily or without due care and attention inadvertently breach the terms of the order. To do so would render yourself subject to serious legal consequences including, but not exhaustively nor exclusively, a possible custodial sentence in conjunction with a fine and potential further sanctions.'

Once the blonde had stopped speaking she turned on her heel and marched back down the hall; the entourage all followed her.

Nathan turned to me. 'What did she say?'

'Beats me.'

'Why don't I understand what anyone's on about today?'

I noticed that Laura had pulled away from the pack and had turned back towards us. She hesitated, then marched back down the hall, her eyes fixed on Nathan. I noticed for the first time that at the end of the hall Millie had appeared, looking around for her mother. She spotted me, and I gave a little wave, unsure of my ground in this weird environment. Hayley often went to court and I wondered how she coped in this strange adult playground. Maybe she did just sit in the café looking at Facebook.

Laura stopped in front of Nathan and said nothing for a moment, just staring at him. She quickly glanced over at me, looking down her nose, then said, 'Nathan, I'm sorry that it had to come to this, but I couldn't have you doing anything stupid to the girls again, egged on by your punk girlfriend here. You had me worried sick for days and the fact you wouldn't answer your phone to me made me mad as hell. What were you thinking, Nathan? What were you thinking?'

'You'd taken the girls away from me; I wanted to see them—'

'You could have asked, you moron; you didn't need to steal them.'

'You stole them, not me.'

'Hardly, I'd moved them somewhere for a better life. You whisked them away in a smelly van.'

'A top-of-the-range camper ... motorhome, hardly a smelly anything.'

'With your stinky feet it would have been smelly soon enough.'

Now I knew where that slightly tangy scent that had pervaded the van had come from.

'My feet have nothing to do with anything. You'd taken the girls and I wanted them back. It's as simple as that. At least I didn't go on TV trying to garner sympathy.'

'Yes, you did.'

'Well ... yes, I did, but not until you'd done it first. I—'

'It wasn't my idea. The local police sergeant said that Lance what's-his-face wanted a human-interest story and we ... *I* fitted the bill. It's probably not the wisest thing I've ever done, to be honest, but too late now.'

'So, what do we do now?'

'We go back to where we were before you started your nonsense. The girls live with me.'

'And I have to make an appointment to see my own kids? I don't think so. That's not going to happen.'

Laura smiled, smugly I thought, but I was biased, of course, and said, 'No, that's exactly what *is* going to happen now. If you want any contact with the girls at all you need to make arrangements via a senior social worker and all visits will be supervised as you are now seen as a danger to them.'

I expected Nathan to explode but amazingly he just wilted, his whole body shrank, and his shoulders slumped as if someone had placed a huge weight onto them. I'd never seen anything like that happen before; I found it fascinating in a strange and unpleasant way.

Laura smiled, pleased at the reaction, obviously enjoying herself, but her smile vanished when Millie ran forward and grabbed her dad around his waist. She cried, 'Daddy, Daddy,' tears pouring down her face.

Laura's eyes narrowed. 'Millie,' she said quietly but firmly. Her daughter ignored her. 'Millie,' she snapped, but again her eldest ignored her.

Laura stomped forward, her eyes blazing and nostrils flaring – she reminded me of an angry, prancing dark horse. I'd endured my fair share of bullying over the years and that was all she was, a beautiful and captivating bully. Before she grabbed Millie's arm I whispered in her ear, 'Don't worry, Millie; everything will work out.'

There, my brain had managed to produce its first ever little white lie. It obviously took an extreme situation for that to happen. It seemed to calm Millie a little as Laura grabbed her arm and dragged her away up the hall.

Nathan stood staring after his wife and daughter, shaking his head. I grabbed him by the shoulders and he lifted his head, his eyes finding mine. 'You can't let her get away with this, Nathan. You need to fight it.'

He lowered his eyes and said, 'I know, I will. I just need some time to work it all out.'

'I'll speak to Hayley again. I'm sure there's lots of ways to fight this. We can get that Dads for Daughters bloke involved and ...'

While I prattled on Nathan sat down on a nearby bench and put his head in his hands. Three seconds later he slumped forward and collapsed onto the floor.

See, I told you he was going to have a stroke.

Chapter 27

Sitting at Nathan's bedside had become something of a habit for me. At least he hadn't died this time and instead looked at me with a strange expression on his face.

'What is it, Nathan?'

'I'm just wondering why you're still here.'

'I can go, if you like. I need to take Hayley's car back to her.'

'No, I didn't mean that. I mean, well, you're amazing, beautiful, sexy and I can't understand why you want to be involved in this mess.'

I'd never dealt well with people complimenting me and my default position always seemed to be disbelief, though I enjoyed it nonetheless. I shrugged and squirmed uncomfortably in the hard plastic chair. 'Aww shucks.'

Nathan laughed, and I liked the fact that I could make him smile even when he was miserable.

'What did the doctors say?' he asked me.

'I don't know. I've not spoken to any of them.'

He could have had a tiny stroke.

'No, he hasn't.'

'Who hasn't?' Nathan asked.

'You.'

'Me what?'

'Never mind. The doctors wouldn't tell me anything anyway.'

'Why not?'

'I'm not next of kin.'

'Who is?'

'Laura.'

'They didn't tell her, did they?'

'I don't think so; she's not here.'

'She never is when I get ill.' He laughed, which, in my book, appeared to be a big step forward from the last time. 'They did all sorts of poking and prodding, then dumped me up here to rest. You weren't watching me sleeping *again*, were you?'

'Well, maybe just for a little while.'

'Funnily enough, I now find that comforting; which means I'm probably losing my marbles. Maybe I should actually see that psychiatrist now that I'm back in here.'

Before I could answer the consultant appeared and stood at the foot of the bed. He stared at me for a moment. 'I know you, don't I?'

'Probably. I work here.' I noted his faded badge said Dr Peter Young.

'Right, nursing staff – I never forget a face.'

'Not nursing, I work in the morgue.'

'Oh, what are you doing here, then?'

'I like to try and visit all the patients before they die, just to get to know them a little better before they end up on the slab. Makes the job that little bit more personal for me.'

'Right,' he said, nodding; unsure if I was joking or not and looking at Nathan with a worried expression on his face. 'Well, um, well, would you mind stepping outside so I can talk to Mr Jones alone?'

Nathan butted in, spoiling my fun. 'She's my girlfriend, doctor, so she can stay if that's all right with you?'

'Oh, right. Oh, I see, that makes much more sense.' He flashed a relieved smile in my direction. 'A little bit of morgue humour.'

I smiled politely.

'Right,' said Dr Young authoritatively now back on firm ground. 'Well, we're still waiting for a number of the bloods to come back but, given that you're conscious and showing no signs of stroke or bleeding, the consensus is that you suffered a syncopal event. Given that you've had recent head trauma, however, just to be on the safe side, we'll schedule an MRI for tomorrow and we'll keep you in overnight for observation.'

Nathan nodded slowly. 'What's a sink pal event thingy?'

'Syncopal event is—'

'You fainted,' I interpreted for Dr Young.

'Fainted?'

'Yep,' I said, laughing, 'like a teenage girl at a Justin Bieber concert.'

Dr Young smiled and left us to it.

'I reckon it all just got a bit too much for you, sweetie, and your brain needed to shut down and reboot.'

'You make me sound like a laptop.'

'Well, there's similarities, I suppose, but you need some rest. I'll come back in the morning and run you home.'

'Not sure I want to go back to my flat, not with the girls gone.'

I smiled at his hang-dog expression. 'Well, maybe you can come home with me for a night. I'll need to do some tests on you just to make sure all your bits are fully functioning.'

'Which bits in particular?'

'Mainly the bits below your waist.'

'My feet?'

'Mm, definitely *not* your feet – well, not until they've had a thorough clean, Mr Jones.'

I left and phoned Hayley to explain why I wouldn't be taking her car back today.

'You're condemning me to public transport. Do you have any idea how it looks for a high-powered lawyer to be travelling on the bus?'

'You're suspended.'

'I know, but still ... How's Nathan?'

'Fine; he fainted with the stress of it all.'

'I did say the abduction idea wouldn't end well, but his situation hasn't changed that much, has it?'

'How do you mean?'

'He wasn't getting to see his girls anyway, so, whilst it's now legal, ultimately he's back to square one.'

'He probably doesn't see it like that.'

'No. What are your plans?'

'I'm taking him back to my flat to look after him.'

'Don't break him.'

'I'll try not to.'

'Any idea when I'll get my car back?'

'Sunday. I'll come early, and we can go for brunch. Then I'll need to go and see my parents, I suppose.'

'Such enthusiasm.'

'Do you want to come too?'

'Has your dad got the llamas yet?'

'I don't think so.'

'I'll think about it. The last time I was there your mum tried to polish my earrings and iron my jeans.'

'She likes ironing.'

'Yeah, but I was still wearing them at the time.'

'You've been with my mum enough to expect the unexpected.'

'Fair enough. Keep me in the loop with Nathan.'

'Ditto with James.'

I returned home and tidied. I really wanted to get my suitcase back and to wash everything, but that wouldn't happen any time soon by the looks of it. Maybe I could go and get the keys from Nathan, but I wouldn't feel comfortable going into his flat with him not there. I made do with cleaning the kitchen, the bathroom and hoovering. I noticed a layer of dust on the coving around the ceiling of the living room, but cleaning that would take me another step closer to my mum's madness and I didn't want to go there.

Later, I made a trip to the supermarket and bought lots of food and got one of my old cookbooks down from the shelf in the bedroom. I felt very domesticated and sophisticated while I planned what to cook tomorrow. However, I realised after ten minutes of reading some of Nigella's suggestions that Nathan might well end up back in hospital with food poisoning if I tried my hand at some of her concoctions, and decided that shoving a pre-made lasagne in the oven with some frozen chips would have to do.

*

Next morning, I collected Nathan from hospital. He'd had his MRI, and, as he'd been fine during the night, they let him out, saying they would phone when the results came back.

We stopped off at his flat on the way as I'd persuaded him that I really needed my things. I felt a lot happier when I knew my case had been safely stowed in the boot of the car.

Back at my place I made some sandwiches while Nathan had a quick shower. I took my spare key from the drawer nearest the cooker and put it on the plate with the sandwiches. He hadn't said much, and I knew he'd be thinking about his kids. I had a plan to take his mind off that and had stripped down to my underwear while he'd been drying off in the bedroom. I opened the door and delivered the food with a jug of orange juice.

'Room service.'

'I didn't order anything.'

'Well, it's here now and you'll have to give me a tip.'

'How much would be appropriate?'

'I think two kisses and a shag might be about right.'

We ate the sandwiches three hours later and I explained the key would allow him to come and stay here whenever he wanted. I wasn't sure he appreciated what a huge thing that was for me but, then again, he was a man, and they didn't get stuff like that.

Our lovemaking that afternoon was feverish and filled with emotion and tears. Perhaps not as full on as it had been in the Highlands, but we didn't have the intensity of an electric storm in the background urging us on.

We'd been through so much over the last few weeks that we'd not had a chance to truly let go. This gave us the opportunity and the pent-up frustration and anxiety had spilled over into the bedroom and beyond. Later, while lying snuggled together in the warmth, the room perfumed with the scent of our sex, I said, 'I love you, Nathan. I've tried not to, I've tried to keep some space between my feelings and you until everything had settled down, but it's too late; I've fallen for you.'

Nathan squeezed my shoulder. 'I love you too. I don't know when it happened exactly. I think Millie knew before I did.'

'Why? Do you talk to her about this sort of stuff?'

'No, of course not. She's just very perceptive.'

'She is. She gave me quite an interrogation that day in the motorhome.'

Nathan laughed. 'To be honest I started to feel something when you made me suck the wine from your fingers.'

'Yeah, that wouldn't be love, that would be lust.'

'Well ... maybe, but I started to think about you a lot after that moment. I love your intensity and the fact that everything with you is black or white – usually black, right enough, but you're always so sure about everything whereas I'm never that sure about anything. Except my feelings for you – they just feel so right.'

'What about Laura – was it not like that with her?'

'Once, yes, but that faded a long time ago. Now ... well, I don't like her, I guess. I haven't liked her for a long time and I'm pretty sure the feeling's mutual.'

We spent the day in bed, only getting up to pee, eat and share a warm sensuous bubble bath.

We slipped into sleep and I woke up a few times in the night and snuggled up next to his warm, hard body. I could get used to this. It just felt right. I'd never had that before and I liked it.

*

Next morning, as we sat sipping coffee fully clothed for the first time in nearly twenty-four hours Nathan's phone pinged.

'Who's that from?'

He looked up from his phone, a worried expression in his eyes, and reluctantly said, 'Laura.'

I felt my stomach drop. After all we'd endured in the last few days and weeks she still texted him. How often had he received texts from her and not told me? No, he would have told me. 'What does she want?'

'She wants to meet up with me.'

'After all that's happened?'

'I know. Maybe she's feeling guilty about everything.'

'As she should, but I don't think she's got the guilty gene in her biological make-up. Maybe she's got the divorce paperwork ready.'

'Really? I thought they just posted that sort of stuff to you.'

'They do normally, but she probably wants to inflict maximum hurt on you.'

'What should I do? I mean, if she wants a divorce then—'

'What do you mean "if she wants a divorce"? Of course, she wants a divorce so she can be with – what did you call him besides Oodles?'

'Sorry, I meant *when*. I'm not thinking straight just now, there's so much going on. His name's Simon.'

'Yeah, Simon.' A nasty thought suddenly appeared in my head. 'What if she wants to patch everything up?'

'Don't be daft, she won't want to do that. That's not how Laura's brain works.'

I wasn't so sure. 'I've learned quite a lot about how your

wife's brain works in the last few weeks, Nathan, and I don't like it. She's had her fun, she's won the battle and she won the war. Maybe she's missing you. It's amazing how attractive a person can suddenly become when someone else wants them.'

Nathan leaned over and kissed me. I couldn't help but respond. 'I don't think so, Kat. In fact, I won't meet with her. I'll just ignore her.'

I sat back and appraised him, taking in his lovely features, his sad blue eyes that always appeared to be filled with regret. He reminded me of a little puppy.

Puppies pee on the floor and chew up the sofa.

'Shhh.'

'I didn't say anything.'

'I know. I wasn't talking to you.'

'Oh, okay.'

Perhaps circumstances had intensified everything, but I knew that I couldn't ever truly be happy unless I knew for certain that I had Nathan all to myself. There'd always be his children, of course, but I could cope with that. What I couldn't deal with would be the spectre of Laura hanging over us. 'No, don't ignore her. Reply and meet with her if that's what she wants. You need to be sure you want to be with me. I can't cope otherwise. I'd rather be alone than always wondering if you're thinking about her and hankering.'

'Hankering?'

'Yeah, hankering. That's my word for the day. Just go and

see what she wants and ...' I paused and gazed into his eyes '... and make sure you know what and who *you* want.'

Nathan pulled me close and we kissed passionately, desperately even. Tears poured from my eyes and he kissed them gently away as we made our way into my tiny untidy bedroom and got naked again. That meant no brunch with Hayley. I'd text her later.

*

Eventually I drove to Hayley's in the afternoon. My mind had morphed into a dreamlike state, thinking about everything that I had going on, and I discovered with alarm that I'd managed to negotiate thirty-five miles of motorway, an A road, about twelve streets and park outside her flat without remembering any of it. I shook myself out of it, locked her car and pressed the buzzer.

'Is that my chauffer?' the tinny voice asked.

'No, it's the maid. Would you like me to turn down your bed?'

'Oh, yes, please, I'll let you in.'

I hugged Hayley, went into her living room and plonked myself on her couch. She disappeared for a minute and returned with wine. 'Hayley, it's only five o'clock.'

'Never too early for wine.'

'I've not had anything to eat.'

'I'll order some Chinese.'

'I need to tell you about Nathan first.'

'Okay, let's talk about our men.' She said 'men' in a deep caveman-type voice, which made me giggle.

'We spent all day yesterday in bed.'

'Aww, sweetie, is he still not well?'

'Oh, no, he's fine. He got lots of exercise.'

'Oh, I see, you little minx.'

'Minx? Now, there's a word I've not heard for a long time.'

'Well, here's another word – ex-wife.'

'Is that not two words?'

'I don't know, it might be, but guess who's refusing to agree to a divorce?'

'Now let me think ... Mrs Cochrane.'

'How did you guess? You must be psychic.'

'She probably doesn't trust lawyers any more. I've got problems with one of them now as well.'

'Lawyers?'

'No, ex-wives.'

'Is she refusing to divorce Nathan?'

'I don't know. Maybe; he's meeting up with her later ... at her request.'

'Well, given the events of recent days I wouldn't worry too much. She's probably wanting him to sell the flat and give her money.'

'Oh, yeah, I hadn't thought of that. I thought maybe she wanted him back.'

'Well, that's always possible, I suppose. You know what us women are like, always changing our minds.'

'Thanks, that's cheered me up no end.'

'Well, that's what happens when we get mixed up in messy relationships.'

'What's James's wife's name again?'

'April.'

'Oh, yeah, so it is. Do you not think it's a little strange calling someone after the month they were born in or the place they're conceived, you know, like Madison or Bognor Regis?'

Hayley topped up my glass. 'Maybe not Bognor Regis.'

'You never know. If my parents had followed that trend I'd have been called "Toyota Corolla" but, given what they ended up calling me, that might have been a decent trade-off.'

'Really? I never know if you're serious or not.'

'No, my dad told me – a bright green Toyota Corolla the year after he started working at the university.'

'Why would he tell you that?'

'You know what my parents are like.'

Hayley nodded. 'The strange thing about April, though, is that her birthday's in September.'

'Really? Weird. Anyway, enough about ex-wives – how are you and James doing after the incident?'

'Okay. It did put a dampener on things, but I still like him.'

'Like, not love?'

'Not love, not yet at any rate, too many uncertainties. What about Nathan – has he proposed yet?'

'Don't be silly. The only person that's ever proposed to me

is my dad's friend Bob, on Christmas Eve three years ago, but he'd been very drunk, so I don't think he'd remember. In any case he'd only want to marry my tits.'

'I don't think that's legal.'

'No, probably not.'

Hayley poured more wine; it hadn't even reached six o'clock yet and I felt decidedly tipsy. I had to remember I had work tomorrow and the Sunday train service wasn't great.

'If Nathan's wife gets him to sell the flat, he'll have nowhere to live. He might want to move in with you.'

I thought about that. 'I could cope for a short while, but my flat's a little on the titchy side. We could rent something bigger, I suppose. We'd have to if he ever gets access to his daughters.'

'What about James – where's he living?'

'At his brother's, though he spent last night here.'

'You little minx.'

Hayley laughed.

'What's he up to today?'

'Having another showdown with April.'

'Right, so while our boyfriends are away spending some quality time with their wives what shall we get up to?'

Hayley started giggling and I followed soon after.

Chapter 28

Nathan had agreed to meet Laura at their flat. She'd been staying at her mother's over the weekend and the girls were still there, meaning they could have some space to talk. She also needed to get some more clothes for the kids.

'Thanks for meeting, Nathan. I know you didn't have to.'

'No, I did. I needed to see you to try and get to a place where we can at least have a conversation without screaming at each other, for the girls' sake if nothing else.'

Laura nodded. Nathan noticed tears pooling in her eyes and she flapped her hands in front of her face to try and fan them away. He sighed. He hated it when women cried; he never knew what to do.

'There's a very thin line between love and hate and it's very easy to cross backwards and forwards over that line in a relationship like ours, Nathan.'

Nathan snorted. 'Yeah, and I know which side I'm on now.'

'You nearly killed our children, Nathan. I'm still not sure I'm finished dealing with that yet.'

'It was an accident, Laura. Very scary and I feel terrible about it but, in the end, everyone is fine, thank God, and it *was* an accident.'

'One that wouldn't have happened if you'd behaved normally. Instead you had to drag them away from me. I can't believe you let that weirdo steal my children, Nathan.'

'What are you on about? She never stole anything.'

'Oh, really? Whose idea was it to get the camper van?'

'Motorhome.'

'Whatever. It was *her* idea, wasn't it?'

'Well, yeah, I suppose.'

'And it was *her* idea to snatch the girls back instead of behaving like a normal sane person and sitting down and talking about it rationally?'

'You didn't want to talk about it, Laura. You said I wouldn't get to see them for months—'

'Weeks.'

'You said weeks *or* months.'

'And you automatically assumed the worst, as usual. So, I say again, whose idea was it to snatch the children?'

'Well ...'

'Yeah, it would've been *her*. Sorry, Nathan, you don't have the imagination.'

'That's not fair. She's been great with the girls and they really like her.'

'She's got the girls being all naughty. They want to go outside and get dirty all the time.'

Nathan stifled a laugh.

'And then you all did that TV thing. That really, really pissed me off. At that point I started listening to Simon's lawyer and started the process of getting you completely excluded from the girls' lives. Up until that point my thinking had been that I wanted you to have access to them whenever you wanted, eventually, but it all changed after that little episode aired. Whose idea would that have been? As if I couldn't guess.'

'Well, her friend's, I think.'

'I think you can see a pattern here, Nathan. That girl's not good for you. She's devious, and full of terrible ideas that put both my girls and you in harm's way.'

'You haven't explained what you think she'd gain by being nice to the girls.'

'Well, for a start she'd get you on her side and then maybe as time went on ... I bet she's broke. I don't think working in a morgue pays all that well.'

'How do you know she works in a morgue?'

'Millie told me.'

'Why is everything down to money with you?'

'It is with most people, Nathan, just not you. She'd get to move into a nice flat and—'

'She says she hates our flat. That it's in Dumbiedykes.'

'It's in Holyrood.'

'That's what I told her.'

'She probably wants you to move, buy a little place that she can put her own stamp on – can you imagine what her taste would be like, all dark and creepy Halloween Land?

Makes me wince just thinking about it. Then she'd turn our beautiful little girls into messy punk-type things—'

'Goth, she's Goth, and I don't think it's hereditary.'

'Doesn't matter, that'd be her plan. I can tell from what the girls have already told me about her and how they've been behaving since they met her, and that'll just be phase one.'

'I think you're overreacting here, that—'

'Am I? Well, stage two would be marrying you, then she'd have a ready-made little family. How else could a girl like that snare a nice man and have children?'

'Kat's beautiful. She'd have no problems finding anyone. She's—'

'She's a freak, Nathan. She's what? Thirty-something—'

'Twenty-nine.'

'Whatever, she looks older and yet still dresses and behaves like a moody teenager. That's not the sort of role model I want for my girls. She would've known that and that's why she decided to snatch the kids away from me. She'd know I'd never allow you access to them with her around.'

'You're just twisting everything, Laura. You were the one who decided that I couldn't see them. You never once mentioned anything about Kat.'

'I didn't know how she'd wormed her way into your life at that point, did I? Don't you think it's odd that she wants to go out with someone she found in the morgue? I wouldn't be surprised if she'd been interfering with you while you were lying in there dead or asleep or whatever the hell you were. She probably makes a habit of it.'

'She wouldn't do stuff like that. Don't be horrible.'

'How do you know? They're probably all freaks in there. Imagine working with dead people all day and night. That would make you weird if you weren't weird already.'

'Laura, me taking the girls had nothing to do with her. I discovered that I might be able to live without you, but not without my girls. My plan had been to return after a week and you'd hopefully realise at that point that you were wrong to do what you'd done and would let me take them home to Edinburgh. But then it turned into a war and—'

'You lost,' she said triumphantly.

'I did, and you were mean and evil.'

Laura nodded and lowered her eyes. This time the tears came for real, and she let them run down her face. 'I agree. I was so angry at you and at that woman.'

She paused and said in a soft voice, 'I've not been fair on you recently, I know that, so I can't blame you for feeling that way.' She sniffed and dried her eyes with her sleeve. 'I was very young when we met, Nathan. I didn't get to do what other girls my age did. I never got to learn who I really was or who I wanted to be, I just became Mrs Jones and a mother, or, at least, I tried to be a mother.'

'What do you mean "tried"? I've never criticised you in that regard.'

'You didn't criticise but I never really got to be one, not on my terms anyway.'

'What are you talking about?'

'You don't get it, do you? You always stepped in with the girls, doing the fun stuff with them that I should have been doing, like soft-play, swimming, and swing parks etc.'

Nathan thought that over. 'Maybe there's a bit of truth in that, but I just filled the void because you were more interested in work.'

'I wouldn't have had to work so much if you'd earned more.'

'Why does it always come down to money? Why is it so important? And why should I miss my girls growing up? Why should I spend every day locked away in an office somewhere missing everything?'

'Because that's the way the world works, Nathan.' Laura sighed. 'I think it's wonderful you've been so hands-on with the girls, but I paid the price for that. I must admit I'm not the most maternal of women – it's just the way I'm made, I guess. But I really believe that, had I not had to work as hard, we would have had a better family life and consequently a better relationship.'

Nathan sighed. 'What *do* you want, Laura?'

'Something's come up, at work. They want me to return to Edinburgh and run the Scottish operation; there's a lot of investment opportunities in the oil and offshore exploration sector now, what with the low price and oil companies looking for different ways to invest and grow. I know you're not interested in all that, but the fact is that most of the oil-and-gas-related firms are based in Scotland or Scandinavia, so I'd be back in Edinburgh. I'd need to travel to Aberdeen and other places, but for you it would mean the girls would be nearby and you could look after them when I'm working.'

'Cheap childcare?'

'That's mean, Nathan – they're your girls.'

'I know, Laura, and I'm not disagreeing with you, but all you can see is a way for you to work while not worrying about them.'

'Yeah, but it would solve our current impasse, wouldn't you say?'

'It would.'

'There's something else.'

Nathan watched his wife take a deep breath and compose herself. 'I'll be on a much bigger salary, so the plan would be to buy a nice big house somewhere. I've started looking and I'm going to view a few places next week.'

'For you and Oodles and the girls to live in? That'll be nice for you all.'

Laura laughed. 'Yeah, well, there's no Oodles any more.'

'He dumped you when you told him about moving?'

'He doesn't know, and I dumped *him*.' Laura took a deep breath and said while exhaling, 'I had grown quite close to Simon, I don't mind admitting that, but there were certain things that didn't add up.'

'That's probably not good for an accountant. Like what?'

Laura managed a sad smile at his joke. 'He was very keen for us to all get together and be a family. Initially, I liked the idea. I thought I might be able to recreate what you and I had at the beginning; you know, the whole "loving family" thing.'

'That's why you were so keen to have the girls with you?'

'Maybe a little, but I missed them too. It's amazing what you miss when you don't have it any more – you really don't know until it happens. But, yes, the whole idea of starting over with Simon appealed. I don't like being alone.'

'You said you left because you wanted to be on your own.'

'I said I needed space.'

'Are they not the same thing?'

'Not at all. Anyway, even up until the courthouse scene the other day I was keen.'

'That's why you were so angry about me taking the girls – it threatened your little family love-nest with Oodles.'

'I wish you'd stop calling him that.'

'I'll try.'

'Thank you. I suppose that's why I also got angry with Millie – she was threatening the whole plan, but I'm digressing. Oodles ... Simon – you've got me doing it now – egged me on to go on TV and stuff, including the enforcement order. I started to sense that he had an unhealthy obsession with the girls.'

'That's weird, and disturbing.'

'Agreed, but not for the reasons you might think. He's been divorced for five years, but always changed the subject

when I asked him about it. Then after our encounter at
the court, Simon and I went out for dinner, I needed to try
and relax. We had a few drinks and he opened up about
his ex-wife and what had happened.'

Chapter 29

'What happened?'

'He and Sarah, his wife, met at university. They'd been together for five years when they got married – he proposed on holiday in Barbados, sitting in a restaurant overlooking the ocean. How romantic is that?'

'Yeah, lovely, what's that got to do with anything?'

'Sorry, anyway ... yes, so they got married and she fell pregnant almost immediately.'

'Sounds familiar.'

'Well, at least they got married first.'

Nathan smiled. 'Fair point.'

'They had a little girl, Abigail, and they both doted on her.'

'I didn't know he had kids.'

'No, neither did I, until this point.'

'That's not something you generally hide, is it?'

'No. He had his reasons and, looking back now, I can probably see why, but he should have been honest about it.'

Nathan knew his wife well enough not to interrupt at this point. Laura continued.

'Just before she was about to start school, Abigail developed a condition called abdominal neuroblastoma, effectively a rare form of cancer. They caught it early but, even so, it spread and, to cut a long and very painful story short, she died six months later, in her mother and father's arms at home.'

Nathan thought about his own children. 'Poor man.'

Laura sniffed back some tears. 'Yeah. He and his wife split up soon after. I'm not sure many marriages could survive that but thankfully I'm not in a position to judge.'

'And you dumped him after he told you that?'

Laura smiled. 'Not precisely at that moment, no. I'm not quite that heartless despite what you think of me, but the next day I explained that I didn't think his obsession with my girls was healthy.'

'What did he say?'

'He wasn't happy, but he understood my point of view, and acknowledged he was trying to recreate something that he'd lost.'

'Isn't that what you were trying to do?'

She nodded. 'Exactly. Not healthy, whichever way you look at it.'

Nathan tried to think that through, but could only feel pity and sympathy for Oodles. It didn't matter how much money you had, some things just couldn't be bought.

Then Laura dropped her bombshell. 'Nathan, despite all our troubles, I've decided to take you back. I want us to start over.'

319

Nathan was stunned and stared open-mouthed at the woman who remained his wife (just). 'What?'

Laura smiled sadly and pushed a stray hair away from her face, tucking it behind her ear. 'I want you back. I want us back – together as a family.'

Nathan couldn't believe it. 'What about all that's happened over the last few weeks ... the last few months? And all the stuff like: "we're broken, we can't be fixed, I need my space and my husband is evil"?'

'I don't think I ever said you were evil and I've had some time to think.'

'Some time to shag, you mean?'

Laura at least had the decency to blush. 'Don't tell me you've not laid a finger on your punk girl.'

'Goth, she's a Goth.'

Laura shook her head. 'Goth, punk, vampires, they all dress bloody weird so what's the difference? Anyway, she'd have been all over you when you were away together. It'd have been part of her plan.'

'We had the girls with us.'

'You're saying you've not slept with her?'

Nathan didn't speak. Laura smiled. 'See, got you. Anyway, it doesn't matter what we've both done, I want us back together, but this time, before you say anything, it'll be different. Especially now we can live somewhere nicer and money won't be such an issue.'

Nathan remembered what Kat had said. 'Is all this because somebody else wants me? You've realised that maybe I'm not such a bad person if someone else is interested?'

'Nathan, I found it very hard to live with you. It's true, part of that maybe could be put down to you not earning enough money to provide the sort of things I thought I needed. Then, after spending time with Simon, who's wealthy but what he needs money can't fix, I realised that what you are is genuine.'

'Genuine?'

'Yeah, genuine. Simon wasn't genuine; nobody I work with is genuine. They're all too wrapped up in themselves – you don't even notice yourself. I know that doesn't sound very good, but what I mean is that all your focus is outward to the girls, me – whoever. You don't need anything, really. You don't know how nice and attractive you are – you hardly ever look in the mirror.'

'I look in the mirror every morning when I shave.'

'That's not what I mean. Anywhere we went, Simon would stop and look at himself. I would too, and when we were together Simon would want to stop and look at us as a couple or as a family group with the girls in shop windows, in mirrored lifts – you get the picture?'

'I think he needs some professional help.'

'Probably, but with you, there's none of that, and that's why I fell in love with you all those years ago, and over time I lost sight of what really mattered and what I had. You wear your heart on your sleeve and I didn't realise how special that is. You're a bit like blood.'

'Sorry?'

'Well, I don't like the sight of blood, I don't like the smell of it very much, but I can't survive without it.'

'That's the sort of thing Kat would come out with.'

'Well, maybe we've got more in common than you think. The thing is, Nathan, I'm the mother of your children – we are a family, no matter what else is going on. I believe now that's what we all need to be again. We need to be a family. That way we can all heal together.'

'In a nice big house somewhere?'

'In a nice big house somewhere.'

'I'm in love with Kat.'

'I don't think you are or you wouldn't be here.'

'I only came because she told me to.'

'Why?'

'She needed to be sure that I wanted to be with her.'

'She's a lot brighter than I gave her credit for. Maybe she does love you, that's why she told you to come – she wants you to be happy no matter the cost to her. That's what love truly is.'

'How would you know that?'

'I sacrificed my youth for you, Nathan, I gave away those years to be with you, so I know. I also gave up Simon to be with you, and, despite his issues, that's still a big step for me. I promise this time it will be different. I've been away from you and what we had, and I now know how valuable and unique that is. I will really work hard to be the sort of wife you want, the sort of wife I used to be.

It'll be easier because we both know what's at stake this time. As much as I tried to forget about you, I couldn't; you still haunt my dreams and, whether I like it or not, there's something about you that pulls me back. I know you feel it too. I can tell just by looking at you and by the way you look at me.'

'Laura, there used to be a time when I was so crazy head over heels in love with you that if I'd owned the world I'd have given it to you just to see the smile of utter joy the gift would bring. I loved you totally and unconditionally but that wasn't enough for you. Some people are lucky enough to find someone they adore and want to be with forever, most never do. I thought I had found nirvana with you, but I hadn't because total love wasn't enough for you. You needed more stuff.'

'Stuff?'

'Stuff.'

'I'm not going to argue with you, Nathan. I'm not proud of myself, but then I still think I did the right thing. I needed to get away for a while to see what life would be like without you and I now realise that I made a mistake, but I wouldn't have known that if I hadn't gone so in a way it makes sense, maybe not to you, but to me.

'The thing is, Nathan, I'm offering you a chance to be with your girls. Yes, I'm part of the deal. It may be not the kind of deal you wanted, but it's the best you're going to get. After all the publicity and carry-on everyone in the country is on my side.'

'I'm not so sure, Laura. James Cochrane did a pretty good job of putting my side of the argument across, with the help of Dads for Daughters.'

Laura shook her head slowly. 'He did until you crashed the bloody camper van. After that I'm afraid everything shifted back my way. You can tell that from what happened at court.'

'I don't know what happened in court.'

'Well, you know the result of it. What I'm saying is that I'll get custody and all you'll ever get to be is a part-time dad. Then one day I'll meet someone else and you might not even get to be that. I'm offering you ... us ... something better than that.'

She stepped into his space and drew close to him. She could sense the heat, the attraction born from shared experience, familiarity and the bond of family. He didn't move. She reached up, took his face in her hands and kissed him. At first, he didn't respond ... then he did.

Chapter 30

Hayley and I had just finished Chinese roast pork, fried rice and an extra portion of bean sprouts. Well, if I was being honest, Hayley had mainly eaten rice and bean sprouts and about two bits of pork and I'd devoured the rest. My recent shagging marathon had certainly worked up an appetite.

James had just phoned to say he was on his way over and needed a drink or six after battling with April most of the afternoon. She'd moved her builder boyfriend into the marital home and was in no rush to move things on with the divorce. Issuing a complaint against Hayley was an attempt at delaying things, in James's view, but Hayley said that her firm, given the complaint, were likely to work even harder in his favour now.

'I'll head off soon, Hayley. I've got early shifts for the next four days.'

'James won't bite, you know,' Hayley said, smiling.

'I know, I'm just not comfortable with him yet.'

I decided to phone Nathan to see how he'd got on

with Laura. I was a little surprised he'd not called already, considering he'd met up with her hours ago.

I dialled his number and waited. I was just about to hang up when it answered. 'Nathan, Kat here, what's happening? I thought you'd have called me by now.'

Silence.

'Nathan, Nathan, are you there?'

'Hello, Kat.'

My heart seized, and my stomach lurched at the sound of a female voice. I'd only heard Laura speak a few times, but I recognised her dulcet confident tone. It took me a moment to respond. Why on earth would Laura have his phone? Then it occurred to me that he'd probably forgotten it and she'd found it and answered it. That would explain the delay too.

'Err, is Nathan there?'

'No, he's in the shower.'

Why would he be having a shower? He only went to talk to Laura about getting divorced.

'Why's he in the shower?'

'Nathan likes to have a shower after making love, I'd have thought you'd have found that out by now.'

Making love ... shower ... what was she saying? 'Laura, I ... I'm not sure I understand.'

'I'd have thought it would be pretty obvious, even for you. Nathan and I are back together, we're a family again. I'm sure he'll want to phone and speak to you at some point, but right now we're a little busy so I'm sure you'll understand if I don't stay and chat.'

Dead air.

I noticed Hayley staring at me. 'What's wrong? You've gone chalk white.'

I couldn't explain and, unfortunately, spilled my nearly full glass of red wine onto Hayley's couch as I rushed off to the toilet feeling sick.

*

I must have looked a mess; well, more of a mess than usual as even Sid reacted to my panda eyes and red nose.

'What's wrong?'

'Nothing.'

'Strangely enough I don't believe you. Has someone died?'

Our default setting could be put down to the fact that we worked in a morgue and were all obsessed with death, or perhaps we were all obsessed with death, which was why we worked in a morgue; whichever way round it was, death remained our first port of call in a crisis.

'Nobody's died, Sid. I just broke up with Nathan, or rather he's broken up with me.'

'What? The zombie's dumped you?'

I nodded and snivelled.

'Has he gone back to his wife?'

I nodded and snivelled.

'Oh.'

That was the nice thing about Sid. He would be the only one *not* to say, 'I told you so.'

'I told you that might happen.'

Okay, maybe not, then.

I felt incredibly stupid and embarrassed as well as hurt at that point. Everybody including Sid had warned me about what might happen. Even my dad had cautioned me, for God's sake, and he knew next to nothing about anything outside his work and sheds and, now, llamas.

'I feel so stupid, Sid. Everybody could see it coming except me. Why is that?'

I knew Sid would be completely unqualified to answer the question, which was why I asked him, but he surprised me.

'I don't know, maybe you had love blinkers on.'

'Love blinkers?'

'Yeah, you know how racehorses wear blinkers some-times?'

My knowledge of racehorses was somewhere close to my knowledge of quantum physics, but I didn't want to appear more stupid than I already felt. 'Yeah, maybe, I think so.'

'Well, that's what happened to you. You had love blinkers on that only let you see a little bit of the big picture.'

'What do I do now, Sid?'

'Well, we've got a post-mortem in fifteen minutes. You need to get the Kugel instrument box, which—'

'Not about work, Sid, about my life?'

'I don't know.'

Sid wandered off to get the instruments himself.

*

'Can you hand me the enterotomy scissors, please, Kat,' Sid said, wiping some gunk from his gloves. I reached behind me and passed them over.

He waved the scissors at me. They were nail scissors, more to the point my nail scissors. Why did Sid have my nail scissors in his hand? Then I remembered, I'd left them lying out earlier after snipping off a raggedy nail. I really needed to focus. As I watched they slipped from his fingers and disappeared inside our patient, slipping down behind the large intestine.

'It's okay,' Sid reassured me. 'I'll retrieve them in a minute.'

'Yeah, well, I'll probably need to buy some new ones now.'

He made a few quick cuts then stopped, and said, 'We need a break.'

'I'm fine, let's finish this then'

'No, I need a break. It feels like I'm doing twice as much work today – your head is somewhere else.'

I sighed and we both changed out of our 'greens' and washed up.

'I take it you're thinking about the zombie?' Sid asked.

I smiled. 'You really shouldn't call him that, but you're

right, I am. I can't believe how stupid I've been. I know I need to snap out of it. He's back with his wife and kids and I'm sure he's happy now. I ... well, I was a distraction, I think.'

I'd known it would be complicated when Nathan met up with Laura. Saying goodbye was never like it was in books or in the movies; it was never a clean break. It was messy, complicated and full of false starts and broken promises. The promises to yourself you broke being the worst of all.

I should have guessed that breaking up with someone he'd been with for that long, would be fraught with danger. Laura was his 'first love' and a big plus on her side was that she was normal – a total and complete bitch but, apart from that, normal in terms of the way everyone, including Nathan, looked at her.

I couldn't be like that. My outlook on life and everything was different, skewed. I'd been called a freak, spat at, had things thrown at me more times than I could count and, although it still bothered me, I'd developed a thick skin and learned to live with it. I'd never adopted a Goth persona to get attention. I'd done it to avoid attention, to avoid having to deal with people. I used it as a mask and it worked, most of the time.

Sometimes people looked at me and instantly formed an opinion. Working with the dead seemed to be an apt occupation according to those who judged me purely on appearance and what little they understood about Goths. The world at large didn't understand me; not that I looked for sympathy – I didn't want or need any – but I wanted Nathan so much it physically hurt. I felt sick when I thought about him meeting up with Laura; I supposed this was what they meant in songs and books about love hurting. I felt physically nauseous.

It even hurt me to think that I might not get to see Nathan's girls again. That surprised me, but they were so lovely and so vulnerable that I found it impossible not to love them. Also, they didn't judge me at all. They were intrigued by my appearance but apart from that they just accepted me. Millie had watched me put my make-up on one morning in the motorhome and asked lots of questions. Nathan too in his own way could be very childlike. He also tended to live very much in the present, which I thought was unusual for an adult. I was pretty sure this was one of the main reasons I liked him – he looked at me with the same eyes that his girls did. When we met he didn't judge me, didn't question me (much) and didn't go and Google 'Goth' to see what it was all about.

Did Nathan truly love me enough to want to be with me regardless of everything?

Obviously not, you silly cow, my inner voice piped up.

'I didn't ask you.'

He'd tried to phone me numerous times yesterday, but I hadn't answered and then I'd blocked him altogether, so he couldn't even text me. He'd hurt me enough.

I became aware of Sid speaking.

'You're talking to yourself again and, if you want my opinion, he's the one losing out. In my experience you don't get many chances in life to fall in love and when you do you need to grab it with both hands.'

I wondered about that, and the fact that Sid seemed to know more about love than me. 'When did that happen to you, Sid? It sounds like you're talking from experience.'

He finished scrubbing his hands and said, 'Let's get some coffee.'

The staff café had plenty of spare tables at this time of the morning and Sid chose a quiet corner. As it was my turn to buy coffee and buns I fished about in my bag for some change and then sat opposite him. He appeared to be distracted, very unusual for Sid.

'I'm sorry about my last question. I didn't mean to pry but, well, you know what I'm like. I just say the first thing that comes into my head most of the time.'

He looked up and smiled. 'I know, with you, there's no shades of grey, everything is black and white – mostly black.' He smiled at me.

'Nathan said that as well.'

'Sorry. In any event, my life is never that straightforward.'

'I suppose not. It can't be easy being gay.' There, I'd said it at last.

Sid almost dropped his coffee cup and stared at me, wide-eyed and slack-jawed.

Oops. 'Foot in mouth Kat' had done it again. I glanced around me quickly and noted nobody had been near enough to overhear. 'It's okay, Sid. I'll never breathe a word about it to anyone. Your secret's safe with me.'

Sid closed his mouth, took a big slug of coffee then said quietly, very quietly, 'I'm not gay.'

Still in denial. 'Well, okay. If you say so; but honestly it makes absolutely no difference to me if you are or not.'

'Yeah, I know, and that's the problem.'

'I don't understand.'

'No, I know you don't. That's part of the problem too.'

'Sid, I'm not following any of this.'

'No, I don't expect you to but I'm not gay.'

'But you've not had a girlfriend as long as I've known you.'

Sid remained silent for a minute, staring into his mug, then he said, almost whispering, 'That's because I've been in love with you, you doughball.'

The sentence didn't register with me initially, so I simply said, 'I don't like doughballs.'

'Well, I love them, and I love you.'

It took a little time, but when someone said they loved you and that person was someone you'd believed to be more camp than Butlin's it was hard to process.

'I don't understand. When did that happen, Sid?'

'From the first minute I saw you I've been smitten; whenever my rota is down to work with you I can't sleep properly the night before. Whenever I'm near you my hands shake – which is not a great thing when you're holding a razor-sharp scalpel or a buzz-saw. The highlight of my day is when you and I get to sit like this in the café and talk. Just being near you is enough to make my heart sing.'

What was it with men and singing hearts, for God's sake? 'I don't know what to say, Sid. I honestly had no idea. I ...' I shut up because my head was buzzing again and I really didn't know what to say to this lovely, kind and warm human being opposite me.

'I'm just a boy standing—'

'No, not the *Notting Hill* line, Sid, anything but that.' We both started laughing as I saw the mischievous smirk on his face. He knew I hated that line with a vengeance, ever since Dr Dave had used it on me the day I'd decided to break up with him.

'I ... this is a huge surprise, Sid. I really don't know ... I need time to think about everything. You've just dropped this on me and there's so much else going on ...'

'It's sudden for you, I know, but not for me and, well, I suppose the only reason I told you is because you looked so miserable and I kind of know how you're feeling.'

Ouch. It suddenly occurred to me that all the times I'd been gushing about Nathan, Sid had had feelings for me and every mention of his name must have been ... well, irritating at best.

We sat in silence, not unusual for us, but less comfortable than it normally was. I recalled all the conversations we'd had over the last few years and the too-many-to-count offers of, 'Let's go out and get pissed,' or, 'What you doing on Friday, Kat? Fancy a few beers?' I'd just thought he'd been bored or trying to be nice.

Eventually we both trudged back downstairs to work. We had a cadaver lying with a gaping chest cavity and had to get that sorted and stowed away before anyone noticed.

As we were finishing up Sid said, 'Kat.'

'Yeah?'

'I know things are a bit confusing for you right now and I don't want to make it worse. I only told you what I did this morning because, well, I ... I hoped it would make you feel better. Also we're not down to work together again until next week.'

'Thanks, Sid, I appreciate that.'

'I don't want it to affect our friendship.'

I needed to process that. Sid blurted out that he had secretly been in love with me for years and got palpitations whenever he was near me. During this time, I'd believed he'd been a closet homosexual (that was more my fault than his but, given his camp nature and lack of female relationships, I didn't think I'd made an unreasonable assumption). Then he chose the day after I'd discovered my boyfriend had had sex with his wife to tell me (that last bit sounded weird even to me).

'Your timing could have been better, Sid.'

'Could it? Sorry, I just thought that ... well, it might make you feel better knowing there are other people, me for one, that think you're wonderful ... Even if the walking dead doesn't.'

I couldn't help smiling.

'Listen, why don't we go out for a drink on Friday after work, just to see ...'

'See what?'

'Well, to see if we get on.'

'We know we get on; we've got on for years.'

'That's not what I mean.'

'I know, and I'm not sure. It feels weird; maybe it's just too soon.'

'I've liked you for years.'

'Not too soon for you, too soon for me after the Nathan thing, you know?'

Just a drink, nothing else, but at least I can sit and talk to you for the first time knowing that you know instead of me wondering if you know and guessing you probably *don't* know because, well, you never told me you know. But now that you do know might you consider, if everything I did pleased you, then, well, you know, might I become your ... err, boyfriend?'

'That's the most romantic thing anyone's ever said to me, Sid.'

'There's no need to be sarcastic.'

'Strangely enough, I wasn't.'

'That's sad.'

'I know.'

Chapter 31

'I don't think that's such a good idea,' Hayley advised over the phone an hour later. 'Your track record with doctors is not good.'

'Sid's nothing like Dr Dave; he doesn't have a bad bone in his body.'

'I know you've had a shock with Nathan. I can still see it on my sofa ...'

I cringed. 'I know, sorry about that. I'll ...' I didn't know what I'd do '... come over and clean it at the weekend,' I offered brightly.

'No need, sweetie, I got white wine on it almost immediately so it's only a slight stain now. I'll get the Marigolds on again later and I've bought some new bubble-gum scented cleaner that I want to try out.'

'That's the sort of thing my mum would say.'

'God forbid. I'm not worried about my sofa. I *am* worried about you, though. I know what you're like when you're suffering from anxiety and stress and it's not pretty.'

'You're saying I'm not pretty?'

'You're deflecting me again; Kat, I care about you.'

I sighed. 'I know you do, Hayley, but I'm fine. Well, I'm not fine, of course I'm not, but going out with Sid will—'

'What's his real name again?'

I tried to remember; I'd become so used to calling him Sid. 'Umm ... David Ingles.'

'Oh, no, you're joking – not another Dr Dave.'

'He's not another Dr Dave ... well, he is ... but not like the last one.'

'Please think about it, Kat. It probably won't end well. Don't you think that if you had a thing for him you'd have known by now?'

'I thought he was gay, so I didn't know that I *could* have had a thing for him.'

'Right, but even still ...'

'We're only going for a drink.'

'I've heard that before. You're hurting and vulnerable; he'll try to take advantage.'

He wouldn't take advantage of me; he couldn't. I was a grown woman with willpower and control. Besides, he wasn't that sort of bloke, well, at least I didn't think so. 'I've been out with him loads of times and he's not tried anything.'

'But this time it's a date. It's different.'

'I don't think it's a date, is it?'

'You tell me.'

'Well, it might be a little date, I suppose, but it'll do me good to get out of the house.'

'Just be careful.'

*

I met Sid just outside Blue Yonder, a little bar tucked away down one of Edinburgh's back streets, a regular haunt of ours and of other hospital staff, being only ten minutes from the infirmary.

We shared a bottle of wine and nibbles and it didn't feel strange at all, but then Sid had been very clever coming here as it felt just like another work's night out. What usually happened was that we'd start out with a group of maybe eight or nine and over the evening this would get whittled down as those with boyfriends, girlfriends or maybe both headed off until usually only the two of us were left.

'I used to like it when everybody else buggered off and left us on our own,' Sid said, almost reading my mind.

'I just thought you were a saddo like me.'

'I am.'

We chatted for a while and it felt good, no pressure, no trying to impress each other and no mention of Nathan. We'd finished the wine and all the nibbles, so what now?

I felt comfortable sitting beside Sid. That, in itself, presented something of a problem, as I shouldn't be that comfortable. I had no twitching or itching in my bits, no reaction at all. Not good. I needed more wine.

'What do you want to do now?' asked Sid, probably sensing my restlessness.

'Let's go back to your flat.'

'Well, all right, if you're sure you're happy and—'

'Have you got wine?'

'Yeah, in the fridge.'

'Let's go, then.'

Sid only lived a ten-minute walk away, which was handy as it looked as if it might start raining. He lived in a new-build block within a stone's throw of the hospital. I suspected most of the apartments were owned by hospital staff. It might be quite nice to roll out of bed and be at work in minutes.

He fetched a bottle of wine (Chablis – good choice) and some glasses from the kitchen and I drained my glass in seconds and refilled it quickly.

Sid watched me. 'If you're thirsty I can get you some water or tea or—'

'Can I kiss you, Sid?'

'What?'

'Can I kiss you – you know, the bit where we press lips together?'

I took his dopey smile as permission and leaned over, pulled his head towards me and kissed him, hard. I shoved my tongue into his mouth and waited for some bit-twitching to happen.

Nope, nothing.

What the hell was wrong with me?

I pulled his hands up and got him to touch the back of my neck, which always drove me crazy.

Still nothing.

I pushed him down onto the couch and French-kissed him again, wondering why it got that name, then chastised myself for thinking about anything except Sid. He was eagerly kissing me back so what the hell was wrong with me?

I twisted my head and guided his mouth towards my ear. 'Can you stick your tongue in my ear?'

Zero reaction, shit.

'Right, try breathing.'

'I am breathing.'

'No, in my ear, gasp into my ear.'

He made a humming sound, which only served to remind me of bloody llamas. 'Sid, gasp, don't hum.'

He sounded like a panting Labrador; that was no use at all.

'Right, stop panting.'

'I'm not panting, I'm gasping.'

'Right, this time can you growl like an angry bear?'

'An angry bear?'

'Yeah.'

'I'll try.'

He pushed his lips towards my ear lobe and growled, but it only tickled, nothing more. Time for desperate measures. Right breast, let's see what that does.

I took his hand and slipped it inside my top, into my bra, still nothing. 'Bugger, that's hopeless, kiss me, Sid.'

'I'm sorry, Kat. I'm out of practice.'

'It's not you, it's me.' Did I really just say that?

One last try. I straddled his lap and kissed him long and deep, with his hand now trapped inside my bra and the other stroking the back of my neck. Nothing. I wasn't getting anything, so incredibly frustrating.

I carried on kissing him, wondering if I could just pretend to be turned on whenever we had sex, but quickly realised that wouldn't be fair on either of us. I had to tell him. I pulled back and looked sadly into his eyes.

Here was the perfect man for me. Intelligent, he adored me, wouldn't expect me to be anything I wasn't, didn't have a wife or kids or any other ties and yet I couldn't feel anything – so unfair.

'I'm sorry, Sid. I so wanted to like you, well, I do like you, obviously, but I wanted to *really* like you, but it's just not happening for me.'

The disappointment in his eyes made me feel worse and I wished I could do something to make it work.

'I'm sorry too.' He smiled. 'I was enjoying that, especially the animal impressions.'

'You're such a lovely man and you've got everything going for you and yet ...'

'It's the chemistry thing, isn't it?'

I nodded, tears forming in my eyes.

'Well, there's nothing to be done about that, I'm afraid.'

'Maybe I can take some drugs to make it happen, like female Viagra.'

Sid laughed out loud but it had been a deadly serious suggestion from me. 'Oh, Kat, the chemistry thing's there for a reason. I'm pretty sure it's an evolutionary block designed to make sure that when people have babies there's as big a gene gap between them as possible. That's why they say opposites attract – there's some truth in that. Maybe we're just too close on the evolutionary gene pool.'

I blinked.

A smile formed on his face and he said, 'Or maybe that's a load of bollocks and I'm trying to find a way to make us both feel better.'

'Sid, why are you so clever? I didn't think you were.'

'I've got a medical degree.'

'Yes, I know, but that doesn't mean anything, well, no, that's not true; of course, it means something, but it's not relevant to this, about you knowing stuff.'

'Well, I know you've still got the major hots for the zombie and, knowing you as I do, until you get that sorted you'll not be able to focus on anything.'

Truth be told, I hadn't really been thinking that much about Nathan, which I took to be a good sign, but it might have had something to do with me trying to get my body to want to jump Sid's bones.

'I suppose as a friend I should really tell you to just give up on him; that would be the sensible advice.'

'But that's not what you're going to tell me?'

'I'll probably regret this, so might you, but the problem is, if you're still in love with him it's going to stop you

343

finding anyone else. Take it from someone who knows.'
He smiled at me and I felt incredibly guilty about, well
... everything.

'I'm not sure if you'll even go for this, but to get Nathan
back, assuming you want him back, you need to compete
on a level playing field. You can bet his wife has played
the "weirdo" card with him, saying you're evil or whatever,
and he's maybe not bought into the whole idea, but he's
bought into it enough.'

'You've said that to me before – so you want me to stop
being who I am?'

'Not me, I love who you are.'

'Right.'

'It's only for a little while, tone it down, then once you're
back together you can go back to normal, or not normal,
or whatever ... well, you know?'

'Thanks for being so supportive after what just happened
... or didn't happen.'

'I do have an ulterior motive. I have to work with you
and I need you to be happy and focused or the contents
of your handbag are liable to end up inside random dead
people.'

'It was a pair of scissors.'

'This time, yes, but next it'll be a lipstick, a phone
or your Silver Bullet Vibrator. Then at some funeral, the
service will grind to a halt, as they try to identify where
the strange buzzing noise is coming from.'

I didn't own a Silver Bullet Vibrator but laughed out

loud anyway, knowing he'd chosen humour to try and cover up the awkwardness of the situation. On that note, 'Sid, you can probably take your hand out of my bra now.'

'Aww, do I have to?'

'I'm afraid so. We can't go about like this.'

He removed his hand and I pulled my top straight while Sid went to make tea. Nothing a good cup of tea couldn't fix.

As we sat nursing hot mugs, chatting as if nothing weird had happened, I sensed that I'd lost something important in the last few hours. Not Sid's friendship, but something else. His admiration? Maybe. His respect? Give our antics this evening, probably, but it wasn't that. Then, with a start, I realised: he'd given up on me. Even I'd not managed to do that yet.

Chapter 32

The next morning, I lay soaking in a hot bath, putting together a plan of action in my head.

I needed hair dye. Well, no, first I needed to grab my razor. I shaved my pits and my legs, then examined my arms and considered turning the razor on them, but they weren't that bad ... and I thought perhaps that might be a shave too far.

I turned my attention to my bikini line – well, line might not be the best description; fuzzy bush would be better. I considered getting the wax out and going for a Brazilian, but in the end plumped for a 'Scottish'– wild and untamed.

After getting out of the bath, I dressed and went shopping. I decided to skip the town centre and headed to the shops at the Fort Retail Park instead – it had everything I needed with the added bonus that I could park my car for free.

I stood in Boots for ages staring at dyes. My natural hair colour used to be dark brown, though it had been jet-black for so long I couldn't remember exactly how it looked. I quickly glanced around and, as nobody appeared to be taking much notice, I sucked my tummy in, pulled my jeans and knickers forward slightly and peered at my pubes. They appeared to be black (with the odd alarming grey exception sticking out – why did they do that? And why didn't I notice them in the bath?). In any event, that didn't help. Whilst I was still examining my aging pubic region a sales assistant chirped brightly, 'Is there something I can help you with?'

I quickly let my jeans go and realised that she'd been watching me watching my crotch. I felt like asking her outright, 'What have you got for grey pubes?' but instead smiled sweetly and chirped back, 'Just looking, thank you.'

I picked up an 'ultra-fun blonde' box of hair colourant, which showed a blonde girl (strangely enough) having a great time on roller blades. I couldn't roller blade, skate or ski so I put that one back. I then looked at 'blonde infusion', which showed a blonde girl again and she must have been standing in a wind tunnel as her hair had blown behind her in an almost straight line. I didn't own a wind tunnel, so I put that back as well. Maybe going completely blonde would be too drastic without an extraordinary sense of balance or a force nine gale.

I picked up a box of 'ash'. I assumed they were referring to the colour and that I wouldn't get home to find a pile of cigarette ends in the box, but ultimately I put 'ash' down as I thought a better description would be 'mousy brown'. I didn't want to be mousy anything.

Along at the end of the bewildering line of hair colour-ants a box caught my eye, mainly due to it being half-price – 'dirty blonde'. Well, I figured, if I'm going to be a blonde I might as well be a dirty one. I picked it up, took it to the till and received a strange look from the checkout girl, who almost did a cartoon double-take when she looked at me and my purchase. 'Miss ...' she said, biting her lip. 'I don't think that this will be suitable for you,'

'What do you mean?' I fired back. 'I can go blonde if I want.'

'You can, of course,' she said, 'but it won't work very well with your colour of hair and with the amount of, er ... treatment it's had, you may not get the result you expect.'

'Why, what'll happen?'

'Well, from experience ... not mine,' she hastened to add, 'people with hair like yours that use this type of product tend to get a ... well, a dark shade of green.'

'Green?'

She nodded.

'But it says, "dirty blonde" on the box.'

'It does, but that's not what you'll get.'

'Why doesn't it tell me that?'

'It probably does on the instructions, but most people don't read them properly.'

'So how do I get to be a "dirty blonde"?'

'You'll need to go to a proper salon.'

'How long will that take?'

'I don't know.'

'Bother.'

I left the box of hair colour behind and went to a coffee shop to search for a salon that might have a free appointment. I figured that if I didn't do it today, I might go off the idea altogether. I phoned three, all within a five-minute drive, and bingo, the third one – Tony Wilkinson Associates (which sounded more like a law firm than a hairdresser) – had a cancellation. I gulped my latte and drove there in three minutes. They greeted me apprehensively and when I said what I wanted, Cheryl – who should have been a model – said, 'Well, it can be done, of course, but ...'

'But what?'

'It's complicated. First, we need to bleach out the black dye. This may take two or ...' she peered at my hair and ran a piece of it through her fingers '... or maybe more applications before we even think about the next step. We normally suggest you wait a week before the next stage.'

'I can't wait a week. I want it all done today.'

She called over Tony, one of the directors – who also should have been a model – and explained my request to him. He raised one eyebrow and looked me up and down. 'Are you sure?'

'I'm sure.'

'We've got a new bleaching agent that they developed in Los Angeles – this might be a good time to try it out.'

'I'll be a guinea pig?'

'Kind of, but we'll give you a discount.'

The money didn't overly worry me, but I had to ask, 'How much of a discount?'

'Well, what you want done would usually cost around £180, but we'll do it for £110.'

'What are the possible side effects?'

'Your hair might fall out.'

'Anything else?'

'Is that not enough?'

'Yeah, probably. Okay, let's do it.'

I had to sign some forms and then I spent the next five hours, yes, five hours, moving between numerous chairs and sinks. They applied the LA bleaching agent twice, dye removers, colours, fixers, shampoos, conditioners, enriching agents and protein emulsified water – but not necessarily in that order. I fell asleep at one stage, so they might have added some garlic and oregano while I'd been snoring away.

When I woke up, I found three stylists/models and Tony staring at my hair with worried expressions on their faces. When they realised I'd returned to the land of the living they all dispersed, smiling sweetly at me, and offered more coffee.

Eventually, they declared me done, and relieved me of £110. The transformation was astounding. A stranger peered back at me from the mirror, but I needed to get some other supplies before I could do a proper assessment.

I returned to Boots and scoured the make-up counters for some darker foundation and a few other bits and pieces. Then it was time for clothes.

Now, I wasn't completely unfamiliar with mainstream clothes shops like Topshop, Gap, River Island, H&M, New Look and Oasis as they all did black garments and I'd even been known to make the occasional purchase from M&S (usually underwear). What I hadn't done for a long time (ever?) was buy normal clothes in normal colours. I wandered about for ages before deciding I hadn't a clue.

I watched loads of people walking in and out of the shops, trying to work out what normal looked like, and decided there was no such thing. Then I spotted a poster in River Island's window depicting a model in a blue and white mohair dress with patent pumps (whatever they were) and chunky jewellery. The poster said 'Retro Look' but what clinched it for me was the girl had 'dirty blonde' hair, like me.

I found the rack of mohair dresses and picked my size to try on. Satisfied with the fit, I then rounded up the rest of the items and headed home.

I put on the new foundation and some powder, but before dressing I had my eyebrows to deal with. I was surprised the salon hadn't offered to do something with them but perhaps my head hair had exhausted them. It was fair to say that my eyebrows were not my best feature. If I left them – which I had for a while – they began to resemble the larvae of the Giant Leopard Moth (thanks to Dr Dave for that little nugget of information) and required drastic surgery. I usually got some poor Eastern European girl to thread them at one of the in-shop eyebrow bars.

I was sure they cringed when they saw me coming and wished they could charge double.

Today I had to do it myself and spent ten minutes plucking most of them out, only to pencil them back in again five minutes later, in the ultimate act of futility.

I removed most of my piercings. I left the one in my left nostril, as having a hole in my nose wouldn't be cool. I also extracted my dark earrings and inserted some cheap silver ones in the shape of little butterflies.

I then carefully applied blusher, mascara (no falsies this time), lip-liner and my RockChick Scarlet, deciding today counted as a special occasion.

I brushed my hair a few more times – it felt dry, but I was used to that. I got dressed in my new outfit, slipped on the chunky jewellery and peered at myself in the mirror.

I honestly didn't recognise the alien vision staring back at me. I think I must have been replaced by a robot and hadn't noticed. I was now KAT-BOT and I had to admit my own bot looked hot in this dress.

I'd never been a vain girl, in fact I never knew that I had any kind of sex-appeal (okay, I must have had something, or nobody would ever have come near me) but it felt incredibly weird, as if I'd, somehow, managed to crawl inside someone else's skin.

Despite the pleasant fright I'd given myself I still felt like a fraud. The person staring out at me from the mirror was an imposter designed with the single purpose of trying to woo back the man who'd screwed up my life. The ironic thing was I'd been doing a pretty good job screwing it up myself before he'd come along and added his contribution.

I shook my head and turned away. Wine; I needed some wine. I glanced at the clock, wondering if it had stopped as it only said 4.30 p.m. It felt much later than that. Screw it. I opened some Pinot Grigio anyway and returned to toast my new image in the mirror. 'Dirty blondes have more fun.' I laughed, raising the glass to myself.

Two glasses later it dawned on me that I could no longer take my car. 'Shit.' Oh, well, public transport it would have to be. I had one more glass and slipped on the white cashmere cardigan I'd bought to go with the dress and headed out, slightly tipsy, into the humid evening.

The sky had darkened a little, but rain didn't look likely, though with my luck I'd end up drenched and bedraggled before I even got to the bus stop.

Due to roadworks and diverted buses I had to go into town and change to get back out to Holyrood. I ended up walking a little way along the very busy Princess Street and got more stares than I normally did, which I found strange. Were they looking at me because I'd got my make-up all wrong or something else? I clocked that it was mainly men staring at me so quickly dismissed the make-up idea. Perhaps I'd tucked my dress into my knickers, but a quick check reassured me I hadn't done that either.

I now had a little insight as to how Hayley must feel all the time – eyes on stalks.

I took the bus to within a street of Nathan's apartment,

and walked slowly towards it.. The closer I got, the more I began to realise the major flaws in my plan. Firstly, I didn't even know if he'd be in and, secondly, if Laura answered the buzzer she might not open the door to me. Also, I didn't want to talk to Nathan with her standing supervising.

I paused, crossed the road and stood in the bus shelter opposite his door, staring through the scratched and graffiti-scored plastic. I remained there for ten minutes, with one eye on the entrance and one eye down the road watching out for rapists and robbers, trying to work out what to do next. What the hell had I been thinking, coming down here alone and on foot? Stupid Pinot Grigio.

Then the first drops of rain splattered down onto the shelter roof. Brilliant, just what I needed. Soon the mini-monsoon had turned the street into a stream and my patent pumps were soaked. I huddled into the corner to try and escape the worst of the splashes and noticed a hooded figure rush out of the flat, clamber into Nathan's car, start the engine and drive off.

I'd only glimpsed it, but it looked female, especially the legs – they'd had tights or leggings wrapped around them and boots on so, unless Laura had completely emasculated her husband, she'd left.

I took the opportunity to rush across the road with my cashmere cardigan over my head, discovering why they didn't make cashmere umbrellas, and pressed his buzzer frantically.

Eventually his tinny voice said, 'Hello.'

'Nathan, it's Kat. I've come for my key.'

'Kat, what ...? I've been trying to reach you, to ... well, explain.'

'Nathan, can you open the bloody door? It's pissing down out here.'

'Oh, yeah, sorry.'

As I squelched up his stairs it reminded me of my first visit here, loaded with Sainsbury's bags, but the baggage I carried this time was much more substantial. As I turned the corner of the stairs Nathan opened his door and I watched him visibly start at the sight of me. Hopefully a good sign and not one of total repugnance.

I stopped at the door and locked eyes with him. The stupid Notting Hill line burst into my head and I made it burst right out again *tout suite*.

I waited for him to speak first.

'You look amazing, I can't believe that's you. You're, well ...'

'Normal?'

'Totally gorgeous. Why the change?'

God, men were so dense sometimes but, rather than point out the obvious, I lied as any self-respecting girl would do. 'I felt like a new look.'

He stepped back, and I manoeuvred round him, trying not to notice his scent or the fizz of electricity between us. He closed the door.

I stood awkwardly holding my cardigan away from my body. We both watched as it dripped rainwater onto his carpet. 'Sorry, I seem to make a habit of dripping on your flooring.'

'It's fine.'

We locked eyes. More sparks. Who was I kidding? My body felt like a raging furnace, heat rushed to my face and I could feel my bits twitching like crazy just standing looking at him.

I broke eye contact and peered past him. 'Where are the girls?'

'With their gran. She took them to the cinema, then for something to eat. They'll be back soon. Laura just nipped out, she—'

'Yeah, I saw her leave.'

'Oh.'

'Where's she gone?'

'She needed something for her outfit. She won't be long. She's got a party tonight.'

As much as I didn't want to discuss Laura, I automatically asked, 'Aren't you going?' I had the thought in my head that maybe I could sneak back later after she'd left.

'No, it's a works do. I'd only be in the way of her schmoozing, plus I'd be bored stiff. She recently got promoted and ...'

Well, yippy-doo-dah for Laura, I thought.

'... it means she's moving back up here, so she feels she has to go to these things now. Another reason I don't want to go is because it's a—'

'Wait, she's moving back to Scotland?'

'Yeah.'

The penny dropped. So that was why she wanted everything back to normal, or at least whatever she considered normal to be. The news made my heart drop and I felt slightly sick again and worried for a moment whether I'd heave up my Pinot Grigio onto Nathan's carpet; thankfully, it passed.

'Oh, right. Well, I'd better be going.' No point in hanging around now.

I registered the disappointment on his face and at that point suddenly felt sorry for him. God knew why after the way he'd treated me, but I couldn't get angry with him, not right now, anyway. I remembered James saying to me when we were in the Highlands, 'Anyone devious enough to get old 'silver spoon' Donaldson flustered must be doing something right.' Laura would have got Nathan wrapped around her little finger or maybe wrapped around something else, but I didn't want to think of that right now.

Nathan broke the silence. 'Oh, your key, just a minute.'

He disappeared into the kitchen and quickly returned, holding my key with the black bleeding-skull keyring in his hand. Halfway down the hall, he stopped with a look of horror on his face. It didn't register at first, but I suddenly realised his eyes weren't on me but on something behind me. I reluctantly turned, and it felt as if time had slowed down, like the time we'd crashed the motorhome. The front door had swung open and Laura had stopped on the threshold with a bemused look on her face.

At that very moment all my sympathy for Nathan vanished, and, in its place, I felt anger, anguish and an overwhelming sense of disappointment. Standing before me wasn't the well-groomed, immaculate Laura Jones from my memory and various TV appearances. Somehow Nathan had managed to persuade her to participate in some twisted fantasy. Perhaps this was the price she'd paid to get back into his life. Laura had gone Goth; in fact, no, she hadn't, she'd gone Vamp.

My emotionally charged brain instantly took in all the details. She'd applied a pale foundation with small dark star transfers falling over her left cheekbone down to the nape of her neck. Black eyeshadow had been heavily applied, she had a nose piercing (identical to mine) red streaks in her hair, and a black studded dog collar encircled her long neck. I couldn't see what clothes she'd gone for as they were hidden under her long coat, but I took in the collar of a cape peeping out from the top of the coat, black patent leather knee-length boots, and false nails that extended out at least an inch from her fingertips, painted blood red. She'd really gone for it. All her ensemble lacked were fangs and I'm sure Nathan had them handy in his pocket, so she could chew down his neck, or whatever else, later.

I lunged back to Nathan, snatched my key from his hand, and, with tears pouring from my eyes, barged past Laura and let go of my feelings with a wail that echoed off the walls. I almost fell down the two flights of stairs in my rush to escape the building. I swore I could feel it closing in around me.

I heard Nathan shout, 'Kat, you don't understand ...'

I also heard Laura say, 'That's the punk? Wow, she scrubs up well, doesn't she?'

I burst out of the front door into the continuing monsoon and ran along the street. Tears gushed from my eyes; the combination of them and the streaming rain meant I could hardly see where I was going, which didn't matter much as I didn't care. I just had to put some distance between me and that ... what could I call him?

Then it came to me: SMACKTARD.

Smacktard? my inner voice asked. *What's a smacktard?*

I couldn't believe I'd started an argument with myself about this.

'SMACKTARD, (all capital letters, thank you very much, if you don't mind). Do you not remember playing that old battlefield game on the computer? The one where these total idiots wander randomly into your gun sights on the battlefield, utter the immortal word 'DUH' and get blown away? They were called SMACKTARDs. And it describes what I'd like to do: give him a big smack.'

Why didn't you?

'His wife was there.'

You could have smacked her as well.

'They're not normal.'

We're not normal either.

'We are not a *we* – we are a *me*, in case you hadn't

noticed. And normal people don't get their wives to dress like their girlfriends to get over them.'

Right.

I didn't like the tone of that 'right'.

Sorry.

'Better. You should be on my side. We can think up another name, if you like?'

No, no, Smacktard is fine.

I sprinted down the road, oblivious to the rain, shouting, 'SMACKTARD, SMACKTARD, SMACKTARD,' at the top of my voice.

At a nearby bus stop an old lady, who bore more than a passing resemblance to the Queen, right down to the long blue coat, cowered away from me as I screamed past. I slowed down for a moment.

'What if she was the Queen? I mean, Holyrood Palace could only be, what, a mile or so away?'

That's stupid; what would the Queen be doing standing at an Edinburgh bus stop in the pouring rain?

'Do you not remember that film about the Queen and how'd she'd gone walkabout during the VE Day celebrations at the end of the Second World War?'

Yeah, but she'd been young then. She wouldn't do that now.

'Unless she's lost her marbles or one of the corgis.'

No, it wouldn't be the Queen, but if it did happen to be her she wouldn't venture out alone again in a hurry. Not with lunatics like you running along the street shouting strange obscenities.

My inner voice fell silent as I ran into Holyrood Park. The rain seemed to have got heavier, if such a thing were possible, accompanied now by a strong wind that lashed the water off my face and body. Still I ran, I had to get away from him and his wife. He'd made me feel dirty, used and stupid, stupid to the point of humiliation. How they must laugh and take the piss out of me when they rolled around in bed together, Nathan with his wife pretending to be me to spice up their pathetic lives. I wondered if she wore the dog collar in bed. I bet she did, pretending she was the dog known as Kat. 'What a dog Kat is.'

As clever as that sounded, I didn't have time to appreciate it. I was the butt of all their jokes; the man I fell in love with thought I was a joke, a pathetic joke, and the sad thing was he was right because I was a joke. A joke of a person, trying to be something I wasn't, trying to compete with someone I could never compete with – what was I thinking?

Lightning split the sky, followed almost immediately by the cacophony of thunder, a million drums echoing across the rocks and cliffs that now towered above me as I ran along the grass verge. I laughed manically; my mind felt as if it had broken loose from whatever held it together. I could feel the threads of my sanity snapping one by one as I ran. I half wished for lightning to strike the rocks above my head to bring them crashing down onto me to end my pain, or to strike me directly, obliterating me completely so that all that was left would be a smudge on the grass, a dark shadow of human dust that would pretty much sum up the impact I'd made on the world. Nobody would miss me, nobody would care. A total and utter waste of space.

I almost fell as another jagged flash lit up the black clouds. It was dark as night now, the sun having surrendered the sky to the impending apocalypse. I'd made the biggest fool of myself during a storm with Nathan and now even the heavens above were torturing my tormented soul by bringing those memories crashing into my mind like the rolling, rollicking thunder.

I ran faster and faster; I'd lost my shoes but didn't give a damn. Stupid, stupid patent pumps. Who wore patent pumps? Who invented such a stupid name for them anyway? Probably a bloke, and I bet his name was Nathan.

I ran on, across the landscape, with and against the storm, the wind and rain buffeting me along or pushing me back as it twisted and swirled against the primeval background – the extinct super-volcano upon which Edinburgh was built. I yearned for the rain to wash me clean, sluice the filth from inside me so that I could start afresh. I felt infected, infected by a dark sadness that rushed up to my brain and poured from my eyes. I felt drenched with sadness, total and utter despair and self-loathing driving me onward.

The road ahead of me seemed to be totally deserted – clearly only a crazed maniac would venture out in this. I stopped running, leaned forward, bracing my hands on my knees, and cackled; that was me, a crazed, cackling maniac.

I must remember to tell Nathan, so he could incorporate that into his sex games.

I set off again. I thought less when running and right then I didn't want to think; I wanted my mind to go blank, completely blank. My thoughts only hurt me, they stabbed at me, gouged at my insides, made me gasp in pain; I wanted to be dead inside, totally and utterly dead so that nothing could hurt me any more. I felt blackness encroaching my vision – surely it couldn't get any darker – but as the darkness closed in I slowly realised that it had nothing to do with the storm and everything to do with me.

I fell to my knees and pain flashed through my head like the lightning through the air and then a cramp in my stomach forced me lower. I rolled onto my side and ended up curled foetus-like on the grass verge beside the road, watching the rain gurgle into the gutter. My mind had reached its limit; it needed to shut down, reset and heal.

Chapter 33

Iopened my eyes and the gutter had gone, to be replaced by my dad's worried face peering at me. Maybe the last twenty years had simply been an incredibly vivid dream and now I'd woken up as a chastened and wise ten-year-old, but my dad's first words dispelled that notion.

'Kat, what've you done to your hair?'

'Sorry?'

'Your hair.'

Oh, yeah, I'd dyed it. 'Err, I felt like a change. How did I get here?'

'A taxi driver spotted you lying in the park in the rain.'

'What happened?'

'Did someone steal your shoes?'

'What?'

'You had no shoes on. Your mum's really freaked out about that. Your feet are all cut and bruised.'

'How did I get here?' I glanced around; a private side room in a hospital, probably my hospital. I would've got priority because I was staff, not fair, I knew.

'Have you been taking drugs? Wacky baccy? Ploppers? Uppers? Downers? Your mother has already examined your arms for needle marks.'

'Needle marks? That's crazy. What are you on about? I don't even think "ploppers" are drugs.'

'Aren't they? See, you're up on the lingo. Your mother's convinced you're a druggie now.'

'Why?'

'What do you mean why? Someone finds you unconscious in the park and you've gone blonde.'

Suddenly the memories came flooding back and I gasped out a sob.

'Don't get upset, Kat. I'm sure it'll come out in time.'

What had I missed? Did he know about Nathan and Laura? Had I been talking in my sleep?

'What'll come out? What have I been saying?'

'You've not been saying anything. I'm talking about hair dye.'

'Oh, right.' I let the tears flow even though I knew it would make my dad squirm. When I used to bawl as a little girl my dad would shout to my mum and say ...

'Janice, she's crying again.'

Some things never changed. The concerned but distracted face of my mum appeared inside the door.

'She's awake. You never told me she'd woken up.'

'Just this minute, Janice, and now she's crying.'

'Why did you upset her?'

My dad raised his hands in a defensive gesture. 'Nothing to do with me, she just started.'

He backed away from my bed as if tears were infectious and let my mum take his space.

She took my hand in hers and couldn't help herself checking to see if my nails were clean. 'The doctors say you probably fell and banged your head, though they can't find any marks or any injuries apart from on your feet. What were you thinking, going out without any shoes on? Have you been taking things?'

I didn't want to explain about Nathan, I wasn't sure I could at that point, even if I wanted to, so instead I just said, 'I got caught in the open in the storm and, well, I think I had a panic attack and started running. I don't know what happened after that. I just freaked out.'

There was a good sprinkling of truth in my explanation, so I probably came across as genuine. 'That's never happened to me before. I just kept running and running and then, well, the next thing I know I'm here.'

My mum smiled, relieved that I'd not become a junkie. 'A nice taxi driver, Tom Phillips, stopped and phoned for help, then phoned me. He works for Comiston Cheeky Cabs so I'm going to make sure I use them whenever I get a taxi. He could have just left you there, thinking you were homeless, or even taken advantage of you, so you're lucky a gentleman found you. Oh, and that's another thing, he used your phone. Why don't you have a pass code on your phone? Any Tom, Dick or Harry could steal it and access all your things.'

'Well, they didn't, did they? And just as well.'

'That's not the point; you need to be more careful, Kat.'

The last piece of advice I'd take in more ways than one. My parents, happy now that I hadn't become a junkie and wasn't about to die, spent the next ten minutes talking at cross purposes to each other and me, just like old times.

'So, what do you think about llamas, Kat?' my mum asked.

'Well ...' I wracked my brain, trying to remember what my dad had said about them. 'I think they hum ...'

'See,' my mum said triumphantly. 'I told you they'll stink the place out, John.'

'No, they don't hum, they hum ... Hmmm Hmmm.' I tried to explain.

My mum frowned at me as if I were daft. 'Yes, well, you've had a nasty bang on the head.'

'I'm thinking of getting another shed,' my dad announced out of the blue.

'What about the llamas?' I asked.

'They don't have much use for sheds, but I can store their stuff in number two, you know, the one I had my easel and paints in.'

'What stuff do llamas need?'

'Food, oats, hay and things. Oh, and saddles; I'll need to get saddles. You can ride them, you know.'

I pressed my head back into my pillow and closed my eyes, trying to stop the tears from suppressed laughter as I pictured my dad perched on the back of a llama. He'd been horse riding maybe twice in his lifetime. My bed must be shaking but nobody noticed.

'I think you might need planning permission, John,' my mum contributed.

'What, for riding a llama? No, I don't think so, Janice, not in your own garden. I might need a licence if I take it out on the road, right enough.'

I didn't think I could take much more without exploding. 'A llama licence,' I spluttered, then felt two pairs of eyes on me.

'I don't think your daughter is taking your llama idea very seriously, John, and I meant planning permission for another shed, not for riding llamas,' my mum said, smiling.

'Well, she should take it seriously. If it goes well I might rent a field somewhere and expand the operation ...'

I felt my eyes closing, listening to them prattle on, and as I drifted down to sleep I heard my mum say, 'Yes, okay, I'll admit the Leg Spreader is quite tasty, but I still think you should take the picture off the handle. I mean, what would Kat say if she saw it?'

'I already offered her some.'

'John!'

'What? It's only beer ...'

*

They let me home the next day. Strangely enough the same doctor came to see me that signed Nathan ... sorry, Smacktard out. Perhaps he had the dubious honour of

368

being the doctor of faints. He didn't comment on our previous meeting and I assumed he'd forgotten all about me. It only occurred to me later that he probably didn't recognise me with the blonde hair and lack of piercings.

My mum wanted me to go home with her for a few days, but I decided that any convalescing I needed to do wouldn't be helped with her buzzing around in the background polishing my toenails or whatever she decided needing doing.

Back in the peace and solitude of my flat I tried to take stock of things. Nathan had made his bed, so he could lie in it with his wife. I needed to move on; I needed normality. My next shift at work loomed large tomorrow morning and I'd go in. I'd initially planned to take a few days off but somehow my mind had cleared, and I didn't feel that mooching about on my own all day would do me any good. I felt the start of a cold coming on but, given my recent exposure to the elements, I'd count myself lucky if that was all I ended up with.

Sid would be there tomorrow, and I'd like to get that sorted sooner rather than later too.

I had beans on toast for dinner whilst watching the *Notting Hill* DVD. I waited for Julia Roberts to utter that annoying line and threw a bean at her. After that I switched it off and got ready for bed. I'd just finished cleaning my teeth and slipped into my fluffy 'I'm feeling sorry for myself' pyjamas when Hayley phoned.

'Hi, how are you doing?'

I'd already filled her in on my misadventures over the

weekend and sent her a picture of myself as a blonde, which made me hang up after she couldn't stop laughing. It wasn't good for a girl's confidence when her best friend laughed at her.

'Yeah, I'm okay, just about to go to bed. Got an early start tomorrow.'

'You're going in?'

'Yeah, thought I should. Get it over with.'

'Sid will understand. After all, you said it was all his idea.'

'Yeah, but it's still weird after I ... assaulted him, I guess.'

'I'm sure he enjoyed it.'

'I'm sure he didn't.'

'No word from ... what did you call him? Smackhead?'

'Smacktard, though I quite like Smackhead too.'

'Where did you get that from?'

'From an old computer game.'

'Right, so you're feeling okay, then?'

'Yeah, I'm all right.'

'I don't have to drive over and tuck you in?'

'No,' I said, smiling. 'I'm so tired I'd be asleep before you even got in your car, but thanks for the offer.'

'I'm a little worried about you. It sounded like you had a breakdown.'

'If I did it could only have been a tiny one.'

'But even then—'

'Hayley, I'm fine, just leave it. I just need some time to get myself back to normal.'

'Back to Goth?'

'Yeah, well, that's normal for me.'

'Your hair will fall out.'

'Probably.'

'We should book a holiday.'

'Should we?'

'Yeah, just you and me, a girly week in the sun.'

'What about James?'

'He's not a girly.'

'Are you cool leaving him on his own for a week?'

'Yeah, we're not Siamese twins.'

'Could've fooled me.'

'Yeah, it's been a bit intense. That's why a holiday away would be good for everyone, especially you. Somewhere hot where we can sit by the pool all day drinking and watching hot men with no clothes on.'

'Are you ovulating?'

'Probably, but seriously, let's do it. I'll look online later and see what's available. We'll need to avoid the school holidays as prices get too expensive, but that's good. I don't want a resort full of screaming brats anyway.'

'One day you'll have screaming brats of your own.'

'Maybe, but they'll be my brats so that'll be all right, and they won't scream. Until then, well, I'll avoid them.'

'How's your couch, by the way?'

'Smelling of bubble gum. It's quite sickly. Your mum wouldn't like it.'

'I'll tell her to avoid that cleaner, then.'

'Kat?'

'Yeah?'

'I wish it'd worked out for you, I really do. You deserve someone lovely.'

'I thought I loved Smacktard and look what happened.'

'You ended up calling him Smacktard.'

'I did, and I scared the Queen.'

'You did what?'

'I'll tell you another time. I'm going to bed now.'

Five minutes later my head hit the pillow and I fell into the arms of the sandman. He was quite dishy, but I didn't shag him,

*

Next morning, I made sure I made it into work before Sid. I needed coffee and some prep time. I got a few comments (all positive) about my hair and general non-Gothness, but in the main I ignored them. Wired from three coffees, I intercepted Sid before he could get changed.

He squinted at me before saying, 'I prefer you dark.'

'That's good, I prefer me dark too.'

'How did it go, then?'

'Could have been better.' I filled him in, including my 'funny turn'.

'You might have a tumour.'

'I haven't got a tumour.'

'If you don't get it treated, you might die, and it would go a long way to explaining your strange behaviour.'

'What, since my tenth birthday? It'd have to be the slowest-growing tumour ever.'

I watched him take a moment to consider that. 'Fair enough, what happens now?'

'Nothing happens now. I'm over him.'

'You're not.'

'Okay, I'm not, but I will be. I just need some time.'

'Fine, and in the meantime, you'll keep your mind on what's happening on the operating table?'

'I will, and I don't think it's an operating table.'

'I operate on it. I do operations.'

'On dead people.'

'I still operate. The fact that I'm not helping them get any better is beside the point.'

'Okay.'

The fact we were bantering like normal lifted a weight from my shoulders. I didn't want my weekend of madness to ruin our friendship and, thankfully, most of the time Sid acted as if nothing had happened between us. I had a huge feeling of emptiness, as if something had been taken out of me. Sid seemed calm, relaxed, relieved maybe. I had to wonder about that. Perhaps he felt he'd had a narrow escape from me. I laughed; maybe he had. I could only wonder at the chaos and confusion I'd have brought into his nice ordered life.

Chapter 34

'Nathan, what's wrong? You've been sitting about for the whole weekend with a face like a soggy fish finger.'

'Breadcrumbs or battered?'

'Either. What's wrong with you? We've just moved into a lovely big house and I need you to help me do stuff.'

'Like what?'

'Hang curtains, for a start – the second spare room has got nothing in the window and anyone can see in.'

'There's nothing in that room except boxes. Why does it matter?'

'It matters to me. I don't want the neighbours thinking we don't have a pot to piss in.'

'We've got three bathrooms, Laura, we don't need a pot to piss in.'

'That's another thing – the bathroom on the top landing, I don't like it.'

'Why?'

'It's got a funny smell.'

'It's probably just unused. A good clean will sort it out, I'm sure.'

'I think we should change it. I don't like the colour.'

'It's white.'

'Yeah, but it's the wrong kind of white.'

'How ...?' Nathan gave up and put a cushion over his face.

'I'm tempted to smother you with that.'

'You won't get the life insurance money if you murder me.'

'I'll say it was suicide.'

'I don't think you can smother yourself to death.'

'Maybe you should give it a go and if you don't succeed then the curtains for the spare room are over there on the table.'

Laura pottered off to do some more unpacking. Nathan's melancholy annoyed her. Everything she'd ever wanted had now come to fruition: a great job, lovely house – well, it would be lovely soon – and she had enough money coming in to do all the things she wanted.

All that seemed to be lacking was Nathan. Well, the Nathan of old, although she had to remember she hadn't liked the old Nathan for a long time either, but that had been more down to her, and her expectations of him, than him.

She'd been sure when she'd got him back he'd forgive her all her transgressions, especially once she got him into bed, and for a while it had seemed to work, but now it felt as if he was missing something. The thought fleetingly entered her head that he might be pining after the punk, but she dismissed it. She had nothing to fear from that freak. What could that bitch possibly offer him that she couldn't?

Laura just wanted him to be pleased for her and to share her enthusiasm for their new life. The girls loved the new place, so that should have been enough for him to smile too. He'd seemed genuinely pleased when they'd sold their old flat and moved in, even though it had been her job and salary that had secured the mortgage. They'd even joked about that.

'So, Nathan, how does it feel to be a kept man?'

'Good, as long as I don't have to clean the fridge.'

'Oh, but being a kept man means that cleaning the fridge is your number one priority.'

'Okay, I don't want to be a kept man, then.'

'Well, priority number two is keeping me satisfied in bed.'

'I like that one.'

'How about we make that number one and the fridge number two?'

'I'd prefer the fridge to be back at number twenty-four.'

'Okay.'

He still worked from home with his advertising agency and even that had picked up recently, so she really didn't understand what had made him so morose.

They got the girls settled, except Millie, who wanted to finish a game on her iPad before going to sleep.

Laura cracked open a bottle of wine and sat down with

Nathan in their big front room and said, 'Okay, Nathan, what's wrong?'

'I don't know.'

'That's helpful.'

'What do you want me to say, Laura?'

'I want you to tell me why you're unhappy.'

'I don't know.'

'Is it me? Is it the girls? Is it this place?' She waved her hand in the air.

'No, Laura, the house is lovely, but it's your dream, your grand plan, not mine.'

'What are your dreams, then?'

'I don't really have any.'

'That's stupid. Everybody needs to have dreams.'

'Why? Why can't I just get up in the morning and see what the day brings? Why does everything have to be planned out in intricate detail?'

'I don't do that.'

'I've seen your spreadsheets, remember?'

A few weeks ago, she'd shown him all her plans for the house, holidays, potential private schooling for the girls if she/they could afford it, plans for their next new car, retirement funds, paying the mortgage off early, and she'd even worked out their household bills over the next four years, adjusting for inflation. She hadn't realised at the time it had disturbed him that much.

'But, Nathan, we need to be organised if we want to have the lifestyle we want.'

'Lifestyle *you* want.'

'What do you want? To live under a bridge somewhere, sleeping every night in a cardboard box?'

Nathan sighed. 'No, of course not. I just tend to, well … well, I like surprises. I like to take one day at a time. It's just the way I am.'

'Well, that's fine; you just do that, and I'll do the planning.'

'It's not just that, Laura. I'm not sure exactly what it is but when we split up, I don't know, it ... I ... I felt betrayed. You betrayed me.'

'Don't be so melodramatic. We needed that break to see what had gone wrong.'

'You needed that break to shag someone else.'

'You had your fling too with what's-her-face, so don't use that against me.'

'I did, and I let her down too.'

'You did what was right and if you're thinking of going back to her, I wouldn't advise it.'

'Don't be silly, Laura, I couldn't go back even if I wanted to. She'd never come near me in a million years after the way I treated her.'

'She served her purpose, Nathan. She made you realise what life would be like without me.'

Nathan pondered on that for a moment before nodding. 'Yeah, she did, didn't she?'

'Daddy.'

'That's Millie shouting,' Laura said. 'What's wrong with

her now? She should be able to go to sleep herself at her age.'

'I don't know. I'll find out.'

*

Nathan walked down the long hall, up the broad winding staircase and into Millie's new huge bedroom. He sat on her bed. 'What's wrong, sweetie?'

'Are you and Mummy arguing again?'

'You must have the hearing of a bat to know that from this distance.'

She smiled. 'I was sitting at the top of the stairs.'

'We were just having a discussion, you eavesdropper.'

'You're not happy, Dad.'

'I'm fine.'

'No, you're not. I can tell.'

'I'm fine. We're all together again as a family – is that not a good thing?'

'Yeah, but—'

'No buts. We're fine. We will be fine.'

'Can I ask you a question?'

'Shoot.'

'Would you give Mum your last bagel?'

He hesitated, and Millie shook her head. 'See? We're not fine.'

Chapter 35

I'd got into work early and plugged my phone into the PA system, which now blared out some dance music. I did this every so often when no one was around. The morgue acoustics were brilliant, though I'm not sure you'd get many bands or DJs wanting to do a gig there, right enough.

I danced around, preparing the tools of our trade for the day. I stopped to fill in some paperwork, doing a quick circle of the room in between sentences. A few months had passed now since my breakdown in the rain and it all seemed like a distant memory. I had started to feel much better about life in the last few weeks and, with a ten-day holiday in Gran Canaria looming, things were looking up. I'd got my mojo back.

The song finished and just as I turned off my phone I noticed Sid leaning against the doorframe, watching me.

'Sid!' I exclaimed, slightly embarrassed at being caught dancing in the morgue; it seemed a little disrespectful, now that I thought about it.

'Don't worry, I enjoyed watching you.'

'Voyeur.'

He nodded, smiling.

'I thought you were supposed to be in court all day?'

'They rearranged it again.'

'Again?' Sid had been called to give his professional opinion on a hit and run case that he'd undertaken the post-mortem for. The driver of the car had claimed he'd only been doing twenty miles an hour, but the state of the corpse told a different story. 'What is it this time?'

'The defendant's ill, apparently.'

'So why are you here? Your shift's all covered today. I thought you'd be enjoying a day off.'

'I wanted to ask you something.'

'Okay,' I said a little warily.

'Can we meet up later after you get off?'

'Yeah, sure, why though?'

'I ... I'll explain when I see you. It'll be easier, if that's okay?'

'Now I'm intrigued.'

'Thanks, Kat.' He smiled and left.

*

Later in the day I got a text from Sid asking if we could meet in the Starbucks just across the road from the hospital. I pottered over at a few minutes past four, ordered a coffee and waited. Another text, '*cu in 2 mins*'.

All this cloak and dagger routine wasn't Sid's style. I'd

David Atkinson

never known two minutes to pass so slowly; it felt like waiting for an eBay auction to end when you'd got the winning bid.

Eventually the door opened, and Sid entered accompanied by a friend – a female friend. His face blushed bright red when he saw me, and he wouldn't meet my gaze, so I looked at his friend instead.

She had bright pink spiky hair, doe-like brown eyes, and a line of silver piercings along both eyebrows. She had a little rosy mouth and smiled with nice, if slightly crooked white teeth.

She'd dressed mainly in black leather, jacket and trousers with black suede calf-length boots. She held out her hand and said, 'Kat, I assume? I'm Jenny.'

Jenny turned out to be lovely, and the punk girl and I chatted like long-lost friends.

'So how did you meet?'

'At a Vibrators gig.'

I glanced over to Sid, who'd gone from pale red to traffic-light red. 'The Vibrators are a punk band from the late seventies, just in case you're wondering.'

'You had me worried for a minute. So, you're into old punk stuff too?'

Jenny shrugged. 'Some of it. I prefer the more melodic songs, to be honest, but I get along to a few things here and there when I'm not working.'

'What do you do?'

'I'm a chemist.'

Okay, smart as well as pretty and chatty. 'What, like in Boots?' I asked, hoping she hadn't been lurking around the day I'd got caught examining my pubes.

'No, I'm an industrial chemist. I work for TXS part of the huge petrochemical site at

Grangemouth, but I'm from Bristol originally.'

That explained the English accent.

'David told me that you and he are good friends.'

I nodded.

'Well, I just wanted to meet you to, well, put my mind at rest, I suppose.'

I nodded again.

'When your boyfriend tells you something like that, it puts your guard up, but, well, you seem very nice and I'm sure I've got nothing to worry about.'

Not now you don't, I thought to myself. She had clearly come to mark her territory and that was fine by me. 'Si ...' If she called him David, maybe I should too. 'David is a lovely person, one of the most genuine and caring people I've ever met, but I'm sure you know that already. He's been very supportive, especially recently when I had a nasty break-up with someone.'

'Yes, I can see him doing that. Sometimes he's a little too nice and I don't like the thought of anyone taking advantage of him, but I'm much happier now that I've met you.'

I nodded for a third time; the cat had well and truly taken my tongue and buried it in its litter tray. She'd obviously picked up on something Si ... David had said about me that had got her antenna twitching. Hopefully when she was with him more than just her antenna twitched and, looking at the two of them together, I suspected it did.

She talked about her work and her childhood in Bristol, which, truth be told, had me yawning until she mentioned her parents. 'They got divorced just after my tenth birthday. My dad moved out initially as he'd met someone else, then he and his new partner bought the house next door. Then my mum met someone, and he moved in, so basically my parents now share the party wall of two semis in Southville in Bristol with my stepbrothers and sisters who all play together and get on wonderfully.'

We sat for a moment considering the oddness of Jenny's parents, then I said brightly, 'You'll fit in perfectly around here.'

Shortly afterwards they left hand in hand and I drove home, delighted for Sid but feeling a little sorry for myself now that the last remaining singleton in my life had left the club. I consoled myself with the thought that I had one more shift, then I could pack my cases and head off for the sun.

*

Three days later Hayley and I stepped off the plane at Gran Canaria airport and the wall of heat that hit us made us sigh with contentment. After an annoying forty-minute journey on a sweaty bus, we were deposited at our hotel and fifteen minutes later were seated by the pool under umbrellas with cold beers in hand.

I had my black bikini on (what other colour would I wear?) and Hayley wore a blue swimsuit with the picture of a dolphin on the front. We were both milky-white; neither of us really took much of a tan but I expected I looked paler because by now my hair had returned to its familiar black. I'd reintroduced most of my piercings too and added a small tattoo on my left calf of a creepy grey skull with glowing red eyes. I loved it; it was almost worth the pain I'd endured to get it applied.

Hayley supped her beer, lay back and closed her eyes, enjoying the late afternoon heat. 'Bliss.'

'Are you not missing James?'

'Not yet. Give me an hour or two and I might. I've got some news on that front, actually.'

'He's not gone back to his wife?'

'No, only men called "Smacked Arse" do that sort of thing.'

'Smacktard.'

'Right. Well, it seems that Mrs Cochrane has decided that she'd rather like a divorce after all.'

I sat up excitedly, spilling some cold beer on my hot skin; it felt delicious. 'That's great. Why the sudden change of heart?'

'We're not sure, but James reckons Bob the Builder's popped the question to April.'

'Wow, that was quick.'

'Maybe, maybe not. James thinks she's been seeing him longer than she admits to, but, whatever, it means he can move on.' Hayley smiled and lifted her sunglasses to peer at me. 'She's dropped the complaint against me too, not that it matters as I got a letter from the Law Society yesterday telling me they hadn't found anything technically wrong with my actions anyway. The words they used were 'unusual' and 'frowned upon'. But that's about it.'

'Frowned upon?'

'Frowned upon.'

'What an old-fashioned industry you work in, Hayley.'

'I know. But I'm back to work in it as soon as we get home.'

'Aww, that's wonderful.' I leaned over and gave her a cuddle, attracting a wolf whistle from some teen boys walking past. Hayley gave them the finger.

*

We spent the rest of the holiday partying and chilling. We both got propositioned, a lot, but didn't take up any offers. That aspect had been good for our egos, well, mine especially, and I arrived home tired, slightly less pale than I'd left and a good bit happier with life.

I returned to work on the Friday, an early shift, and to my surprise waiting for me at the front desk was Sid/David. (I needed to agree what to call him. I'd thought that

I could call him Sid at work and David if his girlfriend happened to be about.)

'Sid, how are you?'

'Good. How was your holiday?'

'Brilliant, just what I needed, some sun, sea and sangria.'

'That's nice. I'm glad for you. Could I have a quick chat with you in the office before we start?'

Uh-oh, that sounded ominous. Maybe his girlfriend wanted him to change jobs to stay away from me, or maybe she wanted me to change jobs to stay away from him. 'Nobody's died, have they?' I asked, smiling, trying to lighten the mood.

Sid stopped walking towards the office door and turned to face me. 'Well, people die all the time, which is just as well, or the world would be even more crowded than it is, and we wouldn't have jobs, but nobody I know personally has dropped off their perch recently.'

He'd spoken with such gravity in his voice that for a moment I wondered if he was being serious, but then he smiled and opened the door. He waited for me to go in, then closed it behind us. I perched on the corner of the desk and he sat nervously on a chair behind it.

'What's up? You look troubled.'

'Troubled? Oh, no, I'm not troubled, I'm ecstatic.'

'You don't look ecstatic, but then you always tend to look the same whatever your mood. You might be screaming with excitement inside with your whole body flooded with endorphins, but your face—'

'Kat, I need to ask you something.'

Not again. 'What is it this time, Sid? Does Jenny want me to sign a document promising on pain of death never to lay a hand on you again?'

He frowned at me, as if giving this serious consideration as a valid idea, then said, 'No, Jenny's cool with us. This is something for me. Jenny and I are getting married.'

The words took a few seconds to register, then I fell on him. 'Oh, Sid, that's amazing. I'm so happy for you.' I kissed his cheek and then went back to hugging him

I pulled back from him and laughed at his smiling face. Wait a minute – how come you're marrying someone you've only known for, what, a few months?'

'I've known Jenny for quite a while, actually, but—'

'You were with her when we ... when I ... well, you know?'

He grinned. 'No, of course not. We met about a year ago and chatted online and met up for gigs and the odd coffee, but I couldn't ask her out, not when I had feelings for you. I knew I needed to sort that out and, well, you kind of did that for me.'

'What if it'd worked? What if I'd liked you?'

'Then I would have loved you forever with the whole of my soul, but it wasn't to be.'

Tears formed in my eyes and spilled down my face. 'Oh, Sid, I don't know what to say.'

'You don't need to say anything, just be happy for me. I'm lucky to have someone who loves me and whom I love back. You and I would've been incredible, but fate decided otherwise, now Jenny and me, well ... now we have the chance to be incredible too. I recently learned that when love calls you have to answer as there's always a danger that it might not ring back.'

'I like your phone analogy. I'm not sure I understand it right enough, but it sounds good.'

Sid laughed and said, 'I wish you could have everything you want.'

'Well, as you say, fate intervened and ... well, it doesn't matter. My two favourite people are happy again and I get to go to a wedding. I am invited?'

'Of course. Who else is happy?'

'Hayley. She's back at work – the complaint thing's been dropped.'

'Oh, that's good. Now, there's something else I need to ask you. I was wondering, well, I'd consider it an honour if ...'

'C'mon, Sid, out with it.'

'Would you do me the huge honour of being my best man ... or best person or whatever it is you would be?'

I had to sit back down in disbelief but missed the corner of the desk and ended up on my arse on the floor. Sid quickly helped me up. 'Sid, that would be a huge honour, but, I mean, is there nobody else who, well, who knows you better? And can I do it? I mean, is it normal?'

'Of course, it's not normal, but what is normal? Certainly not us, we're both well down the slope of the bell curve, but it's what I really want, and nobody knows me better than you. I'd make one request, though.'

389

'Yeah?'

'I'd prefer you not to mention in your speech our night of ... whatever we did, had, you know?'

More tears as I hugged him close. I asked mischievously, 'Does that mean I get to organise your stag do?'

'Probably.'

'Do I get to wear a suit?'

'Jenny would rather you didn't.'

'Oh, so you've discussed this?'

'Of course.'

'She's ... well ... cool with it ...? It is a little unconventional.'

'Kat, the bride's got bright pink hair, is going to wear a dress she bought from Oxfam three years ago and has hired a hall in Bootle for the nuptials. How conventional do you think this wedding's going to be?'

'Fair point. Bootle?'

'Yeah, Bootle. It's halfway between Edinburgh and Bristol.'

'Is it?'

'So she says.'

'Why, though?'

'Well, initially she'd planned to have the wedding in Bristol close to her folks, but her friends up here moaned, so she thought she'd maybe have it in Edinburgh, but then the Bristolites moaned, so she got a map and a ruler and came up with Bootle.'

'Maximum inconvenience for everyone?'

'Exactly.'

'We've set a date. October 31st.'

'It had to be, didn't it? Fancy dress?'

'Of course.'

'So that gives me just over a year to find something other than a suit to wear.'

'It gives you just under six weeks to find something other than a suit to wear.'

'*This* Halloween?'

'Yep.'

'God, you're not hanging about, are you?'

'It'll be a civil ceremony and nothing lavish, so why wait a year? If it's right, it's right.'

'I'm going to be busy, aren't I?'

'Probably, I'll get Jenny to talk to you about everything. I'm not sure what she's got planned.'

'Okay, well, whatever it is I'm sure it'll be an absolute blast.'

'Great, now that's sorted we'd better get to work.'

I skipped into the changing room light-heartedly and donned my greens. I came out and noticed Sid still standing talking on the phone.

He smiled at me as he hung up. 'Just giving Jenny the good news.'

Then his face became serious. 'Now to business – we've got another RTA victim waiting for us.'

'Aww, what happened?'

'I'm not sure exactly, but he's a real mess, so bad in fact

I had to cover him up. I couldn't stand looking at the mess his face had become.'

'Really?' In all the time I'd worked with Sid I'd never known him to be squeamish about anything and we'd worked through some grotty remains in our time.

'Yeah, absolutely, and I think he must've been a pretty ugly bugger before the bus rearranged his features.'

'Ouch.'

'Yeah, huge trauma, I just wanted to prepare you. I got a shock when he came in so ... well, anyway, the sooner we get started, the sooner we get finished. Can you start prepping him while I get gowned up?'

'Sure.'

I walked cautiously into the examination room where the body lay on the stainless-steel operating bench. I had some trepidation from Sid's warning and approached the table warily. I decided the best way to deal with the situation would be to quickly pull the sheet back, take in the full horror, then get to work.

I took the edge of the sheet in my hand and quickly lifted it off.

Nothing could ever have prepared me for what lay underneath. Nothing.

Chapter 36

The 'corpse' lying there had been dressed in a three-piece blue suit with a silver tie loosely tied around its neck. In its teeth it held a single red rose and as I stared, not believing my senses, it opened its eyes, blinked, reached up, plucked the rose from its teeth and handed it to me.

I took it, rendered completely speechless by the sight of Nath ... Smacktard once again lying in my mortuary.

'Sid!' I shouted.

He poked his head sheepishly out of the office.

'Is this your idea of a joke?'

Smacktard said, 'It had nothing to do with him. It was all my idea.'

'I wasn't talking to you. Sid!' He slunk out of the office, scurried quickly past Reception and out of the front door, shouting, 'Take the rest of the day off. I'll cover for you.'

'Sid!'

He didn't look back, leaving me all alone with ... '*Smacktard.*'

'What did you say?'

'That's what I call you now.'

'Why?'

'Why do you think? What are you doing here?'

'I'd like to reset the clock.'

'Reset what clock? What are you on about?'

'Well, this is where we met, and I thought there might be a nice kind of symmetry in being back here again with you and—'

'And what? You think I'll go all whoopsy woo and weak at the knees?'

'Whoopsy woo?'

'Yeah, well, I'm flustered.' The moron smiled, and though I did go weak at the knees I'd never let him see that, so I walked away.

'Kat.'

'Just go away, Nathan. I don't want you screwing up my life again. What's happened? Has Mrs Smacktard left you again and you need someone to make your dinner?'

'I left this time.'

'Why?' I didn't know why I even asked that question. I knew I should just have phoned Security and got him evicted, but I didn't. What a sucker I was.

'I couldn't get over you. I couldn't settle back with Laura; it just didn't feel right.'

I spluttered, 'Well, it looked pretty bloody well all right the last time I saw the two of you. You'd got her to go all vamp, so you could have the best of both worlds.'

'What are you talking about?'

'You got Mrs Smacktard to dress like me.'

The penny dropped. 'Oh, Kat, she was going to a fancy-dress party. She'd—'

'Fancy-dress party?'

'Yeah, at her work. Remember, I told you she had a works do that night and I didn't want to go because I hate fancy-dress parties.'

'You mean you didn't persuade her to go all Goth to replace me? Did you shag her when she was like that?' I didn't know why that mattered to me, but it did.

'No, she came home stupidly drunk and spent most of the night being sick.'

I stood still and silent, staring at him, wondering what to do, then he had to go and spoil it. He came over, took the rose from me and said, 'I'm just a boy standing in front of a girl asking ...'

'Argh.' I rushed at him, pushed him away and ran out of the room into the daylight, tears streaming down my face. How I hated that stupid line.

I ran out towards the front of the hospital and plonked myself down onto a bench, holding my head in my hands. Why did he have to come and see me? I'd just got to the stage where everything felt good again.

I sensed rather than saw him sit beside me. 'Sorry, I didn't know that would upset you. Sid told me it was your favourite movie line of all time.'

I started shaking uncontrollably.

'Kat ...' I could hear his concerned voice in the distance,

but I'd got too wrapped up in the moment and shook even more.

'Kat, Kat, are you all right? Should I go and get a doctor?'

I lifted my head to look at him; tears were pouring from my eyes, partly for the torment he'd put me through but mostly because I'd kill Sid when I saw him. My favourite movie line indeed.

I started laughing, almost hysterically, and the look on Smacktard's face made me worse and I slipped onto the floor, still in hysterics. Sid had set all this up and had set Nathan up too.

It took me a few minutes to regain my composure before I could speak to him. I took a deep breath and said, 'How did you persuade Sid to help you?'

'I came here last week. I needed to talk to him to see if you'd mentioned me at all and, well, he represented my last hope, my only way of finding out how you were feeling.'

'Feeling? How I was feeling? How the hell do you think I'd be feeling? You know what? I'd got over you, I'd got beyond the bit where you used me, dumped me and the bit where you were such a coward that you had to get your wife to tell me you'd gone back to her.'

He nodded. 'Yeah, I can't excuse that. I didn't mean for you to find out that way. I'd wanted to meet you and tell you and—'

'And what would you have said, Nathan? "Oh, sorry, Kat. I think I'm going to go back to my wife. I hope you don't mind. I know she left me, said nasty things about me on TV, took out a court order against me, bullied my daughter and nailed my head to the floor but I can't hold that against her. I deserved it.'

'She didn't nail my head to the floor.'

'I might.'

Nathan laughed, and my heart melted a little bit. 'I think she would like to do that now. Maybe you can both get together and have a "let's nail Nathan's head to the floor" party.'

'I'd like that.'

'If I let you nail my head to the floor, will you go out with me again?'

'I wouldn't want to go out with someone with big holes in the side of their head.'

'No, I suppose not.'

We both sat in silence for a moment before I said, 'I don't know if I can trust you again, or even if I want to try. Where are you living?'

'I've rented a small flat in Meadowbank. It's not much but it's all I can afford just now.'

'So, the girls are with your wife in Dumbiedykes?'

'No, we sold that and bought a big house in Portobello, or, rather, Laura did. I just kind of went along.'

'Like a piece of the furniture.'

'That's what it felt like.'

'So how do you see the girls?'

'Laura drops them at school and nursery and I pick them up. I get them most Saturdays and she has them on

Sunday. They stay over at mine but it's very cramped, not ideal, but it's been okay.'

'What will she say when she knows you're seeing me again?'

'She won't be happy.'

'Why?'

'She thinks you'll turn her daughters into punks.'

'Goths.'

'Goths. Will you?'

'Maybe,' I said, laughing.

'Okay. I probably won't mention that.'

'Will you not miss lording it up in the big house?'

'I wasn't there long enough to "lord" anything really and, another thing, it's always cold and if you lose anything it can be a nightmare. I put my watch down somewhere and it took me three days to find it.'

'You spent three days looking for your watch?'

'No, silly, I gave up after about half an hour, but it was three days before I came across it again.'

'Where was it?'

'Where I'd left it.'

'Where was that?'

'I can't remember now.'

'No wonder you lose things. When did you leave?'

'Two months ago.'

'When are you going back?'

'I'm not.'

'How do you know?'

'I can't. I've tried that. I've learned that you can't go back. What Laura and I had, we lost. A long time ago.'

'So why did you do it, then?'

'I don't know.'

'The little head ruling the big head again? Did she tempt you back with unlimited sex?'

'Her heart wasn't really in it.'

'What's her heart got to do with it?'

'Everything. I love you, Kat. I used to love Laura and I knew as soon as we were back together that I'd made the biggest mistake of my life. I went for what seemed like all the right reasons—'

'Unlimited sex.'

'Okay, for most of the right reasons, but that's not how things work, is it?'

'I wouldn't know,' I said huffily.

He took my face in his hands. 'You *do* know. I tried to do the right thing for my girls, but they knew it wasn't right and even Laura knows ... I think. She won't like the idea of me being with you, but it'll be easier than what we were doing. She can be herself and get another boyfriend if that's what she wants.'

'Did she explode when you told her you were leaving?'

'No, she cried.'

'Oh.'

'I couldn't give her my last bagel.'

'She's crying over a bagel? I mean, could you not go to the shops and get more?'

'Well, yes, but she's not crying about bagels.'

'Good, not many people would.'

'It's all about what the last bagel represents.'

'You're crazier than me. What does it represent?'

'It's like the last chance of, err ... I tell you what, ask Millie. It's the bagel test. She'll explain it to you.' He shut up and stared at me.

I was in trouble here; what should I do? I could tell him to take his bagels and bugger off, but then I'd spend the rest of my life wondering and possibly regretting the decision. The alternative of opening myself up to hurt and possible betrayal again wasn't much better. As Nathan stared at me waiting for a decision I remembered what Sid had said about love phoning and maybe not calling back if you let it go to voicemail or text or ... Well, I understood the gist of it anyway; it was somewhere up there with the bagel analogy. It suddenly occurred to me that Nathan had recently been given a second chance at life so maybe he deserved a second chance at love too.

I smiled at him, he smiled back and my bits twitched so of course I had to take him home.

Later in my dark bedroom he leaned over and kissed me again. 'Mm, I've missed your kisses,' I murmured.

'Me too.'

'You can kiss yourself any time you want.'

'I can't kiss myself. I wouldn't want to anyway.'

'Why not?'

'I don't fancy myself.'

'You should, you're lovely.'

'Not as lovely as you.'

'Flattery might get you into my knickers.'

'You've not got any knickers on.'

'See, told you.'

Nathan laughed. 'Our conversations are still bizarre. I missed that.'

'Did Mrs Smacktard not do bizarre?'

'Not really. She's very matter-of-fact, no time for nonsense.'

'That's a shame; everyone needs nonsense in their lives to make up for all the serious stuff.'

'I agree. I probably never used to think like that, but you've changed me.'

'I've not changed you. It was always there, I just pulled it out of you.'

'Thank you.'

'My pleasure. But I need to be serious for a minute.'

'Do you really?'

'Yes, sorry. I'll be silly again soon and you can get into my knickers again.'

'You're not wearing any.'

'Oh, right. I'll put them back on and you can take them off again.'

'Okay.'

'Right, we need to talk about what we're going to do.'

'About your knickers?'

'You're obsessed with my knickers.'

'I'm obsessed with you.'

'Nathan, I need you to do something for me, and don't mention my knickers.'

'I wasn't going to.'

'You were so.'

'Yeah, I was.'

'I need you to get dressed, walk one hundred yards down the road and get some wine, crisps, milk and bread. Can you manage that?'

'It's not a Tesco's, is it?'

'No.'

'That'll be all right, then. Anything else?'

'Yeah, hurry up. I'll get cold in here on my own.'

He clambered out of bed and I watched his naked backside sway across the room as he gathered up his clothes. As soon as he'd left I grabbed my phone and eagerly dialled Hayley's number. She answered on the first ring; it must be a quiet day in lawyer land. 'Guess what I've been doing.'

'Err, dancing with the devil.'

'Ooh, so close. I've been in bed with Smacktard.' Silence. 'Hayley, are you there?'

'Yeah, just concerned about my couch and, of course, your mental health.'

'My mental health's fine. Listen until I tell you what happened.'

After I'd finished speaking, she said, 'Romantic and creepy, right up your street.'

'Yeah, I suppose.'

'Sweetie, are you sure he's not going to hurt you again?'

'Of course not, how can anyone ever be sure about that?'

'Well, fair point, but you think he's left her for good this time?'

'I think so, but I'll be careful.'

'You'd better be. I suppose this means a kind of happyish ending, then.'

'Not really – happy beginnings maybe.'

'True. Listen, when he needs a good divorce lawyer he knows where to go.'

I giggled. 'I'm not sure I can recommend a firm where the lawyers sleep with their clients.'

'I thought it was a novel way of drumming up business.'

'The other partners didn't agree with you.'

'They didn't so I won't do it again.'

'Okay, then, I'll give Smacktard your card.'

'You can't keep calling him that.'

'I can, and I will.'

'When will you stop?'

'When he proposes to me.'

'That might be some time.'

I smiled. 'I know.'

'Right, this from the girl who thought she wasn't the sort of girl anyone would want to marry.'

'That was a long time ago.'

'You said it only weeks ago.'

'A lot has happened since then.'

'It certainly has, so what's your plan?'

'Well, I've got Sid's wedding coming up and there's nothing like a good wedding when you're madly in love.'

'You're madly in love?'

'I think so. I'm mad anyway.'

'Yeah, no argument there from me.'

'I get to wear black. I might even resurrect my tiara from prom night. It's still in the wardrobe in my old bedroom.'

'I can smell the gloss paint now.'

I heard the front door opening and the general scuffling sound that men made when they came into a house. 'Listen, I need to go, sweetie, he's just come back. I'll call you later.'

I heard him going into the kitchen and stowing things in the fridge. A few minutes later we were curled up in bed again. 'I'm not sure I can trust you again,' I whispered into his ear.

'But we're in bed together.'

'That's lust, not trust. Everything is *not* back to normal.'

'What's normal?'

'Yeah, good point. Not us anyway.'

'So, what do you want to do, then? My heart is in your hands,' he said, sitting up on his elbow and staring at me.

'Yeah, for me, that brings up a whole different picture.'

'Right, sorry, I forgot. Okay, I'd like to spend the rest of my life making it up to you.'

'What film is that from?'

'I don't know, none ... I mean, well, I don't think so, it might be, I suppose, but ...'

I laughed at the panicked expression and realised for the first time in my life that I held the power in a relationship, or at least I'd be on a level footing, and it felt wonderful. 'It's okay, I'm just kidding. What we'll do is take it nice and slow and see how things develop.'

'Thank you.'

'What for?'

'For taking me back.'

'Well, I'm still considering it, to be honest, and I'm going to make you work extra hard to make it up to me. Anyway, I can't let you leave as I've saved your life twice so I'm responsible for you forever and a day.'

'Twice?'

'Yeah, once in the morgue and the second time from a fate worse than death with your wife.'

'I'm glad you didn't stay normal.'

'What are you talking about?'

'The blonde hair and sensible clothes it … well, it just isn't you and it impressed Laura.'

'Wait, my being normal and sensible impressed your wife and you didn't like that?'

'I didn't like that you'd tried to change who you were for me, or for anyone. I love you just the way you are.'

'There's probably a few things you need to know about me if you're going to stick around.'

'Okay.'

'My parents are a bit mad.'

'My mother fell off a boat.'

'Oh, yeah, so she did. Okay, you win that one. I sometimes talk to myself out loud.'

'No, you don't.'

'Don't I?'

'No, you argue with yourself. I heard you in the Highlands.'

'Did you?'

'Yeah, when we were lying together in the morning after the storm, I heard you wondering if I loved you.'

'That's embarrassing.'

'It's not and I should have told you then and there how I felt.'

'But you didn't.'

'No, I didn't want you to know that I'd been listening.'

'Well, at least you know life won't be perfect and orderly with me.'

'I've had enough of trying to do everything perfect and orderly.'

'Good, and, on that note of being unconventional, I've got a stag party to organise.'

'A stag party ... don't you mean a hen party?'

'No.'

'Whose stag do are you organising and why?'

'Sid's getting married and I'm his best man/woman/whatever.'

'Best whatever. I like the sound of that.'

'Yeah, well, if you're going to be around you'll need to help me.'

'I'm going to be around, am I?'

'I hope so.' I lay my head on his chest and murmured, 'I don't plan on going to this wedding on my own.'

'When is it?'
'Halloween.'
'This Halloween?'
'Yep.'
'That's only a few weeks away.'
'It is. You'll love it.'
'Why?'
'It's fancy dress.'
'Aww, no, I hate fancy dress.'
'I know. I've got the perfect costume idea for you.'
'You have?'
'Of course.'
'Go on, then, disappoint me.'
'A zombie.'

Acknowledgements

Thank you to the wonderful Charlotte Ledger for her belief and her editing team for pointing out and fixing my mistakes.